The Bohemian Flats

DISCARD

The
BOHEMIAN
FLATS

A Novel

MARY RELINDES ELLIS

University of Minnesota Press

Minneapolis

London

Published by the University of Minnesota Press
111 Third Avenue South, Suite 290
Minneapolis, MN 55401–2520
http://www.upress.umn.edu

Library of Congress Cataloging-in-Publication Data
Ellis, Mary Relindes.
The Bohemian flats : a novel / Mary Relindes Ellis.
ISBN 978-0-8166-9220-0 (pbk. : acid-free paper)
 1. Germans—Minnesota—Fiction. 2. World War, 1914-1918—Fiction.
3. Germany— History—19th century—Fiction. 4. Minneapolis (Minn.)—
History—20th century—Fiction. I. Title.
PS3605.L468B64 2014
813'.6—dc23

2014004741

Printed in the United States of America on acid-free paper

The University of Minnesota is an equal-opportunity educator and employer.

20 19 18 17 16 15 14   10 9 8 7 6 5 4 3 2 1

For my mother

Relindes Catherine Alexander Berg

*who cared about people from all backgrounds, ethnicities, and races;
who believed in social justice; who cherished hidden stories;
who loved the outdoors; and who celebrated difference*

*For those extraordinary, inspiring, and indomitable people
of the Minneapolis riverfront village once known as
the Bohemian Flats*

*For the Anishinaabeg/Chippewa of Wisconsin
whose continued civil resistance is one of the great examples
of the means of surviving cultural and physical genocide*

We all were sea-swallow'd, though some cast again,
And by that destiny to perform an act
Whereof what's past is prologue, what to come
In yours and my discharge.

—ANTONIO *to* STEPHANO,
in The Tempest *by William Shakespeare*

To be an adult was, for the greatest part, to be in darkness.

—CLAIRE KEEGAN,
"Night of the Quicken Trees"

CONTENTS

PROLOGUE

London

1919

HE IS ON THE WRONG SIDE OF THE RIVER. *He gauges the Mississippi's width, thinks about the strength of the current at that section of the river. A few feet behind him is a tree-covered rise of limestone known as the Father Hennepin bluff. It is an easy walk to the stone arch bridge, north of where he stands and where he can cross on foot. But he decides to swim across because the river is narrow enough here, having been diminished by the St. Anthony Falls. He takes off his dress shoes, his socks, his suit jacket and pants, his oxford shirt and tie, folding each article of clothing into a neat pile on the pebbled shore. He contemplates leaving his underwear on, hesitating only about his undershirt, then pulls it over his head, deciding that it will cause drag in the water. Wading into the water until it is waist high, he then propels himself forward into a breaststroke. He lets the current work for him when he reaches the middle, spreading out his arms and legs to float toward the Washington Avenue Bridge. The bluffs get higher. He drifts past the Mineral Resource and Research Building on top of the east bluff. The river widens into a familiar expanse and he feels the heat of the sun on the water, stares at the goose down of cirrus clouds against the blue sky. Someone shouts and he lifts his head. Two people stand on the western shore. As he floats closer, he sees that one of them is his nephew, dressed in an olive-brown tunic, breeches, spiral woolen puttees, and Pershing shoes. There is something odd about his nephew's appearance. He realizes it is the hat. The boy is wearing an M1917, that soup bowl of a helmet instead of the Montana peaked hat worn for regular duty. His nephew is holding an infant. Next to him is his neighbor from the Flats, Alzbêta Dvořák. His nephew gives the baby to Alzbêta. Then the boy picks up a long pole with a hooked end and wades into the river up to his thighs. He paddles toward his nephew using his left arm. When he is just a hand's length away from the end of the pole, he reaches* out with his right arm. *He swipes at the hook, the pain in his shoulder searing, and misses it.*

"Don't!" *he yells as his nephew wades in deeper. He floats past them. His nephew is shouting but he cannot hear him. Alzbêta is calling him too. The baby begins to cry.*

"MR. DAVIES!"

A nurse shakes him awake.

"Where am I?" he asks.

"In London. In hospital. You had a high fever but it's come down. You were shouting just now. You've had quite a night. For a while there, I thought you were a German. You were shouting in German. But your file says you are English. And just now you sounded like a Yank."

His mouth tastes like the mud of river water. He touches the hospital-issue gown to see if it is wet. It is not. He props himself up on his elbows, looks around at the other beds, and tries to remember where he was before. Kell's office. He pauses before answering, collecting himself.

She laughs. "Are you an actor?"

"Something like that," he says, in the accent of an upper Londoner. "How long have I been here?"

"A week as of this morning," she answers, smiling. "You must be a very good actor. One of the doctors heard you last night and thought the file was a mistake. He's a Brit but he grew up in Germany before the war. He said your German was flawless, just like a native. He thought maybe you were born there."

He gives a weak smile.

"Ah no. I just had a very good teacher," he answers, wanting her to go away. "I'm very tired. I think I'll sleep some more."

"All right then."

He watches her walk away, praying he hasn't blown his cover. It is being ill like this, feverish and hallucinatory, that he has feared the most, that is the most dangerous. He has no control over where or what period of time his mind regresses to, what he might be saying, in what language.

He looks to see if the nurse is watching and sees that she is not.

He doubles the pillow and sits up against it. He does not remember being brought to the hospital, or anything about the past five days except for swimming in the Mississippi, which he now realizes was a dream. *Is* a dream.

Then his eye catches the poster on the wall directly opposite to him, the script in blood red.

ONCE A GERMAN—ALWAYS A GERMAN!
1914 to 1918 NEVER AGAIN
The British Empire Union has wasted no time in making it clear that even with the armistice no German worker is welcome in Britain nor are goods produced in Germany to be purchased.

The cartoon depictions are lurid, exposing what is supposed to be the true German nature behind the dapper German man in tails and striped pants, holding a briefcase: a German bayoneting a baby, a drunken German officer lolling in a parlor chair with a frightened and cowering (and presumably British) woman behind him, a German officer grinning at an executed Allied officer, blindfolded and tied to a post.

**Every German employed means
a British worker idle.
Every German article sold means
a British article unsold.**

He is so focused on the poster, at the image of the executed Allied officer, that he does not hear the approach of Captain Kell carrying a chair.

"Davies."

Kell places the chair next to the bed and sits down.

"I was here yesterday but you were still out of it," Kell explains, sitting on the chair.

"I've been shouting in my sleep," he responds.

"I anticipated that when we brought you in," Kell answers. "I've talked to the doctor and then the specialist—"

"What kind of specialist?"

"A psychiatrist."

"Do you think that's wise? To have a head doctor rummaging his mental fingers through my brains?"

"He won't go that far," Kell answers, putting on a reassuring smile. "You've had a touch of fever but they've ruled out the Spanish flu. It's shell shock. The psychiatrist is only here to treat the symptoms of that—nervousness, insomnia, the rash on your arms and back, and so forth. He is not to analyze any further. I've told the psychiatrist that you are a highly trained soldier, fluent in several languages, and to disregard whatever you say in an unconscious state and to not keep a record of it. Since you are not in physical pain, I've asked them not to give you morphine, which they sometimes do with shell shock."

"How can you be sure that they don't already know?" He lifts his chin at the poster.

"They have those plastered everywhere," Kell says, following his gaze. "Not a very appropriate place to hang such a poster but I have no jurisdiction in asking them to move it. If I do ask, they'll wonder why it is upsetting you."

Kell lingered on the poster for a few seconds more. "Peace is going to be much more complicated than war. I'm afraid that no one will see anything good about Germans or Germany for some time. I know it presents a particular conflict for you. Can you deal with it?"

"Yes. My wits aren't entirely lost. I can still stay in character. I can still separate the realities of this war," he responds and then corrects himself. "This armistice."

Kell claps him on the shoulder. "As soon as you are well enough to leave and before you return home, we'll listen to some new gramophone records. My favorite at the moment is Dvořák's compositions from when he spent time in the United States. Symphony no. 9, the String Quartet in F, the String Quartet in E Flat, and my favorite, the Sonatina for Violin and Piano. I think it is safe to listen to it as he was a Czech and not a German."

"Many people have trouble making the distinction," he says, biting his lip. He looks away, his eyes tearing up.

Kell then stands, hoisting the chair with one hand. "I can't tell you when you'll be released from the hospital. It may be a month or so. I've asked that you be placed in a solitary room today. They can't quite accommodate that, but there is a ward of only six patients, most of whom are in a very unaware state."

"Comas," Davies says.

"Yes. Is there anything I can bring to keep you occupied? Books? A deck of cards? A *special* deck of cards?"

The last question startles him for a moment. Then he smiles at Kell to acknowledge the attempted joke. Their work has not permitted the intimacies of sharing childhood stories, although adolescent boys, regardless of their nationality, share the same surge in hormones that fuel sexual fantasies. He wonders if his old collection of pornographic cards is still hidden in the loft on the farm in Augsburg after all these years. The scent of fresh hay and the wet saltiness of semen is a vivid and visceral marker of youth. How he spread the cards out across the hay so that he could look at exotic and naked women while he masturbated. Their existence for him had only been in the photographs until he boarded the SS *Havel* and met one of them, another strikingly clear recollection that is entwined with his escape at sixteen. He has no knowledge of where Maria is now, only that she is old and possibly dead. But in his memory she is very beautiful and not yet middle age, the emancipator of his body's desires. He can still recall the scent of lily and lavender on her creamy skin, see the green of her eyes, and feel the thickness of her deep red hair. Thinking of her never fails to arouse him, and yet now his penis is flaccid, unwilling or unable to pick up the transmission of his memories.

"Books," he responds, coming out of his mental tangent. "Charles Dickens. I've never read his novels."

"Right. I'll bring those tomorrow. In the meantime," Kell says, "get some rest and don't worry anymore about what you might say in your sleep. I'll be back tomorrow."

✠ ✠ ✠

HE FLATTENS THE PILLOW and turns on his side, away from the nurses and doctors at the other end of the ward.

Kell is right. It is complicated. It was always complicated. He'd been aware as young as thirteen of the contradictions of his nationality, his ancestry, when he confessed to his professor, Immanuel Richter, that his father repeatedly told him to be a good German and that he didn't know what that was.

He shuts his eyes and he is back in Richter's study, the late afternoon sun filtered through the dome-shaped baroque window, full of dust motes and as suspended as professor and student seemed to be as the question of his future arose.

"There is nothing much for you and Albert here in Germany, being second and third sons. Nothing to inherit. You need to become more fluent in English. Albert is nearly there. Because when you become men, you will need to leave this country, leave Europe. It is America you must go to. There at least you will have the chance to find what the French call *joie de vivre*—the joy of life."

HE PULLS UP THE BED SHEET to wipe his eyes. Unlike the cocksure, hormone-fueled sixteen-year-old who left Germany in 1896 and who believed he would always land on his feet, he cannot see ahead this time.

Looking back he realizes it was his ignorance of the future that gave him unimpeded clarity, and that now it is the burden of experience and accumulated knowledge that fogs his vision. He isn't sure who or what he is anymore. Until he leaves the European continent he cannot risk saying or thinking of his true name. Even if he was suddenly gifted with the ability to do so, he cannot wipe out the horror of the past six years. The past two months. Nor will he be allowed to speak of it after the British government releases him from service and he returns home to the Flats.

He flips onto his back and stares at the ceiling. He would like a shot of morphine. Morphine would help quell the questions that keep arising in his thoughts, the answers he does not have that will be expected when he goes home.

In lieu of an opiate, it is the past he will reach back to and think about to provide some comfort and then some answers. He will begin with the day of his escape, that happy day in the Bremen harbor when he, a brewmaster's son, anticipated a future with unlimited options rather than one of the two that his father dictated for his life: a soldier or a priest.

He will move forward from there, gathering like a tinker on the road the missing pieces of what they had done that cursed them.

JOIE DE VIVRE

Minneapolis
1896–1899

RAIMUND WAVERS AT THE TICKET OFFICE. The shipping agent drums his fat fingers, occasionally reaching up to rub the waxed ends of his silver moustache. Raimund reads and rereads the ticket prices. $100 for first class, $60 for second, and $24 for steerage. This may be his only trip on a big ship. He ponders the imagined luxuries of first class.

"Hurry up, young man! They are lowering the gangways."

The *gangways*. He looks out the small window facing the docked ship and sees that two bridge walks are being lowered. The designation of each ramp is obvious from the people being stewarded into the queue for each.

"Steerage."

"Are you sure?" The agent scrutinizes him and Raimund knows what he sees. Good-quality clothes, an athletic body, and a well-groomed face. Then he looks at Raimund's hands and sees the calluses of labor. A farmer's son. He sighs. Another young man leaving Germany.

"Yes."

It dawns on Raimund as he waits to board that he could not have traveled first or even second class. Someone might recognize his last name because of his father's beer. It is less likely that the workers and poor Germans surrounding him in steerage would know the name because they probably had never drunk his father's beer. The Kaufmann Lager is expensive.

"Are you running away?"

He turns around to face a boy about his own age.

"No," he lies.

"I am," the young man answers. "With my parents' blessing. In two days I'm supposed to join the army in Dresden." He holds out his hand. "My name is Erwin Schaeffer."

"Raimund Kaufmann." He sees no flicker of recognition at his name. Erwin tells him that his parents gave him all the money they could spare but that it is not enough. He (like other impoverished men in steerage) is paying for part of his passage by doing menial jobs on the ship. Erwin talks all the way up the gangway and then down the steps to the deck just above the bowels of the ship.

"I'm hoping I'll have enough money in a year to bring my father and mother over," he says, after claiming his bunk and securing his things. Raimund sits on his own bunk, the effect of his escape hitting him with the force of a punch. He wants to sleep. He wants Erwin to stop talking but cannot think of a polite way to say so. They hear a shout from above.

"Have to go. My orders," Erwin says.

Raimund lies down, inordinately grateful that Erwin will be occupied for the trip. He remembers that he was once so irritatingly loquacious, driving his siblings mad with his chatter. *I'm lucky*, he thinks, his eyelids shutting as though weighted with the ship's anchors, *that they didn't drop me in the well.*

FOR ONCE Raimund does not have to work. He does not want to clean cabins or shovel coal in the engine room. Nor does he want to stay below with the women and children. Yet within two days he feels useless, bored, and guilty. So he volunteers to teach English to those in steerage whose fluency does not go beyond being able to introduce themselves.

He is taking a group of children on a tour of the upper deck reserved for first class when he sees her. Lying on a chaise longue about twenty feet away is a woman who looks familiar.

"Her name is Maria Engel," Erwin says that night. "But that is all I know. I wish I knew more." He cups his hands over his chest and raises them as though he is hefting her breasts.

Raimund walks the upper deck the next day looking for Maria Engel and finds her on the same chaise longue. He keeps his distance, discreetly glancing at her and wishing he had brought his cards with him to compare the likeness. The fifth day out, he is leaning over the deck, fascinated by a pod of dolphins cavorting alongside the ship, when he feels a hand on his shoulder.

"You've been watching me. Do I know you?" Her hair is falling from its pins and is blown across her face by the wind. She has green eyes.

"You—you look like someone I saw once. In a photograph," he answers.

"I've been in many photographs. Would you like to see them?"

He is mesmerized by the luxuriousness of her first-class cabin, with its private bathroom and genuine featherbed. She brings out a photograph album documenting her life as a singer and stage actress. None of the photographs shows her naked although she wore scanty burlesque clothing in two of them.

"This is nice," he says, gesturing at her cabin to make conversation. She assesses him while taking the pins out of her thick auburn hair.

"How old are you?"

"Sixteen."

"Ah. You look older. Have you ever been with a woman?"

He hesitates. "No."

"Would you like to be with a woman?"

SHE TEACHES HIM how to slowly remove a woman's clothes, beginning with the unhooking of her stylish boots. Then the unfastening of more hooks and eyes on the bodice of her dress. He is nervous yet his hands do not betray him. She turns around so that he can unfasten yet another set of hooks and eyes on her corset. Finally Maria Engel sits on the edge of the bed, wearing only her stockings and a chemise. She runs her hands down her legs.

"Now these," she says. Only then do his hands tremble as he undoes the garters and rolls down her stockings.

"*Sehr gut,*" she says, reaching forward to kiss his hands. She looks up at him standing in front of her. "None of this matters if the woman is unwilling or forced. A bad encounter with a man can ruin a woman from the pleasure of her own body for life. You are about to learn," she says, unbuttoning his trousers, "never to be such a man."

So begins his education on how to make love to a woman. Maria Engel not only teaches him the fundamentals of physical relations between men and women but also the flourishes: additional pleasures that he could never have imagined when he masturbated in the loft.

"Anyone," Maria says, opening a box of Frossard's cigars, "can perform the act. Look at dogs in the street." She offers him one and he declines. She clips her cigar, attaches an ivory mouthpiece, and lights it before continuing.

"There is fucking and there is lovemaking. The crucial thing to remember is that you don't have to be in love to make love. Every woman should feel cherished regardless of whether you are paying for her or not. Then," she says, lowering her voice and exhaling the sweet-smelling smoke across his chest, "when you part, you part as friends."

She kisses him, her lips and tongue tasting of tobacco and cloves.

She continues his sexual education throughout the fourteen days at sea so that when Raimund disembarks at Ellis Island, he is carnally seasoned beyond his years.

"PSST. RAIMUND!" Erwin is three people behind Raimund in the registration line. He whispers to the women in front of him and they allow him to move up.

"How—?"

"I told them I was your brother," he says, "and that we could not be separated. Where are you going after this? You never said before."

"To find work in New York."

"Why stay here?" he asks. "It would be like getting your foot in the door but never entering the room."

"Where are you going?"

"To the heart of the country! The Middle West! I have a cousin in Minneapolis. You can live with us. There are big mills there and good jobs. Come with me," he urges. "You'll get a job right away in the mills with your background in farming. Wait until you see the sky. My cousin says you can touch the sun as it rises, it kisses the top of your head in the middle of the day, and then you can touch it again when it sets. It is a land like no other."

Raimund smiles, privately skeptical of such a claim until he remembers what Richter had said about the writer Karl May and the validity of his novels about the cowboys and Indians of the American West: *He traveled only to New York City.* Erwin is right. It would be a waste to have come all this way to just wet his boots on the coastline of what is an enormous country.

THEY BOARD THE TRAIN the next day. Erwin talks nonstop. Even when he sleeps in his bunk, words erupt from his lips so that Raimund feels pummeled with noise for the entire journey. Needless to say, he declines the offer to live with Erwin and his cousin, deciding that if he has to he will sleep in a ditch on the outskirts of the city for the silence of mud and grass. After a week of travel, the train enters the city of Minneapolis early one morning, crossing the Mississippi River on a large stone bridge before pulling into the downtown station. Raimund says goodbye to Erwin, promises that they will get together soon, and then enters the station. He asks a white-haired agent where he might find a job.

"Well, there are several mills. Most here on the river are flour mills. But the one hiring right now is the Pillsbury A," he answers. The station agent directs him toward the steel suspension bridge that crosses from the west side to the east side of Minneapolis. "You can't miss it. Big building on Main Street."

He walks across the bridge onto a slice of land, an island in the middle of the river called Nicollet, and then onto the east bank of the river. The station agent is right. The Pillsbury A Mill is a huge Romanesque-style limestone block building standing seven stories high on a cobblestone street that runs parallel to the river. He stops for a moment and scans the gray exterior, feels the reverberations under his feet, coming, he assumes, from the massive machinery operating inside. He places his hand against an outside wall as if to gauge the rhythm of the building's pulse before he steps inside the tiny office on the first floor where he shouts his inquiry for a job. He can see the clerk's lips move but can barely hear him. The machinery roars like lions.

"The water turbines!" the rabbity-looking clerk shouts, pointing to the floor. "Can you read and write?"

"Yes!"

"Sit down and fill this out."

Raimund fills out the form requesting his education and work experience. He hands it to the clerk, who reads it and then whispers to the young boy who is his office assistant. The boy leads Raimund up six flights of stairs to a large room where a short, brawny man with a bushy Souvaroff moustache tends a row of sifting machines. He is nearly bald, the crown of his head tufted with carrot-colored hair. His broad face is the texture of boiled wool and his upper body is massive, with broad shoulders and well-muscled arms. His legs are thick like his arms but short. Almost too short, it seems, to carry a torso that resembles one of the huge limestone blocks.

"The foreman," his young escort says and then leaves. The man gestures him to the quieter end of the room.

"Can you read and write?" he asks in a heavy brogue, examining Raimund with pale blue eyes.

Raimund hesitates, unsure of what the man has said.

"I speak English," he answers.

"So-do-I," the foreman says, enunciating his words. "I-am-a-Scot. I-will-speak-slower. Can-you-read-and-write?" He adds, "In-English?"

"Yes. I can read and write in English. In German and French as well," Raimund answers, his ears rapidly tuning into the man's brogue. "I can fix machinery, too. I come from a large farm in Germany. And a brewery. My father had a brewery." He glances at the automated milling equipment. "I learn fast. I can work one of those."

"And so you shall," the foreman says. "After I train you." He holds out a floury hand. "Name is Gillian McPherson. And this," he continues, "is the most modern flour mill in the world. Thank the Lord that it isn't like the old days where the flour dust was so bad you'd get white lung."

The foreman then briefly explains the machines and tells Raimund to return the next day for work.

"Where should I live?"

"Where you can afford to," McPherson grins. Raimund stares at him blankly.

"I just got off the train," he says.

"My Lord! You *are* fresh! In that case, I would suggest the Flats. There is a house on Cooper Street. One of our men just moved out

of there and so there is a vacancy unless you've been beaten to it.
Go up to Second Street and keep walking east. You will come to the
new Washington Avenue Bridge. Cross the bridge to the west side
of the river. You'll see the houses on the river shore on both sides
of the bridge. Go to the left side of the bridge. Talk to Prochazka,
the grocer. He owns the house but rents it out."

He catches Raimund by the arm as he turns to go.

"Prochazka is Czech and a stubborn bastard sometimes. He'll
pretend he can't speak German and even English but he can speak
both."

IT IS NOON when Raimund crosses the Washington Avenue
Bridge, watching the languid movement of the Mississippi as
he walks. He stops midway to contemplate the clusters of squat
houses, some of which are built into the bluffs like cliff swallow
nests with the rest ranging down to the flat shoreline. They all are
constructed of weathered rough-sided wood with simple peaked
roofs, surrounded by fences made of the same poor grade of lumber as the houses. Each house has its own little yard except for
those that are built up to the shoreline with flat-bottomed boats
roped to hooks pounded into the siding next to the front doors.
Dirt streets bisect the collection of dun-colored houses as if to give
order to what appears to be a human midden of inhabitation. He
continues on, surprised by an elderly woman wearing a head scarf
who appears as though she has walked out of the canopy of trees
at the west end of the bridge.

"Hello," he says, bowing slightly. "Can you tell me how I can get
down there?"

"De shteps," she says, using her walking stick to point behind her.

He shakes his head. All he can see is an abundance of trees
and leaves on the bluff next to the bridge. She walks back with
him, shows him the seventy-nine wooden steps that she has just
ascended and that are hidden from general view. He descends the
steps and then follows Cooper Street until he finds a house that
appears to be vacant. It is a hovel not much larger than his father's
chicken coop, sided by two bigger houses in better condition. He
continues on to the grocery store, where his fear is confirmed: it is

the house for rent. Prochazka is abrupt and distant, his face rough from at least two days of not shaving. Raimund figures him to be anywhere from thirty to fifty in age, his shoulders bent from a previous life of manual labor, his nose latticed red and purple from drinking. Raimund speaks in German but the grocer replies in English.

"What do you want a whole house for? You are only one person and a kid at that. You can stay at Cervenka's boardinghouse on the other side of the bridge."

"A whole house? It is a *bude!*"

"It is a house!"

"What business is it of yours who lives in it as long as I can pay the rent?"

Raimund counts the money aloud as he puts each dollar bill on the counter. It is six months' rent. Prochazka studies the stack of bills. Then he sweeps the dollars from the counter with a rough, tobacco-stained hand and puts them in his vest pocket.

"No trouble, you understand?" he warns. "Your next-door neighbor is Alzbêta Dvořák. A widow. She's been here a long time. Remember that."

Raimund purchases a wool blanket, a loaf of rye bread, a chunk of Swiss cheese, and some ground coffee before returning to Cooper Street. The two-room house has depressingly low ceilings and no furniture. A much-used cast iron teapot is left on the coal-burning stove with a tin cup beside it. He eats two slices of bread and cheese, walking in a circle as if to memorize the space. That night he lies on the floor and listens to the foghorns of the linked barges moving down the river.

Early the next morning he walks to work, crossing the Washington Avenue Bridge to the east side of the river and working his way down to the shoreline, following the river until he reaches the mill. And so begins his first week.

He is recognizably himself when he leaves the house in the morning, but then returns to it in the evening as if frosted with icing. The ivory of milled wheat whitewashes his entire being, even reaching the hair inside his nose and settling in his ears so that the wax he pries out looks like rendered pork lard. The phlegm he coughs up is a pale yellowish-white. The flour dust even seeps inside his coverall so that when he undresses, his body is pasted with the talcum of milled wheat and sweat, smelling faintly of yeast. It is the same for the others who work in the milling district—men coated in varying degrees of whiteness, depending on where they work in the mills. The whitest men are packers and earn less than he does. They exchange silent nods as they pass one another. What they do for a living remains on their clothing and bodies until their nightly baths. The men who work in the two remaining sawmills near the St. Anthony dam are brown from wood dust and shavings and have fragrant slivers of bark in their hair. The two men who load and sell coal on the Flats are covered in its black dust, the whites of their eyes startling in contrast to the midnight-smeared skin of their faces. The snot they blow out of their noses is gray and glutinous. The men passing by sometimes speak to him, offering only the name of where they work.

"Washburn."

"Carpenter–Lamb."

"Pillsbury," Raimund answers.

Then there are the few who work with the water turbines at the bottom of the drop shafts under Pillsbury A. The men emerge from their shifts dripping wet as though they have been swimming all day. They strip off their shirts on their walk home, revealing pale, macerated chests and arms. There are other men from the Flats who work in the mills but their departures and arrivals are not watched as his are. His neighbors are reserved, observing him with caution as if he were an exotic animal. He does not understand this. They may have come from different countries in Europe but they are still Europeans, immigrants like he is. He discerns the different languages spoken from overheard conversations and speculates where they have come from. He asks McPherson if he is correct.

"Aye. You have a good ear. 'Tis a soup of people down there on the Flats. Lived there myself when I first came here. 'Tis mostly Slovaks and Czechs. Some Russians, Poles, Swedes, Norwegians. A few Irish. A few Germans. A Finnish barrel maker and his wife."

The only person who consistently acknowledges his presence is his elderly neighbor Alzbêta Dvořák. She taps on her kitchen window to wave at him as he sets off for work, and then again when he comes home.

A YOUNG WOMAN makes herself known to him on the Wednesday of his second week, leaning out of the open window six houses east of his own on Cooper Street. He acknowledges her but does not stop. On Friday she beckons to him, leaning farther out of her window to display her ample cleavage.

"I see you get one of the best jobs quick," she says coyly.

"I have experience with machinery."

She offers up her name. Branka Cervenka. She does not wear a babushka like the other women, allowing her curly black hair to fall down her back. She tilts her head, smiles.

"I see you go by every day."

"My name is Raimund Kaufmann," he says, noticing that her fingers are ringless. He thinks of Maria Engel, her red hair fanned against the skin of her breasts. "Would you like to go for a walk after supper?"

She looks up at the bluff behind him. He hears whistling and assumes it is the men returning from work on the south side of the city.

"Maybe—yes. Tonight. I come to you," she says, standing up. "I know your house."

Then she closes the shutters. Her sudden change of demeanor confuses him, and he stands in front of the house for a moment wondering if it is custom on the Flats for a woman to come to a man's house. He dismisses it and heads toward his home, thinking that he will find out later that night.

He walks up the three steps to his house and puts his hand on the doorknob. Before he can turn it, a walrus-sized man with a thick beard spins him around and slams his head against the door. He holds a knife to Raimund's throat, swearing at him in what he recognizes as Czech.

"What do you want?" he protests.

Raimund's mind scatters to possibilities. Has he seen him before? Is he going to rob him? Does the big man work at the mill?

No—he doesn't work at the mill. He is not covered in flour. He smells . . . of wood and horses, even has the same large eyes as a horse except that his left eye wanders, confusing Raimund in his focus. And he has a thicket of hair sprouting from his ears. The man slams his head against the door again, and Raimund bites his own lip.

"You!" he yells, his breath reeking of sardines and beer. He bangs Raimund's head into the door a third time. Then the big man shifts the hilt of the knife so the blade is pointed down, held in place by the inside of his cuff. The fingers of his right hand are now free so that he can grab Raimund with both hands. He pulls Raimund forward, lifts and shakes him.

Raimund feels fluid in his eyes and blood trickling down his chin. He cannot think of what to do. Cannot raise his legs to kick the man or manipulate his arms. His head wobbles. It is as though the walrus man has knocked the gray matter of his brain loose from the moorings of his skull and is now shaking it into pudding.

A voice rings out. A thunderous voice. It is the voice of God, he thinks, with a Czech accent.

"Honza! Honza Cervenka!"

The walrus man hesitates but does not take his eyes off his victim. Raimund sees a movement behind them, dimly recognizes his neighbor, her head wrapped in a blue babushka. He cannot believe that a voice of such deep resonance comes from the old woman, and wonders if there is someone with her.

Alzbêta Dvořák crosses the yard between their houses, carrying a broom. She strikes Honza with the straw end of the broom. He shakes off the blow like it is an annoying fly and tightens his hold on Raimund's throat. Then the old woman flips the broom and grips the wooden handle above the straw head with both hands. She swings as if aiming to hit a high ball and smacks Honza in the back of his head. The walrus grunts, dropping Raimund so that his feet touch the wooden steps. But the big Czech still holds on to his throat. Alzbêta swings harder, striking Honza just below the crown of his head. He drops the knife. It bounces once on the steps before falling in the grass. Taking no chances, she raises the broom handle vertically and brings it down a third time, the handle splintering on the top of Honza's head. He releases Raimund, trips down the steps, and falls into the grass.

"Stupid man!" she roars. "Get up!"

She reaches down, grabs the knife, and throws it into her yard. Then she pushes Honza with the broken end of the broom until he stands up and stumbles out into the street.

"How was this boy to know she was your wife? How does anyone know she is your wife? Branka hangs out of that window every day without her wedding ring on, showing her *prsa* like bait to young men like Raimund who don't know any better. You fool! You think you are the only one earning money in your house? You," she commands, pointing a finger at him, "better go home and deal with that Jezebel before you stick a knife into someone."

"Cervenka," Raimund says faintly, his hand outstretched in its blind quest to find the doorknob. "Don't you own the boarding-house?"

"That's his brother," Alzbêta answers. She motions with the remains of her broom as though to sweep Honza on his way. He walks backward, rubbing his head and eyeing Raimund.

"And clean out your ears!" she yells. She turns to Raimund and says, "He's certifiably deaf in his right ear and his left . . . well, he's got the hairy ass of a dog in that one."

The old woman comes up the steps and examines Raimund to see if there are any cuts other than his bitten lip.

"Wait here."

She returns with a wedge of ice wrapped in an old pillowcase and some mildewed-looking leaves.

"Put the ice on your head or neck, wherever it hurts the most," she instructs, "and make two pots of tea with these. Drink all of it."

He slumps against his door and watches her cross the yard. She turns when she reaches the doorstep of her house.

"I want you to go to church with me on Sunday and then come over for dinner," she says. "Make sure you wear a suit."

He boils and drinks the bitter tea, holding the ice against his head until it melts. It isn't until he falls onto his bed that he realizes something.

She said his name.

✠ ✠ ✠

THAT SATURDAY Raimund goes to the city on top of the bluff and buys a used suit and some shoes from an acerbic tailor. On Sunday he escorts Alzbêta to mass at St. Elizabeth's Church in south Minneapolis, and then home again. She is not wearing her usual babushka but a white lace veil, allowing Raimund to see the grainy mix of silver and smoke-gray hair that she has plaited and pinned into two braids across her head. The trip to church and back allows Raimund to observe his elderly benefactor in detail.

Her face is that of a much-used map, the skin visibly soft as though it has been folded and touched many times for guidance. Her large nose is the scale of direction and the mountain peak of her face. The prominent creases in her forehead are north, and the deep lines alongside her nose and mouth are south, creating the concave of age aided by the loss of some teeth. Her cheeks are plateaus, crosshatched with fine lines of what he senses are not just from years of gravitational pull but of work, of knowledge, perhaps sadness. He feels something else upon looking at her, inherent in her voice when she saved him from Honza's assault. Unlike the statue of the humble blue-clad deity of the Virgin Mother, the old woman radiates power and strength, and there is something of the all-knowing about her. Even the priest, Father Hughes, appears to be in awe of her.

Alzbêta's house is in much better condition than his, with clapboard rather than tar-shingled siding, stucco walls, a big nickel-plated stove and oven, more rooms, nice furniture, and polished wooden floors. She serves sausage patties, potato and watercress soup, sauerkraut, fresh peas from her garden, and strong coffee tempered by thick cream and sugar. While Raimund eats, she asks him where he is from in Germany and about his job at the mill. He finds out in turn that she teaches English to new immigrants and has lived on the Flats for thirty years. He stands up to help her clear the dishes from the table.

"Sit."

She opens the oven door, pulls out a large round pastry on a baking sheet, puts it on top of the stove, and dusts it with sugar. Then she slides the pastry onto a clean plate, and puts it in front of him.

"There. Tell me if that isn't the best *Koláč* you've ever had," she says.

He doesn't know what a *Koláč* is but remembers that Frau Richter said that the Czechs were famous for their pastries. He looks at the moon of buttery pastry in front of him, at the deep purple iris of filling in the middle. He cuts a steaming piece, and puts it into his mouth. His mother is an excellent baker and her strudel is considered among the best at local festivals. Yet she had never made anything this rich, buttery, and light, weighed down only by the intense prune filling. Raimund takes a second bite and his eyes well up.

The *Koláč* evokes those early-morning raids to the pastry cupboard and the image of his mother praying on her knees at the kitchen table. He has not yet written his mother a letter. And now he is a boy alone in a strange country and aware of the people he has left behind. His mother, his brother Albert, his sister-in-law Magdalena, and her parents the Richters. The feeling of being unwanted as he walks through the Flats intensifies the loneliness.

"You are thinking," Alzbêta says, "of your mother?"

He nods and wipes his eyes on his shirtsleeves.

"You are fifteen?"

"Sixteen."

"So young," she says. "But so brave to come all this way by yourself. How did you get the money? And does your mother know where you are?"

He tells her the condensed version of what had provoked him to leave Germany and how he had done it. How he expected things to be different but discovered that people could be unfriendly here as well.

"For some of the Czechs and Slovaks, it could be because you are clearly educated and not lowbrow German," she said. "You got a job as a miller while many of the older men are still working as packers. You know the history of Bohemia and the rest of Eastern Europe? The strength of the Hapsburg dynasty in trying to wipe out our native language?"

"Yes."

"They are still probably fighting in Prague as to whether official business should be conducted in German or Czech."

"But that is over there," he protests. "I wanted to leave that behind. I didn't want that here. I'm not an aristocrat!"

"Oh, Raimund," she sighs. "You'll find that you bring your culture with you and that for some people that can include old feuds. It is mostly that you are new, though. And young and single, and handsome. It takes the residents awhile to get used to new people. There are others down here who are not Czech or Slovak. We have at least five German families. We have Irish families, Italian families, Swedish families, Norwegian families, some Russians, and a man from Macedonia who just came this year. We have a Finnish couple—Aino and Kyle Takelo. We even have a Jew."

Raimund isn't sure he has heard her correctly, her accent thickening the language.

"You have a jewel?" he asks, wondering in whose possession it is kept. "What kind?"

"Oh!" she exclaims, covering her mouth with her fist, her body shaking. "That is funny," she gasps moments later, wiping her eyes with her apron.

"A Jude!" she says in German and then repeats in English. "A Jew!"

She wipes her eyes again. "I can't wait to tell Zalman this. He is a jewel. One of the best tailors there is and such a nice man. His last name is Sokoloff. I don't know why he lives here and not with the rest of his people in north Minneapolis. Or why he's not married. He's private that way. Finish your *Koláč*," she says, pointing to his plate, "and then we'll talk."

Raimund eats the rest of his dessert and resists licking the plate free of crumbs. Alzbêta produces a bottle of Slivovitz and two small glasses. She fills both glasses and then sits down.

"I think you are a good boy, with good manners," she begins. "So I'm going to tell you a few things that will make it easier for you to live down here. Things your mother would tell you if she were living here."

He takes a sip from his glass.

"Rule number one," she says. "Don't bed any of the women down here."

He chokes, his throat burning from the plum brandy.

"You've never had Slivovitz?"

"Yes," he lies, coughing, "I have." He gulps the rest of the glass before speaking.

"M-m-my mother would never say that to me."

"She would if she had come across with you," the older woman counters. "I know what happens on ships. It is only natural for a boy of your age. Nothing to be embarrassed about."

"Why should I stay away from the women down here?"

"Raimund! It is just like the Old Country. If you get a girl in trouble or you sleep with someone's wife, they will kill you. Look what happened with Honza and you hadn't done anything but talk to that crazy woman he has for a wife."

She refills both glasses.

"They have a saying here that I like very much," she says. "Do you want to hear it?"

"O-kay," he responds, trying out his new American slang. He takes a bigger sip of Slivovitz, preparing himself.

"Don't shit where you eat." She refills his glass again.

"I should go up to the city—" he begins.

"For that," she finishes.

"If that is the first rule, then what is the second rule?"

"The second rule is to be careful on Sunday nights. Honza and his brother sell homemade beer down here. It tends to get out of hand sometimes. You can get killed that way, too. I don't want you to get mixed up in any of that."

"And the third rule?"

"The third rule is everything else. You'll learn as you go along. But," she adds, looking at his secondhand suit, "when you earn enough money, get Zalman to make you a better suit."

She gives him a loaf of potato bread, a kettle of soup, and another large *Koláč* wrapped in a clean dishtowel. He leaves her house feeling restored, happy, and slightly drunk. Since it is Sunday, the residents on Cooper Street are relaxing outside their houses. His immediate neighbors smile at him. He smiles and nods back. The change in their behavior hits him a few moments after he enters his own house. The first rule is not the first rule. The first rule is unspoken although Prochazka had alluded to it. Alzbêta Dvořák is the matriarch of the Flats. Her acceptance of him assures the rest of the people that he is fit to live among them.

A FEW DAYS LATER, Alzbêta introduces him to Moira O'Flaherty, an ink-haired, widowed seamstress who lives on Mill Street and whose devil-may-care blue eyes seem privy to a joke known only to her. It is from Mrs. O'Flaherty that Raimund learns that there had been other names attributed to the riverfront village, depending on which immigrant wave had settled there for a time. It had been called the Danish Flats, Little Lithuania, and Little Ireland. In the early 1880s, it was known as the Connemara Patch for a while because a group of impoverished Connemaras had lived there, having arrived from Ireland speaking only Gaelic.

"They came over just barely alive. I guess the group was bigger when they boarded in Ireland but many of them died like flies on the ship," she says, looking toward the river from where they sat in Alzbêta's yard. "'Twas only thirty of them that made it. The Connemara are a proud people. *Mara* in Gaelic means 'of the sea.' It takes a lot to separate a Connemara from his land in West Ireland. They looked so bad when they got off the train that a station agent sent a message to Mrs. John Fallon. She and her husband are lace-curtain Irish who lived in one of the nicer houses up there on Seven Corners."

She points up as though the neighborhood of Seven Corners resides in the clouds.

"She's a good woman. She could have ignored them, being well-to-do, but she didn't. She put a family here and there among the other Irish up in the city who were willing to house them. Then her husband and a group of his friends built a big rooming house down here from driftwood they dragged out of the river. You know Cervenka's boardinghouse?"

He nodded.

"'Tis where the original house was until it was torn down by Honza and his brother and rebuilt. All thirty of the Connemaras moved in there until they could make individual shanties of their own. Mrs. Fallon taught them to speak English so that they could get jobs. They hated it, you know. But Mrs. Fallon said, 'It's nothing to balk about. 'Tis American you are learning and you can't live here without it.'"

She sighed and then tilted her head toward Raimund like a canary.

"The Connemaras were only poor, not stupid. American is just another version of the King's English. But they learned it. They had to. Just as I did."

"Are you a Connemara?" he asks.

"No. My man was," she answers. "When we got married, he didn't give me a wedding ring. He gave me this." She draws back her shawl to show him a silver necklace with a large green pendant. "That's Connemara marble. Better than gold or diamonds."

BY WORD OF MOUTH and by reading the two major newspapers Raimund learns within two months that the city people regard the Flats with superstition and fear, based on some truth but mostly stained with the consistent piss of prejudice. He learns that it doesn't matter if you are Swedish, Irish, Italian, German, Norwegian, or any other ethnicity. Once you live on the Flats you become lumped with the Slovaks and Czechs. You become *a Bohemian*.

"If I were you, I'd find a different place to live. There is no intelligence down there. No civilized behavior," the man who sold Raimund his suit had said. "They are emotional. Like women."

He stood back and appraised the fit of the suit.

"They lack a sense of decorum. They are superstitious and they show no moderation when it comes to alcohol. Now that I think of it, they would be better off in St. Paul," he added.

Alzbêta laughed when Raimund told her what the tailor had said.

"I'll bet he's a Presbyterian. You'll find that religion over here isn't any different from Europe. Minneapolis is Protestant and St. Paul is Catholic. If you want to learn more than that, you will have to go up and walk through both of the cities to understand them and their attitudes. But wait until winter is over. You will enjoy it more."

WINTER IS HARSH on the Flats, although the bluffs protect its residents from severe winds coupled with the twenty-below temperatures that kill the unprotected. The cold surrounds and cups Raimund's house, sticks its fingers through the cracks because of the lack of insulation. He buys scraps of horsehair cloth, used for upholstering furniture, from Zalman (whose nail on his right index finger is permanently grooved) and tacks it over the windows. On Honza's recommendation, he purchases and installs a better coal-burning stove. Alzbêta makes him a huge feather quilt and pillow for the mattress and bed he scrounged from the city above. She packs his lunch every day and he eats his evening meal at her house. He learns that this winter is considered a mild one in terms of snow but that the lack of it also makes it colder.

One Sunday in mid-February, crazy with the confinement of his small house, Raimund puts on two pairs of pants and two coats, pulls on thick socks, steps into a pair of cork-bottomed boots, and wraps a thickly knitted scarf around his head and neck until only his eyes show. He walks next door, where Alzbêta gives him knitted inserts for his rough-palmed leather gloves.

"What are you planning to do dressed like that?" she asks.

"See like a bird," he answers.

He walks until he faces the bridge, and looking up he surveys the trestles. There is no wind, just the stillness of winter. Then he begins to climb, the cork soles and gloves giving him the necessary grip to shimmy up the diagonal trusses, resting whenever he reaches a node, the center where two iron trusses cross. Raimund gradually makes his way across the bridge's trestles until he is in the middle of the bridge with the center of the river below. He scans the small channel of open water that the river has become in winter. He looks east and gazes at the imperial buildings of the university, grand in their stature on top of the east bank. Then he shifts focus west so that he can look at his house and the other houses as they appear in winter. The snow has made the river community less dingy and more picturesque with the whitened roofs appearing like the swirled meringue topping of fairytale cottages, with only a trail of black smoke coming from each pipe chimney. A group of people including Alzbêta have walked to the shoreline to peer up at him. Someone with a heavy tread is walking above him on the bridge. The footsteps stop when they reach his position.

"You know," Honza begins, "sane people walk on top of the bridge if they want a view of the river. It's easier that way."

"I know. I needed the exercise."

"How are you planning to get down?"

"Same way I got up here. Climb."

"I don't think so," Honza says. "Those trusses are ice cold and I'll bet your hands are numbing up in those gloves."

A heavy rope is flung over the edge. Raimund hears more boot steps.

"You'll grab it and tie it around you if you know what's good for you."

He hesitates, wanting to prove he can climb down, but the tips of his fingers are numb and even two pairs of pants cannot insulate his legs enough from the cold steel. He ties the rope securely around his middle, intending to climb up and around the deck bridge so that he can grab one of the vertical railings. Just as he reaches for a railing, he loses his grip and is suddenly dangling, the rope tightening around his chest. He can think of nothing but the weightlessness of his body and at the same time the constriction of the rope. Then Honza and three other men heave on the rope, yanking him up and pulling him over the horizontal railing.

He expects the fire of Honza's temper but the big Czech only shakes his head and pushes Raimund into walking toward the west end of the bridge, the rest of the men smirking. Alzbêta and Mrs. O'Flaherty are waiting at the bottom of the steps.

Alzbêta yanks off his scarf and cuffs him hard.

"You stupid boy! See like a bird, die like a bird!"

Then she huffs off toward her house.

"Oh, Raimund," Mrs. O'Flaherty says, her blue eyes somber. "The Good Lord does not like those who play recklessly with their lives, tormenting those who love them."

She linked her arm with his.

"Come to my house and have a hot bath. And then go over and apologize to Alzbêta."

HE IS OVERJOYED when they experience an unusually early spring, the weather warming to the forties at the end of February.

In March, Raimund begins to spend his precious days off roaming both cities. He strolls through neighborhoods, rich, middle class, and working poor, seeing that the definition of each level remains the same. The rich have large and opulent houses set back from the road with large flower gardens and lawns, many gated to keep uninvited pedestrians out. The middle class have smaller but still comfortable houses, sitting on just enough of a lot to command some respectable grass frontage. The poor neighborhoods are like the Flats, people crammed together in brick or wooden tenements or two-room houses, with dirt rather than grass to walk on. If there is grass, its anemic blades grow in and among the refuse of living.

The Flats residents watch with bemused interest when he heads out on these mornings.

"Here," Honza says, putting a pile of coins in his hand, "take the streetcar. Make it easier on yourself."

"I like walking. I can't see anything riding on the streetcar," Raimund says, handing the coins back. "I meet people better that way, see things better that way. The streetcars don't go down alleys and across yards. Don't stop enough. Besides, it's a waste of money traveling by streetcar."

Honza grabs Raimund's hand, pours the coins back into the palm, and then closes Raimund's fingers over the money. He points to Raimund's boots.

"With all the walking you're doing, you're gonna need new boots."

He puts the money in his pocket, grins his thanks. *Walking,* he wants to say, *allows me to think. To smell. To touch.*

RAIMUND WALKS along the east and west shores of the Mississippi to see who else lives and works on the river. He talks to the men on the St. Paul docks and also converses with the men working on the St. Anthony Falls dam, not far from the Pillsbury A and the Washburn C mills. He stares at the opulent townhouses on the north side of Nicollet Island, made with the same gray limestone as the Pillsbury A and graced with huge arched windows.

He crosses to the south side of the island just as a group of

Minneapolis police officers are forcing an Indian family to leave the teepee they had pitched among the trees next to a sash and door company. He watches city workers dismantle the teepee, stack the lodge poles, and pile up the hides that covered them. The Indian family watches impassively but Raimund recognizes the deep reserve of grief. There is an old man with long braids in work pants and boots wearing a deerskin shirt. There is an old woman whom Raimund takes to be the man's wife, wrapped in a colorful blanket with beaded deerskin moccasins on her feet. A younger woman, dressed like the older one, stands next to the old man. She holds a child in a cradle board, a band across its head.

"They just keep trying," a voice says behind him. It is the priest from the Catholic church just four blocks down from the mill on Main Street. "This is the fifth time they've been caught squatting down here."

"Are they Chippewa?" Raimund asks.

"No. They are Dakota. It was their home once," he explains. "But times are different. They must change like everyone else. Adapt. It is the way of the world now. We offered them shelter in the church but they refused."

Raimund bids the priest goodbye, guessing that the offer of lodging was not as simple as it seemed.

RAIMUND PURCHASES Chinese tea from Yee Sing's Laundry and Tea Shop on Nicollet Avenue and buys a bottle of wine from Traeger's Wine House on Bridge Square. Another day he pulls a button off his shirt before entering Marienhoff's Tailor Shop on Hennepin Avenue so he has an excuse to chat with the German tailor while he sews the button back on. Early one morning he takes a streetcar into St. Paul with an ink setter who works at the *Pioneer Press*. He stands entranced by the newspaper sheets as they fly off the large presses at the production plant on East Third Street. He then buys candy at Pellegrini's Confectioner shop on Seventh Street. There he learns that Pellegrini had once worked in the mills and lived on the Flats.

"I like my business and my new house. But it isn't the same. Say hello to Alzbêta. She took care of my wife when our first two were born," he says, giving Raimund an extra bag of licorice for his neighbor.

That night Honza asks him what he did all day. They are sitting on logs near the shore of the river, drinking beer.

"Yeah, I know Pellegrini," Honza says after Raimund mentioned the candy maker. "He's a good man. Didn't become a stick-up-his-ass when he moved to St. Paul and opened his shop. He's not ashamed to tell anyone who asks where he began after he came over. But when some people leave the Flats and move up, they don't want anyone to know." Turning to his brother, Radim, Honza says, "Remember Dobroslav Bartusek?"

Radim nods, grimaces with disgust.

"He lived down here for six years," Honza says, turning back to Raimund. "Did the same dirty jobs in the mills we all did. But then he got a job working up at the Lake Calhoun Pavilion. Told them his name was Don Bart. He worked his way up and now he's the manager of the pavilion. Has a nice house just blocks away on Lowry Street. I took my first wife to the pavilion to see Dobroslav, see how he was doing. I gave him a big wave, shouted out his name like old times. He pretended he didn't know us but I could see he was embarrassed. Then he came over, told us to meet him outside, and made us walk through the service entrance. I asked him what the deal was when we got outside. We used to be good friends. Then he tells us that he's changed his name, that he and his family don't live like they did when they were on the Flats. I asked him, 'Well, how do you live then?' He said he and his family lived quietly, and with manners. Then he tried to give us money to go away."

Honza's ears turn red with the memory.

"I didn't blow up. Wasn't going to embarrass him or my wife. But I told him to keep his damn money because we were never coming back. Told him he was a traitor to Bohemia!"

He stops as if to keep his temper from rising, takes a deep breath.

"Mind you," he says, "I don't begrudge any man who works up the ladder. I would have been happy for him. But to change his name? To pretend he is an Anglo instead of a Bohemian? Christ Almighty! He sold his soul to the devil! That's too high a price for me."

Honza paused to lick the edge of the cigarette he was rolling. "I ask you, what kind of name is Don Bart?"

THE NEXT SUNDAY, Raimund goes back to downtown St. Paul and meanders some more. He stops by Miles Locksmith on Jackson Street to purchase a new lock for his house. Then he decides to walk home via Selby Street. He is waiting to cross the road on the corner of Selby and Dale when he hears a female voice calling him.

"Pretty man. Pree-teee man. Come see me."

He turns and sees a woman leaning out of a second-story window of a well-kept brick house with striped awnings. An older woman appears next to her at the window and gestures for him to come in. It is a brothel that is neither upscale nor lower class, and he spends a blissful afternoon sandwiched between two women. One is the woman who called to him, a Louisiana Creole with caramel-colored skin and black hair that falls to her thighs. The other is a Negro woman as tall as he is, generously proportioned with skin that smells of roses and is the color of the night sky.

After he leaves the brothel, he takes a streetcar to the St. Paul city limits near the university then walks from there, pondering what he has learned. He never identifies where he lives through his sojourns into the cities, bringing up the Flats in a roundabout way. His English quickly becomes flawless and he can mask his accent, sprinkling his speech with vernacular that makes him sound as though he is from generations of settled Americans. He offers the diminutive American version of his name—Ray—which suffices for introducing conversation and familiarity. The dockworkers have no opinion one way or the other about the Flats, living in similar shack communities close to the water. One night after work he casually asked the bartender and owner of the Pracna Saloon just two blocks down from Pillsbury A what he thought about the Flats.

"The mill workers are my customers. Where they live or come from is none of my concern," he said, topping off Raimund's beer. "As long as they pay."

Pellegrini's response is the only positive one. What Raimund hears most is that the Slovaks and Czechs are barbaric for cooking outside in the summer on heated stones and in limestone ovens, for collecting mushrooms and wild herbs on the riverbanks, and for making their own beer, which they sell on Sundays when the breweries are closed. They are thought to lack ambition because they stay on the Flats, salvaging whatever drifts downriver and enduring what hatches from it during the summer to cloud the shore and bite the skin. They hold the most menial of jobs: the men work in the flour and lumber mills, breweries, and factories, and the women take in laundry or climb the steps each day to domestic jobs in the cities or walk alongside Raimund and the other men to reach the North Star Woolen Mill across the river near the Washburn C Mill.

"You live in the Cabbage Patch, eh?" an Irish bartender on East Hennepin said, alluding to the large cabbage gardens that produced the sauerkraut eaten at least twice a day on the Flats. "How do you do it? Jesus, Mary, and Joseph! The smell of kraut is so strong down there it burns your nose. It must feel like fire coming out the other end. Then you have the stink of the river. Rotting fish and mud. The smell of shit. Nope," he shook his head. "I couldn't stand it. But," he added, "those bohunks do make good beer."

ALZBÊTA IS RIGHT. He learns that people bring their culture, cultural feuds, and religious differences with them. Once in the States, they are free to modify their ethnic identities and cultural morals as their fortunes rise, often adapting the disdainful manners of the dominant Anglo culture.

He thinks about Dobroslav Bartusek. Birth here does not, as it does in Europe, dictate one's station in life. A peasant can work his way up to being a prominent businessman or hold political office. Varying levels of social veneer are purchased with the corresponding level of money obtained and as wealth is obtained, so is repression cast as good manners.

One night, after a day off spent in the city, Raimund told Alzbêta his impressions and asked her why she had never moved up to Minneapolis, where she could make a better living teaching.

"Remember what that tailor said? But you tell me this: How can you live a life without passion? Life *is* passion."

He stops midway across the Washington Avenue Bridge,

remembering the pleasure of the afternoon and yet nauseated by the cities. This is not the America he had imagined. Not all who emigrated were welcomed and nowhere was this more evident than on the Flats.

Yet the Flats themselves were not immune to social stratification, evident in the streets that run parallel with the river.

As Honza had once told him, "those who live farther up on the bluff on Mill Street earn the most and have the best jobs. Cooper Street here is just one level down and we make almost as good a pay as those on Mill Street. But those on Wood Street," he shook his head and looked down, "are the new people who just come over. The rent's cheap because, as you can see, those houses sit right on the river. That's why it's called Little Venice, and the people who live there are called wood rats. Every year those closest to the river get flooded out when the river rises. You saw the boats?"

Raimund nodded.

"They live in their houses as long as they can 'cause sometimes the river floods only the first floor. Then they crawl out a top window and climb into the boats, and pole the river to get where they need to be, even if it's the house next door. But sometimes whole houses get flooded and then many of us take in the family till the water goes down. It can get a little tense."

"Tense!" Alzbêta interrupts. "Calling them wood rats behind their backs isn't tense. It's mean. And you, Honza, lived on Wood Street when you came over. You should know better!"

RAIMUND GAZES DOWN in the fading late April light at his new home on the western shore of the Mississippi. He thinks of how those who rise in prominence in Minneapolis and St. Paul adopt the cultural norms he hated in Germany. The cultural dictate to be closemouthed about unpleasant things, to keep up appearances, and to pretend, should something bad happen, that it has not happened even if it means denying the obvious.

On the Flats it is not so. When a problem arises, when there is a fight or a disagreement or unpleasant business, it does not stay under cover for long. The Flats residents, especially the Czechs and Slovaks, react, ask questions, debate the incident or issue over beer or coffee. The question of *why* is asked. Then the men of the Flats chew the juice out of the incident or problem along with their snuff, spitting out the tobacco remains and a conclusion into the grass. The women do the same, talking it through until finally someone puts a fist down on the table, pronounces a solution or at least an understanding, and then coffee and pastries are served. Here Raimund can ask a question without punishment. He may not get the answer, but the freedom to even question is an expected right.

"Think!" Alzbêta roars at him from time to time when he does something irrational.

"Think, Raimund!" is what his former teacher Herr Professor Richter would say to him, pushing him to consider the unconsidered. Richter told him to use his imagination, to think beyond an easy solution to a problem for a better, more creative one. To speak courteously but directly. To be curious. To seek information.

"Life is about asking questions," Richter had said. "And finding answers although you may not like the answers you get. But even those give direction. I don't agree with the proverb that what you don't know cannot hurt you. No one can guarantee happiness, but how do you know happiness if you are ignorant? Happiness and joy is not something that is bestowed on you. It is something you work toward, something that is not consistent but comes with the effort of living. Joy shows up in the most unexpected places."

Raimund has found that unexpected place that holds the *joie de vivre* that Richter told him to look for. The river village is where he belongs. He is certain of this, more certain than he has ever been in his life.

He makes two vows standing on the bridge: to never move to the cities on the bluff above, and to legally change his name to its American version.

Raymond.

HE HEEDS ALZBÊTA'S WARNING about Sundays, as that is the day of the week that gives the journalists from both cities fodder for stories and yet another name for the Flats. While the majority of the houses contain families, the Flats also have a significant population of young and single men who frequently get drunk at night.

They roam the waterfront and the small streets in between the houses looking for entertainment, be it a woman whose husband is working the night shift or a teenage girl disobeying her parents and courting disaster. Fights break out over such prizes, but those too are considered a good time if the men survive to go to work the next day. They posture and swagger with pride to show that despite lost teeth or a pummeled face, they had held their ground. But sometimes the good-time fights turn bad and someone dies from a mortal knife wound to the neck, lungs, heart, or gut. There are the occasional domestic squabbles between husbands and wives and more rarely between neighbors. During the week such violence does not involve anyone from above the river. It is the sale of home-brewed Czech and Slovak beer on Sunday that brings the city dwellers down to the Flats. And the major producers of that beer are Honza and his brother Radim.

"They come down to buy our beer but they never learn," Honza told him. "There wouldn't be any fights if they didn't insult us or tell me my beer is too expensive. I tell them don't buy it then. Go home. But then they buy it. I tell them don't drink it down here. I tell them that they have their beer, now take it home. But it seems to be sport for some of them."

He learns from Honza that the police of the Third Precinct dread Sunday nights on the Flats, christening the riverfront village with the name of an infamous neighborhood in New York City. One Sunday night, Raymond hid in the trees by the steps and watched the police advance.

"It's the seventh day, boys," the sergeant barked as the uniformed contingent walked down the seventy-nine steps with billy clubs and lanterns in their hands. "You may have gotten up with God this morning but if you aren't careful, you'll go to bed with the devil in Hell's Kitchen tonight."

RAYMOND ALSO DISCOVERS that the man who nearly crushed his head is solid in his loyalties when he gives them, contradictory as they may be. Honza owns several horses, drays and riding stock, and keeps them in a horse barn he owns in the Seven Corners neighborhood at the top of the bluff. He loves his horses more than he does his women, leading them down the bluff during warm days so that they can roll in the shallows of the river. He trusts almost no one with his horses, including Radim. But he occasionally needs help when he is hired to haul something in his wagon, or when the outdoor ovens require new slabs of limestone, which must be quarried and dragged down from the upper bluff. He often hires the Finnish cooper, Kyle Takelo. After taking on Raymond several times when Kyle was not available, he notices the young German's affectionate and diligent care toward the animals.

"You are like Kyle," he says one day. "You have a good voice. Horses know men by their voices. Trust them by their voices."

HONZA WAS ON HIS SECOND WIFE when Raymond moved to the Flats, but within three months Branka left him to live "up on the hill" as the Flats people call the southern neighborhoods of Minneapolis. Honza didn't bother to look for her.

"She is where she was meant to be," Honza said, after a neighbor mentioned seeing her in a dubious boardinghouse. They had not been legally married, but few on the Flats considered that a requirement for marriage. Raymond found out from Alzbêta that Honza's first wife, Berta, had died in childbirth. Two months after Branka's departure, Honza finds a third woman, Bozena, marries her, and installs her in his house. People call her Zena for short. She is not pretty like Branka, but neither is she ugly. She genuinely cares about Honza except when he lags behind in his chores. Then her temper is fierce and audible.

"It's a good thing he's partially deaf," Raymond comments to Alzbêta as she shreds cabbage and he salts and packs it into stoneware crocks. They can hear Zena's shrieking all the way down the street. "All of his women have names that start with B. Is there a reason for that?"

Alzbêta picks up a large head of cabbage and halves it with a cleaver on the wooden block they have set up outside. "It is his fate to be stuck with that letter in the alphabet. Never A but B. Could be worse."

ONE FRIDAY Raymond decides not to return home after his shift. He spends a half hour drinking beer at the Pracna Saloon and then crosses the small bridge over to Nicollet Island. He is fascinated by the island and by its locale in the middle of the city. No workers live there, only those who can afford the expensive limestone Eastman Flats and the big Victorian homes on the north side. His presence makes the residents nervous and they make him wary. He stays out of sight by keeping to the wooded areas along the steep shoreline. Raymond sits on the east shore to watch the St. Anthony Falls until the sun is low in the sky.

He returns home by running across the rail tracks of the stone arch railroad bridge to the west shore and then heads south. It is late April and the buds on the trees have just opened, miniature green flags that will grow in a few weeks into dark-green canopies covering the bluffs. He hikes down the bluff to the westernmost edge of the Flats community. He has not gone far when he hears singing and sees the outline of someone standing on the shore. He flattens himself on the ground and crawls slowly toward the figure. It is a woman. He crawls two more feet and is stopped by a sudden sharp pain between his shoulder blades. The tip of a knife is pressed into his back.

"Don't move," a voice whispers. Raymond lifts his hands, palms up from the ground. The man rolls away from him. It is the Finnish cooper. Raymond sees the glint of a large blade.

"I'm not going to kill you," Kyle says in a low voice. "But don't get any closer to my wife."

"I won't," Raymond answers, keeping his voice as low. He stares at the length of the blade, the leather-wrapped handle.

"What kind of knife is that?"

"A big one."

Kyle puts a finger to his lips. He looks back at his flaxen-haired wife singing to the river. Raymond cannot understand the words for she is singing in Finnish but the song is mournful yet rhythmic and lilting. He is mesmerized, feels caught by her singing, as though he were in a net. The song tapers off. Then she turns her head in their direction. Raymond holds his breath. Her face is wet with tears.

☩ ☩ ☩

TWO DAYS LATER, with the cooper's wife's singing running through his head, he walks home from the mill, this time down Washington Avenue from the north. McPherson had told him there was a brothel on the avenue operating behind a storefront of dry goods.

"It's expensive," he said, rubbing his fingers together, "but well worth saving your pay for. The women are," he paused, his eyes drifting toward the ceiling with the savor of a recent visit. "The women are, let's say, fallen daughters of the aristocracy. The door to the brothel is in the alley and it is *pink*."

There are at least three dry goods stores. Raymond walks into the alley next to the first store but finds the service entry dark and grungy from use. He walks the next block over and turns into that alley. There is no pink door there either. Rather than walk back out to the avenue, he continues to the end of the alley and, rounding the corner to the back, surprises two men. After a moment's hesitation, he pretends to have seen nothing and continues on his way. He forgets about his search for the pink door, walks out onto the avenue and toward the west end of the bridge. He is nauseous and sweating when he reaches Alzbêta's house.

"Are you sick?" she asks, directing him to sit at the kitchen table.

"I don't know."

"What do you mean you don't know? Either you are or you're not."

"I saw Zalman."

"So?"

"With another man," he choked out, feeling the delayed revulsion of that brief sight. He can't remember what the other man looked like, only that Zalman was fondling him. Alzbêta does not seem surprised.

"He's one of those—"

"Men with other desires," she interrupts.

"I thought you said you didn't know why he wasn't married?"

"I lied. Or partially lied. He may still like women, too. There are men like that," she says, flipping her hand back and forth. "Fifty–fifty."

He feels a storm roiling up from his stomach and knocks over the chair in his rush to get to the sink. The old woman waits until he is done, and then fetches a bottle of beer from a pail filled with ice.

"Sip this. A little bit at a time," she says. Then she asks, "Did Zalman see you?"

He nods. She sits down. Sighs.

"I've known for about five years. If I thought he bothered children, I'd take issue with it. But he doesn't. He likes grown men."

"Are there others like him down here?" Raymond asks, the beer's bitterness mixing with the bile in his mouth. He can't imagine touching a man in such a way. He's heard talk at the mill about such men. They call them queers or poofters.

"I don't know. And I don't need to know. Zalman does his business, just like you do, up in the city above. The Flats offer him the same amount of freedom that you enjoy."

"Don't you think others have guessed? He is in his thirties and has no woman."

"They may have. As long as he keeps private about it, keeps it away from down here, they are likely to ignore it. But I can't be entirely sure about their knowledge or reaction if you were to say something. Just let sleeping dogs lie. I don't want any harm to come to Zalman. He is a good man and a good tailor. What he does for pleasure is his business. You may not like it but it doesn't interfere with your life now, does it?"

"No."

"You can go on thinking about your women and he can think about his men and the two will not cross paths. What were you doing in the alleys on Washington Avenue anyway?"

He looks down, feels the heat of embarrassment crawl up from his neck to his face.

"I thought so. Now look at me. Do we have an agreement? You will keep your mouth shut?"

"Yes," he answers, looking up and biting his lip. Repulsed as he may be, he has no desire to hurt Zalman unless Zalman should take a fancy to him.

"If you're worried that he's interested in you, I can tell you that he is not," she says, an amused look on her face.

"How do you know?"

"I know. Now get it out of your head and keep your mouth shut. Or I'll come over to your house and beat you with something worse than a broom."

THE PREVIOUS YEAR Raymond had arrived on the Flats too late to experience the Morena—the Eastern European ceremony of spring held in the month of May. His seventeenth birthday coincided with his first Morena, and he considered the celebration to be the greatest birthday party he'd ever had. Unbeknownst to him it was also the beginning of an annual drunken argument with Honza about the gender of winter.

"It's Old Man Winter," Raymond tells him, drinking a glass of beer. They watch as a group of young boys carries a straw dummy in the shape of a woman down to the river's edge.

"Not in Bohemia!" Honza proclaims, raising his glass. He wipes a crest of foam from his moustache with the back of his hand.

"Honza. This is America," Raymond argues. "Winter is a man here. Traditions have to adapt when you move or else they die. The kids don't make snow women. They make snowmen."

"You have it all wrong," he counters. "A nigger on the docks in St. Paul told me the Mississippi River is a man. Would it make sense to throw a man into the river? Would that bring spring? Make things grow? No!"

He walks away to get a fresh glass of beer. Raymond finds the straw dummy strange. It seems a violent gesture toward the women in the village, although they don't appear to mind because it is tradition. But most women on the Flats rule the households. They banish winter with spring cleaning and the planting of gardens. He has learned that from the beginning of the village's existence there had never been a declared patriarch on the Flats, only a matriarch.

"So throw a female straw pig or donkey into the river. Not a straw woman," Raymond says, picking up the thread of the argument when Honza returns with a full glass of beer.

"It is tradition," he answers. "This is the Flats, not all of America. If we changed it, it would no longer be Bohemian. Now be quiet. The boys are ready."

They swing the dummy back and forth three times before throwing it into the water with the cry, "Drown the winter!" A second cry goes up among the people on shore. "Drown the winter!"

And with that, the celebration begins. Raymond sets up the log tables with Kyle Takelo. The women follow, placing bowls of sauerkraut and sour mushroom soup, platters of carved roast pig and smoked fish, rye, potato, and black bread, Bohemian goat cheese, potato dumplings, something called potato dreams, and potato rolls next to trays of prune- and poppyseed-filled *Koláče*. Raymond and Honza roll out barrel after barrel of Bohemian beer, and then they sink pails of cow's and goat's milk into tubs of ice for the children.

Raymond laughs with the children over the muffled belching and the occasional seam-busting rattle of flatulence, and he receives the same scolding from the women. He dances with Alzbêta, who identifies the band with its strange mix of instruments and people. The piano is played by fat Mrs. Dusek, the accordion by Gabriel Balducci, the harmonica by young Joe Pisek, and the violin by Birgitta Andersson.

"And Zalman on the cello," she says, waving at the tailor. The tailor's luxuriant red beard is combed out and trimmed. Raymond lifts his hand as well, and the two men exchange a quick glance that settles the knowledge between them. *I did not see you.*

Then Alzbêta tells him the story about the piano, how Honza "found it" up on the hill two years ago and how they lowered it by ropes from the bridge down to the Flats. They then built a sturdy hand truck wide enough to accommodate Mrs. Dusek and the piano, with wheels that made the instrument and player mobile.

Today, the band stops playing only when a fight breaks out, as a couple of them do that day.

The first is a knife fight between two young and drunk men, a Macedonian and a Slovak. Honza groans.

"This always happens. These young idiots think they are invincible just because they made it over in one piece. They think they can shit fire."

Raymond recognizes both of them as packers at the Pillsbury

A Mill. He guesses that it is big-mouth Reznik who has started the fight by insulting another worker named Kosta.

"Donkey!" Reznik sneers, holding a fillet knife in his hand. He brays at Kosta, who pulls a small Cretan dagger from his boot. The two men are simultaneously caught by Honza and Kyle before either can make a lunge. Kyle holds his own knife to Kosta's throat and Honza twists Reznik's wrist so that he drops the fillet knife. Kyle takes the dagger away from Kosta while Honza gestures for Raymond to pick up the fillet knife. The two young men are then dragged to opposite sides of a table and forced to sit down. Alzbêta places a mug in front of each of them.

"Milk," she says. "That's all you are drinking from now on."

Reznik cannot let the fight go. He looks at Kosta at the other end of the table and begins to say something. Honza cuffs him hard alongside the head.

"That stupid boy is asking to be killed," Kyle comments. He glances at Raymond. "Never get into a knife fight with a Macedonian." He looks at the knife in Raymond's hand. "Especially not with that."

He remembers the big knife and its handmade leather hilt that Kyle threatened him with a few weeks ago.

"Can you make me a knife like that?" he asks, nodding toward the Cretan dagger in Kyle's hand. "But with the same hilt you have on yours. I'll pay you."

"You don't want a bigger knife?"

"No. I want a knife I can hide in my boot."

"I can do that."

The second altercation is a fistfight between two Czechs and is more good-natured in its aggression. The crowd watches them like any boxing match, letting the fight go on for just so long before Honza and his brother break them up because of the police patrolling the Washington Avenue Bridge. Then the band takes a break at about five o'clock and Mrs. O'Flaherty's nephews take over with their Bodhrains and fiddles.

RAYMOND FALLS INTO BED at midnight, exhausted, drunk, and euphoric. He listens to the buzz of the mosquitoes and the pinging of the river gnats as they bounce off the shut windows again and again. The insects have effectively ended the spring ceremony, clouds of them rising biblically from the river shore to plague the stubborn few who tried to hold on to the day. The day had been warm and the night remains so. He sits up, takes off his shirt, and lies back again. He thinks about the Karl May novels he used to read and laughs aloud at his naïveté, at the strange circumstances of his present life.

He has left Europe and yet come home to it. He works in the city and lives in a rural village. He's never seen such poverty and at the same time felt such wealth. There are rumblings of a labor strike at the mill but even that does not frighten him. The possibility of workers striking is amazing, incomprehensible in his previous life. Here, even with the darker things he has observed, is still the possibility of change. Here is the chaos of creativity, and at the same time a strange harmony. Here is where conformity is only for the sake of getting things done by a large group of people, not a cultural dictate ruling one's entire life. Here he can fashion his own ways, think ahead without prescription.

He finally understands what his former professor was trying to tell him. That joy came in acquiring not the tangible but the intangible.

Then he remembers something else Richter had said, quoting the American president Thomas Jefferson during one of their tutorials: "I like the dreams of the future better than the history of the past."

Raymond sits up and stares out the small window. While he is dreaming of his future, in fact living it, the people he loves the most are stuck in the mire of the history he escaped, still wrestling to break free of a futureless future.

"I agree with Jefferson," Richter had gone on to say, "but even he must have known that one's history is the navigator of one's future, including rebelliousness to change. Something, somewhere in our childhoods is the presentiment, whether taught or acquired through experience, that allows us to make those dreams. And then at the right opportunity, to enact them."

Raymond picks up one of the two beers he brought home with him, opens the bottle, and takes a long swig. He thinks of the conversation he had with Alzbêta that previous Sunday after their noon meal.

He had told her that he would continue to accompany her to church on Sundays if she liked but that he did not believe in God.

"But you must believe in faith," she had countered. "For you would not be here if you did not."

"Not faith," he had said, feeling slightly embarrassed. "Miracles. I believed in miracles when I was small. And history. I have always been fascinated by history. But I don't believe in miracles anymore. Obviously the two don't go together."

"You are wrong," she had said. "The two are not incompatible. If I were you, I would retain some belief in the miraculous. I think the two beliefs have to do with your mother, am I right? You say she is a devout Catholic. But I also think that she is a seeker of the truth. Would you say that is incompatible?"

He was startled. Although Alzbêta has never read tea leaves or coffee grounds for him, he is aware that the all-knowingness he had first sensed in her is attributed to her sense of the unseen, the unknown. All on the Flats regard her abilities with respect, not derision. At one time or another everyone has consulted with her, with the exception of Raymond, who feels no need because the old woman tracks his thoughts with uncanny accuracy.

"Not with my mother," he had answered.

He takes another swig of beer. There is enough distance now—literally, for he is an ocean and half a continent away—to think about what it was, and how it was in his childhood.

Not only for him, but for Albert and Magdalena.

HISTORIE

Augsburg

1881–1896

IT WAS THE DAY BEFORE THEIR TENTH birthday. Raimund was talking about miracles with his best friend, Leo Kritz. Wasn't it a miracle, he said, that Leo was born in the same year, on the same day, and nearly the same hour as he was?

"Maybe," Leo answered. They were sitting on the steps of the Rathaus, the regal town hall in Augsburg. Leo had a deck of cards so that they could practice the American game of poker.

"You Lutherans don't believe in them."

"We do so," Leo responded without looking up from what Raimund suspected was a winning hand. "We just don't talk about them all the time like you papists do."

Raimund looked at his own cards and knew Leo was right. The Lutherans in Augsburg saw miracles as flamboyant displays of Catholic mysticism and a shameless way to peddle holy relics: something the Protestants had gotten rid of with the Reformation. Two weeks ago, they had learned about the Peace of Augsburg agreement in 1555, allowing the two religions to coexist with uneasy duality. During recess, Raimund pretended to be Pope Marcellus II, and Leo, Martin Luther. They walked around the playground, bowing to each other and saying "peace" before verbally dueling over their differences. Then last week, their teacher began to lecture on the Thirty Years' War. Leo pretended to be the Lion of the North, King Gustavus Adolphus of Sweden, who sent his armies to help the Protestants take the city. Raimund was a general in the Catholic army and they fought with leafless oak branches. The headmaster saw them in mock battle and recognized the branches as belonging to the tree that he had planted fifteen years earlier to shade the south side of the school.

"This war is over," he shouted, dragging both boys by their ears into the building.

"But we don't know that yet!" Leo protested.

"Then you will find out!"

They lost playground privileges for the rest of the week, staying inside to read the remaining history of the war. Leo finished the reading first, closing the book with a long face. Raimund did not jeer when he found out that the Catholics ultimately won, surrounding Augsburg with their troops in October 1634 and starving out the Swedish garrison over the winter. Leo took the 247-year-old defeat personally until he triumphed with repeating the story he had told Raimund many times before.

He swore that one of his great, great, great—he wasn't sure how far back it went—grandmothers who was then a Catholic married one of those starving Swedish soldiers, thereby saving his life. But to do so, she had to convert.

"That was a miracle," Leo insisted every time.

Raimund told his mother Leo's story the first time he heard it and of his declaration that it was a miracle. She lifted an eyebrow.

"There is nothing miraculous about it. She fell in love and lost her common sense. The soldier was cunning enough to take advantage of that. He got his life saved and added a convert to his faith. She was the one who was conquered in the end. But don't tell Leo that. Every family has a right to their stories, right or wrong."

"Look! You can see the Swede in me," Leo said, pointing to his white-blond hair. Then he palmed his face to pull his skin taut so as to emphasize what he claimed was his Nordic bone structure. His pale blue-gray eyes reminded Raimund of ice on an overcast day. Leo had fair skin that burned from the sun rather than tanned, and hence his parents made sure he wore a hat, long sleeves, and long pants while the rest of the boys wore the school's uniform breeches. Leo wanted to be a Viking when he grew up but he was a short boy and eventually would grow only to a height of five feet five inches. He was a fastidious child, despite being a farm boy like Raimund, and he washed with a soap that smelled of peppermint. Because of that he was called "Peppermint Drop" and was picked on at school. Raimund didn't mind his clothes or that he smelled like candy. He liked Leo because he was smart and loyal.

"Could be," Raimund remarked, studying Leo's face. Then he playfully tapped Leo's nose. "But your beak is German."

They had just learned that morning another reason why the Thirty Years' War ended. Both sides, exhausted and demoralized, recognized that they had a greater enemy than their spiritual differences. Germany not only lost one-third of its population in the war but it had destroyed the nation's centrality in trade. The threat to the great commercial industries of Augsburg and its place in the world market brought a cautious but necessary unity. Still, Germany's economy stagnated.

"You boys have no idea how fortunate you are to have been born after 1850," their teacher, Herr Professor Schmidt, commented. "We gained back our trade power and stability only in the past fifty years."

Raimund glanced at Leo's felt hat. He never asked his friend how the Lutherans differed that much from the Catholics. The Kaufmann family rode in a buggy behind the Kritz family on Sundays. They entered the same church: the Basilica of St. Ulrich and St. Afra. But Raimund's family entered the larger, more gilded part of the Basilica known as St. Afra while Leo's family entered through a door on the north side of the church into the small preaching hall that was St. Ulrich. He asked his brother Albert what made them different.

"Their priests can marry and have children. And they don't move around as much," Albert said, pantomiming the Catholic calisthenics of kneeling down, standing up, sitting down, dipping fingers in holy water, and making the sign of the cross. "They don't have statues either and they think art is decadent."

His brother grinned, sure that Raimund didn't know what the word *decadent* meant. He didn't but he wasn't going to let Albert know that.

"What do you want for your birthday?" Leo asked Raimund.

"A miracle. But I can't say what it is. It might be a sin."

"Can you whisper it?" Leo asked. "I won't tell anyone. I promise. Then I'll tell you what I want."

Raimund leaned over and cupped a hand over Leo's ear.

"That's what I want!" Leo claimed. "And to grow taller."

"Really?"

"Ja," he answered. Leo looked past Raimund and saw Albert approaching on a horse. "Your brother is coming." He grabbed both hands of cards, put them with the rest, and slid the deck into his pocket.

"We have to pray for it tonight. Which prayer are you going to use?" Raimund asked, standing up and wiping the dust off his school breeches.

"I'll say the Our Father," Leo said, "and you say the Hail Mary. Then we'll see which one works."

Raimund was pleased. His mother favored the Hail Mary, saying the Virgin had a greater understanding of mortals because she had once been one.

Albert reined the horse to a halt and waited while the two boys swung up onto the saddle behind him. Leo was dropped off at his family farm two miles south of Augsburg, then Raimund and Albert headed the last mile home.

"Don't forget!" Raimund yelled as Leo ran down his road.

"Forget what?" Albert asked.

"His homework."

Raimund prayed in bed that night with the blanket over the top of his head. When he got up early the next morning and measured his penis with a ruler, it was the same size. His brother turned over in his bed, and Raimund slid the ruler under the mattress.

"Your *Schwänz* isn't any bigger. You can pray all you want but it won't help. It happens naturally when you turn twelve," Albert said with the sleepy authority of a thirteen-year-old. "Maybe thirteen," he added, squinting at Raimund. "Go back to sleep."

"so?" he asked Leo at recess. Leo hedged. Worked the toe of one shoe into the dirt.

"No," he answered with obvious disappointment. "You?"

"Didn't work for me either," Raimund said. "Maybe next year."

Yet Raimund felt bigger and stronger when he did chores after school that day. He decided the Blessed Virgin had not completely abandoned him and so recited the Hail Mary while herding his father's sheep into a new pasture. He nudged the last ewe in, shut the gate, and then went to the courtyard pump to wash up for supper.

His father came home two hours late. They listened as he rode his horse past the house and to the barn. It would be another half hour before his father entered the house, as the animals, particularly the horses, always came first. His father would unsaddle the horse and sponge down the animal with warm water so that the sweat from the ride would not dry and paste the gelding's coat, making it difficult to curry later. He would put oats in the trough and fresh water in the pail before stalling him.

The family sat at the table waiting. Dinner, according to his father's rule, was to be served at six o'clock. The food had been dished up and was ready to eat at the required time. At six thirty, his mother and his sisters removed the pork roast and side dishes from the table and returned them to the stove and oven to stay warm. They were quiet. The oldest son, Otto, worked a rubber band between his hands. Albert dozed in his chair. Greta and Liliane returned to the table and sat in resignation. Raimund glanced from the birthday torte waiting on the kitchen sideboard to his mother. His father had been late before, and while his mother didn't like it she bore it like the rest of them, urging them to drink glasses of water to stave off their hunger. But that day she got up several times to look out the kitchen window. She even checked the brewery, a large addition to the back of the house where his father made, drank, and sold his own beer.

Heinrich Kaufmann finally came in, pulling off his boots in the entryway. Raimund watched his mother and sisters rise to put the food back on the table. His father walked into the kitchen without greeting or excuse, pumped water into the sink, washed and then wiped his hands on the pastry towel. Raimund could smell the beer and liverwurst he must have snacked on in town mingle with an intense scent reminiscent of roses, cloves, and almonds.

Otto snickered, stretching the rubber band and letting it go so that it hit Greta in the back, causing her to nearly drop the dish of potatoes she was carrying. Albert pretended to smell nothing and looked at his hands. Their mother detected it, though. She sucked in her cheeks, something she did when she was angry. His father had pulled out his chair and was about to sit down when Raimund asked, "Why do we have to wait for you?"

His mother and sisters froze, the dishes of steaming food held in their stilled hands. His brothers gripped the sides of their chairs. Heinrich pushed the chair back in and glared at his youngest son. Then he walked to the entryway, pulled on his boots again, and picked up his riding crop. He reentered the kitchen, lifted Raimund out of his chair by one arm, and dragged him outside where he shoved him up against the house.

"Take off your pants."

Raimund braced himself against the wall, jerking every time the crop hit the back of his legs and buttocks. He heard Otto cackle, saw out of the corner of his eye his oldest brother as he leaned against the house. Raimund kept his head down and would not cry out even though it made his father strike with more force. When his father was finally satisfied, he picked up Raimund's trousers and threw them at him.

"No supper for you!" he spit out. "Go to the barn and clean out the stalls. Brush the horses down again."

"Moron," Otto hissed just before their father shoved him toward the kitchen door.

"Fat pig," Raimund whispered.

The whipping was a punishment. Being banished to the barn was not, although his father didn't know that. He did his chores and climbed with stinging legs up to the half-story loft and its gable window to wait for sundown. From there, he could see everything on the farm. The stone fences built by past Kaufmann generations and maintained by the present generation. How each pasture and field was a jigsaw of green and gold enclosed by the fences whose three-foot-wide tops Raimund could walk on, encircling the entire farm that way. In one pasture was his father's herd of Brown Swiss cows, in another the sheep, and, in the third, the farm's draft horses. Four golden Belgians and a three-year-old Percheron whose muscular blackness and enormous size stood out from the rest, thus earning him the name of Aherin—lord of the horses. Against the backdrop of the horses were fields of wheat, rye, barley, oats, and trellises of hops. Raimund watched the ducks and geese settle onto the pond for the night; he watched the chickens wander back to the coop to roost. Otto came out of the house and lit the single oil lamp in the middle of the courtyard.

Finally the lamps were lit in the brewery. The rest of the house was dark except for the bedroom Raimund shared with Albert. He crawled down the ladder, wincing because the bloody welts had dried to his pants and every step pulled the fabric away from the skin, causing them to bleed again. Limping across the courtyard, he slipped into the house through the kitchen door and made his way up the stairs to the bedroom. His mother and Albert were waiting for him.

"I'm sorry—"

"Shsh."

She removed his clothes and helped him into a pajama top. Then she told him to lie on his stomach.

"You are so hard-headed, Raimund. I told you before never to question your father," she said but without her usual conviction, spreading camphor ointment onto his wounds. Albert sat on the chair next to the bed. He held a glass of milk and a plate containing a pork and rye bread sandwich and a slice of torte.

"It isn't right," Raimund said, his eyes watering because of the ointment. "It isn't fair."

He didn't expect his mother to respond. She had little more leeway than her children in questioning her husband's authority, but Raimund said what he thought anyway because at least his mother tolerated hearing it. They were no different from most other families. His parents had been taught, as had their parents before them, that God was their Father in Heaven but the father in most households was god.

"Life is *not* fair," she said with sudden bitterness. She screwed the lid back onto the jar and studied the welts on her son's backside. "Sleep on your stomach," she advised before leaving, bending forward to kiss the side of his face not submerged in the pillow.

He waited until she left and then swung his legs off the bed to sit up. Albert put the plate on the bedside table. He lifted the glass of milk to Raimund's lips.

"You were born with a big mouth and no sense," he said, watching his brother drink. He cut the sandwich into four pieces and gave Raimund one of them.

"You don't like it either," Raimund said. He chewed and watched Albert's face for signs of anger but saw exhaustion instead.

"No, I don't. Just shut up for now," he answered. "And quit measuring your *Schwänz*. Someday it will be bigger than his and then you can tell him off."

As he chewed on his sandwich he considered his mother's bitter tone. Considered his mother. About who she was and what was between them.

HER NAME WAS ANNALIESE. She awoke earlier than the rest of the family to prepare breakfast. She wove a rosary through her hands and knelt next to the kitchen table before she went out to the barn to collect eggs and bring in a fresh pitcher of milk. Raimund was also up early, drawn to the dark silence of the house. He imagined himself invisible as he walked the hallway and down the stairs, through the parlor, and finally to stand next to the closed kitchen door. He listened to the murmur of his mother's voice as she recited the prayers of the five cycles of Redemption, her fingers working from bead to bead.

One morning he slipped into the kitchen after she had left the house to collect eggs. He opened the pantry cupboard in the hopes of finding a piece of *Kirschkuchen* from the day before. The pastry was gone but there was an open book laid face down to mark the page. He read the spine: *Anna Karenina* by Leo Tolstoy. A month later he squeezed into the narrow pantry to avoid the wrath of his father over a chore he had not done and discovered a thinly bound essay behind the flour bin. He had just read the author's name and the essay's title—*The Subjugation of Women* by John Stuart Mill—when his mother opened the door, reached in for a jar of plums, and found her youngest son instead.

"Put that back," she whispered, "as though you never found it. And I'll not tell your father where you are."

It became an unspoken agreement and bond between them. He told no one of his mother's secret reading. Raimund remembered the titles and the authors but he did not understand the word *sub-jugation*, although he did gather that *Anna Karenina* was about a woman. Reading for pleasure was not done in the Kaufmann household. The only two books considered acceptable by his father were a large and heavy leather-bound copy of the Bible and *Das Volk in Waffen* (A Nation in Arms) by Baron von der Goltz, both openly displayed on a shelf in the parlor. He contemplated his mother's secrecy, knowing that she did not waste time on unnecessary activities. So he concluded that they were holy books of a sort, providing his mother with another kind of spiritual sustenance.

RAIMUND WAS REACHING for a second piece of sandwich when they heard shouting. It wasn't coming from inside the house. Albert went to the window that overlooked the courtyard.

"It's Ma," he whispered.

Raimund pushed himself off the bed, turned the wicks down on the lamps, and limped to the window. They listened with a mix of shock and fascination as their parents argued in the brewery. Their mother's voice, normally so low and patient, was raised to such a pitch that they both shuddered. Then the door to the brewery was flung open and their father stumbled out, trying to make a run for the courtyard gate. Their mother followed, striking her husband across the back with a steel poker from the fireplace. Heinrich went down, covering his head with his arms and hands. She hit him across the legs. Their father howled, causing their St. Bernard, chained to his doghouse by the barn, to commiserate with his own canine yodeling.

"I know why you were late!" she shouted. "You came home stinking! On your son's birthday no less! And then you whip him for asking why he could not eat on time? Son of a pig!" She stood over her husband with the poker raised as if thinking of where to hit him next.

"Whore!" she yelled, kicking him in the side. She turned to the barking dog. "Shut up!" Then she looked up at the house. The boys ducked below the sill.

They listened as she entered the house and locked the main door behind her. Listened as she locked every entryway into the house, including the brewery. Albert shut the window and they both crawled into bed. The house was as silent as the courtyard. Raimund wondered where their father would sleep now that he couldn't get into the house. The barn, most likely.

"Do you think Mama will be all right tomorrow?" he asked Albert, fearful that his father, who had never struck his mother, might begin to do so.

"Ja. Better than all right," Albert answered. "For once your big mouth did something. I don't think we'll have to wait for Pa to eat on time again."

"Why was he late?"

"Did you smell the perfume on him?"

"Ja."

"If I tell you will you stay quiet about it?"

"Ja."

"Swear on it."

"I swear on my life," Raimund said, making the sign of the cross in the dark.

"He's been going to a *Frauenhaus*," Albert said.

Raimund had heard that term from some boys at school. He pretended to know what it was and laughed along with them. He asked his oldest sister what it meant when he got home. Liliane told him that it was a house for women of ill repute. He wasn't sure what "repute" meant but the "ill" made him think it was a special house for sick women.

"How do you know?" Raimund asked Albert. "Does Otto know?"

"Otto is the one who told me. Pa took him to a *Frauenhaus* last year when he turned sixteen."

"Why would Pa and Otto visit a house full of sick women?"

Albert snorted. "You don't get it, do you?" He propped himself up on one elbow. "It is a house of whores. You know. Women who sleep with men for money. Like Mary Magdalene."

"Pa does that? He did that to Otto?"

"Ja. Otto said it was to break him in."

Raimund leaned over the edge of the bed, picked up the slice of torte from the nightstand, and, pondering his brother's words, began to eat.

"It couldn't have been too difficult," Albert went on. "Pa's gelding is smarter than Otto. He's not doing that to me when I turn sixteen. You can get *diseases* from those women. The kind that make your *Schwänz* rot off."

Raimund licked the sticky sweetness of the torte's walnut filling from his fingers and then wiped them on the side of the bed. He could just make out the outline of his brother's face. The onset of Albert's puberty seemed to happen overnight before he turned thirteen. His voice deepened, his penis became longer and thicker, and he acquired a forest of pubic hair. Once when they were washing outside, Raimund saw Albert glance at their father to make sure his change was normal. Their father's belly hung obscenely over his penis, which would have been obscured had it been small but it was not. Heinrich caught his second son looking and grinned.

"Even the best bull needs shelter," he said. He threw Albert a towel. "So you are a Kaufmann man after all. In two years I'll take you to someone who will show you how to use it."

Raimund lay back and wondered what had gone wrong that day. Should he and Leo have met at the church instead of the city hall and made their pact there? Did playing poker invalidate their prayers? As far as he could tell, the Our Father, while not giving Leo what he wanted, didn't appear to cause him or his family any harm.

"Raimund?"

"What?"

"Who did you pray to?"

He hesitated. Albert was not cruel and sarcastic like Otto but he did enjoy teasing Raimund from time to time.

"I said the Hail Mary."

"Ach!" Albert muffled his laughter with a pillow. Raimund raised himself on one elbow, drank the rest of his milk, and put the glass back on the nightstand. Albert pulled the pillow from his face.

"Raimund! How could you be so stupid? Think about it. Why would you pray *to a virgin* for your *Schwänz* to grow bigger? Do you think the Virgin Mary wants your *Schwänz* to grow bigger? She's a virgin! And a holy one! She's not supposed to have anything to do with *Schwänzen*."

"Saying the Our Father didn't help Leo!" he protested.

"Of course not! The Holy Father doesn't want your *Schwänz* to grow big before its time or you'll sin with it."

"Well who do I pray to then?"

"No one. At least not for that. It's nature," Albert said. "Herr Professor Richter says you can't force nature. That our bodies come into being in their own way. And that there is nothing to be ashamed of."

Albert paused and chewed his lower lip. Herr Professor Richter was Albert's hero, scholarly and otherwise. If Raimund continued to do well in school, he too could look forward to being Richter's student. He stopped thinking about his ambitions for a larger penis and pondered for a moment Albert's teacher.

THERE WAS THE INFORMATION that all of Augsburg knew. Immanuel Richter was the son of Friedrich and Alexandra Richter, wealthy owners of a porcelain factory and a textile and a paper mill in Augsburg. The oldest son, Bernhardt, was groomed for inheritance of the factory and both mills, something Bernhardt welcomed as he had a keen interest in business. Immanuel, the second son and last child, had no aspirations to run the family business. Convention dictated that he, as the second son, either became a man of God or a soldier of Germany. Friedrich Richter, however, did not always obey convention, having profited from being progressive in his business acumen and his overall view of life. His wife was the more conventional anchor that kept him in respectable limits, but even she enjoyed the freedom that wealth accorded them in ignoring some cultural expectations. Her chief desire, above all, was the happiness of both her sons. So she joined her husband in encouraging Immanuel to fulfill his wish to become a scholar and to travel. The only condition his parents placed on him was that he return to Augsburg when he married and started his family, so that he could sit on the family's board of directors and assume ownership of the businesses should something happen to his brother.

Immanuel received his first degree in history from the University of Tübingen and, with the reluctant blessing of his parents, his doctorate in literature from Oxford. As part of his studies and to indulge his wide-ranging interest in other cultures, he traveled to many exotic places, including Peru, Argentina, and Chile in South America; Morocco and Egypt in North Africa; and a six-week expedition into the Congo. He then taught at Harvard University in the United States and in Oxford, Berlin, Budapest, St. Petersburg, Vienna, Prague, and finally Bucharest, where he met his wife, Adelinde. Adelinde was the focus of much gossip—gossip that Raimund did not hear at home because their mother detested hearsay and did not allow it.

ALBERT FINALLY SPOKE.

"I don't think your praying was wasted, though. It just went to Ma."

Raimund's mouth fell open. Albert was right. His prayers to the Virgin had taken a necessary detour to answer the prayers of the one who needed them the most in their house. Their mother. Raimund was merely the conduit through which the Virgin Mary had worked, opening her holy hand and dropping the illuminating card that revealed his father. The ace in the hole that gave their mother a ripe and justified reason to revolt.

A miracle had occurred after all.

IMMANUEL AND ADELINDE RICHTER returned to Augsburg just after their honeymoon in Paris that spring of 1877 so that Immanuel could accept the post of headmaster at the prestigious Augsburg Gymnasium.

That first glimpse of what Friedrich Richter described as Adelinde's entrancing loveliness, and then hearing her low and sensuous voice, sent the gossips, the *Klatschbasen*, into fits of speculation. She was already suspect, being a Romanian, but it was her dark beauty—her thick and abundant black hair, heavily lashed, brown almost black eyes, and olive skin—that they declared was a clear sign of gypsy ancestry. She brought two horses with her from

Bucharest, a magnificent thoroughbred jumper and a black Andalusian that she used for leisurely riding, occasionally participating in an official race as the animal was a fast runner. She was the only woman that autumn to participate in the jumping category of the Augsburg horse show, winning easily while riding sidesaddle. The *Klatschbasen* scrutinized her at the show, watched how the horse responded to her. She rode the thoroughbred with an intimate assurance, clearing the obstacles on the course as though she was a female centaur. One of the judges was a well-traveled man and a former colonel in the German army. No one had that kind of skill with a horse, he said, except Mongolians, Turks, and gypsies.

Then there was another camp that did not believe that Adelinde Richter was a gypsy. Instead they declared that she was a Jewess hiding behind the Catholic church. The small Jewish population in Augsburg thought so as well but did not say so publicly, not having any proof and sensitive to centuries of having characteristics attributed to them that were not true.

Alexandra Richter became exceedingly annoyed at the whispering and the less than discreet stares when she introduced her daughter-in-law to the high society of the city. Yet it was Alexandra who unwittingly fueled further gossip after her son and his wife returned from a trip to London in September 1878. She told her closest friend, Elsa Schneider, a self-appointed matron of arts and culture in Augsburg, that her son and his wife would have drowned on the SS *Princess Alice* had Adelinde not stopped them from taking the "Moonlight Trip" to Gravesend and back on the Thames River paddle steamer. Adelinde and Immanuel were standing on Swan's Pier near the London Bridge waiting to board when Adelinde suddenly felt queasy and asked Immanuel to take her back to the hotel. The next morning they awoke to the horrifying news that the *Princess Alice* had collided with the *Bywell Castle*, an enormous coal-hauling ship coming back from having been repainted at dry dock. Six hundred fifty passengers on the paddle steamer drowned.

"What the devil was a big coal hauler doing on the Thames?" Immanuel asked the concierge, only to learn seconds later that the man's silence was because of grief. His brother had been the captain's assistant on the *Princess Alice*.

☩ ☩ ☩

"DON'T YOU THINK IT ODD that she got queasy even before she boarded?" Elsa asked.

"Absolutely not!" Alexandra responded, suddenly aware of the ominous twist in the conversation. She eyed Elsa with a prohibitive look. "I hate to travel on water. I won't even go boating on the Lech or the Danube. It makes me sick just thinking about it. To my knowledge Adelinde has never been on a ship of any kind."

But Elsa retold the story the next day at an afternoon tatting party, lacing the story with her own perceptions just as her hands were creating lace. Alexandra heard the embellished story from one of her maids the next morning. She walked the two blocks from their mansion on Maximilianstraße to the more modest but still large baroque house where her son and his wife lived to make her apologies and strategize stemming the damage.

"Elsa Schneider is no longer a friend of mine!" she huffed after telling her daughter-in-law. Adelinde laughed.

"Don't worry, Mother Richter," she said. She placed a hand on her midriff. "There was a reason for the queasiness. I am pregnant."

"*Gott im Himmel!* How wonderful!" Alexandra cried, thrilled at the actuality of becoming a grandmother and simultaneously overjoyed with having ammunition to dispute Elsa's disgusting conjecture.

"I'm so glad you're pleased," Adelinde said. "But this won't stop people from talking. I might have to hold the baby up naked at her baptism to show that there are no marks of the devil on her."

Alexandra hinted, as her daughter-in-law became visibly with child, that she maintain a quiet life at home until the baby was born. Adelinde, however, did not believe in retiring from public view just because her belly was getting larger. She walked briskly every day and did most of the market shopping rather than leave it to a maid. She and Immanuel continued to ride horses at the family's country home twenty miles outside Augsburg. This, the *Klatschbasen* declared, was another sign that she was of dubious, common stock. Only gypsy women were careless and hardy enough to ride a horse while pregnant.

"She is not Romanian," Alexandra Richter would answer when

asked, refusing to say the word *gypsy*. "Her family is Hungarian. They are known in Romania as the Csángó."

Immanuel told his mother to cease and desist her explanations of his wife's origins, saying that it only gave the ignorant tinder to add to the fire. Richter did not answer inquiries about his wife's ethnicity, saying only, "She is whom you see."

But there were rumors about Immanuel as well. Some said he was an atheist, his belief in God stripped away by all his education. Yet he attended mass with his family on Sundays and honored all the holy days. Others said he was a transcendentalist or a Darwinist, the latter being as bad as an atheist because really, who could believe that humans were descendants of monkeys? Immanuel also believed in equal education for women, something that conservative Augsburg had yet to grasp although it was accepted in the northern part of Germany. But there was a boundary to the rumors about Immanuel because he was a son of one of the most prominent businessmen in Augsburg. He was also the headmaster of the strenuous and secular secondary school the Augsburg Gymnasium. Those who wanted their sons (and some of their daughters) to achieve academic and social prominence through education treaded carefully in their stated opinion of Herr Doktor Professor Richter.

Magdalena was born the following February. When the priest held the baby up as an offering to God during her baptism, Alexandra Richter suddenly remembered what her daughter-in-law had said, wondering if Adelinde had known she would give birth to a girl. *I might have to hold the baby up naked at her baptism to show that there are no marks of the devil on her.*

She dismissed it as coincidence after they placed the newly baptized baby in her arms, the weight of which made her teary with joy. Finally, she thought, looking down at the abundant black hair and almond-shaped eyes, someone to buy dresses for.

BUT THAT WHICH MAGDALENA'S MOTHER and father ignored found another route into the family. A new baby was excuse enough for the tattling battle-axes of Augsburg society to toady up to her mother when she was out pushing Magdalena in a pram. One of them kept her mother busy with chatter while the other two or three bent over the carriage and, under the subterfuge of maternal cooing, whispered their observations and opinions. If they felt safe enough doing so, they plucked at the blanket framing Magdalena's face, drawing it away so that they could see more of her facial features. Occasionally one of them would insert a sly finger inside the bonnet to check the shape of Magdalena's ears, the roundness of her head. She may not have understood their words but as she grew into a toddler she perceived through the tone of their voices the negative connotation of their whispers. She squirmed from their touch, refused to respond to their baby-talk inquiries, eyeing the women and the occasional man with silent scrutiny. Her grandmother, though, understood her grave public countenance. She saved Magdalena from such examinations on days when she took her out for a daily stroll or to the market. Her grandmother covered the pram with a blanket when Magdalena was an infant, refusing anyone a glance on the pretense that the baby was sleeping. When Magdalena became a little older, Alexandra hoisted her out of the carriage and held her when they stopped, her grandmother's aristocratic bearing effectively eliminating any idle talk, inappropriate references, or the dreaded unwanted touch.

Her father was startled one day when during a casual conversation a colleague expressed sympathy over Immanuel's having a sullen, taciturn daughter. He told his family of the conversation during a Sunday dinner at the elder Richter's mansion. Magdalena looked up from where she was playing games with the maid in the parlor, the dining and parlor doors both open so that the adults could keep an eye on her. Her mother's and father's backs were to her but she could see her grandmother's face as she sat on the opposite side of the table, one eyebrow raised in exasperation.

"I was amazed," her father went on. "She is a very cheerful, talkative child here and at home."

"Good Lord, Immanuel! How can you be so educated—both of you—and so ignorant at the same time," Alexandra admonished. "You do not let *those people* speak to Magdalena without being right there. Do you think she hears nothing? Understands nothing? I sincerely hope not, because then you would be as bad as they are. Magdalena is a very intelligent girl, has been since birth," she said.

"Are you saying that we should shield her?" her father said. "Keep her locked in the house? I don't remember you doing any such thing with me."

"This is different," her grandmother insisted.

"I don't think it is as bad as you make it out to be," he replied. "She will have to deal with *those people* for the rest of her life. Like we all do. In fact she has gained the experience she will need to survive in this city. We can't protect her from every bit of ridiculous gossip. She has learned the best defense to such encounters. Stare back and say nothing."

"Immanuel is right," Adelinde added. "Magdalena is fine when she is at home and among people she trusts. She laughs and plays like any other child."

She passed a plate of cherry tarts to Magdalena's grandfather.

"I'm not as callous as you think. I do love, and will protect, my daughter. I had to endure the same thing. But I learned that none of us is allowed just one life," she said. "We all have to adopt at least two lives, one public and one private."

"Of course," her grandmother answered. "I am just saying that there are gentler ways to teach that, to ease into that. You could have just wet her toes, so to speak, rather than drench her in the water. I'm worried that she might become withdrawn, dislike people overall."

"I don't want her to become withdrawn, Mother Richter," Adelinde said. "But a healthy dose of caution toward people is necessary. What and who is to be feared most in this world?"

"Other people," Friedrich Richter answered. He looked past them in the direction of the parlor and winked.

Magdalena was standing in the dining room doorway.

HER GRANDMOTHER WAS ALMOST CORRECT in her assessment. Magdalena developed a deep antipathy for adults who considered children as uncomprehending beings, unable to interpret the subtleness of tone let alone conversation. But rather than become bitter, Magdalena daydreamed them into their true roles, envisioning the *Klatschbasen* as fat and hovering witches and warlocks that she threw rocks at in the garden and deflated. But she in turn also had dreams she had no control over, dreams of such vividness that she had difficulty believing that she had not lived them. Her earliest dream was of struggling in a dark place for an indeterminate amount of time before being blinded by a white light. She was five years old, playing in the walled garden behind the house after a soft rain, when she tentatively identified what it was. She was observing earthworms as they emerged from the ground to crawl through the wet grass, occasionally lifting their eyeless heads under the opalescent light of diminishing rain clouds. Then the sun came out in full and she watched them shrink from it. She picked up one of the squirming worms and closed her fingers over it so that it was sheltered by darkness again. She concluded, feeling the muscular wriggling of a subterranean life, that she had once been a worm.

She held that belief for one week until her mother, a month away from giving birth to her second child, explained as factually as she could, given the age of her daughter, how babies were made and born.

"This is something that you shouldn't repeat," her mother said. "Not that it isn't true. Your father and I believe in telling the truth whenever possible. But other parents aren't as comfortable telling their children certain things like this and we must respect that."

Magdalena was silent with astonishment. Her dream was not a dream. It was a memory.

She put a hand on her mother's belly.

"It's dark in there," she said.

"I imagine it is."

"She can't see me."

"Why do you say *she?*" her mother asked in a strange tone of voice. "It could be a boy."

Magdalena looked at her mother, her hand still on her mother's belly. She knew she was right. It was a girl. But saying so had upset her mother. She paused, rethought her answer.

"I *think* it is a girl."

"That's better," her mother said tensely. "No one can be certain of whether a baby is a girl or a boy until it is born."

Her mother was lying. She had seen her mother bring out the clothes that Magdalena had worn as an infant, including the ribboned bonnets and lacy nightgowns. The three sets of booties she had knitted were pink. Even if she hadn't seen the clothes or paid attention to the booties, she still knew her mother was lying. This sudden certitude gave her a mysterious feeling, one she couldn't decide was good or bad, much like the sensations she experienced at times when she was alone in the garden sitting on the tree bench. Then she felt suspended in space as though the bench and all the greenery around her was a dream she was momentarily in and not her real life. She would get up, walk to her mother's roses, and thrust an arm into the bushes to feel the thorns. The blood and pain from the scratches brought her back, proved to her that she was mortal and that she was in her garden, on the earth. Magdalena felt her mother's heightened scrutiny, further confirming that she was right about the sex of the baby.

"If it is a girl," she said to her mother, "I would like to name her Rose." She did not tell her mother that two more babies would be born after Rose, and their names would be Amalia and Eva.

ON HER SEVENTH BIRTHDAY, she discovered that her mother had told another lie. They did not live two lives but three. She accompanied her mother to the Fuggerei, a housing district for the poor within the city of Augsburg, built nearly four centuries before by Jakob Fugger, a wealthy businessman and devout Catholic. They entered the walled-in district via the arched gateway on Jakobstraße and emerged on the main cobblestone street called Herrengasse. It was early in the morning on a cold but sunny Thursday in February. There was no one about except for a one-legged man sitting on a stone bench near the marketplace. He wore a black homburg hat and the brown woven wool coat of the working class. Instead of wearing pants the same as his coat or like the suit pants worn by Magdalena's father, the man wore breeches that had once been white but now were gray with age and wear. The right breech pant was folded and pinned up near the groin, as there was not a leg to fill it. But the man's left leg showed what the other had once looked like in its entirety. The breech stretched over a long, muscular thigh while the lower leg and foot were encased in a black leather boot that was cut low behind the knee with a large flap that covered the front of the knee. Magdalena recognized the boot from the family's visit to Berlin the previous fall where, among other things, they watched a military procession. It was the boot of a cuirassier. She wondered what had happened to the rest of his uniform, the plumed helmet and the gleaming sword.

"Josef! It is too cold to be sitting out here dressed like that," her mother said.

"I'm just as warm as I need to be," he answered. Then he looked at Magdalena and smiled as if he knew her.

"Hello, princess," he said. He was older than her father, she decided, but not as old as her grandfather Richter. "You are as lovely as your mother."

"We aren't here to look pretty," her mother said. "We are here to help." She lifted the large bag filled with books to be distributed among the Fuggerei's children.

"But it is her birthday," the man answered. "She must be allowed to play, too."

"She will after we finish our work," her mother said. Their work involved three half-days a week spent in the Fuggerei, delivering used but clean clothes, or fresh bread, vegetables, fruit, or meat—links of sausage or a ham. Her mother also taught the children and some of the adults to read and write. Magdalena liked playing with the other children in the housing district. Here she did not feel scrutinized or different, did not feel ill-will from any of the inhabitants given that she came from a family of wealth.

"Be sure to do that. All children must have playtime," he said, smiling again at Magdalena.

She wondered how he knew it was her birthday. She had never seen him before in the district, did not hear him mentioned by either her father or mother. Her mother bid him goodbye and they proceeded down the street. Magdalena sensed the man was watching them. She stopped and turned around. She did not see the man they had just spoken with sitting upright on the bench. Instead she saw the soldier he had been, lying on the ground, moaning and with one hand clutching his bloodied leg, which was bent at an awkward angle. There were voices and shadows . . . shadows of men lying around him. She heard the scream of a falling horse but did not see it. Then she watched as he withdrew a pistol from within his chest armor and put it to his head.

"Magdalena!" Her mother grabbed her arm. "It is rude to stare!"

She could not say what occurred, only that her mother's voice and touch startled her. She blinked. Josef was sitting on the bench just as he had been. He waved to her. Her mother waved back, mouthing *I'm sorry*.

Her mother waited until they were beyond Josef's sight before stopping again. She frowned and put a hand against Magdalena's forehead and then against her cheek.

"Did Josef frighten you?"

"No."

"You look so pale. Do you feel all right?"

"Yes . . . what happened to him?" Magdalena asked.

"He was a soldier in the war against France. Josef was in the Battle of Gravelotte. It was a terrible battle, one of the worst for both sides. Josef was shot in the leg and it shattered the bone. He was left for—" her mother suddenly stopped. She picked up the bag of books. "Enough of that. We have work to do before we go home and celebrate your birthday."

An hour and a half later, they had left a house on Ochsengasse, having delivered the last book. They were halfway to the district's main street when they met a tired-looking woman whose gray-flecked brown hair was loosely wound into a simple chignon at the base of her neck. Her face lit up when she saw Magdalena and her mother.

"Adelinde! How good to see you! Thank you for the lovely batiste that you left last week. And this," she said, bending down to kiss Magdalena on both cheeks, "is your oldest daughter—yes?"

Her mother nodded and laughed. Then the woman and her mother began to speak not in German or Hungarian but in Romanian. Her mother rarely spoke Romanian in public and not much more at home. But she spoke the language enough for Magdalena to recognize it even though she comprehended little. Magdalena noticed that the woman's coat was threadbare in some places with scruffy fur on the cuffs and collar that looked as though a small dog had chewed on it. Yet she smelled of cardamom and cinnamon and not like washing soap or the sweat of manual labor like many of the other women in the Fuggerei. Just then the sun hit her face at a sharp angle and Magdalena shut her eyes against it. That is when she saw, in the darkness behind her lids, the woman's folded and rosary-laced hands, closed eyes, and solemn mouth. She opened her eyes, listened as the women spoke again in German to say goodbye. The woman kissed Magdalena once more, her breathing whistling and labored. For a few seconds, Magdalena was overwhelmed with the panic and dizziness emanating from her. They waited until the woman reached her house, waving again before the woman shut her door.

"Who was that?" she asked.

"Frau Mueller. Josef's wife. She works in the market bakery and sews first-communion dresses for those families who cannot afford them. She's had a hard life, working and taking care of her husband."

"She is going to die," Magdalena said. Her mother's face paled.

"How do you know that?" she asked tersely.

"I saw it."

Her mother stood transfixed as though frightened. Then she grabbed Magdalena's hand and, turning around, walked back to where they had been, near the end of Ochsengasse. Her mother pointed to the gatehouse.

"Do you know what happened in that house in 1625?" she asked. Magdalena shook her head.

"A woman named Dorothea Braun lived there with her daughter. She was a nurse in the Fuggerei clinic. Her daughter, for unknown reasons, claimed her mother was a sorceress—do you know what that is?"

"A witch."

"Yes, a witch," her mother said, pausing to take a breath. "They believed the girl and tortured her mother, forcing her to confess to something she was not. They convicted her, beheaded her, and then burned her body."

Her mother knelt down and held Magdalena by the shoulders.

"They had no proof, just the word of an eleven-year-old girl who was probably angry at her mother for a trifling thing. But those words killed her mother."

"That was a long time ago," Magdalena answered, confused as to why her mother was telling her an old story that had nothing to do with them. They were not witches.

"People don't change much. When there are hard times, like there have been for the past ten years, people need to blame something or someone. And they usually go after those people who appear to be different or are more intelligent. Or say something," her mother added, "that sounds suspicious."

"But I saw her—"

Adelinde Richter clasped her daughter's chin.

"You saw nothing."

Frau Mueller died of pneumonia two weeks later. Distraught at the death of his wife, Josef Mueller shot himself in the head the day after her funeral.

HERR DOKTOR PROFESSOR RICHTER was a second son, too. He pointed that out to Albert on the first day of his personal tutorials at the Richter home.

"It's a tough lot being the second male in the family," he said. "First place is already gone. We second sons have expectations put on us and yet with no clear directions. We have to make a life for ourselves. But!" he continued with a grin of affinity, "that means we get to make choices, take control of our lives. And with a brain like yours," he patted Albert affectionately on the head, "the world is full of possibilities."

Richter did not usually hold tutorials at his home after the school day but he found Albert to be an exceptional student at age thirteen. It was both an enormous honor to receive extra tutoring from such a prestigious scholar and a hard-won battle his mother fought with his father who believed the rumors about Richter and his wife. Albert and Raimund had listened through the shut door of the kitchen while their parents argued about the education of their children.

"You refused to let Greta and Liliane go on to school because they are girls. I had no say about Otto's education although I agreed that he should at least go to *Realschule*," their mother said, referring to the technical school that allowed their oldest son to concentrate on modern agricultural methods. "Even if he isn't doing particularly well there."

"Die Pfeffernüsse," Albert whispered, and they covered their mouths to silence their laughter. They knew that although their father approved of vocational schooling, he had no choice as Otto had little academic talent or interest. Even those people the family associated with had recognized that the oldest Kaufmann boy was dim.

It was the blacksmith and shop owner Klaus Geringer who gave Otto his nickname when he was a humorless, unimaginative, and pudgy five-year-old with white skin, hair, and eyelashes. He jokingly called Otto "Die Pfeffernüsse" because he physically resembled the hard, round, pepper-nut cookies traditionally made at Christmas, covered with confectioner's sugar.

"Except he has more pepper than sugar and very little spice," he commented after Heinrich and Otto had left the shop one day. The name stuck, although it was rarely said to Otto's face.

Their mother continued. "You heard what the headmaster at the *Grundschule* said about Albert and Raimund. He would not have taken the time to talk to us if he thought any less of the boys. This extra tutoring is an excellent opportunity for Albert."

The boys' headmaster had previously risked Heinrich's temper by telling him that Albert and Raimund excelled at school, that it would be a terrible waste if both boys were not enrolled in the more rigorous and prestigious Gymnasium, where they could focus on Latin, the modern languages, history, sciences, and mathematics. Their father had finally agreed to the boys' switching schools but the extra tutoring galled him.

"Two days a week spent overnight, in addition to five days of school? No!" Heinrich shouted. "He doesn't need that much education."

"You will be seen as ignorant and backward if you don't allow this. Everyone knows how smart Albert is," their mother countered.

She then listed all the prosperous landowners, merchants, and industrialists from Augsburg who sent their sons to Gymnasium, and added, telling a little white lie, that other sons received extra tutoring. That did it. Their father had built a successful brewery in addition to a productive farm, and both his pride and reputation were at stake. He could not be seen as doing less. But he remained uneasy with Albert spending two nights each week at the Richter home.

ALBERT HAD BEEN EXCITED and simultaneously nervous about his first tutorial at the Richter home. He knocked on the massive door of the house on Maximilianstraße, his knees quaking.

Frau Richter opened it instead of the maid and said, "Hello, Albert! Welcome to the castle!"

He stumbled into the hall, unable to coordinate his hands or feet. Frau Richter took his satchel from him.

"I don't like living in such a big house," she said, ignoring his nervousness, "on such a well-known street but it is as it is."

Then Richter appeared, and after pushing two large black dogs out of the way he ushered Albert into his study.

"My wife may call it a castle," he remarked after he sat behind his desk, "but I call it a circus. Those two bears outside the door are only part of it. We also have six canaries and two cats." He sighed, ran a hand through his thinning hair. "As you will see, my wife and daughters have a great affection for animals. One of these days I'll come home and there will be a monkey hanging from the hallway chandelier."

IT WAS NOT JUST A WORLD of possibilities but a universe that existed for Albert on Tuesdays and Thursdays. He worked hard to sustain his avenue to knowledge on Wednesdays and Fridays, the days after his nights spent at the Richter home for private tutoring. His father would quiz him, wary of what Albert was learning. But Heinrich underestimated his second son, not seeing that the stubbornness attributed to him also existed in Albert. Albert pretended to be ignorant of what went on in the Richter household. The harder Heinrich probed, the more it solidified and strengthened Albert's loyalty to Richter, for he not only received a formal education from Richter but an affectionate, liberal one from his family.

The Richters *talked* while they ate dinner. Their four daughters were encouraged to express their thoughts and opinions, to comment on the events of their day. Albert listened slack-jawed as decisions were arrived at by way of discussion, sometimes passionate but never angry. There was nothing, it seemed, that could not be talked about: politics, religion, history, the city government, Frau Richter's six canaries, should they get a third dog, and so on. Richter would ask the daughter who initiated a particular debate "Why do you think that?" and forced her to give a logical and astute answer in defense of her view.

Albert found Frau Richter especially fascinating. Her first name, Adelinde, was melodic when said aloud. Her almond-shaped eyes were as dark as the roasted coffee beans she ground and brewed for dessert. Her hair under the evening light appeared black, but in the sunlight it showed the iridescent reflection of many colors, much like that of a starling's wings. She often wore it in a braided chignon but on special occasions would gather and pin it on top of her head so that a waterfall of curls draped her shoulders. Sometimes she looped her hair and captured it into the beaded netting of a snood at the nape of her neck. She wore earrings every day, crystal drops that accentuated her long neck. When she turned to talk to her daughters, he saw her profile as that of the ancient Egyptian queens he studied in school. Her figure was a youthful hourglass and had not, like other women who had more than one child, become a loaf of bread, the middle slightly compressed into a waist with the help of corsets so reinforced that they could have served as breastplates for women warriors. He described his impressions of Adelinde Richter to his mother.

"She is a beauty," his mother said with undisguised admiration. "Prettiness can only last so long but true beauty in a woman lasts until death. But, more important, Frau Richter is generous and kind."

Adelinde Richter read the same number of newspapers and books as her husband and spoke four languages fluently. She regaled

Albert with stories of their visits to Budapest, Rome, Paris, Berlin, Moscow, and London. Her particular area of interest was art and art history. She took him on a tour of their home to look at original paintings of unknown artists and copies of famous painters.

"It takes courage to convey truths with a painting," she said, leading him into the family's private parlor. "Painters have the greatest power because they reach those who cannot read but can see. And what do you see here?" she gestured at the paintings on the wall. Albert stared at the replicas of Rembrandt's *Bathsheba*, da Vinci's *Leda and the Swan*, Botticelli's *Birth of Venus*, and Caravaggio's *Raising of Lazarus*.

"There is something wrong," he said, pivoting to consider each painting again. "It is like having too many stories told to you at the same time. And Lazarus is the only man."

"Oh you darling boy!" Frau Richter said. "I have said the same thing to Immanuel. It is the conflicting themes. There is birth, death, adultery, rape, and resurrection in the same room. And you are absolutely right about Lazarus. I have asked Immanuel to remove the Caravaggio."

"On the contrary," Richter said, standing in the doorway with a bottle of anise liquor. "These are the themes of human reality and beliefs. Good and bad."

"Why not Caravaggio's *Death of the Virgin*," Albert suggested. "Then at least all the realities and themes would be represented by women. Except, of course, the swan, who is Zeus."

"That is a very good suggestion. Even though Zeus is present in the da Vinci, his actions represent a kind of death for women. Do you see what I mean?" Frau Richter said. Albert was momentarily confused. Then he thought of something his mother once said.

"Rape is death," he said.

"Exactly!" Frau Richter said. She turned to her husband. "I think he is your brightest student."

"He is," Richter said, standing next to Albert. He surveyed the paintings. "Hmm. It does appear that Lazarus is the odd man out."

FRAU RICHTER DIFFERED FROM HER HUSBAND in that she did not always believe that facts and reasons could ascertain truths.

There were discussions in which Frau Richter's response would be "some questions cannot be answered with facts or logic, only intuition." Then Richter would throw up his hands and playfully lament about being the only man in a house full of females. Yet Frau Richter's intuition prevailed in the face of illogical circumstances. Albert witnessed Frau Richter's ability to casually speculate about another family's fortune or misfortune. When her speculation came true, nothing much was said about it except to feel happiness for the family if they were fortunate or sympathy if they suffered bad times or tragedy struck. Frau Richter decided the destinations of their holidays and even the dates when they would travel. She had, as did his own mother, a room off the kitchen where she hung drying herbs, ropes of onions and garlic, and other plants from the walled-in garden behind the house. Albert thought nothing of it until the day he arrived at their house feverish and struggling to breathe. She put a garlic and mustard pack on his chest but also made him drink a chicken broth boiled with a twisted cheese-cloth bag full of herbs from her pantry. He woke up the next day as though he'd never been sick. Albert never mentioned his illness and overnight recovery to his parents nor did he give any indication that supported the rumors of her prescient abilities. He found it curious that Richter and his daughters never mentioned Frau Richter's unusual abilities, but sensing the family's implicit silence on the subject he did not make inquiries about it.

MAGDALENA RICHTER WAS THE SAME AGE as Albert and attended Gymnasium as well. Her demeanor there was quiet and she would have been invisible were it not for her striking resemblance to her mother. Although she was animated with her family, she remained aloof and distant with Albert. It was only at her mother's urging that she provided him with company after the Tuesday and Thursday night dinners. One evening they put on their coats and walked within the confines of the large walled-in garden behind the house.

"You are lucky to be living on Maximilianstraße," he said.

"Why?" she asked, running her long fingers over the bricks of the wall.

"Because it is historical. It is an ancient road built by the Romans," he answered.

"Who conquered the Germans," she said without looking at him. "The barbarians," she added.

"Is that what you think we are? Barbarians?" he asked, wondering what her hair looked like at night with the braids taken out and brushed. She turned around.

"No. That is what *you* think we are," she answered. "You are the Romans." It took him a second to understand that she was referring to his father's claims of their ancestry. She also used the plural you, including him with the rest of Augsburg society.

"I am not a Roman," he said, hurt and angry. "I am a German like you." He paused, thinking of his discussions with her father about German history. "Whatever that means," he said.

They faced each other in silence, exhaling white clouds. He didn't like being included in the faction that held her family suspect, but he understood her protective defiance.

Magdalena stepped forward, crossing her arms.

"Now you've seen how we live, how we are," she said. "Some of what is said is true. Mama is Catholic but not devout. She doesn't believe in original sin or the virgin birth. And I think you've noticed that she has a way about her. But that doesn't mean she is a gypsy."

"Yes, I've noticed. Do you have—"

"And it is true that Papa is an atheist," she went on, ignoring his words. "He goes to church only so that people will leave us alone."

"But he knows the Bible better than the priest does," Albert said.

"Because he is a scholar. He respects the Bible as a book of literature but does not believe it to be the word of God. You are here," she said, "because my father trusts you. He doesn't care what people think about him but he worries about Mama and us. You could hurt us with what you know."

Albert knew what his own father would do with such knowledge. He would be withdrawn from Gymnasium, from this precious two-day existence during the week.

"I am not my father," he said. "And I *like* the way you live."

To his embarrassment, he broke down and cried. Years later he would tell his granddaughter that he felt as though Magdalena had cupped his head, read its contents, and then fractured his skull, relieving the pressure of having lived concussively until that moment. She smiled and reached forward, clasping his hand.

"No, you are not," she said, leading him toward the house. "Mama is right. You are like your mother."

AFTER DESSERT, Magdalena and Albert went into Richter's study. She pulled three immense books from the shelf.

"This," she said, opening the first book and sitting next to him on the small divan, "has paintings by Goya." She grinned as Albert turned a deeper shade of pink with each page. "Papa has many books on erotic art in here—Degas, Courbet, Bouguereau," she explained. "We know he's looking at them when Mama says, 'Don't disturb your father. He is with his ladies.'"

"Really?!"

Magdalena burst out laughing.

"Don't worry," she said. "He loves Mama very much. Papa says the body's function is not only to work but to be an instrument of love, and therefore it is not something to be ashamed of."

Before she could open the next book, he reached for and picked up his book by Goethe, left on Richter's desk, and placed it over his lap.

"So I won't forget it," he explained. He listened and suffered while she talked about the other two books. Finally he excused himself, claiming fatigue. He ran up the stairs to the guest bedroom and, after shutting his door, unbuttoned his pants and masturbated. Then he undressed and drew a hot bath. He looked down at his penis in the water, stiff and upright for the second time.

Everything he had been taught to believe about family, about men and women, about the possibilities in his own life had been altered. While such liberality did not exist at home, his parents were progressive for their time. Sex was never discussed at the Kaufmann home but it was understood as a natural act. The priest might drone on about the evils of masturbation but their father mentioned such evils only in passing and then made jokes about it. From time to time, their mother told Albert and Raimund not to become too "preoccupied with themselves" but it was one of her lesser worries. Albert and his brothers did not suffer as some of their friends did, having their hands tied to the bedpost or having to kneel on a rough floor saying prayers all day. Still, Albert had never witnessed affection between his parents, and certainly could not imagine them naked and having sex. His parents stopped sharing the same bedroom the night after his mother beat his father with the poker.

Here he felt differently. Sex and nudity were art and were to be respectfully enjoyed, even talked about.

"An instrument of love," he said aloud, pleased that he could think of himself without shame. He imagined that when a man and woman came together, a symphony commenced, audible only to the lovers. It was evident that a symphony existed between Richter and his wife. He held her hand or put his arm around her shoulders. She brushed his cheek with her fingertips when they passed each other in the hall.

He stepped out of the tub, toweled off, put on his pajamas, and climbed into bed with the depressing knowledge that he would be at home the following evening.

JUST AS HIS BROTHER HAD PREDICTED, Raimund's penis and his height began to grow when he was twelve, thus relieving him of the fear that he would not be a true Kaufmann man: tall, muscled, and, most of all, well endowed. The onset of adolescence gave him a robust mental and sexual curiosity that not only enlivened his fantasy life but also caused him to look at the world beyond himself.

Ernst Geringer, the son of Klaus and now the owner of the blacksmith and adjoining hardware shop, winked and gave Raimund two postcards for his thirteenth birthday.

"What Monsignor says is not true. You will not go blind and your hand will not turn black and fall off," he said. "But don't ever say where you got them from."

He lied to his family, telling them that he needed more time alone in the hayloft to study, as the house was too noisy. He was granted that privacy because of his stellar grades and faithful service as an altar boy. Surrounded by the aphrodisiac smell of fresh hay, Raimund masturbated while looking at the two naked women.

Then three weeks later while he was cleaning the brewery and its small office, he found his father's own abundant collection of pornographic cards hidden in a wooden box underneath the steel legs of the safe. He filched a random selection and stuffed them inside his shirt before his father could walk in. Raimund was both aroused and appalled when he examined them later in the hayloft. The women were not the blonde, blue-eyed virginal models of German womanhood that Heinrich Kaufmann espoused for his sons. They had kohl-rimmed eyes and rouged lips. Their skin color ranged from tawny to olive to mahogany, and their brown or black hair was tousled as though they had just arisen from sleep. All of them were small waisted, heavy hipped, and had firm breasts with nipples rouged as heavily as their lips. The only exception was a redhead whose skin was the ivory of clabbered cream. Raimund looked at them and wondered if his father still went to a *Frauenhaus* and whether the women who lived there looked like their postcard counterparts.

"Describe them," Ernst asked. He was shoeing a horse and they both sweated in the heat of the forging room. Raimund told him, adding that the only fair-skinned woman had red hair and that for his father, red hair was the mark of the devil.

"The ones you think are evil are the most exciting," Ernst commented, pounding a nail into the last shoe. He stood up and wiped his face on his shirt. "At least for some men." He paused. "I carry those cards. But your father has never bought them from me."

Raimund watched as Ernst led the horse to a stall, then fed and watered it. Ernst was thirty years old, unmarried, and took care of his elderly parents. His mother said that if a woman could look past Ernst's physical appearance she would have a loyal and kind man. He had nearly all of the physical attributes of being handsome. A woman could enjoy a pleasant survey of his features if she began at his feet and moved her eyes slowly upward. He had long muscular legs and a narrow waist that widened into a broad chest and shoulders. Despite his work as a blacksmith, he had beautiful hands with long fingers and clean, oval-shaped nails. But his face was that of a bulldog, broad and thick-boned and with jowls usually seen on an older man. Ernst had one rope-like eyebrow that extended down

both sides of his face as though it were a tributary of hair emptying into the basin of his beard. He did not go to school after the
age of twelve because he was the only child of older parents who
were at the bottom of the mercantile class.

"A pity," Annaliese Kaufmann always said after seeing the blacksmith, noting that Ernst was an intelligent and inquisitive man who
read constantly to educate himself. He imported various publica-
tions and items from other parts of the world.

"From France," he answered, when Raimund asked him where
he purchased the cards. "Sometimes England or Austria but France
has the best ones."

Albert, Raimund, and Leo frequently stopped by Ernst's shop
on their way home from school. Ernst sold Karl May's Wild West
novels to Albert, telling him, "This is the life you should seek someday. Free from rules."

He let Leo and Raimund peruse the legitimate postcards on
display, featuring cities from all over the world: New York, New
Orleans, Paris, Brussels, Vienna, London, Prague, and even Shang-
hai. One postcard featured a drawing of the Statue of Liberty. The
caption read: A MIGHTY WOMAN WITH A TORCH.

Albert gave the Karl May novels to Raimund when he was
finished reading them. Raimund's brain expanded and floated on
chaos and canyons, Indians and cowboys, arrows and guns, sand
and sagebrush, and, most of all, freedom. His teachers punished
him for inattentiveness. They rapped his knuckles with rulers and
made mental notes among themselves. Yet they were unable to enforce their perceptions on Raimund's school record or in a written letter to his father because Raimund finished his homework
with complete accuracy, and none of them wanted a confronta-
tion with Heinrich Kaufmann. Raimund was blessed with the
mental agility to answer a sudden question while in the depths of
daydreaming. To the teachers' astonishment, Raimund answered
the question put to him like a magician, as though he had reached
behind the teacher's ear and pulled out the undisputed answer
rather than a coin or egg.

Raimund began to turn inward. He learned to become judicious in asking questions, much to the relief of his brothers and sisters. Only his mother was disturbed at the change in her once talkative son. She asked him questions to draw him out, finally admitting that she thought he had melancholy.

"I'm *fine*, Ma. I'm just thinking," he said, knowing it bothered her as she had an uncle who had committed suicide, in addition to his father's brother.

Fortunately being thirteen meant that he graduated into becoming Herr Doktor Professor Richter's student and was in the same school as Albert. Albert worshipped Richter, spending much time in tutorials at the professor's home. Raimund knew Richter considered his brother an uncommonly thoughtful and intelligent boy. But Raimund was, as Richter later told him, an academic challenge. He was a boy with a combustible mix of appetites interwoven with a high aptitude that, if guided correctly, would rise above conformity and mediocrity to do great things. Richter did not say what would happen if Raimund was not correctly guided.

Raimund had been thrilled when Richter suggested that he join Albert in the tutorials. He walked with idiotic giddiness as he and Albert made their way from school to the Richter home. Albert grabbed his arm, forcing him to stop.

"Don't be such an ass," Albert said. "And don't embarrass me. And don't talk about the Richters no matter how hard Papa or anyone tries to weasel it out of you."

"And, and, and," Raimund parroted.

"I mean it," Albert hissed, twisting his fist into the fabric of Raimund's shirtsleeve. "I'll beat you worse than Papa ever did."

He behaved well for the most part, exaggerating formal manners to conceal his instant infatuation with Frau Richter. His only digression that first evening was when she kissed him on the cheek. He became dizzy with the softness of her lips and the smell of her perfume. He grabbed the back of a chair to steady himself while Richter coughed over his amusement, and the Richter girls and Albert smothered their laughter.

Dinner at the Richter home was an especially enlightening experience for his palate. Raimund and Albert ate good food at home but nothing out of the ordinary for Bavaria. Frau Richter served, among other delicacies, Brie cheese with pears and nuts, and Stilton with port wine for dessert. A first course to a meal might be olives and bread or foie gras. The latter tasted faintly of the *Leberwurst* they were used to but was silkier. They had wine with every meal. Birthdays were celebrated with champagne. Raimund tasted a pomegranate for the first time, his hands and mouth stained red from each seed, and listened while Frau Richter told them the story of Kore and Demeter.

"WHAT ARE YOU THINKING?" Richter asked him one day. Raimund had skipped lunch and stayed in the classroom, staring out the window.

"I don't understand my father," Raimund answered. "I never have. He always tells me to be a good German. But he is not always good. What is a good German? What makes that so different from being a good Swede, good Frenchman, good anything?"

"Come to my desk," Richter said. Raimund followed him to the front of the room. He took two books from one of the desk drawers and placed the first, a slim volume, in Raimund's hands.

"These are essays about Germania by the Roman historian Tacitus. Read them at least twice." Then he gave him the second book, which Raimund recognized right away. *Das Volk in Waffen* by Baron von der Goltz. "Read that too and we'll discuss both of them in a week," he said.

He read the first book that night in the hayloft, and the night following he read the von der Goltz book. Rather than indoctrinate him the latter book was revelatory, and it dovetailed with the observations of Tacitus. Von der Goltz's most famous quote—*We have won our position through the sharpness of our sword, not through the sharpness of our mind*—revealed to Raimund the mindset that had created his father and dominated all of Germany. But it was Tacitus who spoke to him. He reread the volume on the third night after chores, resting on a bed of straw near the gable window of the loft. Raimund occasionally looked up to watch his father as he inspected the fields. For the first time, he was able to see his father in a more personal *and* ancient light.

✠ ✠ ✠

"YOUR FATHER COMES from one of the few families who owned their land rather than rented it from the aristocracy," Ernst Geringer had told him one day after Raimund bemoaned not living in Augsburg. "It has been in the Kaufmann family for generations and for good reason. It is next to the Lech, has rich soil, and is only three miles from Augsburg. Like your grandfather, your father set some of the land aside as pasture for his livestock, but unlike your grandfather, your father cultivated the rest into barley, hops, and rye in addition to wheat. Growing his own supply allowed him to build his own brewery, and the rest is history."

Raimund thought of the beer that made his father famous in Augsburg and Regensburg. Before Raimund was born, his father had perfected a medium-brown brew with a creamy head described as both velvety and crisp. It was known as the Kaufmann Lager.

Yet when Raimund looked at the daguerreotype of his parents' wedding, Heinrich at six foot three and a muscular two hundred thirty pounds looked less like a farmer and more like his hunting, gathering, and warring ancestors. There was also a daguerreotype in the parlor of Heinrich with the Augsburg javelin team. Tall and broad-houldered then, he had the chest and midriff of Michelangelo's David, giving some credibility to his claims that the Kaufmanns were descended from Roman as well as German stock. Raimund could see it in the tintype. His father's chiseled face was like Michelangelo's David with its patrician jaw, nose, and brow line. His hair was curly then, bleached white in the summer sun. He was thirty years old when he married, and thus Raimund knew him only as a middle-aged man who caused his own physical decline by mastering, instead of the javelin, years of smoking cigars, beer drinking, and overeating fatty sausage, cheese, buttery spatzle, and pastries. He had reduced himself to a thick-fingered, heavyset, bellicose braggart. His father rarely visited a doctor, but three years earlier after showing his sons how to properly throw a javelin his chest cramped up, causing him to be short of breath. It scared him enough to go to the doctor, and he took his youngest son with him. Raimund sat outside the doctor's office and listened.

"Quit smoking. And practice moderation in your eating and drinking. If you don't, you'll never live to see your grandchildren," the doctor said. Heinrich loudly dismissed the doctor's advice, saying he knew his own body better than the doctor did.

Since he could no longer participate in the sport he loved, Heinrich required that his sons learn the art of throwing the modernized spear. He also demanded that they learn to fence and to handle a firearm. Raimund and Albert excelled at all three. Much to Heinrich's dismay, Otto failed at the javelin and he lacked agility in fencing. He redeemed himself only on the use of firearms, proving to be at least competent at loading, aiming, and firing a pistol and rifle. Heinrich was disgusted.

"It doesn't take any brains to shoot a gun!" he said, pointing the pistol in the air and firing. "But to use the sword you have to think ahead of your opponent. Be fast and agile. The javelin is the same. You have to gauge the pitch of the spear, think about what might knock it off course. The direction of the wind. How fast it is blowing. Will it land where you want it to. Do you understand?"

"Why would I need to throw the javelin? Or use a sword? Especially if I can use a gun during battle?" Otto had responded.

"Because, you idiot," Heinrich flared. "Fighting requires thinking. When you run out of bullets or your rifle jams, what do you do then?"

"Use your bayonet," Albert answered.

"And any other knife you are carrying," Raimund added.

"Exactly," Heinrich said, pushing the spear end of the javelin into the ground before walking away.

Otto glared at his two brothers.

"I'd shoot both of you dead before you could even pull out a knife."

"Not if your rifle jams," Albert said. "You just don't get it, do you?"

Albert and Raimund followed their father, ignoring Otto's vocal imitation of shots being fired into their backs.

RAIMUND CONTINUED READING. In his essay "The Warlike Ardour of the People," Tacitus articulated what Heinrich in his limited education could not have explained about his own inner being.

Nor are they as easily persuaded to plow the earth and to wait for the year's produce as to challenge an enemy and earn the honor of wounds. Nay, they actually think it tame and stupid to acquire by the sweat of toil what they might win by blood.

Raimund stopped reading and observed his shirtless father as he walked through his rye field. His hands restlessly swept through the stalks every now and then, his eyes focused on something in the distance. He now often worked naked from the waist up when it was warm, acquiring a tan more golden than brown, fading the scar on his chest. His father turned briefly, raised a hand to shield his eyes against the sun, and looked back at the barn.

Honor, Tacitus whispered in Raimund's ear. *Blood.* He recalled the story of the scar that his father had once told them about their Uncle Gunter.

"We came out in the wrong order," his father said in a rare moment and with undisguised resentment. Albert, Raimund, and Heinrich were resting after milking, drinking water from the courtyard pump. "Gunter was never good with a rifle. How can you be a soldier if you can't shoot? He cried when he fell down. Hated blood. How can you be a soldier if you are afraid of being hurt?" Then he took off his shirt. There was a foot-long scar across his chest. "I got this protecting your uncle."

"Were you stabbed?" Albert asked, awestruck.

"No. Not stabbed," he answered, and extending the rare moment of disclosure he told them the story of his wound.

"Just before Otto was born, I was invited to go boar hunting in the Black Forest with three other landowners and four merchants from Augsburg. I wasn't going to pass it up. It was a once-in-a-lifetime opportunity. The boar populations were low and leases to hunt were expensive, especially in the Black Forest. We each contributed to a group permit for four days. Your Uncle Gunter was home on military leave and I talked him into joining the hunting party. We fanned out into a large circle and walked toward the center to trap a flushed boar. Your Uncle Gunter was next to me. We heard a shout from one of the other men, heard the sound of brush being trampled, and then the boar ran out from under the brush and toward us.

"Your uncle was in the best position to shoot but he just stood there. Terrified. The boar charged him. I couldn't shoot because I was afraid of hitting Gunter. So I used my knife."

He then told Raimund and Albert that he intercepted the charging animal, stabbing it in the neck and then through the ribs. He held the boar down until it stopped struggling. It wasn't until the other men arrived that he realized some of the blood covering him was his own. The wild pig had slashed his chest with its tusks. They found a local doctor who sewed up the wound, telling Heinrich how fortunate he was, as a wealthy businessman from Hamburg had died two days earlier when a boar punctured his lung. Gunter left the next morning and returned to his military post in Berlin. A month later he shot himself.

"Gunter was a coward even in death. He was not born to live up to his name," their father said. He put his shirt back on and then silently waved them back to their chores.

"I don't believe him," Raimund said when he was out of hearing. "I'm going to ask Ma."

Their mother was scrubbing the parlor floor.

"Gunter's name means *war*," she said, wiping her hands on her apron and sitting back on her heels. "Only people like your father put such stock in the meaning of those names. The story is true but your father's attitude is not honest. You can't blame someone for the order in which they are born. Even if Gunter had been born the oldest, he didn't want to be a farmer. He wanted to be a scholar. He loved books. But your Uncle Dieter was chosen to be a priest and so Gunter had to be a soldier. As to why Gunter took his life, only God can place judgment. I don't know why your father thinks his fate is so terrible. He inherited everything, and Gunter and Dieter got nothing."

Raimund stuffed the book into his shirt as his father approached the barn. He felt something he had never associated with his father. Sympathy. Beneath his father's pastoral exterior was the aggression and arrogance of his ancient brethren. It was what drove him to succeed at what he had inherited and what was expected of him, and simultaneously permeated and twisted his beliefs and his thoughts. Understanding his father better did not, however, help Raimund or Albert weather the community's opinion of him.

Although Heinrich was not well liked, he was respected for being a successful and wealthy farmer. He was politely described as eccentric to Raimund and Albert. Raimund would later tell his nieces and nephews that eccentric was a gracious way of saying the old man was nuts. They knew he was called a stewed Catholic for his extreme righteousness and allegiance to Pope Pious IX and then Pope Leo XIII, and considered the irony of their father's position for he did not like to go to church. Yet they also knew their father held a strange allegiance to Otto von Bismarck, whom many in Bavaria considered to be the devil.

"Why are the schools secular?" Richter asked his class of boys one day.

"Because Bismarck believed that government, not the church, should determine what was right and wrong," Raimund answered, reciting almost from memory what he had read in his textbook. "It was the only way he could unify the German states into the Second Reich. That is why schools became state sponsored and secular."

"And what happened when he did that?" Richter asked.

"A lot of Germans left the country and went to America so that they could have religious freedom."

"Correct. The first wave of Germans going to America were called the 1848'ers. You can see from our lesson today why Bismarck has reversed his policy somewhat. Leo, can you tell us why?"

"Because he's losing men who would serve in the military," Leo answered.

"Has it worked?"

"I don't know. Has it?" Leo answered earnestly, and the boys around him laughed. Richter smiled.

"It has slowed immigration but not stopped it," Richter answered.

Raimund knew his own father's opinion of Bismarck's policies. Heinrich recognized the dilemma but thought Bismarck unimaginative in his solution. He believed the United States to be a holding pen for mongrel races, and he saw those who left the Fatherland as traitors and human *Müll*—garbage.

To Raimund and Albert's embarrassment, he was not afraid to state his beliefs in public. After they were done at the market, buying equipment, or getting a horse shod, Heinrich insisted that his sons come with him to sit in his favorite beer garden, the Charly Braü. There he and the other men present fomented over the subject of Bismarck and the Germans who left the country.

"Let them go!" he shouted, becoming more argumentative with each beer. "This country needs a good cleaning anyway!" His answer to building up the numbers of soldiers was to encourage loyal Germans to produce bigger families, and for the government to offer them financial incentives to do so, especially if they had sons. It was something the Catholics had always known: you gave birth to your own army of soldiers and workers.

While his father predicted that Bismarck would go to hell when he died, his father also believed that someday Germany would look back on the chancellor with pride for his shrewd leadership and his acquisition of other lands to make Germany a world power. Raimund knew it was why his father had named his oldest brother Otto and doted on him almost to the exclusion of the children who followed. His father regretted it later, however, as Otto grew into a tyrannical horse's ass who lacked the intelligence credited to his namesake.

He flattened himself into the hay as his father entered the barn and felt again a twinge of sympathy. He and Albert often wondered if Richter resented his lack of sons but they saw no evidence of it. Perhaps, Raimund thought, it was because Richter had become close to them and thus could partake in veiled father and son discussions. The boys knew that it was not their father's fault but his fate that he could not be the kind of male figure they yearned for and found in their professor.

"WHAT DO YOU THINK about von der Goltz's position," Richter asked Raimund when they began their tutorial session a week later, "especially in light of what Tacitus observes?"

"It makes us sound as though we are still barbarians who cannot think. As though we are still fighting the Romans," he answered.

"Exactly," Richter responded. "And you know what happened

to us then." They were sitting in the study. Raimund watched as Richter plugged his pipe with tobacco and lit it.

"Human beings are still a primitive species. Until we evolve further," he said, "we will only attain some measure of civilization through supreme mental effort and ethics. But never peace. At least not in Germany. Germany has always unified and gloried under war but suffered uneasily under peace. It has been cursed for hundreds, even thousands of years with the cultural trait of being single-minded. I don't particularly like Bismarck or his methods—especially his hatred of socialists of which I'm one. But I can't deny that he did unify Germany and he has an adroit grasp of foreign diplomacy and policy, and at least some world vision. The kaiser does not. We will eventually have another war in Europe because Kaiser Wilhelm is arrogant, stupid, and greedy."

"My father says we will have a war, too," Raimund answered, "because Germany is superior in everything it does and should rule Europe."

Richter leaned back. He took the pipe out of his mouth.

"There's that single-mindedness again. Your father isn't alone in thinking that. Our education is the best, the most rigorous in Europe. We study and support science. We have high culture, magnificent music, and a strong belief in work done well. So that part is true. Your father is not a stupid man. Far from it. He is a very intelligent man. In the last twenty years, many farmers lost their farms because they had no vision and no sense of management. Your father is a shrewd businessman. What he lacks is a liberal education. I do agree with him in that we will have a war eventually. But not because we are superior. It is a fight between the royal families of Europe. The kaiser wants a bigger empire but will not go up against his grandmother, Queen Victoria, at this time. He's biding his time until she dies. Then he will try to get a bigger empire but it will bring about the ruination of Germany."

Raimund thought about his Uncle Gunter's fate.

"You are the third son?" Richter asked.

"Yes."

"And Albert is the second. That means the farm will go to your brother, Otto," he said, thinking aloud. He tapped out the ashes from his pipe and refilled it. "Your English is passable but you must work at it so that you are completely fluent. Albert is nearly there. When you both come of age, you will need to look beyond this country. Not to Europe but to America. It is the only place where you both will have what the French call *joie de vivre*—the joy of life."

Raimund considered the professor's advice. He had no idea how he was going to do that but thought that the Karl May novels might give him some direction. Then Richter spoke as though he had read Raimund's mind.

"The United States is *not* like a Karl May novel. He traveled only to New York City and was there for a very short time. I doubt he encountered any Indians and cowboys in that city." He paused to adjust his glasses.

"I suggest," he continued as if he were going to explain why a beloved pet died, "that you throw away those books. There isn't one bit of truth in them. And he's a terrible writer."

ALBERT HALF-LISTENED TO RAIMUND speak of the future as they mucked out the large chicken coop. His brother's lips and hands were chapped from having been washed with lye soap. It was the only way Raimund could get rid of the stain from the pomegranate he had eaten the night before. Albert wiped his face against his arm and looked over at his thirteen-year-old brother who did not like farming or farm work. A passing stranger would not have known that about his brother today. Today, Raimund loved everything. He could tolerate the acrid chicken shit and dust in his nostrils because it was temporary in the scheme of things. The world was larger than what they had been raised to believe. Albert knew that feeling, could see himself at that age in his brother.

He stopped working, cleaned one of the dust-covered windows with a rag, and looked through the glass at the wind rippling through the wheat and creating waves on the duck pond. *His* expanded view of the world included the farm. Unlike his older and younger brother, he loved the farm and liked farming. When he fantasized a future as the farm's owner, it was with his father's same progressive agricultural methods. But unlike his father, Albert would not shirk the life of his mind. He liked the English concept of being a "gentleman farmer," of believing that working the land and expanding the mind complemented each other in making a whole life.

"Here you go."

He felt something cold against his shoulder.

"Oh no you didn't—"

Raimund had filled two empty beer bottles with water. His brother grinned, the sweat creating a seersucker pattern of dirt on his face.

"I'm not that stupid. Besides, Pa is in the brewery with a buyer."

"A buyer from where?

"München. From the Nürnberger Bratwurst Glöckl."

"München!" Albert was stunned. München was famous for its breweries. Restaurants there served beer only from brewmasters within the city. And the Nürnberger Bratwurst Glöckl was among the most famous.

"Where is Otto?"

"Far from Pa," Raimund answered. "He took Otto to the train station yesterday while we were at school. Otto is spending two weeks with Uncle Dieter at the monastery in Regensburg."

He spoke in reference to their father's discovery two days earlier that Otto, not the seasonal workers he had fired, had been pilfering crates of beer to drink with his friends at neighboring farms. It was the latest in a growing line of offenses. Two months earlier their father had found Otto sleeping in a field that he should have been plowing. Not long after that, Heinrich had sent him to Ulm to buy oak kegs, only to have Otto come home late with the wrong kegs and overpriced ones at that. Just last week, Otto suggested that they hire more farm labor rather than do the work themselves. Heinrich struck his oldest son, knocking him into the manure-filled gutter.

"How does that make a profit!" the old man had roared.

Otto made no attempt to get up for fear of being knocked down again. Manure splattered his face and slicked the front of his shirt. Albert looked at his older brother, wondered for the umpteenth time how his parents had produced such a being. It was not a question of his mother's fidelity—even if he knew little else about her, he could be sure of that one thing. Otto resembled their father but something had gone awry. He had premature jowls on his face and his pudginess of youth had hardened into a stockiness that would not last, as a hint of corpulence was discernible through his chest and belly. Otto was cunning and sly, and yet stupid and lazy. Worse, he was disturbingly cruel. He had once killed a barn cat—a favorite of their sister Liliane—and her kittens by strangling them with twine and then tacking the bodies to the chicken coop wall so that she would see them when she collected eggs. When Raimund was three years old, Otto threw him into the pig pen and told him to run. Unbeknownst to Otto, their mother was in the courtyard and heard Otto's laughter and Raimund's screams in time to rescue her youngest by beating the pigs off with a stick. On both occasions, it was their mother, not their father, who whipped Otto until he blubbered. Albert held his terrified younger brother and watched their mother deliver the punishment.

"What is wrong with you!" she screamed as she raised the strap. "He is your brother! If I didn't know better, I would think that you tried to kill him!"

Albert did not believe his brother was a mistake of God but rather an evolutionary flaw that corrected itself with the children who came after. A freak of nature like an albino foal born to a brown stud and mare. He saw that his father suffered the same bewilderment, although he likely attributed it to God or bad luck rather than Darwin's theory of evolution.

Then Heinrich shocked them.

"You came out in the wrong order," he said, still heaving with rage and pointing a finger at Otto. "Albert should have been the first. He can manage the farm on his own *now*."

ALBERT AND RAIMUND LEANED against the chicken coop wall and drank their water. Then Heinrich emerged from the brewery with the buyer. The two men shook hands before the buyer mounted his horse. The boys straightened up as their father approached them, a rare grin on his face.

"He made the sale," Raimund commented.

✠ ✠ ✠

OUT OF FEAR, Magdalena suppressed in herself that which her mother had forbidden on that February day and it was never mentioned again so directly. The Richter daugters practiced their parents' example in establishing a public face when at times they wished to be just their private selves. They knew, for example, the routine when one of them became ill.

A doctor was called. He examined the child in question and then gave Frau and Herr Richter a diagnosis and treatment. Sometimes he was correct and sometimes not. If their mother disagreed with the doctor's opinion, she did not say so. She waited until he left and then treated the sick daughter in question with her own remedies, grown in the walled garden behind their house.

Their mother was also adept at sensing pain in others. Magdalena and her sisters observed their mother diffuse anger in a social situation before it was obvious that someone was angry. They watched as men especially gravitated toward their mother, holding conversations and revealing things about themselves that they would never have told their wives. On any given day, they would come home from school to find a male relative, a former scholar, or a workman who had delivered a crate of wine or some other goods sitting at the kitchen table with their mother. They eavesdropped behind the closed kitchen door, hearing the men speaking in low tones, their faces, they knew, twisted with emotion. Frau Richter listened to each man, poured more coffee, and finally upon being asked, gave a sage suggestion that neither spoke to the past nor the future.

"I thought we'd agreed that you would not do this anymore," her father said during one of their rare arguments. The milkman had sat in their kitchen that day, lamenting his marital woes. Magdalena had flattened herself against the wall next to their shut bedroom door in the hopes her mother would reveal something.

"Do what? They ask for my opinion and I give it to them."

"Other people will see it as fortune-telling."

"I hardly do that. Any fool who took the time to listen could discern the answer from the talk. Most women instinctively know how to do that. Whether they choose to listen is their choice. Given the number of unhappy men in this city, I would guess many of their wives do not hear what their husbands have to say. *And,*" she added, "*vice versa.*"

MAGDALENA TRIED to confront her mother when she turned twelve.

"You are different with me," she said. She sat next to the mirrored vanity in her parents' bedroom and watched her mother brush her long hair into segments for braiding.

"How so?" her mother asked, picking up a lank of hair and braiding it. Magdalena considered a less-ambiguous response. She was now sure that her sisters did not have the unnamed and unexplained ability that Magdalena shared with their mother. They were empathetic and intuitive but exhibited nothing out of the ordinary. Rose, Amalia, and Eva did not appear to sense anything further in their interactions with others that burdened them. Furthermore, their mother's relations with her sisters proved it.

"You have more fun with them," she answered, thinking of her mother's face when she interacted with Magdalena's sisters. Her mother was relaxed, confident in knowing that her other daughters saw the world on its surface whereas she seemed perpetually on guard with Magdalena.

"That's not true," her mother said, pinning up a coil of braided hair. "We have fun, don't we?"

When Magdalena didn't answer, her mother said, "I don't mean to be different with you." She finished coiling and pinning up her braids into a small monument of coiffed beauty before speaking again. She shifted on the bench to face Magdalena.

"Perhaps it is because you are the oldest. I was the oldest child in my family and I was aware of being apart from everyone else. Different things were expected of me. I was the first child to experience everything. I felt like the carved figurehead of a woman at the bow of a ship. I had to break through the waters. I was the first to take the pounding and freezing waves of my parents' decisions."

Then her mother looked past her in contemplation of something else, something that made her look sad.

"I was the child most closely watched," she said.

"Why?"

Her mother sighed.

"Here I thought I would be a different mother to my firstborn and I see that I have repeated my mother's mistakes."

"It's not that," Magdalena began. But her mother stood up and was moving toward the armoire to pick out a dress. Her words trailed her.

"I think you and I have not had enough time together. We'll go shopping this afternoon. Just the two of us." She held up a dress. "What do you think of this color?"

And with that, Magdalena was silenced.

SHE TRIED AGAIN at sixteen.

She was peeling potatoes at the kitchen table and watching her mother's back as she kneaded bread. Magdalena had been moody lately, something both her parents attributed to the general uproar of adolescent bodily change. But it was more than that. She was sick of the artifice of their lives, at the lack of rational answers in what was otherwise a family that prided itself on being open and rational; of transcending the inane and embracing the sublime.

"You are your mother's daughter," her Grandmother Richter had said before she died three years earlier. Magdalena thought that her grandmother was alluding to the physical resemblance between the mother and daughter. It was true. The similarity was so strong that when they traveled elsewhere in Europe they were mistaken for sisters. She dropped a potato into a pot of salted water and thought of her mother's analogy of being the oldest child. Her mother had explained it in terms of the psychological and not the physical experience. The physical was different and often disturbing for Magdalena.

As the oldest and first child, Magdalena saw her herself as the first printing of a second edition. A sentence or two might have been changed but the overall appearance was the same; the pages dark with the abundance of ink from the press's first run. Her sisters resembled later editions, later printings, their hair not as black, their skin not as olive. Their father's physical attributes appeared more in them. Eva had his jawline, Amalia had his ears, and Rose his patrician nose.

She finished the potatoes, concluding that the time for ambiguity was over.

"Why have you never talked to me about that day in the Fuggerei?"

Her mother's back stiffened but she did not turn around.

"What day in the Fuggerei? We've been there countless times," her mother answered.

"You know which day. My seventh birthday," she said, and then added, "the deaths of Frau and Herr Mueller."

Her mother kneaded the bread dough into a ball and placed it in a buttered bowl, covering it with a tea towel. She turned around, wiping her hands in her apron.

"Their deaths were sad. Like so many."

"I saw them. I knew they were going to die."

Her mother crossed her arms.

"You are very intelligent, Magdalena. But that can sometimes lead to fanciful illusions. There was nothing there that wasn't obvious, even to a child. Frau Mueller was sick that day even though she put on a brave face. And Josef sat on that bench nearly every day. He couldn't do anything else. He was depressed—it was obvious to all who lived there. Frau Mueller became sicker and then died. In his depression, Josef saw no further reason for living. You imagined what everyone else saw and knew."

"Then why did you scare me with that story of Dorothea Braun?"

"Because you had to learn the consequences of misinterpretation. Of saying the wrong thing in public."

Magdalena seethed at her mother's skillful subterfuge.

"You know, Mama, you can't fool us. We see what you do. Why do you practice something that you won't acknowledge? Why won't you talk to me about it?"

She watched as her mother briefly touched her forehead. One of her headaches. Magdalena faltered. None of her acquaintances at school would have been allowed to question their parents' reasoning. As liberal as her family was, there was still a requisite need for respect for one's parents.

"I'm not going to discuss this anymore or indulge in your illusions," she said, removing her apron. Her hands were shaking. "I'm going upstairs to lie down and do not wish to be disturbed until dinner. Please finish the bread."

MAGDALENA REMAINED AT THE TABLE, thinking of what she could have said, of what she didn't say. The irony of it was she had learned the consequence of misinterpretation, not from anything said publicly and by her but from her mother. Magdalena had, from that day in the Fuggerei on, behaved impeccably in public. They all did and yet the rumors continued.

"Can you tell me my fortune, Mag-da-lene?" a boy had snickered just a week ago at school during the lunch break. He stuck his hand out, palm side up. She stared at him, wishing his disappearance.

"I'll tell you your fortune," Albert interrupted, slapping the other boy's hand down so hard that it hit the table with a crack. The boy was their same age, sixteen. He stood there, tears welling, holding his injured hand.

"Your fortune is this," Albert said. "Ask stupid questions and you will get painful answers." Then Albert sat down as though nothing had happened and proceeded to eat his bread and cheese.

She was grateful for Albert's intervention, but it was not the most hurtful incident she had faced. No single incident or collective ones had been as terrible as her mother's continued denial.

She heard a noise in the hallway. A moment later her father appeared in the kitchen.

"Come into the study," he said. She followed him down the hallway, went through the open door, which her father then shut. He motioned for her to sit down.

"You've had a disagreement with your mother?"

"Yes." She paused. "I didn't mean to hurt Mama. I just wanted some answers."

"Rightly so. I'm as guilty as your mother in not providing them," he said.

She paused. It occurred to her that she had never sought counsel from her father on the subject.

"I never asked you, Papa," she said.

"True. But then I should have approached this subject sooner. I was hesitant to do so because it felt to me to be your mother's domain. But I can see that it has now come to a head."

"We never talk about what Mama knows. What she does. What *it is*," she said. "I see things too. I have since I was very little."

"I know," he answered, surprising her. Then he continued.

"What *it is*, is a kind of intelligence. When we were first married, I dismissed it as feminine illusions," he said, wincing. "Which I regret in retrospect because I fell in love with your mother more for her intellect than her beauty. I considered it a socialized feminine trait that she was not entirely aware of. But as the years went by, I realized that your mother had an intelligence different from mine."

"Better than yours?"

"Not better. Different," he answered. "I am a rationalist. I believe in reason. But in teaching history and mythology, I cannot ignore what is done to people when they are perceived as being different and therefore dangerous. Did you know that the famous astronomer and mathematician Johannes Kepler had a mother who was a healer? She was accused of witchcraft when one of her patients got sick. Her son defended her at the trial and it was his defense—as a rational and well-known thinker—that saved her. I'm convinced that he arrived at the same thinking I have. I can't explain it or understand it. I don't know where it comes from but I know for a fact that it exists and therefore I cannot deny it. In your mother or anyone else. There are other cultures that revere such intelligence. But not our present culture. We still live in a time of religious superstition and persecution. The clerics of this city would consider your mother's abilities to be satanic. They can't and won't look at it rationally. Your mother fears for your safety, hence she won't discuss it on the premise that the less you know about it the better."

"That doesn't make sense," Magdalena said. "You of all people have said repeatedly how damaging ignorance is."

"Yes, and I still believe it. But so is a little bit of knowledge—like thinking that one species of fish can give you all the answers to what is in the ocean."

"I don't know what to think or do with what I see," she said.

"Your mother says it is an inherited trait among the women in her family and so I am not surprised that you have it. You are so much like her," he answered.

"Is that why she doesn't love me as much as Rose, Amalia, and Eva?"

Her father was taken aback.

"You must never think that. *Never*. On the contrary, your mother loves you very much. It is fear that dictates her behavior toward you. She sees herself in you and wants a different life for you. But she cannot talk to you about it and I'm asking you not to press her on the matter. I don't agree with her about this but I have to respect her wishes. I'm not of much use to you either as I don't know what it is like to see another dimension, so to speak."

"Do you believe that I have fanciful illusions?" she asked.

"No. You are a realist. You were even as a young child. Which I suspect makes it even more difficult when you sense things other people cannot."

"It does."

"What I can tell you is this: use this gift with discretion but always use it for good, like your mother does." He paused and smiled. "I understand that Albert came to your rescue last week."

"He told you?"

"No—Raimund did. Albert is very fond of you and I think you are of him. But don't tell him until you are absolutely sure of his trust. Don't tell anyone else outside the family. I realize I'm asking you to bear what feels like a continued burden. My hope is that someday people will embrace difference, not hate it. In the meantime," he winked, "indulge in some fanciful illusions. Try not to become too realistic. Hardened realists cannot see the creative in anything."

HEINRICH, ALBERT, AND RAIMUND worked into the night loading kegs onto two wagons. The boys then drove the wagons and their father to the train station the next morning. After the kegs had been moved into a boxcar, Heinrich took Albert aside and told him to plow under a small field in the southeast corner of the farm.

"That field hasn't produced a crop of hay in two years now. We have to make it productive again." He rolled a cigar between his fingers. "Use Aherin. He needs the exercise," he said. "After you are done plowing, work a good load of manure into it. You and Raimund will have to miss school tomorrow and maybe on Monday but that is the way it has to be. The farm comes first."

Then Heinrich boarded a passenger car, uncharacteristically turning to wave goodbye to his sons.

The next day was Friday. It was the day that their mother typically drove into Augsburg to purchase necessities such as sugar, soap, and cloth, and she left in her single-horse buggy after breakfast. Albert lifted the plow onto a small cart with help from Raimund and then hitched up the Percheron. The field was near a section of the Lech River with a natural sand beach. They had swum in it as small children but not since then. Albert was halfway there when he realized that he had forgotten to pack a lunch. He had resigned himself to going without food until dinner when he suddenly remembered a stone cottage nearby, going to ruin because no one had lived there for several years. He would search the vegetable garden behind it, looking for wild remnants of onions or carrots.

He worked until noon. Albert was leading the horse down to the river when he heard voices. He stopped and listened again. The sound was clearer: the splashing of water, the laughter distinctly female. He tried to think of who it might be. Both of their neighbors on the opposite sides of their property had access to their own section of the river. One neighbor had small children but it was spring for them as well; too busy a time for someone to oversee children swimming. He led the horse away, making a wide circle so that he came up behind the cottage unnoticed.

He tied the Percheron to the old hitching post. The horse lifted its sweat-stained head, flared its nostrils to catch the scent of water nearby, and then lowered it. The animal was more tired than thirsty and grateful for the shade cast by the cottage. Within minutes the horse was dozing, one hoof pointing down. Albert walked around the building, dropped to his hands and knees, and crawled through the long grass to the bank above the beach.

He saw Frau Richter first, watched as she swam in from the depths, waded through the shallows, and walked onto the shore. Had he not see her face he might not have recognized her. Her chemise clung to her body, the thin cotton made transparent by water. Her breasts, neither large nor small, retained the upward slope of youth. The only evidence of her having borne four daughters was the sensuous swell of flesh above her hipbones. She picked wet strands from her face, gathered them into the rest of her thick hair, and twisting the entire mass, wrung out the dripping water. She let it fall like a heavy rope down her back. He looked for Magdalena, saw her submerged with her sisters so that only their heads were visible. The youngest swam closer to shore to stand waist deep in water, her chest as flat as a boy's. She jeered at her sisters, held her hand threateningly above the surface. Then she struck the surface with her palm, shoving a spray of water at them. They swam toward her until their feet touched bottom and began a water fight, the shriek of their voices echoing.

His chest burned. He had been holding his breath unconsciously. Cupping his hands over his mouth, he exhaled, then dropped his hands and inhaled. He might have been shocked had he been thirteen instead of sixteen, had he not been exposed to the artistic nudes of ancient India and his own European culture. It was less shocking than it was surreal. He had stumbled into a painting that had suddenly come to life. Women bathing in a river. It was a scene from antiquity, alive in front of him.

Then Magdalena waded into shore. Her wet hair fanned out, covering her breasts, and it was so long that it hid her pelvis. She stood next to her mother, lithe and supple, and wrung out her hair in the same way. He shifted to lie on one hip, the arousal he felt both painful and pleasurable.

Albert heard a familiar voice and became aware that there was a sixth female in the river. He looked away as she swam into shore, and then glanced back to see if she was dressed. His mother walked onto the beach, her light-brown hair wet and loose and not in its customary crown of braids. Her chemise was made of thick cotton and hung more like a wet towel on her, for which he was grateful. He had seen her in a nightgown, buttoned up to her neck, but had not, since he was very young, seen her bare shoulders, arms, and legs. He could not stop watching her, and felt immense shame for doing so. His mother's body was also lovely with the same swell of flesh from having borne children. Hard work had kept her lean although it marked her hands, the skin calloused and the knuckles red. Frau Richter said something to her and she laughed like a young girl.

He crawled backward until he could safely stand up and then returned to the cottage. He unhitched the horse, and hoisting himself up began the ride home. Albert mulled over how to handle the situation. His mother would panic, seeing the partially plowed field and the plow left behind. He would tell her that he had been in the field but had quit early because he had forgotten his lunch. He would say it as if he'd seen nothing remarkable. Then he'd come back after dinner to work the field alone and into the night, finishing the plowing and spreading the manure. His father would not think anything of it except to know the job was done. As Albert approached the barn, he wondered how long his mother and the Richter women had been swimming there.

He went back to school the following week although he was still putting in late nights on the farm. He fell into bed unwashed, splashing water on himself the next morning before leaving for school. During the day he became aware of dirt under his nails and the distinctive odor of cow manure every time he shifted in his seat. That afternoon he knocked on the Richters' front door, so tired that he almost fell onto his professor when the door opened. Richter watched him stumble into the hall, then immediately dismissed the tutorial and sent Albert up to the guest bedroom to take a bath and sleep.

They teased him during dinner and then asked questions about his work on the farm. Afterward, he and Magdalena went for their customary walk in the garden.

"I envy you," she said, "living on a farm."

"You want to smell like manure?"

"Be serious."

"I am serious," he answered, thinking of her seminude body, the water dripping from her hair. The finely made chemise. "You don't want to farm," he added. She pulled away, her fury such that he felt as though he'd been pushed although she had not touched him. He stepped back.

"How do you know what I want?" she said.

"I thought—"

"Oh, I know what you think," she answered. "And I suppose I shouldn't be angry. It is only natural you would think that. We have nice clothes, a beautiful house, and good food. We go to the symphony and other social parties. But that life is not for everyone. Do you know what this is?" She swept her arm in a semi-circle to indicate the garden. He shook his head.

"This is my mother's compromise with my father. This is the only way she could have survived in Augsburg. If she could grow things in winter, she would be out here. When they moved here there wasn't a wall. My father had it built so that she could garden without the neighbors watching her. So that she could get as dirty as she liked, plant what she liked. My mother sometimes works in only her chemise and a skirt. She doesn't do it alone. I am out here with her."

"But there is so much to do in town, to enjoy," he answered. "I envy you that."

"That's true. But it is only here, in the house and garden, that I can be myself." She put a hand around her throat. "It is stifling here. When we go for drives in the country I can hardly stay in the buggy. I want to get out and run through those fields."

"Running through fields and working them are different. Have you ever seen my mother's hands?" he said. She studied him for a minute before answering.

"Yes. I have seen your mother's hands. I have *seen* your mother," she said.

"On Sundays," he said, his face impassive.

He involuntarily shivered. She was doing it again. Reading him. He stared back. The impasse was broken when she led him to the circular bench around the only tree in the garden. Then she told him about the Lech River.

"We have been swimming there for at least four years. Your mother has afforded us that luxury. She tells my mother at Sunday mass when your father will be away from the farm, selling his beer." She laughed. "We swim naked! It is heaven. My mother is so grateful. Your mother swims with us sometimes and your sisters did as well before they left. Then we swim in our chemises because your mother is so modest. But you should see her. She has such fun. We have picnics afterward. We always bring the food. And we laugh because you all think that she is in town. So yes, I have seen her hands."

"Does your father know?" he asked.

"No! Papa would be furious. Mostly because he is afraid for us."

Albert had never seen Richter really angry, had no idea what his professor would be like in such a mood.

"You think I don't trust you," she said.

"Not that," he answered. "Jealous maybe. I would like to go swimming with you, too."

"And we will someday. Just you and me," she said. "Please don't say anything. It means so much to us. And it means even more to your mother. It is something she can do without your father's permission although she risks much. It is like giving a gift to herself and to us at the same time. A secret that hurts no one. Last summer was hard on your mother. Your two older sisters were busy attending socials, hoping to meet husbands, and she was so lonely. She *is* so lonely."

Magdalena got up and walked around the tree.

"I love school as much as you do. But since I was little I have wanted to live on a place where I can walk outside in my nightgown without anyone looking at me. Where I can grow things. I love my father but can you imagine him as a farmer?"

He tried to picture Richter trudging behind a horse and plow. "No."

"Can you picture your father as a scholar?"

"Jesus, no."

They heard their names being called, looked at the house and saw her mother waving them in for dessert. He walked behind her. They had never talked about the future although he thought about it, contemplating how to reconcile his conflicting desires of farming, going to university, and being with Magdalena. Since he was thirteen he had known what he wanted but not how to achieve it. She turned around before opening the door.

"Your father isn't very likeable but he does make great beer," she said.

ALBERT HAD BAITED HER. She looked in the mirror, brushed her hair, and smiled. But he had not expected such a reaction. He deserved her fury, wounding her like that. She was not a crier. Instead her pain came out in anger, almost rage. Rage at being thought of as a pampered and wealthy girl who did not or could not get her hands dirty. But somewhere in her fury, she saw that he was looking at her differently. It was when he said "Sunday" that she knew he had been at the river last Friday, that he had seen them. She was there at the river for a few seconds, looking through his eyes. But she wanted to be sure of his knowledge. So she led him to the garden bench and told him what he already knew. She watched him for signs, guilt or perhaps remorse. But he gave nothing away except the intensity of how he looked at her.

For the good. She put the brush down, took off her robe, and crawled into bed. She did not see heavenly visions like the twelfth-century mystic Hildegard von Bingen. Nor, did she think, did her mother. They were earthly women, feeling and sensing earthy fears, desires, wants, and needs. Except that she suspected her mother had known her own future. Magdalena's sense of her future life was hazy.

She blew out the light and settled back into her pillows. What she did know was that Augsburg would not be home for her when she was an adult. And that she had answered Albert's unasked question. She wanted a farm, too.

A FATEFUL SEQUENCE OF EVENTS began when Raimund was fifteen years old and Albert eighteen.

Otto impregnated and married a neighbor's daughter. She gave birth to a son six months after the wedding and was pregnant again four months later. They lived in the large stone farmhouse with the rest of the family and there were nights when the noise of their intimacy was embarrassing.

"I guess Die Pfeffernüsse *is* smarter than Pa's gelding," Raimund said to Albert as they watched Angelika waddle from the courtyard well to the house. His brother grimaced.

"Think again. It's Angelika who has the reins. She managed to get Otto's pants down and secure her future," Albert replied.

Angelika was not an appealing woman although she was, superficially, everything their father found acceptable in a wife for his son. She came from another well-to-do farm, had thick, yellow hair, and was used to working hard. She had a broad, bland face with no features to distinguish it except for her prominent nose. Heinrich accepted her but didn't like her much. She was coarse and dictatorial, sometimes ordering Annaliese around in her own home. Otto was cuckolded from the beginning, which only irritated Heinrich more. Raimund and Albert privately referred to her as Die Queen Pfeffernüsse and it was evident by her Teutonic bones and short, wide-hipped frame that she would be stout by the time she was thirty. But even Heinrich had to admit that Angelika did what he had been unable to do: harness Otto into domesticity. Faced with the responsibilities of a family, Otto had to work on the farm, although he still required supervision.

Raimund's sisters Greta and Liliane met their future husbands at a social function in Augsburg the summer before. Much to their relief, their husbands were men who did not farm, who were sons of businessmen from Berlin and Hamburg, and therefore could afford more than comfortable homes and a life away from drudgery. Both of their courtships were brief and both married as quickly as was possible within the strictures of the Church banns, grateful to be leaving home.

Albert was close to taking his entrance exams at the University of Tübingen. Since he continued to work hard on the farm, his father didn't question the time he spent at the Richter house in preparation for his exams. He had told his mother about his feelings for Magdalena, knowing she would be an ally, but summoning up the courage to tell his father was difficult. And he had to do it soon. He finally came out with it during a midday break on the first day of March.

"I'm going to marry Magdalena Richter."

Heinrich didn't react right away. He and Otto sat at the kitchen table, eating slices of summer sausage. Raimund and their mother stood by the kitchen sink. Otto half coughed, half laughed.

"Sure you are," he sneered.

Heinrich took a long drink of water and then stared at Albert with the intent of making his son flinch.

"You don't tell me when you are getting married and to whom," he said. "I tell you. And my answer is no."

"Did Otto ask permission?" Albert responded, lifting his chin at his older brother, "Or did Angelika? Or," he said, focusing on Otto, "were you too stupid to realize she was taking permission when she was yanking your pants down?"

His father rose from the table, his weathered face mottled as though rage had given him a sudden rash.

"You selfish ingrate!" he shouted. "Richter may be German but his wife is either a gypsy whore or a Jewish one or both. That makes the daughter unacceptable to this family."

"How do you know that?" Their mother stepped forward, startling both of her sons. "Are you speaking from your extensive experience of going to a *Frauenhaus?*"

Heinrich Kaufmann leaned over the table, breathing too hard to speak.

"They have my permission," she continued. "I have talked to Monsignor Mann. The banns begin this Sunday."

Tradition dictated that the father give permission but Heinrich never bothered to endear himself to the priest. He almost never went to confession, and even on occasion through bad manners he insulted Monsignor Mann. His mother, well respected and liked, had the local hand of God in her favor.

"You what?"

Heinrich coughed. He coughed again, took a deep breath, and couldn't stop coughing. They watched him with detached sympathy. The forces of bodily neglect were now upon Heinrich. The realization was on his face. He could no longer regain his breath or stand up easily because his will no longer lorded over the mechanics of a body too heavy for its depleted organs. And he also realized that no one had made a move to help him, not even Otto who sat slack-jawed.

"Damn you all," he choked out as the coughing eased up. He stood up and wiped his mouth with a napkin. Pushing Raimund aside, he walked around the table and stood in front of Albert.

"You *Schwein*," he said hoarsely before walking out of the house.

"You marry that whore and it will destroy this family!" Otto proclaimed, getting up to follow their father. "She will curse this family."

"Whore?" Raimund said. "Look to your wife. Angelika has been in the hay with every farmer's son within a ten-mile radius. You were the only one stupid enough not to figure that out. You're the one that got the used goods."

Otto stomped out, slamming the back door. Their mother then turned to Albert.

"You better go to town now," she said. "Get Magdalena and go see Monsignor."

Albert changed clothes while Raimund got his horse ready and led the animal up to the house. Albert swung himself up and gathered the reins.

"Your *Schwänz* must be big enough now," Raimund teased. "Did you measure it this morning before going up against the brewmaster?"

Albert grinned, reached down, and punched Raimund in the shoulder. "It's been big for a long time now. And I've never had to measure it." Then he heeled the mare in the ribs and took off for the main road to Augsburg.

RAIMUND LISTENED as his father kicked pails and posts inside the barn. His mother came outside with a basket of wet linens. She struggled with the weight of it, and he took it from her. She had won another round with his father but looked tired rather than satisfied. Raimund noticed the gray streaks in her hair. He thought of their wedding daguerreotype hanging on the wall in the parlor. His mother had dark-blonde hair then, pinned up with modest curls framing her face. She wore a simple but well-made blue dress—a dress she could still fit into. Standing next to his father, she appeared serious and composed and older than her seventeen years. It was not a marriage of love but of connections. Her father had been a farmer from Ulm and had done business with Heinrich's father. She became a transaction that would cement the two families. His mother rarely talked about her feelings on the subject of marriage, but Raimund and his siblings did know that marriage was not what she wanted. She had wanted to be a nun, a better alternative to a life of wifely drudgery. She resigned herself to her fate and did it well, loving her children if not her husband. Raimund realized that it was that love, that sense that marriage could be happy, that drove her up against his father. If it had been possible in her youth, she might have wanted what Albert was soon to have: a marriage of love, of partnership.

He glanced at the barn. If his father belonged to an ancient time where he might have been happier killing enemies and wild boars with a javelin, then his mother belonged to a time Raimund couldn't have identified then but suspected was the distant future. They listened as Heinrich bellowed. His mother retied her apron.

"Your father is acting," she said, "like a stallion that's lost a fight."

MAGDALENA'S WISH was to live in the stone cottage by the river. So in the six weeks before the wedding, Magdalena left the minutia and even the larger details of the event to her mother, and rode out early every morning to help Raimund and Albert fix up the old cottage. They gathered fieldstones to replace those missing in the walls and foundation. Raimund mixed the cement. He waited as Magdalena sponged water onto the stones surrounding the damaged area so that the stones would not leach the water from the cement, preventing it from drying properly. Then Raimund spread the cement inside the gap with a trowel and Albert placed the clean fieldstone into it. Raimund finished by sculpting the stone into place with more cement. They fixed the smaller cracks in the interior walls the same way and repaired the fireplace before moving on to replace the slate roof. When the outside was done, they moved inside, covering the stone floors with hardwood. Annaliese joined them to sand the planks by hand before Albert and Raimund varnished them.

"The ceilings are lovely," Magdalena remarked one day, looking up at the pine beams cross-hatching the ceiling. "And so high. Isn't that unusual for a cottage?"

"It is," Annaliese answered, taking off her work gloves and sitting back to look up at the ceiling. "Heinrich cannot bear small spaces because he is tall."

"But he was never going to live here."

"It is one of the funny things about Pa," Albert said above them. He was on a ladder, plastering a section of wall. "I remember when he built this cottage. He said no man, after working with dirt all day long, should have to feel like he's living in a burrow."

THEY DID NOT SPEAK OF IT but all of them recognized the time spent working on the cottage as a suspended state of grace. Heinrich, still opposed to the marriage but resigned to accept it, would not contribute any effort, thus rarely coming to that part of the farm. Magdalena brought a sumptuous lunch every day, packed by her mother. Annaliese brought a crate of the family's bottled beer, and breaking the tradition of drinking it warm, she had Albert sink the crate into the cool shallows of the river so that they could drink it cold.

Spring had arrived early and the days were warm. They ate lunch on the bank by the river. Raimund and Albert listened as their mother and Magdalena talked about books, politics, and religion, and laughed over the latest gossip from Augsburg. The uncensored atmosphere gave Raimund the courage to ask his mother about the books he had long ago found hidden in the pantry cupboard.

"I will give them to you tonight," she said, winking at Magdalena. "And then you can find out what is in them."

They watched as the women removed the cotton scarves from their heads and shook their braids loose. The exhaustion and defeat that Raimund had witnessed earlier in their mother was gone, replaced with a relaxed happiness.

"You would think they'd known each other for a long time," Raimund remarked later to his brother.

"They have," Albert replied.

WHAT THEY ANTICIPATED about Heinrich did not come true. Rather than hate his new daughter-in-law he lusted after her instead. He eyed Magdalena with disturbing interest when she was working at the main house. Annaliese noticed it and made sure Magdalena was never alone in Heinrich's presence. One day while working in the garden behind the cottage, Magdalena caught a movement in the periphery of her vision and looked up in time to see her father-in-law on horseback turning to leave at the far end of the field. She said nothing to Albert, hoping it was an isolated incident. But two days later Heinrich showed up again, sitting on his horse at the far end of the field. Her mother was visiting and observed him from the kitchen window.

A week after that, both her parents came for a visit with the gift of two English mastiff puppies, already big at three months and becoming massive at six. Magdalena named them Erebus and Nyx. The dogs patrolled around the cottage and the immediate field like hulking spirits, scaring Heinrich enough so that he ceased his visits. But Heinrich's shadowing of Magdalena continued when she worked at the main house.

"The old goat," Albert exploded one night, standing on the riverbank. "He follows Maggie like he's in rut." He turned to Raimund. "Does it make sense? You'd think he wouldn't want to even look at Maggie. Especially now that she is pregnant!"

But Raimund knew what it was.

Magdalena had the exotic, illicit beauty of the postcard women. Raimund could not confront his father about his obvious hypocrisy without revealing his own knowledge of Heinrich's collection of pornographic cards. Nor did Raimund want to endanger the pictures he possessed because they had become dear to him. His chances of a real sexual encounter in the repression surrounding him were nil and even if he found a girl so willing, he did not want to risk becoming a father. Raimund did not see himself getting married for some time. Apparently his father didn't either.

On the eve of his sixteenth birthday that May Heinrich informed Raimund that he intended to place him in a seminary to become a priest in the tradition that one child should be returned to the service of God.

"I don't want to be a priest," Raimund told him.

"Oh, you'll want to be a priest," his father responded, "given your other choice. Would you rather be a soldier?"

Raimund didn't want to be a soldier either. He knew that his father compared him to his Uncle Dieter, although Raimund had no idea why. He had risked his father's wrath so many times that he had scars on the back of his legs. He did not shrink from blood. But outside of testing his father's rigidity, Raimund avoided provoking fights and only resorted to a physical brawl in the protection of his friend, Leo, who still suffered taunts about his size and his studiousness.

His father didn't say exactly when Raimund was to enter the seminary, only that it would be after the upcoming Augsburg beer festival in mid-August. His father's mind was preoccupied by the festival because he had perfected a pale wheat-colored beer and was anxious to see how it would do in the competition. He called it *Kaufmann Gold*.

There was a dance in the afternoon before the beer tasting that night, conducted by judges from Munich. Albert and Raimund stood with their mother and Magdalena to watch the dancing. Magdalena tapped the floor with one foot, one arm instinctively wrapped across the bump of her belly. Heinrich had just finished dancing the *Schuhplattler*, the Bavarian folk dance that required hopping and the rhythmic striking of the thighs, knees, and the soles of the feet. He was breathing hard when the dance was over. But then the band began to play the Bavarian version of the Flying Dutchman polka. Seizing the opportunity, Heinrich grabbed Magdalena as his partner. Halfway through the dance, he made an exuberant leap, stiffened in midair, and crashed to the floor like a chunk of granite. A local doctor—the same one who had examined Heinrich years earlier—pushed through the crowd. Kneeling next to the fallen man he put a stethoscope to his chest. Raimund didn't need the doctor's pronouncement to know the old man was dead, that his heart had imploded while he was briefly airborne. Otto, drunk, stumbled forward and stared down at their father on the dance floor. He looked up at Magdalena and pointed a finger at her.

"You dirty gypsy bitch! You killed him."

The doctor stood up.

"Don't be an ass. I warned your father long ago that such a day would come. She had nothing to do with it." He motioned to Ernst Geringer. "Take Otto outside and then come back and help Raimund and Albert carry their father."

They buried him two days later. Before the priest began the funeral liturgy, he noted the irony of Heinrich's departure from this world without knowing that his beer had won first prize. It was an era where death was something to be expected and his father had lived, by all accounts, a good life. Raimund and Albert respected him for his accomplishments, honored Heinrich in the official way that sons were supposed to honor their fathers. They did not grieve over the paternal love that was never made evident to them. Raimund instead grieved his father's misplaced life and the way it ended. Raimund and Albert soberly observed the casket being lowered to the bottom of the grave while the priest droned on. He leaned over, spoke in a low tone to Albert.

"For all that Pa was," he said, "he still deserved a better death. Dying while dancing and wearing lederhosen is like being shot in the *Scheißhaus* with your drawers down."

"Ja. It would have been better if he had died while walking through the fields," Albert agreed.

The solicitor read Heinrich's will four days later. The farm was left to Otto in accordance to the laws of primogeniture. The inheritance law at that time also prevented Otto from dividing up the farm among his five siblings. Not that he wanted to. Otto, like his conservative namesake, believed the unity of the Kaufmann family and farm relied upon one leader only. Just minutes after the solicitor left, Otto stood up and quoted Bismarck's famous saying that "one sword keeps the other in its sheath" in his demand that the rest of his siblings work the farm under his direction. Raimund's two older sisters and their respective husbands refused and made it clear they had no legal obligation to him. Albert did not want to leave their mother alone, harnessed to the will of Angelika, and Magdalena did not want to be far from her own family.

"We're going to stay and hope that Otto will change his mind and make me co-owner," Albert told Raimund. "And we have to protect Mama. It isn't her house any longer." They were alone in the solicitor's office.

"You and Magdalena will be dead before that ever happens."

"Maybe not. Papa knew that Otto wasn't capable of running the farm. He told Ernst at the reception that he thought Otto didn't have the smarts. Papa died before he could change the will." He tugged at the sleeve of his new serge suit. "If Otto gets into trouble—and he will get into trouble—he'll need me. You have school to escape into. You can take the university exams now, even though you are only sixteen."

So Raimund began preparing for his university entrance exams, thinking he had escaped his father's scheme to turn him into a religious eunuch. But late one afternoon, one week after Heinrich's death, Otto told Raimund to pack his things as he was to be sent to St. Michael Seminary in Traunstein the next day. Raimund stared past him at the courtyard and said nothing. Otto interpreted his silence as acceptance of his fate.

He waited until they were all asleep. He couldn't say goodbye to Albert, Magdalena, and his mother without implicating them. Fortunately, Otto had forgotten to change the combination on the safe in the brewery. Raimund stole a considerable sum from it and added the money to that he had saved under the floorboard beneath his bed. He slipped from the house like the thief he had become, took one of the finest horses in the barn, and rode hard for four days, reaching Bremen just as the SS *Havel* was getting ready to sail back to the port of New York. He sold the horse and the saddle on it. In the hours before boarding, Raimund bought a new pair of pants, a shirt, and a vest with secret pockets in which to hide the rest of his money. Then he had his medical exam and acquired a passport and the necessary papers he would need to establish himself in America. An hour before boarding, he ran to the harbor office to buy his ticket.

ROLLING BILLY

Voyage to America

1899

OTTO'S REACTION TO RAIMUND'S DISAP-
pearance was volcanic. He sent petitions to authorities in
all major cities of Europe, believing his brother still on
the continent. His pig-eyed rage propelled more changes in the
family. Annaliese, freed from the tyranny of her marriage and not
wishing to endure a second dynasty of control by her oldest son
and his equally domineering wife, was permitted by the priest to
break convention and enter the Franciscan Kloster of Maria Stern
in Augsburg. Otto declared his mother dead to him and refused
to visit her in the convent.

Ten months after Raimund's disappearance, Albert and Magdalena received a letter from him, passed to them by Ernst Geringer.
The teenager had settled in the Middle West of the United States,
in a city known as Minneapolis. He urged them to join him, and
repeated that desire with every letter they received from him. In
August 1898, a flyer arrived with one of his letters.

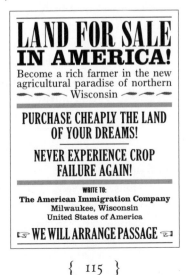

A month later a book titled *Northern Wisconsin: A Hand-book for the Homeseeker* arrived at the Richters' home. Immanuel read the book and Raimund's letter before Sunday dinner. He was somber throughout the meal, saying little. After the table had been cleared, he and Frau Richter asked Albert and Magdalena into the parlor. Magdalena's sisters took three-year-old Eberhard and one-year-old Frank upstairs to play.

"I think it is evident to both of you," Richter said, "that Otto will never include you in the farm. You work like serfs earning very little while the rest goes into Otto's pocket. Just look at Albert, at the shadows under his eyes. I accepted, four years ago, your decision to put off your university entrance exams in favor of working the farm. While Heinrich was a difficult man, he gave Ernst Geringer some indication at your wedding of his concerns about Otto's ability to manage the farm. So I thought perhaps he might legally change the Kaufmann will after all. But he died and we'll never know what he intended."

He paused, tented his fingers against his mouth, and looked at the Persian rug underneath his feet. Then he dropped his hands and spoke.

"If I thought Germany was going in a positive direction, I would ask that both of you prepare again for the entrance exams at the University of Tübingen. But Germany is in trouble. The kaiser is taking this country toward destruction."

He took off his spectacles and rubbed his eyes.

"What are you saying?" Magdalena asked.

"This has been on our minds for some time now," her mother answered. "We think you, Albert, and the boys should join Raimund in the United States. We have been setting money aside for you to leave and to get off to a good start once you are there. You can have an even bigger farm in the United States. Something that is your own."

"Don't you think you are exaggerating, Papa?"

"No!" Richter stood up and began to pace.

"Magdalena! Think!" he said. "We have a vain, immature, and egotistical monarch who wants an empire. What happens when a king wants an empire? Remember Napoleon? Kaiser Wilhelm is building up the army. He is establishing a huge naval fleet. What does that tell you?" He threw up his hands. "Even Raimund knows what is happening in Germany and he is on another continent!"

He stopped pacing, and sat in the chair opposite his daughter.

"We are thinking of leaving too," he said. "But we can't do it at this time. Your sisters need to finish school. And there are other things that need to be taken care of. But you two need to go as soon as possible. Albert does not own any land. He is in danger of being conscripted."

He directed his attention toward Albert.

"I'm sorry, Albert. The farm has been in your family for generations. Had it been left to you, it wouldn't be in the poor condition that it is now. If your father saw the land now—"

Albert thought it was exhaustion at first. But at the mention of his father, he shocked himself and everyone else by weeping. Love was never a word he applied toward his father and yet he had longed for Heinrich over the past year, the grief of his absence palpable every time Albert looked at the diminished fields, the crumbling stone fences, and the ill-used animals. His feelings put him in an uncomfortable state of confusion. The old man had been an embarrassment, had been tyrannical, bigoted, lustful, loud-mouthed, and sometimes capricious, but never when it came to the farm. There his closed mind opened to change and possibility but only after careful deliberation, plotting out a course of action before acting upon it. He worked with the land, and not over it, with a tenderness not given to his family. It was the one thing Albert and his father had in common: the love and husbandry of land. But if Heinrich had been in the barn a week ago, he would have beaten Otto to death. For Otto intended to give up planting the fields to wheat, barley, and hops and instead purchase the grain at the market. Albert could not make his brother understand the economics and independence of growing the supplies for the brewery. Then he realized that his brother understood very well.

"You are such a lazy ass!" Albert shouted. "You don't deserve this place!"

"The old man worked hard, not smart," Otto responded.

He tackled Otto, knocking him to the barn floor. Otto swung, his right fist glancing off Albert's left cheekbone. Albert jabbed Otto in the groin with a well-aimed knee, rendering his brother momentarily unable to fight back. Albert then beat Otto with his fists until Otto cried out for him to stop. Albert pulled back and it was then that Otto surprised him, hitting Albert in the chest with a massive fist. Albert was momentarily stunned. The two rolled free of each other with Albert getting up first. Otto had barely rose to a squat when Albert shoved him down so that he landed on his side.

"You're too damn slow. That's always been your problem," Albert heaved, kicking his older brother in the ribs and the back until Otto blubbered for him to stop. But Albert didn't. He hauled Otto up against a stall post and struck him in the face over and over, breaking his nose, splitting his lip, and blackening both his eyes. Albert stepped away from his moaning brother and simultaneously felt his chest for any broken ribs. He was almost to the door when his brother called after him.

"It's her! That gypsy whore! She's turned you into a madman!"

RICHTER GAVE ALBERT A HANDKERCHIEF. He wiped his eyes and blew his nose. The weeping was cathartic. He felt freed by it and by his father-in-law's advice.

"It isn't what you think," he said, wiping his eyes. "I want to leave. The farm I love, my father's farm, no longer exists."

He looked at Magdalena. He saw the anguish on her face, understood and shared it. The Richters had been their only family with the exception of visits to his mother in the convent.

"Your mother," she asked. "What about her? We can't leave her."

"Sister Hildegard," Frau Richter said, using Annaliese Kaufmann's religious name, "left for another country just like Raimund did. But her new country is within her. I doubt she will leave. Still I think you should ask her to be sure."

They visited Albert's mother two days later. It always startled him to see his mother in a habit, her head completely covered except for her face. To address her as Sister Hildegard and not as Mama. Yet he had supported her decision and was always gratified to see the serenity of her chosen life reflected in her face.

"Frau and Herr Richter are right," she said. "My place is here now. But you must go. Raimund needs you. You have always been close as brothers, closer than the other children." She cupped Albert's face. "I know how much you loved the farm. But our lives on this earth are very short. Ownership is an idea that men aspire to but in the end cannot have."

She then turned and hugged Magdalena. "If it is true what they say about America, you can live without anyone caring what you look like, where you come from, what you know. You deserve that."

OVER THE COURSE OF THE YEAR at the Richters' home Albert and Magdalena planned their departure. Immanuel made a solo trip to Bremen in the spring of 1899 on the pretense of doing scholarly research, and he purchased their second-class passenger tickets there. Over the summer her mother casually mentioned to neighbors that the family would be going on holiday to Berlin in late summer and had purchased the train tickets ahead of time. Albert and Magdalena visited Sister Hildegard the week before they were to leave. Their sons, unaware of where they would be going, talked to their grandmother as if they would always see her. Albert's mother gave him a sealed letter for Raimund. She gave Magdalena the silver rosary that had been in her family for generations. Then there was a knock at the door, indicating that the allotted visiting hour was up.

"Be careful," she warned. "Otto must not know that you are leaving. He does not forgive and he suffers the sin of vengeance. I fear that he has no moral compass." She made the sign of the cross over both of them and said, "Give Raimund my love and go with God."

THE DAY BEFORE their departure, Frau Richter went to the train station and had the destination changed from Berlin to Bremen. Magdalena and Albert waited until midnight and then bundled their sleeping sons into a buggy and left the farm to meet the Richters at the train station. They all took turns entertaining the boys during the two-day rail trip. Magdalena's sisters sang lullabies. Frau Richter read to them aloud. Herr Richter regaled his grandsons with details about the ship, showing them a postcard of the SS *Wilhelm der Grosse*, built two years before.

"It is an enormous ship. At twenty-two and a half knots, you will fly like swallows across the ocean." Magdalena watched her father spread out his arms to emphasize the ship's proportions, knowing that he was using his fascination with mechanical details to keep them all from brooding on the parting ahead.

"The *der Grosse* is 684 feet in length, 66 feet in breadth, and weighs 14,349 tons. It has four funnels and two masts," he said, holding up two fingers. "It has triple expansion engines that eat 560 tons of coal a day!" He comically opened his mouth wide, and the boys did the same before dissolving into giggles

He assured them that she was the safest ship built, although her nickname was "Rolling Billy" because she was slightly top heavy. Magdalena cleared her throat, raised her eyebrows at her father. It was not reassuring to travel on a ship with such a nickname.

They spent the night in Bremen, telling family stories over and over again during the evening meal. After the boys were put to bed, the men stayed in the inn's dining room to talk about future plans, while Magdalena, her mother, and her sisters returned to their rooms where they talked as if nothing was happening while simultaneously bracing themselves for the separation the next day.

WHEN ALL THE PASSENGERS and crew members were accounted for, the gangways were pulled in and the chains anchoring the ship were released. Albert, Magdalena, and the boys watched and waved to her parents and sisters on the dock below. They were waiting for the final blast of the horn that would signal the tugboats to begin leading the ship out of the harbor, when suddenly Otto rode through the crowd, scattering people. His horse skittishly revolved in a circle as he surveyed the ship's deck. Then Otto saw them and began screaming.

"You belong in America! Take your mongrel brats and your gypsy whore of a wife and go to the land of garbage. You," he pointed at them, "will fail. You will die. Your children will die. But she will live on! The witch will live on! You wait and see!"

The boys covered their ears and cried.

"Take them to the cabin," Magdalena said.

Albert picked up their sons and carried them below. She turned back and stared at her brother-in-law. His mouth foamed and spit with saliva just like the horse he had whipped into exhaustion. She watched as her father summoned a shipping official who notified a police officer. The officer called for more help when Otto refused the order to dismount. Then her mother did something that astonished Magdalena. She walked toward the frantic horse, grabbed the animal's halter, and said something. Otto stopped shouting as though she had put a hand over his mouth. The police then pulled his inert body from the horse and took him away.

THREE DAYS IT HAS BEEN LIKE THIS. He fed her some milky tea and plain bread earlier. He places a hand on her stomach. She nods. The food is staying down. He wedges a small bowl into a space between the wall and her body. Then he settles in the bunk below and waits.

They listen to the noises of the ship. Of people murmuring, of crying children, of the ocean itself like a steady cadence underneath the muted hiss and grind of the engines. He is grateful to the Dresden woman from steerage who offered to watch the boys during the day.

"I'm sorry," he says. She extends a hand over the bunk. He reaches up and holds it.

"Don't be. This is what we agreed to do. What we wanted."

She has misunderstood him. He is apologizing for what happened three days earlier. She holds his hand for a few moments longer to reassure him before letting it go. He lies back, helpless against her illness, helpless against her will. He reaches up and touches the ceiling of his bunk and the floor of hers.

She shifts in her sleep and a lank of her hair falls over the bunk. Albert resists touching it. He relies on her for so much. When they meet new people, he watches her instead of them, her face giving subtle clues as to who is genuine, who is suspect or superficial. He knows what they see: an unsettling beauty, a calm and self-assured young mother, an educated and articulate woman. They do not know that she carries a heightened, almost painful, awareness of her surroundings, an aptitude to sense things unseen.

"Can you . . . I mean do you . . . see things about me?" he asked her after their engagement was announced.

"No." She became unreadable then, her skin ashen. He was terrified over his blunder.

"I am not my mother," she said. Her face softened. "It isn't like that. We cannot be married with you always thinking of me in that way. I know you as you are now. Do you understand?"

It was his mother who brought it up in an offhand way three days before the wedding when the two of them were alone in the cottage, painting the windowsills a deep blue.

"You must protect Magdalena. From strangers and family," she said, dropping her paintbrush in a bucket of kerosene. She reached behind her head to work the knot out of her scarf and spoke as though thinking aloud. "It is strange that gypsies are said to have prescient abilities and thought evil because of it. But in saints and holy people, such abilities are called visions. And they are venerated for it."

HE GETS OUT OF BED and quietly unwraps a loaf of rye bread and a hunk of Swiss cheese, cutting a slice from each. He sits on the boys' bed so that he can watch her, and chews, savoring the caraway seeds in the bread. There is a dining room reserved for first- and second-class passengers but he does not like to eat alone. They are breaking the rules, keeping food in their cabin. He asked a deckhand why it was prohibited.

"Because of rats," the man said, pointing downward. Yesterday evening, he went down to steerage, first to the women's dormitory to see if they wanted to learn English. He saw the same deckhand working below, heard him yell at a group of children, apparently playing in the path of his work.

"Goddamn rats! Get out of the way," he shouted. A chorus of women's voices screamed at the deckhand. He had heard stories about traveling in steerage but the third-class accommodations on the *der Grosse* are better than he expected. There were clothes hanging on lines between the iron beds stacked three, sometimes four beds high. Then he went to the men's dormitory and saw nearly the same thing. The two sexes came together in a general hall with long tables and benches. Still, the conditions were limited. It was only the second day at sea and the air was already foul with the smell of unwashed bodies, with vomit, and with the smell of alcohol in some quarters.

He pours water from a stoneware jug into a glass and drinks it. He looks at his sleeping wife, wonders when she will awaken from what he hopes is a temporary state of ennui. He thinks about the day they boarded, feels the bile in his throat. He pours another glass of water and drinks it.

If he ever sees his oldest brother again, he will not beat him. He will kill him.

SHE DRIFTS, rises to the present, and leaning over, vomits into the bowl that Albert has provided. She can still hear Otto's words. Magdalena wipes her mouth, and falls back into the pillow and back to sleep.

A few hours later, she awakens to the sound of her sons' voices. They are chattering like sparrows.

"Tempy's hand," Eberhard asks. "What happened to it?"

"I don't know. And it isn't polite to ask," Albert responds about someone they have apparently met. She shuts her eyes so that they will think she is still asleep. She considers her mother's parting words as she embraced Magdalena. "We will see each other again."

"Yes, we will," Magdalena answered. But both women knew it was a lie.

SHE WAKES UP EARLY and dresses in the dark. Her husband, exhausted from his four-day vigil of tending her, is asleep. Her sons are sleeping just as soundly, their excitement of being on a ship having boiled down their energy. She slips out of the cabin and walks up to the deck with her mother's olive-wood rosary threaded through her right hand, her mother-in-law's silver rosary in her left.

The deck is dimly lit. Most of the passengers tend to crowd the bow during the day and so she walks toward the stern. It does not occur to her that it is not safe, a woman roaming alone in the dark on a ship full of strangers. She does not feel vulnerable because she does not feel real. She cannot sense or see ahead, although she can hear the sound of her footsteps. It takes her a while to reach the chest-high deck near the stern. She leans over it and waits. She wants to witness the sun rise from the endless water around them. See proof that they have not embarked into an abyss of sky and ocean without direction.

The sky lightens. She can now see the surface of the ocean. Having lived inland all of her life she does not know the ocean, although her father taught her various terms pertaining to it. One fathom equals six feet; a nautical mile is 6,080 feet; a sounding is the measurement of the depth of water.

"Do you miss your God?"

At first, she thinks the voice has come from below; from the constant roil of white-tipped waves cleaved from the ship's advance through the water. Then she turns around and sees a black man. He is sitting on a footstool, drinking coffee and eating bread with a piece of cheese. Three fingers are missing on his right hand. He puts the food down, stands up.

"*Sprechen Sie Englisch?*" he asks when she doesn't respond.

"I speak English," she answers. He wipes his hands on his pants.

"I apologize if I startled you. Usually only certain members of the crew are up this early. Sometimes passengers but not at this end of the ship," he says, sitting down again.

"My sons have talked about you," she says. "Your name is Tempy."

"Yes, I have met them. Eberhard and Frank. Very polite boys," he answers.

"My name is Magdalena," she says. She walks toward him, to be at a closer distance for conversing.

"Don't! Stay where you were." He looks behind him. She steps back until she feels the railing again.

"Are you sick?" she asks.

"No. It isn't that," he answers. "Crew members are discouraged from getting friendly with passengers. Especially those from first and second class."

She thinks that odd, given how much her sons and Albert have talked with him. Maybe she heard wrong but she doesn't think so. This is the man who showed them the enormous coal furnaces, the massive pistons of the engines. Albert said he was a Negro but looking at Tempy, she is not sure that is true.

Then the reason occurs to her and she is embarrassed. She is an unescorted woman for one thing. He has politely avoided stating the obvious and she obtusely didn't realize it at first.

"Is it because you are a—"

"Colored man," he interrupts. "Yes, that most of all."

She watches as he mops the coffee from his pants with his jacket sleeve and then picks up the tin cup, gripping it with the little finger and thumb of his right hand.

"Your hand," she says. "Do you know why it still works?"

He shrugs. "I make it work."

"That too." She smiles. "I meant it works because you still have your thumb. It is called opposing motion." She demonstrates with her left hand, touching her thumb to her little finger and then every finger.

"Opposing motion," he says, looking at his hand. "I'll remember that."

He looks up at the sky, points to the sunrise.

"I must get back to work."

SHE WALKS BACK to their cabin, opens the door. Albert is still sleeping. Her sons, half-dressed and with breadcrumbs around their mouths, leap up from their bed and hug her.

"I have met Tempy," she says.

HE WAITS FOR HER the next day but she does not appear. He first saw her when she boarded the ship and it caused him to dwell on a mother he can barely remember. That this woman should appear so unexpectedly yesterday morning is a sign, although he cannot divine what its significance is. Only that it means something. Only that he feels compelled to talk to her. She is an uncommonly beautiful woman but it is not lust that nags him, or fear. She will not hurt him. That he is sure of. Still, it is dangerous for him to talk to her and yet he has the overwhelming, inexplicable need to do so.

Luckily, his work assignment is near the stern and so he will continue to wait for her early in the mornings.

TWO DAYS AFTER MEETING TEMPY she gets up early, walks to the stern of the ship, and is disappointed to find he is not there. She wonders if he is in trouble. She threads the rosaries through her hands, leans over the deck, and ponders the sea below. The cabin is stuffy and the sea air is refreshing, reviving. She feels suspended in time, no longer at home but not yet at her destination. She puts the rosaries in her skirt pocket. Then she loosens the single braid that drops to her waist, runs her fingers through the clumped strands to free them. A gust of wind suddenly lifts the mass of hair, so that it is alive with movement. She pulls out the rosaries and weaves them through her fingers again. She closes her eyes and lifts her face. She is Amphitrite, the Queen of the Sea.

"Do you miss your God?"

She turns around, astonished that she did not hear him approach.

"The engines," he says. "You can't hear footsteps because of the noise from the engines. It is why so few passengers come to this part of the ship." He gestures to her hands.

"Not my God," she says. She holds up the olive-wood rosary. "This rosary is from my mother and this," she says, holding up the hand with the silver rosary, "is from my mother-in-law. I miss both of them very much."

"Where you are going has many Gods," he says, leaning against a bulkhead. "Not just one."

"Isn't the United States a Christian country?"

"Not for everyone. There were old Gods there before the Christians came."

She wonders if he means the American Indians and their myths, of which she knows little. Seeing her confusion, he says, "I'll tell you about one. It is a river. One of the most powerful rivers in the world. It is a Man–God and he splits the country into two pieces. In Minnesota at Lake Pepin, he is over two miles wide."

He stretches out his arms. She notices the deep grooves on his wrists.

"What happened to your wrists?"

He drops his arms. He meets many people and yet no one asks about his scars save for the abolitionists who rescued him. He assumes it is because most people don't really see him or if they do, consider it part of his being a colored man and leave it at that. He looks back at her, at her long, black hair fanned out by the wind. He thinks of his mother again.

"These," he says, showing his wrists, "are from the white man." He holds up his right hand with the missing fingers. "But this is from the River God. I was sold when I was about fifteen just before the war broke out . . ."

HE WAS BEING TRANSPORTED on a small steamer down the Mississippi to a plantation in Louisiana, chained to the boat's railing by iron cuffs on his wrists, his cuffed ankles chained to each other. The new owner's overseer had beat him the day before to establish his authority. Tempy slept on and off as a wedge against the pain, hunched next to the railing. He briefly came to and saw the overseer standing near the bow of the steamer, smoking a cigar. When he awoke again minutes later he heard shouting, and after listening he did not hear or feel the rhythmic pulse of the engine. He pulled himself up and looked over the railing. The boat was drifting. Worse, the river's current suddenly shifted, trapping the steamer so that it was pushed toward a large deadfall of trees off the starboard bow.

He watched as the overseer kept smoking his cigar with the arrogant stance of thinking the engine would begin working again just because he thought it should. Then the steamer slammed into the dead trees, the bow went down and the river reached up and swallowed the man, cigar and all.

The immense jolt knocked over the stove in the kitchen quarters and started a fire. Tempy saw a deckhand he recognized and shouted for help. The man vanished into the interior of the steamer. Tempy pushed against the railing with the energy he had left, hoping to break the steel frame from the wood. But then the deckhand came back. He had gone to the overseer's cabin and found the keys to the cuffs. He unlocked Tempy's hands, freeing him from his attachment to the railing and his hands to each other. But the smoke from the fire was overtaking them and the steamer was sinking. He shoved the key ring into Tempy's bloodied right hand.

"Swim," he screamed before diving into the water. Tempy followed him. While using his arms to stroke toward shore, the key ring slipped from his hand and sank into the riverbed. With his feet still shackled, he hobbled through the woods for two days before reaching a farmstead. That night he stole a splitting maul from the barn and used it to break the two chains connecting his feet. He followed the Mississippi north, stealing chickens, a sack of ground corn, and a ham from a smokehouse along the way. When he reached St. Paul, he was befriended by a faction of underground abolitionists whose leader, Miss Jane Grey Swisshelm, lived in St. Cloud. The group, one of many, lived close to the river in St. Paul, knowing runaway slaves on foot would use the Mississippi to guide them north.

A sympathetic blacksmith removed the iron cuffs from Tempy's ankles. Then the abolitionists gave him a place to live, created free papers for him, and found him employment on the St. Paul river docks.

His job abruptly ended five years later. He was roped to the pilings one day so that he could swim underneath the dock to repair it. He wasn't under there long when a strong eddy pulled on his legs and feet. The rope around his waist became undone and the current began to take him. He called for help as he drifted out from underneath the dock on the other side. The other workers threw him the only rope that was handy; the one attached to an engine-driven pulley. He grabbed the rope and wrapped it around his right hand. It was a tug of war in which the river appeared to be winning until one of the men cranked the engine to pull him in hard and fast. They hauled him up and laid him on the dock. His right hand throbbed and he saw that the rope had slipped and wrapped around his three fingers. There wasn't much left to them except bloody pulp and broken bones. He was taken to a doctor who amputated what was left to prevent gangrene.

A week later he stood on the dock and observed the water, observed the calm surface that hid the powerful currents below. The

River God had punished him for being so cocky. For thinking he was favored because the Mississippi had saved him once. He had two chances with the river and decided not to test a third. He was twenty years old by then. He left St. Paul and went farther north to Duluth where he worked on a freighter that crossed Lake Superior and Lake Michigan.

IT HAS BEEN MANY YEARS since he has talked that much or spoken of that part of his life. Only now is he aware that he has been staring at the ocean the entire time and not her. He looks at her, then back at the sky and panics. The sun is halfway above the eastern horizon.

"Oh no," he says, turning his face away. "You must leave right away."

SOME OF HER DESPAIR LIFTS as she walks back to her cabin. Tempy has given her a story to put her grief into perspective. More than that, he has risked much in telling her about his life. She thinks back to the men who sat drinking coffee in her mother's kitchen, spilling information about themselves that they had told no one, not even their wives. This will be her destiny, too. She senses that from now on she will be the receiver of such stories, regrets, and secrets. The receiver of mythologies and Gods.

IT IS THREE DAYS before she can get away. Tempy looks at her bare hands.

"Please take out your beads. That way if someone should come up on us, they will think you are praying and I am here working," he says, remembering the voyage with the six German nuns going to America to begin their own religious order. Their black-and-white habits rendered them invisible as women, allowing him the freedom to address them and they him. She removes the rosaries from her pocket and threads them through her fingers again.

"You said you worked on the Great Lakes. Do they have Gods as well?" she asks, intrigued by deities not sanctioned by the Bible.

"Yes, they do," he answers, taking out a pipe and a pouch of tobacco from the inside pocket of his jacket. "May I?"

She nods. He covertly glances at her as he tamps the tobacco in the bowl of the pipe. It has been a long time since he talked to a woman he didn't pay for and even then, not much was said, the physical need outdistancing any cerebral stimulation. It is a pleasure he misses, as conversation with the other deckhands is limited to drink, work, cards, and sexual failures or gains with women.

"Are they Man–Gods too?" she asks.

"No, no. Those are She–Gods," he answers. He strikes a match against the metal joist on the pole next to him, lights the pipe, and draws in a lungful of smoke.

"I call them the Sisters," he says, exhaling. "Sister Superior, Sister Michigan, Sister Huron, Sister Erie, and Sister Ontario. They are cold but passionate. It does not make sense, does it?"

"No, it does not."

"We are on the North Atlantic right now. She is freezing cold. But when a storm hits, there is no mistaking her passion." He pauses, draws from the pipe. "But," he continues, "there is nothing like a storm on the Sisters, especially Sister Superior. She does not roll a ship like the ocean does during a storm. She punches and punches on all sides of a ship with her waves."

He puts his pipe down, and smacks his left fist into the palm of his right hand repeatedly.

"Until she has broken all the bones of that ship. Then she takes the ship and the men on board down so that they freeze in her womb. I survived three storms on Sister Superior and that was enough for me. I transferred to a ship that took me through the St. Lawrence and then I made my way to New York. Now I work on ships that cross the Atlantic."

"You must either like water or danger," Magdalena says. "What about the Ocean Gods?"

"So far," he grins, moving the pipe to the corner of his mouth, "those women have been good to me."

Magdalena looks at his worn boots. She read *Uncle Tom's Cabin*. He didn't speak like the slaves in that book.

"May I ask how it is you speak English so well? And, it appears, German."

"One of the abolitionists was a Czech woman who taught me to read and write. Then she taught me German, some French, but not Czech, because she said I would need German and French more one day. And she was right. I've learned to speak German better because this route seems to be the one I'm on the most. America to Germany. Germany to America. A lot of Germans leaving Germany."

"For good reason," she comments. She looks at his red-brown hair, his high cheekbones. *There are continents in his blood.*

"What—" she begins hesitantly. "What is your ancestry?"

"I can count on one hand," he says, "the number of people who have asked me that. And not as politely as you just did."

"Which hand?"

He smiles.

"The left," he answers, raising that hand as if to confirm it. "Most people assume I'm a black man. A Negro," he says. "But my father was Irish and the owner of the plantation that my mother lived on in Georgia. My mother was a quarter Cherokee, a quarter white, and half African. Your hair—hers was like that. Black and long. I used to hide in it when she brushed it at night. I remember her as being very beautiful."

He looks past her, at the ocean.

"It is better to be ugly, I think. Beauty can be a curse. It can trap the one having it. My mother worked in the master's house. What they call a house nigger. The last time I saw her was when I was eight. The master sold me to a plantation in South Carolina."

"Your *father* sold you?"

"Had to. His wife would not tolerate my presence. The red hair, the freckles. It was obvious that her husband was my father. A few years after he sold me, he sold my mother to a plantation in Alabama. I only know this because fifteen years ago I met a man who had been on the same plantation. It seems the master there liked her too," he says. "She killed herself," he adds without emotion.

Magdalena doesn't know what to say. Her current difficulties are miniscule in comparison to his life. She turns toward the deck, ashamed.

"You have been sick," he says. He knows what it is, what the slaves called it. The Misery.

"It is nothing now," she answers.

"I saw that man on the dock."

"That was my husband's older brother," she says. She draws her arms in and turns around. "I think everyone on the ship saw it. It was upsetting."

"You could have gone below," he says, "with your husband and children but you stayed and faced him."

"You heard what he said? What he called me?"

"I did."

"It hurts me more that my sons heard that," she says. "Heard me called that. *A whore. A witch.* They will remember that about me."

"They might," Tempy answers. He stands up. "But it won't be a memory they hold against you. That woman who stopped him— was your mother?"

She nods.

"I thought so," he says. "You look so much like her. Do you know what she said to him?"

"No."

He had not seen such a sight in a foreign port. The man behaved as a slave owner, shouting as though he had a right to his brother, his brother's wife, and his brother's children. And then to see that older woman grab the horse's halter with such confidence, and say something that frightened him into speechlessness. Tempy didn't have to smell or see it to know that the fat, raging devil on horseback had shit in his pants. He had seen a woman do that only one other time.

He was twelve and on the plantation in South Carolina. A Geechee woman had been stripped to the waist and tied to a post so that she could be whipped for some infraction. How she worked her hands free from the post, no one could say. She suffered ten lashes, but turned around on the eleventh and caught the end of the whip, jerking the overseer toward her. With blood running down her back and breasts, she cursed him in a language that Tempy did not understand. The man stared at her for a minute or so before his knees buckled and he fell to the ground, jerking and working up the dust with his kicking legs, piss and shit staining his pants. The Geechee woman was locked up in a windowless shed while the owner pondered what to do with her. The morning after, the house cook told Tempy that the overseer had been "stroked" and that the Geechee woman had escaped during the night.

He looks at Magdalena, at the olive brown of her skin, the dark-brown eyes.

"I think your mother sent her God after him," he says.

HE SEEKS HER OUT just as the ship enters the port of New York, most of the passengers standing at the bow, mesmerized by the Statue of Liberty. Albert is below fetching the rest of their things from the cabin.

"Your husband told me where you are going to live. I know that place. There is woman there who will help you get settled. Alzbêta Dvořák."

He gives each of her sons a piece of hard candy.

"Remember what I said?" he asks, looking at Eberhard.

"Don't swim in the river," the boy answers.

He smiles. Then Tempy disappears back into the milieu of the ship.

THE FLATS

Minneapolis

1899–1905

RAIMUND, ALBERT, MAGDALENA, AND THE two young boys stand on the Washington Avenue Bridge and look down, their eyes squinting against the slant of the October sun. Magdalena does not see the mighty Mississippi that Tempy had said was two miles wide. Instead she sees its more juvenile but no less muscular self, a quarter of a mile wide. The river, aided by centuries of time and given additional thrust to its volume by the St. Anthony Falls before it was dammed, cuts a deep channel between two limestone bluffs. The bluff on the east side of the river juts up steeply and is covered with wild grasses, river birches, butternut, river oak, and cottonwood trees. On its crown are the imperial buildings of the University of Minnesota. Raimund then points to the west side of the river where he rents a house and where they will live for now. It has a wide and precipitous brow of flora-covered limestone at the top. Then it slopes down to the river in a series of natural benches with the most prominent of these called the upper Flats and the lower Flats. It is there that their eyes rest on the cluster of fifty or so houses below.

"That," Raimund says, "is the Flats."

They finish walking across the bridge and then march down the steps of a crude wooden staircase to the upper Flats where Raimund lives on Cooper Street. Frank and Eberhard run ahead to a huge pile of coal near the shore. They stop and watch the boys attempt to scale the coal.

"I forgot to tell you that no one here calls me Raimund," her brother-in-law says. "I've changed my name to the American version. Raymond. They call me Ray. The only one who still calls me Raimund is my neighbor."

"Will we have to change our names?" Albert asks. "Do our names have an American version?"

"No. They are the same. But you will probably be called Al because Americans tend to shorten names," Raymond answers. "You," he nods to Magdalena, "will probably be called Maggie."

Albert calls for the boys. Presentable and clean when they stepped off the train, they run toward their parents with coal-smudged faces looking like orphans from a novel by Dickens. Magdalena pries nuggets of coal from their hands, and wipes their hands and faces with a handkerchief before they proceed down Cooper Street.

They stop near the end of the street and Raymond points to a small house.

"I rented it my first year here and then bought it from Prochazka. I haven't had time to fix it up like I've wanted to," Raymond explains, "but now that Albert is here, we can make it much nicer."

Magdalena puts a hand to her throat.

"A shack with windows," Albert says with forced enthusiasm as they walk up the steps, "is better than a cage made of gold."

Magdalena steps through the doorway, sees the one bed in the corner of the kitchen, a rickety table with matching rickety chairs, and the old coal stove.

"Speak for yourself," she says. And faints.

WHEN SHE COMES TO, she is lying on the bed and an old woman is wiping her face with a cold cloth. The men and boys are standing in the farthest corner of the kitchen.

"You are pregnant," the old woman whispers in German. Magdalena stares at eyes resembling the coal nuggets she removed from her sons' hands. The woman's face is concave, wrinkles gather toward the mouth like smocking on a dress.

"I'm just hungry," she says, trying to sit up. "I didn't expect this. I must be crazy." The old woman pushes her back down.

"*Nicht*," she answers. "The crazy one is Raimund. You are just pregnant."

The old woman stands up and turns to the men and boys.

"Raimund! How many times did I tell you to fix this place up!" she yells. "Stupid boy! You can't live like a bachelor anymore!"

Raymond is stiff with shame, Albert with shock. Frank and Eberhard press their faces into the men's legs.

"Don't just stand there!" she roars. "Go up to the city and find some beds and more furniture!"

The boys run out of the house, followed by Albert and Raymond, singed by the bullwhip of the old woman's voice.

"Are you Alzbêta?" Magdalena asks, propping herself up again.

"I am. I assume Raimund told you about me."

"No. A man on the ship told me."

"A colored man? With freckles and red hair?"

"Yes."

The old woman looks pleased.

"So Tempy is still alive. The water hasn't gotten to him yet." She places her hand on Magdalena's belly. "It is early. Maybe two months. No queasiness?

Magdalena shakes her head.

"Stay there," Alzbêta says. "I'll be back with some food."

Magdalena eats chicken soup with slices of buttered potato bread. Alzbêta cuts steaming pieces of prune *Koláč* with a fork and feeds them to Magdalena as though she is a child. The old woman then pours a large glass full of homemade beer. Magdalena drains the glass, and the old woman refills it. She drinks the second beer nearly as fast as the first.

"Sleep," Alzbêta says, pulling a blanket over Magdalena.

THE MEN AND BOYS spend the rest of the day roaming the neighborhoods in the city above, scavenging for castaway furniture. Honza, Radim, and three other men join them and they come back at dusk with three more beds, a solid pine table with five chairs, chipped dishes, and a set of old silverware from the rectory's housekeeper at St. Elizabeth's Church. Alzbêta ushers them over to her house and feeds them supper because Magdalena is still asleep. Only Raymond stays.

When Magdalena wakes up, Raymond is asleep in a chair next

to the bed. His face is dirty and tear-streaked, his breath sour. She sits up and leans over. There are three empty bottles on the floor, a fourth that is half-full, and a fifth that has not been opened. She picks up the fourth bottle and takes a drink. It is beer but not as good as what Alzbêta gave her. There is a fishy taste to it, a mineral heaviness that suggests mud. She wonders if it has been made with water from the river. No matter, she thinks, tipping the bottle back and drinking the rest. She picks up the fifth bottle, pulls out the protruding cork. Swigging intermittently, she studies her brother-in-law. She hopes the house is the only thing he has lied about, and takes inventory of their present circumstances.

They have come across the Atlantic, suffered a long and tiresome train trip to the middle of America, only to end up in a village that resembles the thatched-roof houses of peasants living next to the moat of some baron's castle in medieval Germany. It is a squatters' haven at the bottom of a river ravine.

She contemplates hitting Raymond in the head with the bottle. He has done one good thing, though. Albert already has a job at the same flour mill where Raymond works. He begins in the morning and because of his education and experience, will receive a higher wage. She finishes off the bottle, thinks of Tempy when she puts it on the floor next to the others. *Where you are going has many Gods.*

"May one of you take pity on us," she says aloud.

A WEEK LATER, Aino Takelo claims that their arrival has given the Flats an Indian summer. Magdalena does not understand the significance of this.

"More time to work on the river and on the bluffs," Aino says. "Come, Maggie, I'll show you. Bring the boys. They can work, too."

And so Magdalena learns how to hook billets of wood, logs, mill ends, and other sawmill waste with a long metal pole. She and the boys walk from the river shore to the house and back again, building a substantial pile of planks. One night she leads Albert and Raymond behind the house to show them the cross-stack of mill-cut boards.

"They will need a week to dry out," Raymond says. "Then I promise we will fix up the house."

They work at night by kerosene lamp after their long days at the mill. They flatten tin cans and nail them over knotty holes in the wood, climb the roof and patch it with the shingles Eberhard found on the shore next to a docked barge. More wood comes down the river over the ensuing days, and Albert decides that they will have enough time before winter to build onto the house at least one room if not two. Aino gives Magdalena some raw wool to fill the holes inside the house before Albert covers them with tin.

Not just wood but all manner of useful and even treasured things float to them or are fished out of the Mississippi. A distribution house upriver dumps fruit one day so that oranges and bananas wash up on shore. Magdalena and the boys bring home sacks of the fruit in a small hand wagon. Alzbêta spreads the oranges and bananas out on a crude worktable that Albert and Raymond have built outside. Kyle and Aino walk over, having seen Magdalena and the boys trudge up from the river with exotic booty. They have all tasted an orange before but not a banana, although the adults have heard of them and know they are edible. Kyle takes out his knife, peels an orange and eats a segment of it, the juice running down his hand.

"Tastes very fine," he says. "I don't understand why they dumped it." He then cuts a banana free from its cluster, slices off the green top and peels it. He breaks off a piece and eats it.

"Not bad." He points to the green tinge on the peel. "They are not ripe yet. A couple of days in the sun and then they should be better."

Little Frank reaches for a banana and Alzbêta lightly slaps his hand. "Not now. Eat the rest of it, Kyle. If you don't get sick, then the children can have one."

They laugh, watch Kyle eat the rest of the banana. He does not get sick and two days later they all peel and eat a banana for the first time.

NEXT TO ALZBÊTA, the Kaufmann family becomes especially close to the Takelos. Aino is slender, fair skinned, and fine boned with hazel-flecked green eyes that change to a startling aqua in the right light. Kyle has the blue eyes of a Nordic man, with a long and muscular torso but short legs. His hair is flax colored like his wife's but his beard and moustache are a chestnut brown.

At first Magdalena thinks the boys are drawn to Kyle because, unlike most of the other men, he is home during the day working as a cooper. He makes high-quality barrels in a workroom behind his house that contains a brick furnace, allowing him to work through the winter. The boys come home with stories of a magic mill called the Sampo, of mystical lands where only women live, and of a God known as Väinämöinen and a Goddess called Lohi who battled each other over centuries of time.

"Those are stories from the Kalevala," Albert says one night during supper. "Remember? Your father talked about it. We didn't study the Nordic myths as much but we read some of the Finnish runes. He said the Finns had a mythology of their own and that it was called the Kalevala."

"Aino was a rune singer in Finland," Raymond says. "Wait until you hear her sing." He breaks a slice of bread in half, and with his knife covers both halves with butter. "It isn't just a mythology to them," he continued. "It is their religion. You've probably noticed that Kyle and Aino do not go the Lutheran church like the Swedes and Norwegians. They believe in the older Gods of the Kalevala."

Magdalena is fascinated by the Finnish myths but the Takelos are a private couple and so she does not inquire further. Kyle keeps the boys occupied with his stories and for that she is grateful. He shows her and the boys the limestone smokehouse a few feet from his workshop in which he cures all kinds of meat including fish from the river. He teaches the boys how to fish from a platform he has built up over the water, the four logs supporting it sunk deep into the muddy shallows. He catches Buffalo carp, catfish, crappies, and sunfish, smoking them with maple wood that he buys up in the city where he also sells most of what he cures to a butcher on East Hennepin Avenue.

In the beginning of November, Kyle changes his fishing tactics. He drags the river from his platform, using a steel pole with a long and heavy wire welded to the end of it. At the end of the wire is a four-pronged hook. He sings in Finnish while he drags the river. Eberhard explains to Magdalena and Albert that Kyle is courting favor from Väinämöinen. He fishes mostly on weekends so that he can get help from other men.

"Look at that hook," Albert observes. "Is he going whaling?"

"Wait and see," Raymond says. Nothing prepares them for what Kyle snags and tries to pull ashore that second Sunday. Raymond and four other men wade into the river with gaffing hooks. Ropes are tied around their waists and held by men on shore.

"It is a whale!" Eberhard shouts.

"*Nicht*," Raymond says. They stare at the fish that has been dragged up onto the grass. "It is a sturgeon."

"What do you think?" Kyle asks. "A hundred pounds?" He measures the fish's length with his hands. "Six feet."

"Feels closer to two hundred," quips one of the men who has helped drag in the sturgeon.

"Better than that dead cow he hauled in two years ago!" someone shouts.

"That dead pig, too," Alzbêta adds.

The next Sunday, Kyle catches two sturgeons and a paddlefish. The children take turns trying to lift the fish by its paddle-like snout. Kyle assures them that although it is strange looking, it is delicious to eat. It has become a tradition since the Takelos moved to the Flats for Kyle to provide a smoked sturgeon or a paddlefish for the community Christmas feast and another for the Morena. Aino and Kyle depend upon harvesting at least three sturgeons and two paddlefish. Magdalena learns from Aino that the smoked fish brings a high price in the city above.

"We need the money. We hope to leave here in two years or three," Aino says. "We put a claim down on a homestead near Pine City up in northern Minnesota. We can't afford to buy land south, and anyway Kyle and I feel more at home among pine trees. We'll do a little farming and some logging. Raymond tells me you are also saving for a homestead."

"In northern Wisconsin. We have a booklet on it. The land is cheap and farming is supposed to be good there. We already have some money from my family and so we are hoping it will only be a year or so before we move. We want to start farming soon," Magdalena answers and then asks, "How long have you been here?"

"Five years although it seems longer. We've made good friends here and you will too. It will make it difficult to leave when the time comes."

THE WOMEN WORK HARDER as the days grow shorter and the weather colder. Alzbêta and Aino show Magdalena how to search the bluffs for late-season mushrooms, wild onion, garlic, and various herbs. She learns how to dry and store them for use in winter soups and stews. Staples such as flour, salt, sugar, and meat are purchased from Prochazka's grocery store. Milk at five cents a quart and butter at seven cents a pound comes from Mrs. Karitish who keeps seven cows housed in a cave on the bluff not far from the village. She and her young son haul a twenty-five-gallon can every morning and every evening to each household. The son leads the cows down to the Flats to graze on whatever grass is there. They lumber in single file behind him and their collective bovine gait makes the bells around their necks ring in a crude but soothing harmony.

The coming of winter is as quirky as the prolonged autumn. The temperature drops suddenly while it is raining on the last day of November. The river birches, used to waving in the slightest wind, are stiff with ice. The house is cold despite the wood reinforcements and the copious amounts of coal burned in the stove. Two-and-a-half-year-old Frank and nearly five-year-old Eberhard are very proud of their contribution to heating the house. They scamper after the coal wagon every day, picking up small chunks that fall off the back, putting them in a burlap sack to drag home. Their faces are streaked with coal dust, their hands as black as a chimney sweep. Magdalena watches them sometimes from the window. She thinks of the copy of the painting by Jean-François Millet in her father's study, *The Gleaners.*

"They look like street urchins," Albert says one night after the children are in bed. "It isn't dignified. And what if they get caught?"

"I don't think there is anyone who cares to catch them," Raymond counters. "It has nothing to do with dignity. How is picking up coal different than shoveling manure? We did dirty work at their age."

"But not in public."

"This isn't 'public' down here. Everyone has to work. The children here have chores. How different is that from our childhood? There is no one here who looks at them as street urchins. All the children find things that are useful to their families. Besides, Eberhard and Frank have made a game of it."

Albert looks to Magdalena for an opinion.

"Deuteronomy 24:19," she says. "Remember?"

But it is Raymond who responds and repeats one of the few Biblical verses that Richter had liked.

"When thou reapest thy harvest in thy field, and has forgot a sheaf in the field, thou shalt not go back to fetch it; it shall be for the stranger, for the fatherless, and for the widow; that the Lord thy God may bless thee in all the work of thy hands."

"They are not fatherless and Magdalena is not a widow," Albert comments.

"We are strangers," Raymond says.

"I doubt the American laws recognize Deuteronomy," he shoots back.

"I don't think American laws pertain to the Flats," Raymond grins.

THE COLD DOES NOT SEEM to bother the boys. One Saturday, Albert and Magdalena watch from the kitchen window as the boys play outside. She turns, coffee pot in hand, to Raymond sitting at the table.

"How did you survive the last three winters?"

"By sleeping in some woman's bed up in the cities," Albert says. "Where do you think he is these nights when he does not come home?"

He steps away from the window, reaches over and ruffles his younger brother's hair.

"You take after the old man," Albert teases, putting on his coat. "Like a dog after every bitch in heat."

He leaves the house and joins the boys. Magdalena pours herself a cup of coffee and sits at the table.

"You don't pay for it, do you?"

"Sometimes. Do you think it immoral?"

She does not answer right away. He is not the same boy who ran away from home to escape his deceased father's dictum to make him a priest. The frantic, bottled-up teenager who told them he was studying in the hayloft when he was really masturbating while looking at pornographic postcards. Magdalena found the cards after he left, wedged between two beams in the hayloft, and understood the ruse.

When she stepped off the train, she saw the man he had become; a man who moved with confidence and ease, who tipped his hat at the other women descending from the train. She felt his sexual vibrancy when he lifted her and spun her around. He has grown into his body and resembles Albert except that his dark-blond hair is longer. He has the same masculine jaw and chin as her husband, the same broad chest and beautifully shaped hands. Raymond tilts his head and smiles disarmingly at her. She picks up the coffee pot, reaches across the table, and refills his cup. She wonders if Raymond has one woman or many. Many, she decides, and then wonders how he can afford them.

"For the women or for you?" she responds. "I don't know what to think about that. Just be careful that you don't get into trouble."

"Too late. My first week here I almost got beaten to death. I flirted with Honza's second wife. I didn't know she was married. Alžbêta stopped Honza before he cracked my head open," he grins, leaning back in his chair. "Do you know what she told me?"

"To keep it in your pants?"

He laughs.

"Yes and no. She told me to never get involved with the women on the Flats and to look for women in the city instead. She's never judged me. Do *you* think it is wrong?"

She frowns at him. He knows the liberality of her parents' ideas on sex.

"You are forgetting who you are talking to. No," she answers. "And Albert doesn't either. He's just teasing you. Obviously he doesn't suffer from lack of affection or desire." She glances down at her belly.

"I enjoy women. I always have," he says.

"And they evidently enjoy you," she responds. "You are fortunate. You have the freedom a woman could never have. It suits you, Raymond, as long as you don't get serious or get someone pregnant. I don't think that you should ever get married." She gets up from the table to slice a loaf of bread. "You will only cause and suffer heartache if you do. You like women too much to settle down with just one."

"Are you so sure of that?" he asks.

"I am."

"God dammit!" he says. "Alzbêta told me the same thing. But you both could be wrong."

RAYMOND HAD LIED about another thing.

"You never said anything about Alzbêta other than she was a teacher."

"She is a teacher," he says evasively. "She teaches many things."

"You mean she is a seer," Magdalena says mildly irritated. She avoids using the word *witch*, and wonders how she will do her weekly bread and kuchen baking. She is often at Alzbêta's house, using her oven. It is only a matter of time before the old woman detects the same ability in Magdalena.

"She does no harm by it," he answers. "In fact she is revered for it." He adds, "It is not the same here, Magdalena."

Raymond is right. It is not the same. Still, when the other women arrive for a visit, Magdalena stays out of sight in the big room off the kitchen where plants hang upside down from clotheslines and nails. She recognizes peppermint, lavender, rosemary, and chamomile. Alzbêta points out some of the others. St. John's wort, blue vervain, bergamont, feverfew, Culver's root, and prairie sage. She sits in the room mending clothes or stringing wild garlic and mushrooms, but listens as Alzbêta reads tea leaves and coffee grounds, scattered on saucers, to the women.

They come to her with problems or to confess. They ask questions such as how to deal with a benevolent drunk who cannot hold a job, a philanderer, or a child in trouble. They ask: He hit me. Am I not right to crack his skull with a frying pan? They ask: He is a cock in the city but a hen at home. What can I do? They ask about children, the lack of or too many: Why do I have all boys and no girls? Why do I have all girls and no boys? Or they lower their voices, speak in whispers: I cannot have this baby. Where do I go?" They ask about their children's futures: Will she marry well? Will he get a good job? Will they be generous or greedy? Will they take care of me when I am old? Those who have saved enough money ask if they would do better if they left the Flats to live in a nicer house up in the city. If Alzbêta says yes, they are anxious. The tradeoff might be a nicer house but not nicer neighbors. No one to talk to over the fence or clothesline, and, of course, they would not be close to the river. When Alzbêta says no, they sigh, mull it over, and then perk up, thinking of new and different ways to fix up their houses.

Men too come to see Alzbêta but usually at night when no one can see them slip in and out of her home. Magdalena saw Zalman walk up Alzbêta's steps just the other night and knew the fabric draped over his arm was a subterfuge for his visits.

Alzbêta gets paid in kind. Mrs. Karitish gives her free milk, cream, and butter. Else Janikowski does all of her ironing. Larissa Zacharov sews for her as does Zalman. Grateful men do repairs on her house.

One day walking back from the grocery store, Magdalena asks her if she uses cards.

"Cards!" Alzbêta huffs. "What do you think I am? A circus performer?"

"But you're Catholic. You go to mass," Magdalena says. "What does Father Hughes think?"

"I don't know," she says, opening the door to her house. "I've never asked him."

They sit down for coffee. The boys stick their heads in the door, are given a piece of kuchen and sent back outside, eating the warm coffee cake as they run. Alzbêta watches them from the window for a few minutes. Finally she speaks.

"You are upset by what I do."

"Not upset. It is just unusual, that is all." She knows the older woman sees through her lie.

"Let me tell you what my grandmother told me," Alzbêta says.

"She said that such an ability came from God and exists among the persecuted people of the world. The Irish, for example. They call it 'second sight' and Lily O'Brien who used to live on the other side of the bridge had it. My grandmother told me it was God's way of compensating what he had set in motion with Cain and Abel. If Abel could have sensed his brother's hate instead of being blinded by love, he would not have been killed. Except that it is usually women, not men, who have it."

Magdalena turns her coffee cup in its saucer.

"Silence is often a necessary sword," the older woman remarks. "Unfortunately the sword with time becomes heavier than the thing it is protecting." She reaches across the table and holds one of Magdalena's hands. "You are here now. I respect why you want to keep such a gift private. But don't deny it in yourself. It will twist on you. The Americans call it 'gut instinct.' I don't care what it is called. It is your best compass in knowing what is right and what is wrong. Not just with people but out there."

She sweeps her arm to indicate what is beyond the house. The river, the trees, the sky.

IN JANUARY the river freezes over near the shore and the men create an ice-skating rink, marking the perimeters with poles stuck into the ice. Raymond finds used ice skates for the boys. But Magdalena can't concentrate, watching them instead of doing laundry or cooking some days. She stares off into space and cries for no reason.

"Get outside for an hour every day. Just walk," Alzbêta advises. "I'll watch the boys. Go now."

Magdalena puts on her heavy winter coat and thickly knit mittens. She wraps her head and face with a wool scarf. Then she leaves the house and walks toward the Washington Avenue Bridge.

Life is glass, she thinks, watching the people on the bridge above her. Some of them are sturdy and some are as fragile as china. A man, sometimes a woman, looks down from the bridge, one hand sliding across the top of the railing. Magdalena feels the flirtation of their suicidal notions as they peer at the surface of the frozen river, looking for a patch of thin ice that will not sustain the weight of their self-flung bodies. She stands still, stares up at them until they become aware of her. She lifts her hand, waves. *I see you*, she mouths. *I see you*. It is enough, that small gesture. After a few moments, they slide their hand back from the railing, lift it and hesitantly wave back. Someone notices that they exist in the world.

A couple of days later, she makes her way down to the grocery store and observes Prochazka lick his ink-stained fingertips as he tallies up her bill. He sucks on a saliva-soaked cigar wedged into one side of his mouth. The wetness, color, and shape of it reminds her of what dogs leave behind, steaming and moist in the snow. The following Monday, she finds Ivan Zacharov drunk and lying in a snow bank with icicles hanging from his nose. She fetches Aino and together they hoist the old man into a wheelbarrow and push him home. His arms and legs drag on the ground as they wheel him. She looks at his face. He will die in a year, maybe less.

One day she accompanies Mrs. Karitish on her rounds delivering milk, butter, and cream. Mr. Karitish is working at the mill and their son is skating on the river with the other boys. Her milk cart is pulled by an old cow past bearing calves and milk but still able to do this work. They talk about Sunday nights, about the danger.

"You should have seen the fight last spring during the Morena," Mrs. Karitish says. "Raymond was involved in that one."

Ten men from the city had stood on the western end of the Washington Avenue Bridge, unzipped their pants, and holding their penises as horizontal as possible sent long arches of urine onto the Flats below. Raymond heard Alzbêta cry out, saw the yellow stream that hit her and looked up to see the ten men engrossed in jeering at the people below. He and nineteen other men slipped into the trees near the steps, bounded up, and caught the offenders by surprise. The fight ended quickly on the bridge. They dragged the offenders down the wooden stairs by their feet, their heads concussed by every step.

"You can't wait until Sunday, eh?" Honza said to the beaten men, opening the fly on his pants. "Well here is your beer."

The rest of the men did the same, pissing the digested remains of good Czech beer onto the semiconscious men as they lay at the foot of the stairs. Someone shouted and they looked up. Several officers from the Third Precinct came thundering down the steps to interrupt their revenge. Honza pulled Raymond out of the fight after he sustained two billy club strikes, and the two ran and hid in the bluffs.

On the last Friday in January, Magdalena walked to the nearest city neighborhood known as Seven Corners to shop and see what is there. To her dismay, she is approached first by a woman whose religious overtures Magdalena halts by simply staring at her. The second is a somberly dressed Mormon, pleading with her to convert to the Mormon Church. The man is about her age, with crusted eyelids.

"Daughter. Let me guide you to the true faith," he says.

"I am not your daughter," she snaps and pulls out her mother's rosary from underneath her shirtwaist and lets it fall for him to see. That makes it worse. A papist, apparently, is in more need of conversion than a gypsy or Jew. He follows her for two blocks until she hails the policeman standing on the corner. The third time is in the fabric shop a block away from St. Elizabeth's Church. A woman sidles up next to her and asks if she tells fortunes.

"I don't know what you are talking about," Magdalena answers. "I do nothing of the kind."

Even Zalman asked her a month after they arrived on the Flats, "When did you convert?" She is mystified by what people see when they look at her, what they interpret based on her physical appearance. Why not mistake her for being French, Spanish, or Italian?

DURING A DAILY STROLL in early February, she sees Aino standing by the shore of the river, watching the children skate. Her head is hooded by a large black scarf, her long gray coat monastic in its lack of styling. Magdalena hesitates and then walks until she stands next to her neighbor.

"Winter here makes me sad sometimes," Aino says without looking at Magdalena. "Too many people. I miss walking where there are no people. I need to get out of the house like you." She tilts her head up to stare at the eastern bluff. "But at least there is the river. I need to live near water. And it helps to watch the children."

A child calls out and waves. *Auntie Aino!* Then several children do the same. Aino waves back.

"We had children," she says. "Three babies. Two girls and a boy. We had a farm. Kyle was a sawyer but nothing ever went right. A drought one year, crop failure the next. We lost a stand of timber to a fire. The first baby died of a fever. My milk dried up too soon for the second, and she couldn't tolerate cow's milk. We moved to Helsinki with the third baby. Kyle found work as a fisherman. We thought it would be easier close to a doctor but it wasn't. Our son died of cholera. He lived the longest. Two and a half years. We took him back to where we buried his sisters in the forest. And then because we were childless, Kyle was threatened with conscription into the Russian Army. We borrowed money from both of our families and left Finland."

"Aino—"

The Finnish woman will not tolerate any sympathy or pity. She takes Magdalena's arm and, turning around, leads them back to their respective houses.

"Alžbêta says I have reason to hope. So things will get better," she finally says, lightly touching the cumbersome bulk of Magdalena's belly. "In the spring we will celebrate this."

ALTHOUGH THE DAILY EXCURSIONS outside help, Magdalena cannot recall being so vacant when she was pregnant with Eberhard and Frank, so lost in her thoughts that she could not keep track of the days.

"What day is it today?" she asks Eberhard, drawing at the table.

"Saturday," he answers, looking up. "February twenty-first," he adds, watching her.

"Where is your brother?"

"At Aino and Kyle's."

"Go get him. I have to start supper."

"I don't want to walk over there in the dark."

She looks at her precocious oldest son. "Eberhard! You've walked over there in the dark by yourself until now."

"I don't want to today." He brightens up. "But I'll go if you come with me."

She reaches over and feels his forehead. Sighs.

"Alright. But we have to be quick about it. Your father and uncle will be coming home any minute."

Eberhard knocks twice on the Takelos' front door and then repeats the staccato of two knocks. Frank opens the door and behind him stands Aino, Kyle, Alzbêta, Albert, and Raymond.

"Happy Birthday, Mama!" Eberhard shouts. Frank takes her hand and pulls her into the house.

"You forgot your own birthday!" he giggles, leading her to the dinner table.

Kyle made a trade with the butcher and acquired some brook trout to smoke; the flesh delicate and white, the flavor sublime. There are boiled potatoes with butter and dried dill, pea soup called *hernekeitto*, cabbage rolls called *sarma*, Finnish flatbread, and for dessert, a sweet bread flavored with ground cardamom seeds known as *pula*. Aino opens a precious jar of loganberry jam sent by relatives in Finland, and Kyle brings out Koskenkorva—Finnish vodka.

The talk varies. Jokes are told, there is some political discussion, and then talk of future land. Aino sips a glass of Koskenkorva and holds Frank on her lap. Eberhard sits on a small bench next to Alzbêta and rests his head against her shoulder. The boys ask for a story.

"Aino," Raymond says. "Tell them the story of your name. In English."

She hesitates, her green eyes lustrous in the candlelight. Kyle nods and lights his pipe. She begins, her voice with its lilt and rhythm, sounds like something between a chant and a song.

I am named after the girl who drowned herself and then turned into a salmon to escape a marriage she didn't want. It was her older brother Joukahainen who caused it to happen. He dared the God Väinämöinen to a sing-spelling contest. He knew that if he lost, Väinämöinen would kill him. Joukahainen did lose. To avoid death, he promised his sister as a bride for Väinämöinen. He went home disgraced and upset, knowing what he had done. He cried to his mother:

I have given my sister, Aino,
pledged my mother's child to care for Väinämöinen
to be mate to the singer,
refuge for the dodderer
shelter for the nook-haunter.

But the mother was happy because Väinämöinen was a God and to
have him as part of the family meant they would not suffer famine
anymore. She told her sobbing daughter that it was a great thing to
be married to such a man, that she would never be without food to
eat, she would have beautiful clothes and a beautiful house. But Aino
knew that no young woman wanted to be married to Väinämöinen.
She warned her mother that if she forced her to go through with it,
she would become a sister to the whitefish and brother to the fishes.
Her mother didn't listen. So Aino left home and traveled three days
until she came to the seashore. There were three water maidens
sitting on a rock not far from shore, gesturing to her to join them.
Before Aino dove into the water, she took off everything that was
human-made while the animals on the forest's edge watched her.

She cast her shirt on willow
Her skirt upon an aspen
Her stockings on the bare ground
Her shoes upon the wet rock
Her beads on the sandy shore
Her rings upon the shingle

Then she swam out to the rock. While she was sitting on it, the
rock slowly sank below the surface. To the animals on the shore, it
appeared that she drowned. None of them would tell her mother
except the hare. He ran to the farm and found the mother and her
other daughters in the sauna where they laughed and threatened to
roast him. When he told her, "your daughter has become a sister to
the whitefish and a brother to the fishes," the mother began to weep.
She lamented for days and finally she said:

Don't, luckless mothers ever in this world
Don't lull your daughters

Or rock your children to marry
Against their will as I,
A luckless mother have lulled my daughters
Reared my little hens.

But Aino was not dead. When the water covered her head, she turned into a salmon. Soon Väinämöinen found out that Aino was alive as a fish and he tried to catch her with silk nets, certain he could return her to her human form. He caught a salmon but didn't realize it was Aino until he was about to cut her with a knife. Then she flipped free of the boat and raising her head above the waves, said,

O you old Väinämöinen!
I was not to be
A salmon for you to cut
A fish for you to divide
For meals at morning
For breakfast tidbits
For salmon lunches

Väinämöinen then asked her what she was to be? And she responded,

I was to be a hen tucked under your arm
One who would sit for ever
A lifelong mate on your knee
to lay out your bed
to place your pillow
to clean your small hut
one to sweep your floor
to bring fire indoors
to kindle your light
to make your thick bread
bake your honey-bread
carry your beer mug
and set out your meal.

I was not a sea salmon
A perch of the deep billow:

I was a girl, a young maid
Young Joukahainen's sister
Who you hunted all your days
Throughout your lifetime longed for.

You wretched old man
You foolish Väinämöinen
For you knew no way to keep
The Wave-wife's watery maid
Ahto's peerless child!

He begged her to come back but she never did.
She had become a daughter of water.

Magdalena cannot sleep that night. Albert and Raymond drank too much vodka and are snoring. The boys too are asleep. She dresses, leaves the house, and walks to the shore of the river. The ice is thinning. She hears it, hears the current underneath working to break it into pieces. The water has a voice like Aino's. Both lament being held back by ice and by land.

SHE GIVES BIRTH to a daughter in early April, assisted by Alzbêta and Aino. The baby is a robust seven and a half pounds with black hair, dark eyes, and rosebud lips. Albert is besotted with his new daughter. He cannot stop looking at her, holding her.

"Have you named her?" Aino asks a week after the birth.

"Not yet. I thought I'd wait until the baptism."

Alzbêta is nervous in the days that follow. When Magdalena asks her what is wrong, she says, "I don't know. Maybe it is the weather. It is too early for it to be *this* warm. It feels like the air is . . . what is the word?" She puffs out her cheeks.

"Fat?"

"A balloon?" Aino offers.

"Swelling," Alzbêta says. Albert dismisses her comments after she leaves.

"She is old. Her bones ache when the weather changes. That is all."

He and Raymond sit at the table in their underwear, having taken off their flour-coated clothes outside. When Albert leaves the house to wash up, Raymond tells her that he has never known Alzbêta to be wrong.

"She's probably feeling the river. It will be high this year and that means the lower levee will flood out. Those people will need a place to stay until the water goes down."

But the men are wrong. The inflated sensation that Alzbêta feels bursts and delivers itself two weeks later. Typhoid breaks out on the Flats.

Minneapolis city officials blame it on the wells of the levees' households and most of them are shut down. Albert and Magdalena forbid their sons to play at the river's edge, fearing like everyone else that the contamination has come from the river. Magdalena is less concerned about the baby whose appetite is excellent and whose only source of food is the prodigious amount of breast milk that Magdalena produces. They scrub everything in the house, washing their clothes with boiling water and lye soap. Their neighbors do the same and yet they watch in horror at the coffins that go by every other day, carried on the shoulders of family members as they trudge to Holy Emmanuel Lutheran Church on the second levee. The quarantine will not allow the Catholic residents to bring their dead to the city above, and those victims are buried in the Lutheran cemetery as well.

The Kaufmanns are not spared. Eberhard comes down with it first and then Frank. Magdalena leaves the baby with Aino between feedings, as Alzbêta is ill as well. Two days after the boys fall sick, Albert and Raymond complain of stomach pains. She spends frantic days keeping their fevers down with ice wrapped in blankets, coaxing them to drink sterilized water, and removing their feces-soiled clothing, scrubbing them clean in a vat of boiling water outside. She washes her hands and breasts with soap and the hottest water she can tolerate before feeding her daughter. The men and boys survive.

Ivan Zacharov dies from it. And then Alzbêta. As she is the oldest and longest-living member of the Flats, the sorrow that follows can be heard throughout the village. Sick as he is, Raymond hears the collective wailing and knows the old woman has died. He is carried to her funeral on a litter, his grief silent and deep.

Just when it seems the disease has run its course, the baby spikes a fever at the beginning of May. Magdalena sends the men and boys to stay with Kyle and Aino so that she can concentrate on her daughter. Kyle brings over a washtub filled with chipped ice. She rubs the baby with alcohol but the fever climbs until the infant begins to convulse, her back arching, her arms and legs jerking like a strung puppet. Magdalena prays aloud, wrapping the baby in a blanket and nestling her in the washtub of ice. *God help us, God help us*, until it is reduced to *help us*, over and over again. The ice brings the fever down just enough to stop the convulsions. She wraps the baby in dry blankets, sits in the rocking chair by the stove and sings lullabies. Sometime during the night, the baby quiets down. Magdalena, exhausted and thinking the fever has broken, falls asleep. When Albert wakes her the next morning, she feels the limp weight of her daughter's body. Sees the face that mimics the peaceful sleep of a contented child.

She pushes his hands away and begins rocking as if the motion might induce breath into her daughter. Albert leaves and a few minutes later, Aino enters the house. She pulls up a kitchen chair and listens while Magdalena rocks and sings to the baby. Finally she leans over, stops the rocking of the chair by grabbing one of its arms.

"Maggie. The baby is dead," she says.

"No!"

Aino grips Magdalena's upper arm with her other hand.

"I know. Three babies, remember?" she says. Magdalena palms one of her daughter's hands and looks at the pasty white fingers. There is a blue hue around her daughter's mouth.

"I should have seen this. But she was so strong," Magdalena begins, her voice unnaturally high. "So healthy. The boys got sick. Raymond and Albert got sick. But not us. Not us."

She looks about the room and at Aino with feral eyes.

"I'm cursed. I've cursed her by being her mother," she rambles on. "He said my children would die. That's what he said. He screamed at us even when the ship was pulling out of the harbor. I thought only the boys heard it. But she heard it too."

"He? Do you think Albert's brother has that kind of power? If you think," Aino says, "that this would not have happened if you stayed in Germany you are wrong. Typhoid happens everywhere. Babies die. Alzbêta lived here a long time, survived many things, and she died. You did everything a mother could do."

Magdalena unwraps and then rewraps the baby in her blanket.

"The baby needs to be buried today. Albert is making the funeral arrangements."

"She is not baptized," Magdalena says. "The Church won't recognize her life. I don't want her buried." She wipes her face with her free arm. "I don't want her buried in a cemetery. Any cemetery."

She suddenly thinks of the funeral pyres of the Celts, of the Hindus, of her own German ancestors. How they sent their dead to the afterworld on a raft, shot a volley of fire-tipped arrows once the pyre was afloat so that the body would burn and be taken up by both the air and the water. Then she thinks of the girl in the story, the girl that Aino is named after. The Mississippi is powerful. It could transform her daughter, possibly give her life again.

"What about the river?" she asks.

"She can't go into the river. Her body would contaminate the water and it is against the law."

"I will not bury her in a cemetery. You did not bury your children in a cemetery."

"Kyle and I belong to a different faith. We are at peace with what we did because it was acceptable to us. And to my mother's people, the Sami. You will be breaking the laws of your Church and disobeying your husband. Can you live with that?"

Magdalena looks for a resemblance to her husband in the baby's face and sees only her own face. She and Albert agree on many things but religion. Her husband has found a balance that is acceptable to his faith and also to his education on evolution and nature. But he retains a strong belief in the afterlife, obeying the Church's precept on burying the dead. She cannot find fault with that but neither can she agree. Especially now having come to this sudden and inexplicable truth. Who is God to decide where the soul of a child should reside?

"Albert doesn't need to know." She looks up at Aino.

"I need your help."

AINO RUBS A WATER STAIN on the table's surface. If she had not experienced it herself, she might think Magdalena's reasoning to be the madness of grief. But Aino knows the feeling of holding a dead child, knows that a mother is still a mother even when her child is dead, and in being so is still the protector of her child. That pain of this type can bring a clarity, not a muddling, of reason. She swallows against her own pain. They need Alzbêta. The old woman would have been a ballast and a rudder to this decision. Aino hesitates, and then says, "We cannot do this alone. You need someone you can trust. Kyle will help us as well."

"Raymond," Magdalena says. "He doesn't believe in God. I will ask him. He will do this."

SHE STANDS RESOLUTE against her rage during the funeral service at St. Emmanuel's Lutheran Church. Raymond is quiet while Albert doesn't bother to wipe away the tears running down his face, his grief doubled by the quarantine that prevents his child from being buried in the consecrated ground of the Catholic Church. Magdalena feels the love and support of their neighbors who overcome their fears to attend the service. But she also knows they believe that God, after a pause, may have signaled the end of the horror that swept through the community by taking this last small life, an innocent who, unlike Isaac, was not spared at the last moment. She silently speaks to God as the coffin is lowered into the ground. *You did not ask me. I did not agree. You will not have her.*

RAYMOND IS THE FIRST to leave the house that night after arguing with his brother. Albert stays outside and drinks Koskenkorva and Slivovitz until he cannot stand upright. Magdalena helps him into bed. She gives the boys hot chocolate laced with whiskey. They wander through the small kitchen, dreamy-eyed and falling asleep on their feet until she guides them to bed as well. Then Magdalena leaves the house. She meets Aino and Raymond near the community hall. Aino carries a shovel wrapped in a blanket. The streets are empty and quiet because people have cocooned themselves in their houses, the death of the baby making them feel the betrayal and terror of what might still be out there. They enter the Lutheran cemetery with no one to witness them.

Aino and Raymond take turns with the shovel. Magdalena digs at the fresh mound of dirt with her hands. Raymond lifts the coffin out, removes the baby swaddled like a mummy, and hands her to Magdalena. He reburies the coffin. Then Aino leads them to the highest part of the upper levee to avoid the streetlights. They walk on what appears to be a deer path until they reach a grove of river birches beyond the western edge of the village.

"Here," Aino points. "But not until dawn."

THEY SIT THERE, sometimes looking at the river in the distance, sometimes at each other. Raymond stares at Magdalena illuminated by the full moon, sitting cross-legged with her long hair loose, and cradling the dead infant. He thinks of how she takes the pins out of her hair at night and lets it fall to her waist for Albert to brush. It is a silent, hypnotic ritual that is witnessed by Raymond and his two nephews. To entertain his sons, Albert winds one hand in the thickness and length of their mother's hair until it covers his arm up to the elbow. Some nights Raymond is tired enough so that he falls asleep after the ritual hair brushing. Other nights he becomes so aroused that it is unendurable to be in the same room. He waits until the rest of them have fallen asleep before slipping out and walking up the wooden steps to the city to visit a brothel, to find a woman with hair like Magdalena's, a woman with coffee-colored eyes fringed with lashes like lace, a woman whose skin is not a Victorian white but a Mediterranean brown. A woman who can keep him from betraying his brother, from insulting his brother's wife.

He is tired. More tired than he has ever been and, perhaps, a bit crazed. The workdays that he and Albert have missed because of illness will cause some financial hardship. But it could have been worse. They could have all died but had not because of Magdalena.

He could not refuse her request, however strange or torn about it he felt. Finally Aino speaks.

"What did you tell your brother?"

Raymond glances at Magdalena.

"I told him I was going up to the city to visit a friend," he answers. "He didn't take it well. He said I was denigrating the memory of my niece by fucking around—I'm sorry."

It is the adolescent embarrassment on Raymond's face, the apology for a word he doesn't think they should hear or know. Magdalena covers her mouth and tries to hold it in but she shakes from the effort. She leans into Aino who realizes what is happening.

"You think we don't know that word? Fuck?" Aino says. "It is so odd what language you men will use with each other and then think we don't know it."

"Aino is right," Magdalena gasps. She takes a deep breath. "But your accent," she says to Aino, "makes it sound so funny."

Raymond stares at them, unsure of how to react. He can't tell if Magdalena's tears are from laughter or grief.

"I know it is terrible to laugh," Magdalena says. "But I can't cry anymore."

"Why shouldn't you laugh?" Aino asks. "Raymond, don't look so shocked. Think of it. We buried the baby today, and then we unburied her tonight. We climbed up into the woods here, are sitting in the dark, and your brother thinks you are out with whores. If I hadn't gone through it three times, I wouldn't have understood it either. Something has to fill the place crying empties out. You can't stop certain things. You have to laugh against them. It is a sign of life. So is fucking," she adds matter-of-factly, thinking of the sexual frenzy that followed her and Kyle in their grief. "Not such a bad thing to do after all the deaths of this past month. It means you are alive. You almost died too. So it is a normal thing to do."

"Laugh or fuck?" he asks.

"Both," she replies.

He shivers. It is what he wanted to do. He wanted to go up to the city, have aimless sex, and get lost in feelings other than sorrow.

"I'm sorry Albert took it out on you," Magdalena says. "I'll think of something to tell him. Still, that was the best excuse you could have given because that is where you go most nights."

"I wish it were true," he admits. "I would like to be doing just that. But I'm not myself yet."

"Can't make wood, eh?" Aino says.

Their hysterical laughter echoes down the bluff to the levees, causing people to later comment that they heard wolves until Honza corrects them, saying a wolf hasn't been seen on the Flats in years and that it was coyotes.

"Did you know," Raymond says, "that Alzbêta used to tell jokes at funerals? I forgot that she did that. Her timing was good too, just when people needed to laugh." He tilts back his head and looks at the night sky. "She used to curse like a sailor when she was really angry. I mean red-hot mad. The first time I heard her, I thought my ears were going to fall off."

"You were the source of that anger your first year here," Aino notes.

"I know." He drops his head between his knees. "She used to say," his voice breaking, "'What were you thinking? *Were* you even thinking? How can you be so smart and so stupid at the same time?'"

He hides his face from them. He remembers the day he and Alzbêta stood on the frozen riverbank four months ago. She pointed to the university buildings across the river and said, "Do not work in the mills for the rest of your life. Both you and Albert are too intelligent for that. But his passion is land and farming. Your passion is knowledge and history. The history of where people have been, where they are going. You have a talent for understanding what shifts countries and their people. You were meant to be one of those people. A scholar."

"I won't ever leave the Flats," he answered. She cuffed him.

"Did I say you had to leave here? Don't be stupid now. You can still live here although they might think it is strange. An educated man among poor Bohemians. But that would be good, I think. You will represent us. Through you they will know that we are a good and intelligent people."

THEY BEGIN DIGGING when the night sky turns gray. The ground is full of rocks. When Raymond becomes tired, Aino takes over. Then, at the first glimpse of the rising sun, Magdalena lays her daughter into the new grave and puts a lock of her own hair on top of the bundled body. They stand, not knowing what prayer to say until Aino says something in Finnish. They put the soil back into place and cover the mound with leaves and branches so that it looks like a natural brush pile.

"Kyle is borrowing a horse from Honza. He is going to the caves later this morning," Aino says, "with a pick and hammer to get some limestone slabs for our summer oven. He will take one of those slabs and put it here so that animals can't get at her. Then he'll cover it up again with leaves." She puts an arm around Magdalena's waist. "He knows how to do this."

Except for what has happened, what they have done, nothing has changed. The new green of the birch leaves dapples their faces and makes the river look new as well. Magdalena can't think of anything to say and turns to Raymond who is leaning against one of the trees. He cocks his head, puts a finger to his lips, and then points up. The sound is faint at first and then grows into a chorus of rusty hinges.

"They are going north to nest," Aino says as the flock comes into view. The geese drop in altitude as if to land on the river. They watch them for a few minutes before breaking up. Raymond climbs up higher on the bluff so that he can walk across the top of it and then down the steps as if returning from a night in the city. Aino and Magdalena head back to the Flats. They are prepared to say they were hunting for spring morels. But the village is quiet.

"It's Sunday," Aino says. "Are you going to church?"

"No."

She did her praying through the long night of sitting in the trees. When the geese appeared, she knew what she had done was right. Her daughter is not lost. There is no God among the wild birds that will condemn her baby for not being baptized. The only thing that mars her sense of peace is the secret that she has to keep from Albert for the rest of her life. It is the trade she has made for her daughter's soul.

They stop in front of Alzbêta's house. When the old woman knew that she was dying, she sent for Prochazka to write down her will. That was when they learned that she owned her house rather than renting it like most residents of the Flats. In the will she had signed over the house and all of its contents to Magdalena and Albert. Upon their departure, it was then to go to Raymond.

"We only knew her for seven months and yet it feels like a lifetime," Magdalena says. Still she is certain the old woman is not quite gone because she had felt her presence throughout the night.

"What are we going to do without her?" Aino says, mirroring what the rest of the people are wondering.

"She is here," Magdalena says. "We won't be without her."

MAGDALENA'S WORDS are prophetic. There is no one who can fill the void of wisdom, bawdiness, holiness, bossiness, and general power that Alzbêta has left behind. Hardened realists, the Flats dwellers do the opposite of reality, preferring to believe that if they talk to Alzbêta, she will hear them from wherever she has gone after death. The most church-abiding among them cannot imagine the old woman in heaven or hell. So they decide that she is still in their world spiritually but not physically.

Larissa Zacharov is heard talking aloud to Alzbêta as she walks up the stairs to the city, and no one thinks it strange because they do the same, talking to Alzbêta as they would to God when they need help. The women forget sometimes and knock on what is now Magdalena's door, wanting to have their fortunes told. She invites them in for coffee and something to eat, listens to their woes and their triumphs. But she does not give them her sense of their lives. It is enough for the women to be in Alzbêta's kitchen, to sit for fifteen minutes or a half an hour. She tells Albert that they can offer at least that measure of solace.

A week after her own daughter's death, Magdalena and Aino attend to a young Slovak woman on Mill Street who is in prolonged labor and weak. She dies but the infant boy survives. The husband, unable to cry or speak, holds his two other children on his lap. A city official, his mouth and nose covered with a large handkerchief, stops by the house. He has been walking through the Flats that morning to survey the loss from the typhoid. He advises the husband to put the infant and two toddlers in an orphanage. Magdalena pushes him to the door.

"We don't do that here."

The two toddlers go home with Aino. Magdalena takes the newborn, unwrapping the binding cloth from her breasts to feed him.

THEY ENTER THE SUMMER CAUTIOUSLY. The outbreak finally forces the city to place a hydrant line from the city mains so that it runs down to the river village. In July Aino discovers that she is pregnant after a five-year hiatus of not conceiving. Sundays are strangely peaceful with no fights incurring over the selling or drinking of beer.

"Who wants to fight" Raymond says, "after a springtime of death?"

Albert forgives his brother for disappearing the night of the baby's funeral. But his grief expresses itself in an unexpected way. He waits until Magdalena is physically willing. Then he makes love to her as often as he can, sending the boys over to Aino and Kyle's for time and privacy. One night he comes home late from the mill too tired to bathe but not to make love. It isn't until after they are lying in bed sated that he looks at the black hair of his wife and sees that it is gray with flour. Her pubic hair is the same. They laugh like crazy at the flour that seems to spill from his pores. And then Albert cries.

MORE IMMIGRANTS move to the Flats that summer. Among them is a Cornish man in his middle twenties who entered the United States through Canada, fearing rejection at Ellis Island because of his blind left eye. Ian Brock has a countenance that borders on mournful until he smiles. Then his right eye and that side of his face glow, eclipsing his cloudy left eye as though it is the sun covering the moon. Three weeks into his new life on the Flats, he focuses his good eye on Larissa Zacharov. Their courtship and engagement is swift. There had not been a Morena that spring and so Ian and Larissa's wedding in September is its replacement. Zalman Sokoloff makes Ian's suit as a wedding gift and Birgitta Andersson does the same, embroidering the wedding dress that Larissa has sewn herself. The wedding reception is down at the river. Father Hughes evokes the blessing of both Ivan and Alzbêta, not realizing that the Flats' residents consider the dead Russian man and Czech woman already in attendance.

In October, Magdalena weans the motherless infant from her breast as the young father is remarrying and will have a complete home again. The following March, Aino gives birth to a healthy boy. Three months later, the land deal that Kyle has been waiting on comes through earlier than expected, and the Takelos leave the Flats to move to northern Minnesota that July of 1901.

"We will see each other again. Kyle promised that we would put aside money, no matter what, to come back and visit here. He says we may need to come to the cities from time to time for supplies depending upon how he does with logging. Write to me and I will write to you," Aino says at the train station, wiping her own face and then Magdalena's.

"I will." Magdalena knows it is truth. She will see Aino sometime in the future.

FOUR YEARS LATER in February 1905, Albert makes the final payment for a homestead in northern Wisconsin near a town called Chippewa Crossing. Enclosed in his payment to the land agent is a request for three skilled men to help him build a story-and-a-half Pennsylvania-style log house immediately after their arrival on May 3. He also asks that a trusted man purchase a flatbed wagon and a good team of horses and meet them at the train station. The night before they are to take the train, Albert tries to persuade Raymond to come with them.

"I'm not a farmer. My life is here. But I'll visit as often as I can," he says, sitting on a trunk that will be loaded onto Honza's wagon in the morning.

"Albert! Raymond is still attending the university," Magdalena admonishes. "He is a scholar. Why would he throw away the years he has already invested?"

Raymond is grateful for her support. He had entered the University of Minnesota as a sophomore in the fall of 1901, upon the recommendation of Richter, who had sent a letter to the president, Cyrus Northrop, and to Wallace Notestein, a faculty member in the Department of History. To prove Richter's claims of his advanced education, Raymond had voluntarily tested out of his freshmen-level language, history, literature, and math studies, finishing his bachelor's degree, summa cum laude, in three years. He was enthusiastically accepted into the doctoral program in history in the fall of 1904.

"Don't worry about Albert. It is fear that makes him behave so," Magdalena explains after Albert leaves the house in seeming fury. "It was hard for him after you left the first time."

She looks at a photograph of her own family. Her Uncle Bernhardt is making it difficult for her father, insisting he stay in Augsburg. She wraps the framed photograph in tissue paper and places it with the others in a box.

"What will the future bring, Maggie?"

"Don't ask me that. I'm not Alzbêta." Her voice is sharper than she meant it to be. "I don't honestly know. Good things, I hope," she adds.

MAYBE IT IS THE FULL MOON, Albert thinks, standing on the bridge and seeing its lunar reflection in the Mississippi below. He ran down the street, scrambled up the wooden steps in the dark, ashamed of his forcefulness in trying to change Raymond's mind. He watched himself arguing with his brother and then his wife, knowing all along that his brother was going to stay on the Flats, completing his education to the fullest as he would have in Germany. Albert's single-minded dream in pursuit of a farm of his own is about to happen, and he is excited and nervous. But he is a little unhinged as well and frightened. He does not want to lose his brother again.

He looks down at the black surface of water, at the refracted moonlight. He knows from his own education the power of the lunar cycle especially upon water. Although the Mississippi has no tides like the ocean, Albert has noticed over the last five years that under a full moon the river seems stronger. Alzbêta told him that first year that the current in the spring and summer was the strongest and therefore the most dangerous under a full moon, as though the moon's light pumps the Mississippi's watery muscles. Most everyone else believes it too. Beer selling on such nights has a supernatural feel to it, a heightened sensation that everyone feels but cannot name. They feel a potential loss of control, over the way they think, over what their bodies might do.

Albert has prided himself on being a rational man not given to superstition, and he is frequently consulted or asked for help because of his level-headedness. He had worked his way up into the position vacated by Gillian McPherson, Raymond's first boss at the mill. It has never been a secret that his family would not be on the Flats forever, that a farm was their goal. Yet leaving hits him like a punch to the gut.

They came to the Flats and were welcomed, quickly becoming beloved members of the river community. Magdalena is especially revered, much like Alzbêta was. His sons have thrived in the community's social fabric, learning to speak some Czech, some Slovak, and some Finnish. The boys think nothing of the difference, assume that the world is like the Flats, filled with so many people from different and fascinating backgrounds.

He wipes his eyes and, for the first time, silently begs Alzbêta to help him. Does he have the right, he asks, to put his dream first, to uproot his wife and children from this poor but loving enclave of people, to take them away from their much-loved uncle. He waits and then hears something. He thinks it is coming from the river but can't be sure. Then the whisper is as clear as the moonlight.

Do you have the right to deny them the dream?

He reaches out an arm in the direction of the voice. He wants to feel her touch, to know for sure. But all he feels is the night wind ruffling his hair.

The morning of the Takelos' departure, Kyle had warned him that it wouldn't be easy to leave.

"The unknown is always frightening," Kyle had said. "I failed in Finland as a sawyer and a farmer. I could fail again at farming and logging. But I don't plan to. I'm going to give it all that I have. Remember, Al, we would never have land of our own had we stayed in Finland, in Germany. Nothing to give to our children, or their children. I love the Flats and so does Aino. We have lifelong ties here. But we need land that we know is ours, that we can work, that will guarantee independence for our children."

Albert wipes his eyes with the back of his hand and begins walking back to the steps. It is a good thing after all, he decides, that Raymond will stay. He will be the tie that keeps them connected to this home in Minneapolis.

HE SLIPS UNNOTICED from the house after supper when his father and uncle began arguing, and follows a deer path above the upper Flat until he reaches a grove of river birches that he discovered two summers ago. There are pieces of limestone and a large limestone slab that he assumes have been discarded by men like Kyle who harvest the stone from the nearby cave to build the outdoor ovens used in the summer. He sits on the largest slab and releases the sorrow of departure that has weighed on him for months. When the worst of it has passed, Eberhard wipes his face with the bottom of his shirt and looks down at the waterfront community, its shanty housing and muddy streets softened by the scrim of horizontal clouds filtering the light from the setting sun. It has been his home since he was five years old.

He picks at a dried patch of mud on the knee of his pants. He is ten years old now. It occurs to him just then that his life has changed in five-year increments. He was nearly five years old when they left Germany, and his memories of his father's family farm and his mother's family home in Augsburg are still vivid. He learned to walk, with the help of his father, across the top of the stone walls that surrounded and bisected the farm. On his own, he crawled up the ladder inside the barn to the loft window to peer at the physical world of his father's and Uncle Ray's childhood. From that height and without his parents' knowledge, he once watched a fight between his father and Uncle Otto. His father, breathing hard and with a bleeding upper lip, was agile and accurate in his jabs. His Uncle Otto was bigger and thicker, with fists like beef joints. But he was slow on his feet, grunting initially against his brother's blows and then braying like a donkey when he was unable to deflect his younger brother's fists.

Then there was the genteel but bustling activity of Augsburg and the luxurious home of his grandparents Richter. The walks to the various parks, pushed first in a pram by his grandmother and aunts, and later running ahead of them to the man who sold flavored ices and had a monkey on a leash. He could still recall the smell of sweet pipe tobacco on his Grandfather Richter's breath, and the wonders of his study including the large world globe atop a carved wooden stand. His grandfather took one of Eberhard's hands and, guiding his pointing finger, spun the globe slowly to reveal a round earth full of oceans and continents.

"There are other people and other countries," his grandfather said. "And maybe someday you'll have the chance to visit them all."

He remembers the excitement at crossing one of those oceans and feeling the spray of its waters. Of the dark man, Tempy—he would never forget his name—with three fingers missing on one hand, who showed them the engines that drove the ship through such a vast body of water, who gave him and Frank hard candy, who warned them about the River God. He remembers the long train ride that kept them riveted to the cabin window until they fell asleep, only to wake up hours later and repeat the cycle.

And then they were on the Flats with Uncle Ray and their parents. He and Frank faced the big river, remembering Tempy's words not to swim in the water. But the river brought forth wonders from its waters such as fish, wood, and even fruit. They skated with apprehension on its surface in the winter, looking down at times to see if the River God was watching them from beneath the ice. If they were thirsty, they did not have to walk home but could stop by a neighbor's house and ask for a glass of milk or water, or if hungry, a bowl of soup with bread. When they trailed the coal wagon with burlap bags, they collected as much coal as possible, delivering what they didn't need at home to their neighbors. He remembers the delirium of being sick, of thinking he was going to die. He dreams of his sister. It still frightens him. She was born and then suddenly died. His mother and father do not talk about the baby who died. But he secretly talks to her, his sister who would have been nearly five now, and to Grandma Beta as he and Frank called the old woman they'd only known for seven months.

Now they are to leave here too. It is not a surprise. He has known since they arrived that his parents were saving money for a farm. When he was six years old, he declared to Kyle Takelo that he would not go when the time came. The Finnish man stopped working the board he was slowly bending into an arc and said, "Don't say that, Eberhard. Your father and mother want to give you a future you would never have had if they had stayed in Germany, or if they stay here. You should be the master of your own destiny. Your father will teach you what it is like to build a farm rather than just inherit one. You will have neighbors just like you do here. Besides, your Uncle Ray is staying here and that means you can come back for visits."

Then Kyle went on to tell him stories of the huge pines he would see in northern Wisconsin, and what he knew about the Indians who lived there.

He stands up, brushes the limestone residue from the seat of his pants. He will give this new place another five years of his life. Then at fifteen, if he doesn't like northern Wisconsin, he will come back to the Flats to live with his Uncle Ray. Come back to this grove of river birches and to the big river.

CHIPPEWA CROSSING

Northern Wisconsin

1905–1912

A BURLY MAN WITH A DIRTY KNIT CAP, tobacco-stained teeth, and a crumb-flecked beard meets them as they step down from the train in Park Falls.

"Are you Roman Zelinski?" Albert asks.

"I am! And you are the Kaufmanns!" he booms. Stench envelops them as he reaches forward to shake Albert's hand. Magdalena nudges the boys. They suck in their breaths and shake the man's hand. Then they step back and stare with squint-eyed fascination at the scarred lid that covers Roman's left eye. The skin is blistered and thick as though it has been fried like an egg.

"You are very kind to meet us. You must have come directly from your job?" she says, hoping he'll catch the meaning of her inquiry.

"Oh yeah. I was afraid I'd miss the train." He steps back from them, removes his cap and twists it in his hands. "Sorry for the stink. Been tanning hides. I can't smell it myself after a while. If you folks don't mind, you can have tea and coffee in the station there," he says, pointing to the building behind them, "and I'll just run up the street and wash myself good at Zoesch's hotel."

Roman returns in an hour, driving a team of horses hitched to a wagon so newly built that pine sap dribbles down its boards. His wet hair is slicked back and he has shaved his beard.

"I got your wagon here," he says, still smelling of hides and hemlock tannin but tolerably so. "I got two men besides me ready to build your cabin. Good men, hard workers. One's an Injun. Do you object to an Injun?"

Albert pauses.

"Indian," Eberhard whispers, knowing his father, like the rest of them, has heard *engine* instead.

"No," Albert answers. "As long as he works hard."

Roman helps them load their belongings into the wagon. Magdalena sits with the boys on a blanket-covered trunk in the back of the wagon. Roman hoists himself up, taking the reins from Albert who sits alongside of him.

"It's a day-long ride to Chippewa Crossing. You'll stay at the hotel in town tonight and tomorrow we'll get your supplies at Fishbach's store before heading out to your place. We'll need to pick up some hoops and canvas to tent the back of the wagon for you to sleep under while we work on the cabin."

THEIR FORTY ACRES has a natural clearing on top of a slope that rolls down to the shore of the Chippewa River. The boys are fascinated by the Indian whose name is unexpectedly European, Jacob Bleu. But they are disappointed that he does not wear what they had envisioned of an Indian: a feather headdress, beaded clothing, moccasins. The other man's name is Eddie Charbonneau. They watch as the men walk the clearing to determine where the well should be dug and then where the cabin is to be built in proximity to the well.

"You'll need a drilling outfit from town," Jacob says, "because of the rock." After that he speaks very little, working in near silence. They begin by felling big pines, red and white, and hewing them into notched timbers.

The cabin and outhouse are done in a month. Albert pays the men to stay on and build a temporary shed for the horses and cow until a proper barn can be built the following summer. They build a chicken coop, and ice house as well. Magdalena cooks meals on a wood stove outside. She glances from time to time at the trees along the river.

"We are being watched," she says, giving Roman a cup of water from the new well. He drinks the water, his lower jaw swollen with a plug of tobacco.

"Probably," he says, wiping his mouth. "Nuthin' to worry about it. It's likely children from Fox Lake—the reservation's about two miles from here." He spits a long stream of brown juice into the grass.

"Does Jacob live at Fox Lake?"

"Nope. He lives by the bottomlands. He's got some French in him, been among white people more. Was sent away to school, if I remember right. His wife is a Métis too. She is a Cadotte from La Pointe, the main town on Madeline Island. Thank God he don't work on Injun time, which'll drive you crazy if you don't get used to it."

"He doesn't talk much."

"True. But he's one of the best damn carpenters I know."

The men work hard and Albert pays them well on their last day. Magdalena asks them to visit when they can, as they will miss their company, rough as it is. After they leave, she walks up to the chicken coop to check on the pullets they had purchased in town a few days before. Jacob is standing a few feet from the door when she steps out of the coop.

"Your husband said you spoke French."

"*Oui. Et vous?*"

"Only a little," he answers. "But my wife does. She is from Madeline Island and misses the language of her childhood. Would you be willing to visit with her, to speak in French? I am usually gone on logging jobs. This was the first job close to home that I've had in a long time."

His request is not that of a humble man or an arrogant one. She sees that he is a proud man in addition to being reserved. The reserve, she senses, is not natural but cultivated to keep people at arm's length.

"I would be happy to visit with your wife."

"If you get a piece of paper, I will draw you a map to our place. It isn't that far once you know how to get there and back. How soon can you come?"

"Friday."

THEY GET A LETTER from Aino and Kyle just a week later. In September, they begin to attend mass on Sundays. They could have tolerated the ignorant and righteous rants from the surly old priest, Monsignor Fitzgerald, as they were limited to one day a week. But they cannot tolerate the caning the boys receive in school for speaking German. They confront the priest after mass one Sunday.

"They do not speak it during class," Albert says. "Only during recess to each other. As do some of the other German children."

"Is that what your sons tell you?" the priest replies, enraging Albert.

"Are you saying our children are liars?"

"Parents don't know their children as well as they think they do. Some children," he comments, looking at Magdalena, "can't help lying. The Jews, for example. It comes natural to them and they must be broken of it."

He draws himself up, gives her a look that usually withers and silences his female parishioners.

"That is blasphemy," she answers. "Jesus Christ was a Jew and so was his mother. I think you are deliberately mistaking freedom of speech with deception."

The monsignor's face turns red. The broken capillaries on his face are illuminated by his mood, appearing like ant trails across his nose and cheeks.

"Do not tell me what is blasphemous!"

"This discussion is clearly pointless," Albert interjects. "We are withdrawing our sons from the school. My wife and I will teach them at home. Good day."

"Then they will be cast into ignorance," the priest shouts as they walk away. Magdalena turns around.

"I doubt that very much. It is you who is ignorant. *Damnant quodnon intelligent.*"

The old priest stares at her. She reads his thoughts as though he has spoken. *The Jew speaks Latin.* He makes the sign of the cross with a shaking hand.

THEY ARE RELIEVED in having their Sundays free. Every waking moment is spent clearing the remainder of their acreage and preparing for the coming winter, except for the one day a week when Magdalena rides over to see Marie Bleu who is much less taciturn than her husband but speaks a pidgin French.

"*Vous êtes français aussi?*—Are you French?" Marie asked on the first visit. It was not an inquiry of suspicion, of judgment, or of underlying motives. It was a question of recognition, of wishing to establish a common bond. Marie Bleu's ancestry announces itself pentimento-like in her features, the native blood inheritance more pronounced in the color of her skin while the French is more evident in her fine bones. *Yes*, Magdalena wanted to answer with the simplicity of one origin, *I am French.*

"*Ah non. Ma mère était roumaine et mon père allemand*—Oh no. My mother is Romanian and my father is German," she answered, pleased to be able to speak the truth and not fear any connotations. But Marie's New World French is difficult to understand at times. It takes Magdalena three visits to grasp the pidgin expressions.

They purchase the state paper, the *Milwaukee Journal*, on their visits into town to pick up mail and things at the store, but they rarely have time to read it. Their news of the world, personal and public, comes through the mail from Raymond or Magdalena's parents. Her mother writes that two of Magdalena's younger sisters have been accepted to the University of Tübingen and will begin their studies in the fall. In July, her father writes of the forced resignation of the French Foreign Minister Delcassé by Kaiser Wilhelm. They learn from Raymond of the Portsmouth Treaty, bringing an end to the Russian–Japanese War. They already knew about Bloody Sunday—the January revolt by Russian workers in 1905 and its lethal consequences. They learn of the second uprising by Russian workers in St. Petersburg in a letter from her father in early November.

"Marx predicted such a revolution," he wrote, "and said that it would come from within Russia. This is only the beginning."

Two days after that letter, Magdalena receives one from her mother, meant only for her.

We learned from Ernst that Otto knows that Raimund—and he thinks you and Albert—lives in Minneapolis. I doubt he can do much with the information but it disturbed us nonetheless. It is his obsessiveness and hatred that bothers us. I have told Sister Hildegard. She can't do anything about Otto but she keeps aware of his doings in Augsburg. It is amazing what she hears and knows. The Kloster is not so closed after all. We are relieved that you are in northern Wisconsin but I worry about Raimund.

She folds the letter and puts it into her skirt pocket. She

wonders why Otto thinks gaining information about them is so important. There is nothing he can do short of leaving Germany to look for them, and that is something he would never do. Surely her mother must know that and yet she is worried about Raymond. Magdalena doubts that Otto has friends in the United States, given his feelings about Germans who leave the Fatherland. Even if he had, no one will take the time to seek out Raymond. And if they did, they would not go unnoticed on the Flats.

IN EARLY DECEMBER, a letter comes from her sister, Rose. She has fallen in love with a fellow student named David Katz, and barring complications between their two respective faiths she hopes to marry in the spring of '07.

Then one morning in the middle of December, Magdalena wakes to find she cannot tolerate even a light cotton chemise against her nipples, and after a few moments realizes that she has not menstruated in three months. She counts back. The baby will arrive in late May or early June. Albert is overjoyed.

"It will be different this time," he says.

"We don't have an Alzbêta or an Aino here," she says, pinning up her hair. "I've not heard good things about the doctor in town. He also delivers calves and foals and apparently he doesn't do that well either. So you will have to help me when the time comes."

The next morning she rouses herself to ride over and visit Marie. She knocks on the door and when it opens, Marie's face is flushed and Magdalena catches a whiff of vomit.

"*Êtes-vous malade?*—Are you sick?"

"*Oui et non*," she replies, weakly smiling. "*Je n'ai pas eu mes règles depuis un mois. Je crois que je suis enciente*—Yes and no. My blood has not come for a month. I think I am pregnant."

Two days later while Magdalena is shopping at Fishbach's store, Alexandra Fishbach gestures her to the back of the store.

"I prayed and prayed for a baby," Alexandra whispers, "and now God has granted me one."

Magdalena is astonished by Alexandra's sudden confiding intimacy. Righteous and arrogant, Alexandra has shown little desire to get to know Magdalena before this moment.

"Do you think it will go all right?" she asks. "My husband so wants a boy but I want a girl. What do you think it will be?"

Magdalena's astonishment turns to anger. It is evident that Monsignor Fitzgerald has voiced his opinion of her background and ventured that she could be gypsy as well as Jewish. But it is clear that Alexandra, devout as she may be, suddenly regards Magdalena's supposed gypsy ancestry as a positive.

"I don't know. I don't think any woman knows how her pregnancy will go," Magdalena answers and then quickly adds, "But I'm sure it will be fine. As to a boy or girl, it will be God's grace just to have a healthy child."

Before she can write to Aino, Magdalena gets a letter from her. Aino is pregnant as well. Their five-year-old son is thrilled and so is Kyle. She hopes for a daughter.

"How is it possible that we can all be pregnant at the same time?" she wonders aloud to Albert. "It feels eerie."

"I would say it feels magical," Albert says, "and a sign of good things to come."

Although mystified by it all, she is nonetheless grateful to have Aino and Marie share the experience with her. It makes her feel less alone, less apprehensive about her own pregnancy. She writes back to Aino immediately. *You told me the clean northern air would do me good*, she writes, *and it appears you were right.*

THE EYES STILL WATCH from the tree line by the river. She hikes through the snow three days before Christmas with a basket of eggs. They had purchased more pullets than they needed, knowing from experience that some of them would die before they feathered out. To their surprise, only three chicks died and now they have a surplus of eggs. She turns and walks sideways down the slope, getting as close to the river as she thinks safe, and nestles the basket in the snow.

"Fresh eggs," she calls and then repeats, "*Oeufs frais.*" She hears movement in the trees, then a whisper, a giggle. She trudges back, hoping they will leave the basket when they take the eggs.

The basket is on the doorstep the next morning. Roman comes out later in the day to wish them a Merry Christmas.

"Probably kids. Could be Zeke Smith taking the eggs. He's not well," Roman said, tapping his head, "but he don't hurt nobody." He glances at the basket on the kitchen table. "Basket came back, eh? Was Fox Lake people then. They musta liked the eggs. They want more."

THE FOX LAKE PEOPLE thought it was over, the removal of children from the reservation, sent away to boarding schools. The last time had been fifteen years ago when the Board of Education took three boys with the promise that they would come back with skills to help the tribe.

"For their own good," a Wisconsin State Education official had said.

The officials stood up in the wagon then, too, as though to step down onto the ground might reduce their perspective on the matter. The boys were sent to the Carlisle Indian Industrial School in Pennsylvania. One of them, a Two Knives, never came back and no one knew where he was or if he was alive. The second one came back with the Christian first name of Ezekial and last name of Smith. White people from Chippewa Crossing said Zeke Smith was not right in the head. The Fox Lake people shook their head at his new name, stumbled over the hard z in its pronunciation. They pronounced the shortened version of his name as "seek," and said his spirit had been cut and divided, some of the pieces gone forever and the rest scattered with edges that didn't match inside of him. Zeke did odd jobs when he wasn't drinking, wandered on and off the reservation, and frequently spent nights in the town jail. The third one came back as well, silent about his experience, touchy and ill at ease but able to cope. He was given a Christian first name as well. Jacob. They did not change his last name, Bleu, because it was an acceptable American name.

The sheriff had ridden out in a wagon with two Wisconsin State Education officials a year earlier to inform the reservation elders of the federal law that required their children to be sent away to school for their own good. The Fox Lake people, knowing the flip side to that good, decided otherwise. This time the sheriff stepped down from the wagon and lit a cigar. Ilmarinen Stone, son of a Finnish mother and a Ojibwe father, tried to negotiate. He pointed out that his mother taught the Fox Lake children to speak, read, and write English, and they were therefore schooled.

"There is more to school than that. She is not a certified teacher," one of the officials said. He pronounced teacher as "tea-cha." He moved like and resembled a horsetail reed, his tall and thin body put together in segments with skin the texture of sandpaper. He stared down at Ilmarinen. "Are you what they call a half-breed?"

"What school would you send them to?" Ilmarinen asked, ignoring the man's question.

"The industrial school at Lac du Flambeau," the sheriff answered. He tapped his cigar to shake off its rim of ashes. "It's on a Chippewa reservation, same as you all."

"We'll be back in four days to pick up the children," the tall man said, sitting down on the wagon seat. They watched as the sheriff climbed into the driver's seat, slapped the reins, and steered the horses back in the direction of town. Joe-John Two Knives, father of the son who had never returned, spoke first.

"Lac du Flambeau is not Fox Lake," he said. "I've heard of that school. The parents aren't allowed to see their children except on Fridays even though the building is on the reservation."

He turned to look at his wife. Every fall she burned dried cedar in remembrance of their youngest son. Her hands rest on the shoulders of their grandson, Mika. She shakes her head.

"No," he said. "They are not taking the children."

The men rotated in groups of posted sentries on the reservation boundaries and near the roads and passable entries to watch for the sheriff or any other person who looked suspicious. The officials came back four days later. Ilmarinen's father saw the wagon first. He began whistling a series of melodic notes, imitating a hermit thrush. This alerted the young boys waiting farther inside the boundaries who then ran to each household. The children were carried or bounded alongside their mothers who took them deeper into the reservation's interior.

Their strategy worked for a year with the help of a snowy winter, but collectively they knew they could not elude the authorities much longer. They were desperate. The nightmare came back and promised an apocalyptic vision into the future.

ILMARINEN STOPS to let his mare drink before crossing the shallow part of the upper Chippewa that the whites call Shell Lake. It is where his people spear walleye and northern pike in the spring, after driving them up from the deeper end of the river with torches to light the surface of the water. Sated, the horse tosses her head and he prods her across and heads west along the river until he reaches a small clearing near the bottomlands.

Jacob is sitting outside on a woodpile, smoking a cigarette. Ilmarinen notices the whiskey bottle near the axe before dismounting. He ties his horse to the fence post near the kitchen door of the house, an L-shaped clapboard building that Jacob had built.

"You've caused me trouble, building such a nice house," he jokes, handing his cousin a twenty-pound sack of smoked venison. "My wife wants one like it."

"Learned it in school," Jacob answers. They hear a paroxysm of coughing from inside the house. It stops briefly and then starts again.

"My wife," he says. The coughing stops again. The two men remain silent, anticipating another bout but it does not come.

"You know what is going on at Fox Lake?" Ilmarinen asks.

"I do."

"Is there anything you can tell me . . ." He pauses awkwardly. "Is there something you know, from what you have been through, that might help us?"

Jacob drops his cigarette, grinds out the burning remains with the heel of his boot. Ilmarinen smells the whiskey on him.

"Upriver on that slope where we used to grouse hunt lives a German couple. Magdalena and Albert Kaufmann. They came here a year ago to farm forty acres. I built their cabin with Zelinski and Charbonneau. They took their boys out of the Catholic school last fall because they were punished for speaking their own language. Magdalena," he adds, flashing a rare but brief smile, "is not afraid of the priest."

He takes another cigarette from his shirt pocket and lights it.

"The woman who leaves the eggs?" Ilmarinen asks.

"Yes. She gives us eggs, too," he answers, pausing to remove a flake of tobacco from his tongue.

"They are not like so many of the others who come here. They are well educated and speak English," he continues, exhaling smoke. "The wife—Magdalena—also speaks French. She comes over here to visit Marie."

It is the most he has heard his cousin talk since he returned home from the boarding school. On the day they went grouse hunting, Ilmarinen spoke to Jacob in their native language until he realized Jacob's silence meant that his cousin could not remember the language and was ashamed. Jacob had picked some up some Chippewa since, but not much else has changed about him. He keeps his hair short. He does not eat the maple sugar candy they make every spring, preferring the licorice that he buys in Chippewa Crossing. He works for the Krueger Lumber Company—the same company that continually tried to advance onto the reservation to strip it of its timber. Jacob works as a cutter and is gone for weeks at a time. Although he does participate in the harvest of wild rice and occasionally joins his relatives in hunting and fishing, he remains distant and wary. At first they had taken offense when he returned to the area with his wife, but since then they realized he is the same with white people.

"Can they help us?"

"In what way?"

"To talk to the officials," Ilmarinen replies, feeling doubtful. His mother is white and they didn't listen to her.

"Maybe. They might know of a way." He draws a lungful of smoke. "She is different."

"Different how?"

Jacob exhales smoke and makes a circle around his face with one hand.

"What does that mean?" Ilmarinen asks, irritated by his cousin's obscure reference.

"You'll see."

ALBERT AND THE BOYS are in the field nearest the river. Earlier that morning, their father explained to Eberhard and Frank why he refused to clear the land down to the shoreline of the river as their neighbor did.

"You need something to stop the soil from being swept into the river during heavy rains or during spring melt," he said, throwing a rock to the edge of the field. They have been fortunate in their forty-acre parcel in that it contains more alluvial soil and less of the type from glacial moraine that their surrounding neighbors had to contend with.

Frank leads the Belgian mare while their father works the steel-beam walking plow. Eberhard follows them, picking up and throwing rocks to the side. All three smell from a mixture of sweat and the sulfur-smelling concoction purchased in town that is supposed to repel the clouds of gnats, black flies, and mosquitoes. Frank is wiping gnats from the horse's nostrils when he sees an Indian man with a dove-brown braid emerge from the birches near the riverbank. He is leading a horse and carrying a rifle in one hand.

Frank jerks on the halter. His father, so into the momentum of synchronized movement, trips over the plow and lands on his knees.

"Why—," he begins and then looks in the direction of his son's nod. He stands up and brushes the dirt off his pants. Eberhard walks up until he is standing beside his father.

"Do you know him?" Eberhard asks.

"No. Stay here."

Their father loops the reins around the plow handles, takes off his gloves and gives them to Eberhard. Then he walks casually down the slope. The boys stand in the field with the horse, straining to catch the conversation. Finally their father turns and shouts, "Frank! Unhitch the horse and take her up to the barn. Eberhard, tell your mother we have company for lunch."

Eberhard runs to the doorway of the cabin. Before he can call out, he sees a fifth place-setting on the table.

After stalling the horse, the boys strip off their clothes, taking turns pouring a bucket of water over each other. They dry off with a towel their mother has placed on the porch next to clean clothes.

Frank stays outside, lying on his back in the grass, but Eberhard watches his father and the man from inside the doorway of their cabin. It takes them awhile. They walk, then stop, talk and then begin walking again, only to stop and talk some more.

"How did you know we would have company?" he asks his mother whose belly causes her to stand sideways so that she can maneuver the frying pan.

"It is a nice day. People are bound to be out and about. Why," she turns and smiles, "did you catch so many fish last night?"

He and Frank caught ten large northern pike. After scaling, gutting, and filleting them, the boys wrapped the fish in waxed paper and put the parcels in the icehouse. His mother had taken them out when she got up that morning. She dusts the fillets with flour, wraps them in bacon, and fries them in butter with tarragon she grows in a pot on the south-facing window. There are bowls of fresh peas and sauerkraut. On the sideboard are loaves of rye and potato bread and two pans of kuchen with custard and choke-cherry preserves. She wipes her hands on her apron before joining him at the door.

"He's Indian," Eberhard says. His mother studies the two men approaching the house, one hand on her belly and the other supporting her lower back.

"Not all Indian," she answers. When his father and the stranger enter the house, Eberhard sees that his mother is right. The man has gray eyes. His father introduces the visitor.

"Ilmarinen? You are Finnish?" his mother asks.

"Yes. Half. My mother is Finnish," he answers.

"Ilmarinen is the name of the blacksmith who made the magic Sampo," Frank says, coming in the door.

"You know the Kalevala?"

"We do," his mother answers. "We had friends when we lived in Minneapolis who were Finnish. Aino and Kyle Takelo."

"You know the story of Aino?" Ilmarinen asks the boys.

"The girl who turns into a fish," Eberhard answers, "so she doesn't have to marry the old god Väinämöinen."

They sit down and eat lunch, the boys listening while the adults talk. When lunch is finished, their father tells the boys to go outside.

Eberhard and Frank walk down the porch steps and off to the side of the cabin. Then they run around the back, hoist themselves up on the porch floor, and crawl until they are under the window nearest the table. The adults are so engrossed in talking that they do not notice the boys peeking over the edge of the windowsill.

"THE CHIPPEWA have never made war on the U.S. government," Ilmarinen says, "although my great, great grandfather was one of the Chippewa warriors that joined Tecumseh's army to fight the British."

He tells them that the Chippewas' overall strength lies in passive resistance. Every time they were removed, the people wandered back until the state gave up and established reservation land in northern Wisconsin. The Fox Lake people had hoped it would work this time, keeping the children away long enough for the state to give up. He tells them about Joe-John Two Knives's son. About Ezekial Smith who cannot remember his birth name, Ka-ka-ke Stone, who does not answer to it, who wanders, who watches. About Jacob, whom they know.

He tells them their opposition is wearing thin.

"Jacob says you took your sons out of school because they were punished for speaking your language."

"We did," Albert answers. "But we just learned that the old priest and mother superior are retiring and leaving in a month. They will return to the Archdiocese in Milwaukee. A new priest and mother superior will be arriving two weeks after that. We have heard that the new priest is young and has an advanced education. We are hoping he will be more tolerant."

"So you will put them back in that school?"

"Only if they agree to what we ask," Magdalena replies. "We understand that this is an English-speaking country and we have never fought that. We want our sons to speak as many languages as possible. We will agree that the boys will not speak German during class but that they should not be punished for speaking it to each other during recess or lunch."

She hesitates to give advice, still new to the politics of the town.

"Have you considered having the Fox Lake children attend the school in town? That way they could still live at home."

Ilmarinen recalls visiting the school. He and his wife had gone with the rest of the Fox Lake people when the old priest and mother superior had invited them to attend the church once. The Fox Lake people found the name of the church and school strange—*Our Lady of Perpetual Sorrow*—and after seeing a man nailed to a cross-hatch of logs inside, concluded that the Catholics were obsessed with sorrow, death, and punishment.

"We have thought about that," he answers. "But we fear they will take the children as well. The Catholics have their own schools." He paused. "We have our own school. My mother taught me to speak, read, and write in English. But they will not accept her as being a teacher even though she is white."

"How can we help?" Albert asks.

There is a sudden thud on the roof, wild laughter from outside. Excusing himself, Albert leaves the cabin to find out what the boys are doing.

Magdalena shifts in her chair. Albert's question hangs between them. He wants more from her, a solution that is more appealing. But she doesn't know him or his culture. Still there is the sobering evidence of what happened before. The desolate figure of Zeke Smith wandering through town, drunk. And Jacob, his reserve now explained.

"If we can exact a promise from the new priest that the children will not be taken away, that they will go to school and come home every day like the other children, will that be acceptable?"

"None of their promises are real," he says. "To you maybe, but not to us. Even if the new priest agrees to let us keep our children, we will still have to obey the rules of—"

"Catholicism," she finishes. "That is true. It is a Catholic school. The children will go to mass every morning. They will be baptized and asked to renounce their own beliefs when they take First Communion. I too went to a Catholic school but my parents had other beliefs. I—we also have our own beliefs although we are still Catholic. It is not an easy way to live but that is what we have chosen."

ILMARINEN WANTS TO KNOW what those other beliefs are but feels it rude to ask. He understands his cousin's reference to her. All of them are tan from the sun but the husband and younger son are still visibly white with light-brown hair and blue eyes. The oldest boy, like his mother, has crow-black hair and eyes, and skin that is naturally brown. He remembers that Jacob said she spoke French. He wonders if she is Métis instead of German, and where her people are.

"You must have some understanding of what it is like to live between two cultures?" she says, startling him.

He nods. He thinks of what he is called when he is traveling outside the reservation. Finndian, half-breed, and a more polite word, Métis. Yet he is regarded with more credibility than others in his tribe, and hence he is the one sent forth to negotiate business in town and to speak on the tribe's behalf. He knows where his mother is from, knows the stories of her culture, and understands the basic tenants of Christianity because of her Lutheran upbringing, which she has since abandoned. She was the one who had explained to him the significance of the man nailed to the cross.

Magdalena leans forward.

"It is not the best solution but it is the only solution as far as I can see. They will eventually have to live with two cultures, as I am sure you know. But if the children get sent away to a boarding school, you will lose them. They may never come back. Of this I am sure. Teach the children to pretend during the day at school. Being home at night will help them stay grounded with your beliefs."

Ilmarinen realizes that his cousin's reference to her is more than the way she looks. *As far as I can see.* Then she winces and grips the edge of the table, sweat beading her forehead. Ilmarinen stands up, embarrassed that he did not see her discomfort before.

"Your baby is coming," he says, rounding the table to help her to her feet. "I will get my mother. She takes care of all the women at Fox Lake. Will you be all right for the next hour or so?"

"Yes. The boys didn't arrive very fast and this one won't either."

She insists on wrapping a loaf of rye bread and pan of kuchen to send with him.

ILMARINEN SPURS HIS HORSE into a gallop. Eberhard visually
follows him down the slope until he enters the tree line. He hears
his mother's voice, turns and sees that she is on the porch with his
father and brother.

"I'll be fine," she says. She takes their father's arm and stiffly
walks down the front steps. "Just help me walk around. It feels better to walk outside. What else did Ilmarinen say?"

"He told me how to make something better to keep the flies and
mosquitoes away. It will work on the horse, too," their father answers, supporting the weight of their mother as she leans into him.
"In a few days we'll go into the woods with buckets and knives and
score the pine trunks and let the sap drip into the buckets.

"The sap will stick. We'll never get it off," Eberhard says.

"The secret is to boil it with bear fat. We don't have that but we
do have venison lard in the icehouse. He said that would work until this fall. Then he will take us bear hunting."

SHE IS WRONG about the pace of the labor. The contractions rip-
ple across her middle as though the child is running its fist against
the wall of its housing, anxious to be born. But after an hour the
contractions slow to a more normal pace. Albert wipes a cold cloth
across her face and neck, unbuttons the top of her chemise. He
pours a glass of water from the pitcher on the bed stand. The cabin
door opens and she hears her sons' voices. Then a small woman
walks into the bedroom, wearing an ordinary shirtwaist and skirt.
Albert stands up, whispers to the woman before leaving. He comes
back only to bring a basin of water, soap, and a towel before leaving again.

"My name is Marjaana."

Magdalena recognizes the lilting sound of Finnish-accented
English. She searches the woman's face for ethnic familiarity. Marjaana's face is broad and flat but with the same high Nordic cheekbones as Aino, and gray eyes with an epicanthic fold of skin. Her
thick, gray-flecked brown braids are pinned into a coronet on her
head. She puts both hands on Magdalena's belly, moving them to
ascertain the baby's position.

"A few more hours. When did the contractions begin?"

She tells her that they came on suddenly, that for an hour they were so painful and urgent as to be frightening. Marjaana gestures for Magdalena to pull her knees up and then washes her hands. She lifts the chemise and gently inserts two fingers.

"It is a large baby and it might come sooner. But all is fine," she says, returning to the basin to wash her hands. She opens the bedroom door just enough to tell Albert to boil at least two large pots of water. Then Marjaana pulls up a chair and sits, occasionally leaning over to wipe Magdalena's face, to give her a sip of water. She asks about Albert, the boys, where they lived before, and before that. At first Magdalena thinks the older woman invasive but realizes that she is trying to keep her from dwelling on the pain. It gives Magdalena leave to ask questions back, questions she could not ask Ilmarinen.

She learns that Marjaana came over with her parents when she was eight, first settling in the Upper Peninsula of Michigan where her father worked in the copper mines. They moved to Chippewa Crossing when she was fifteen, her father having saved up enough money to buy a homestead adjacent to Fox Lake. Her mother died of pneumonia when Marjaana was seventeen. Her father died two years after that when a white pine he had been cutting fell the wrong way and crushed him.

"Did you farm the place by yourself then?" Magdalena asks, gasping as another wave of contraction overtakes her.

"No. I married Ilmarinen's father."

"How—" She cannot finish her question, the contraction visibly rolling across her belly. She shuts her eyes against it.

"The usual way."

Magdalena opens her eyes. Marjaana grins.

"It is a legitimate question. A white man can still marry an Indian woman by having her simply move into his house, although that is changing, too. But not then, not for a white woman. He had been courting me—without my father's knowledge—a few months before my father was killed. The Lutheran minister at that time wouldn't marry us unless my husband converted. I wouldn't have cared about being married in the church except to honor my mother—my father was not much of a church-goer. But there were other reasons. I had to get officially married to keep the homestead, and I had to face the reality that I would not be accepted in town if we married in the Indian way. So my husband went through the motions because we would also be married by Fox Lake customs."

She sighs.

"The minister baptized him and named him *Luther*. But we insisted on his Indian name for our last name. In Chippewa it is Keesh-key-mun, which means Sharpened Stone. But on our marriage certificate it just says 'Stone.' We decided not to fight anymore battles and left it at that."

"So you and your husband are Lutheran?"

"Not anymore. But there isn't anything they can do about it now."

"Do they accept you in town? I have not seen you there, although we are not in town much, only once a week."

"Not really. But Chippewa Crossing didn't have a doctor for a long time and now it has a terrible doctor. So I am called for when one of the town's women goes into labor or someone is sick. Otherwise my life is out here at Fox Lake. Did you know Ilmarinen and his wife just had a boy a week ago? I delivered my own grandchild!"

They spend the night talking intermittently. About four o'clock in the morning, the contractions come fast and hard. Marjaana pushes the chair away and places a basin on the floor.

"I'm going to grab your arms and when the next pain eases up, I want you to turn and sit up so that you are on the edge of the bed."

Magdalena pushes hard for half an hour. Finally the head crowns and the rest of the infant slides into the older woman's hands.

"A girl. A big girl."

She places the infant belly down on her knees and pats her back until the child cries. Then she cuts and ties off the umbilical cord. Magdalena remains upright, waiting for the placenta to pass into the basin below. It drops like a cow pat, thick and bloody into the white enamel of the basin. She weakly swings her legs up on the bed and lies back against the pillows. Ilmarinen's mother washes the baby from the new basin of water that Albert has brought in. She wraps a blanket loosely around the infant before giving her to Magdalena to breastfeed. Then she attends to Magdalena, washing her and pushing a wad of thick cloth between her legs. She sits down. They watch the baby suck. Marjaana leans over, draws back a corner of the blanket hiding the baby's face.

"What an old face. Fierce." She sees the dismay on Magdalena's face. "Ah. That could change though."

Magdalena looks down at the nursing infant who has hair so fair that she appears bald. The child looks nothing like her or even Albert. She does not resemble her brothers at birth either. At that moment the baby releases the nipple, her mouth settling into a haunting and familiar grimace.

"Do you have name for her?"

She and Albert had talked about several names with Albert torn between his mother's given name of Annaliese and her religious name. *Hildegard*, she decides. She will give the baby the religious name of her mother-in-law as a first name to serve as a bulwark against the child's eerie resemblance to Heinrich Kaufmann. Then her own mother's name, *Adelinde*, as the middle name and second line of defense. She explains the histories of the names.

"Let's hope she will earn those names," Marjaana comments. "I'll be back in a day or so to see how you and the baby are doing."

"Thank you. I thought I would have to do this alone. Albert will pay you."

"No," she says. "We will take it out in trade."

"You don't want money?"

She laughs. "I take money from the women in town but for the women out here, it is in trade. You have this high ground, good for growing vegetables that won't thrive at Fox Lake. And eggs, milk, and butter."

She listens as Marjaana and Ilmarinen say their goodbyes to Albert and the boys. She looks down at the sleeping infant, notes the unyielding line of her lips. Albert will not wait this time. He will want the baby baptized that Sunday, which means enduring the righteous, clawed hand of Monsignor Fitzgerald.

TWO WEEKS after she gives birth, Magdalena drives the buggy into town to see the old priest off at the newly established train depot in town. It is mostly the women and younger children of the town in attendance as the men and older children are at work. Most of the women are sorry to see the priest leave, their eyes moist with tears instead of sweat from the stifling heat. Magdalena holds her fussing daughter and wonders if the women could articulate, if asked, what they will miss about the priest. They do not realize that it is the loss of familiarity, even a disagreeable familiarity, that makes them sad and not because they had true feelings for the old priest. Magdalena looks around to see if any of her rural female neighbors are there and they are not. She wipes her forehead with her free hand and considers the weather appropriate for Fitzgerald's departure. She has sacrificed a day of farm work to witness the leaving of the rigid and querulous old Irishman who had snidely said, after the baptism, "She doesn't look like either of you. Must be a changeling."

"Must be," Magdalena answered, smiling wickedly at the priest.

A WEEK LATER Magdalena is back at the depot, where it is cloudy and cooler than before. Albert and the boys come along this time as does Ilmarinen. Again, the waiting crowd is mostly the female members of the parish from town. They watch the train enter the depot; listen to the crow from its whistle when it comes to a complete stop. People begin to descend from the Pullman cars. A man of about twenty-five years of age steps down from the first car, and had he not been wearing a black cassock would not have been identified as the new priest. Alexandra Fishbach, wife of the owner of the grocery and dry goods store in town, raises a gloved hand to her mouth.

"My God," she says. Magdalena hears her and steps to the side of the crowd for a better look. *My God*, she echoes silently. He is of medium height, has a head of black curls, a pronounced cleft in his chin, and jaws that bear a five o'clock shadow. The cassock emphasizes broad shoulders, hints at a slim waist. But it is his eyes, cerulean blue, that hush the female crowd. Then he smiles and says, "Hello. I'm Father Boland, your new priest."

There is a collective gasp. Not only is it the cerulean blue eyes but a deep voice with a light Irish brogue, unlike Monsignor Fitzgerald, who was born in Philadelphia. The women lean against one another and stare. Ilmarinen moves past all of them, past the women too stunned to feel aghast at who he is or his rudeness. He holds out his hand and Father Boland shakes it. Albert gives the baby to Magdalena and pushes his family forward to meet the priest. Father Boland greets them and then looks up at the sky.

"The Lake Superior effect. Cool air from the Arctic," he says. "Was it hot here last week?"

"Hotter than hell!" Frank answers. Magdalena and Albert are mortified but Father Boland and Ilmarinen laugh. Alexandra Fishbach clears her throat in disgust.

"Yes, when you have heat with humidity, that is what it feels like," Father Boland says to Frank.

The priest graciously turns to the rest of the crowd and asks them to meet him at the rectory in the evening where there will be food and refreshments. He then gestures to Albert, Ilmarinen, and the boys to follow him back to the Pullman car where his luggage is being unloaded onto a handcart. Magdalena walks after them, curious to see how much the priest has brought with him. He takes a long tube from the porter and asks Ilmarinen to carry it.

"My fishing rods," he says. "Bamboo."

Then the porter hands him what is unmistakably an expensive gun case and he gives that to Albert. Magdalena leans over to look at the insignia on the leather case.

"A Purdey," Albert says. "Very nice. You hunt?"

"I do. That was my father's shotgun," he replies. "I like to hunt grouse, quail, duck, woodcock, and pheasant."

Albert considers the gun case in his hands. Magdalena knows what he is thinking. Upland game hunting is the sport of the aristocracy, not for people who traditionally survived on meat or, like themselves, supplemented the dinner table during a bad year of farming.

"No pheasant here," Albert comments, "but plenty of grouse, duck, and goose."

"We hunt deer and bear, too," Ilmarinen adds. Father Boland briefly considers the information.

"I'd like to learn how to hunt deer and bear," he answers. He looks at his gun case. "I guess I'll be needing a rifle for that."

"You will," Ilmarinen says.

UNLIKE HIS PREDECESSOR, Father Boland is affable and quick to laugh. He enjoys the out of doors and prefers whiskey to wine when not performing mass. They feared that his youth as well as being a Jesuit would also make him a zealot, and they are pleased to find out that he is progressive. Still they remain cautious of his intentions, knowing that he cannot stray too far from the Church's doctrine.

"I don't agree with the practice of removing native children from their homes," he says when they meet with him in the rectory a few days later. "Of children from any culture. But before I say any more, I must examine the judicial language before I meet with the state officials. If I'm right, they cannot enforce the law if there is a viable school nearby. Unfortunately," he says, pausing to refill their coffee cups, "parochial schools are often not considered viable to laws that are Protestant in their origin."

Magdalena glances at Ilmarinen, who is skeptical. The priest bends forward in his chair to address him.

"I'm told your mother is Finnish and that she educated you."

"That is so."

"I do understand a little of your dilemma. I grew up being forbidden to speak Gaelic, the language of the Irish. We could not speak it in school and in public. I was sent to a boarding school in Dublin. I didn't like it but at least my own people, my own culture, and my own religion surrounded me. Had I been forced to go to school in England, I'm not sure I would have survived. Most of my family died in the potato famine or fighting against English rule."

"So Ireland is like my mother's country?" Ilmarinen says.

"Yes! The two countries have a parallel history in many ways," the priest answers, astonished at Ilmarinen's quick grasp. "Finland has been fighting for independence from Sweden for decades and has a history of suffering through extreme famines. I noticed before I left Chicago that the number of Finlanders emigrating to the United States is rising and that this area has a substantial population of Finnish people."

He stops, sips his coffee.

"I understand your mistrust. I won't pretend to know your culture but I look forward to learning more about it. I won't lie to you. If the Fox Lake children go to school here, they will be taught Catholicism. I cannot disobey the Church in regards to that. But I think we can come to some middle ground of understanding. If we win this battle with the state, it will allow the children to remain at home, which is the most important thing."

THE STATE CAPITULATES to the priest's crusade and so the Fox Lake children begin attending the Catholic school in town. Chaffed with the rigidity of rules and at being confined for seven hours each day, the Fox Lake children dub the school Our *Lake* of Perpetual Sorrow, which Magdalena finds amusing. Father Boland, though, finds it worrisome, as he has inherited some nuns whose methods and loyalty are to Monsignor Fitzgerald. Still, as the year goes on, by not being righteous he gains the trust of those stung by religion, but scandalizes the pious who think his activities improper. He wears a cassock when visiting housebound or sick parishioners in town. When he rides out to see the rural members of the Church, he wears a work shirt, trousers, boots, and thick gloves. If the weather is cold, he also wears a fur-lined cap, heavy wool coat, and scarf. He hears confessions and gives communion if those rites are requested. He dons rubber boots and, wearing only the upper half of his vestments, blesses the fields in the spring, walking across plowed land swinging a thurible of incense while a designated boy dips his hand into a bowl of holy water and flings it to the right and left. Then the priest returns to the homes of the farmers who need the most help on that particular day and takes off his vestments to assist with all manner of chores: plowing and seeding fields, milking cows, collecting eggs, churning butter. He is invited to Fox Lake to participate in the early fall ricing and in the spring to the run of maple sap and the syruping that follows.

Although the priest finds all of the reservation fascinating, he is enthralled by Joe-John Two Knives's cousin, Henry Two Knives, by his stories and his knowledge, by the mere fact of his existence. The first time they met, Father Boland flinched at Henry's disfigurement, recognizing the scars of smallpox. The older man acknowledged the priest's reaction.

"I was young, about five years old when I caught it," Henry said. "As bad as it may look, I am fortunate that it didn't blind me. But it killed my parents and my older sister."

The disease left the skin on Henry's body and face pebbled and pitted as though his body had boiled internally, the furious bubbling rising to the surface and hardening there into a brown shell.

The priest, too, like many European children, had been entranced by the stories of Karl May concerning American Indians. Embarrassed by his boyhood notions of Indians and the obvious inaccuracies of May, Father Boland discovers that Henry is no tintype medicine man, no poetic rendition of a Longfellow sage or chief. He is not a medicine man at all, although he participates in the Midewiwin ceremonies and the Dream Dance. Henry is moody, sometimes gregarious, and sometimes belligerent.

"He was wild when he was younger," Ilmarinen tells him. "Drank and got into fights. Didn't support his family. Then my father persuaded him to stop drinking. He worked for one of the lumber companies for a couple of years to support his family. But he hated it and gave it up."

Father Boland is careful with his questions, having been told by Magdalena that Henry suffers fools not at all, having been in his youth one of the biggest fools on the reservation. It is then the priest realizes that although Henry's stories are surreal and symbolic, his wisdom is that of any man who has made an ass of himself for years, and learned from it.

It is not just the content of Henry's stories that fascinates Father Boland but Henry's way of telling them. His English is magnificent. He learns from Marjaana that after Henry quit drinking, he taught himself to speak and read English from a primary and secondary school reader packed in a box of donations to Fox Lake. He then bought a large Merriam-Webster dictionary to increase his vocabulary, and after years of practice he now spoke the English of aristocrats, intimidating the local whites, many whose literacy in English is still questionable. The stories and how they are delivered mesmerizes the priest so much that he spends the night on the reservation when the storytelling goes beyond ten o'clock. One night they talk about hunting, the meaning and need of it.

"You need a proper rifle," Henry tells him, "if you are to go deer hunting."

"I know. But I can't use the Church's funds to buy a rifle," he says. "I'll have to find another way to acquire it."

To the priest's surprise, Henry asks Ilmarinen and Luther Stone, as well as Albert Kaufmann, to contribute enough money to buy Father Boland a Winchester.

The priest learns quickly and is as good at deer and bear hunting as he is with duck and grouse. The sisters at the convent rebel, give in, rebel again, and finally accept, mastering the art of roasting or canning whatever Father Boland brings back to town after a hunt.

IT IS FROM THEIR NEW PRIEST that the others discover the origins of the area they settled.

"Theology and geology," he jokes, referring to both his doctorate from the University of Chicago and his passionate interest in geology. He tells them that Chippewa Crossing is built on the northernmost belt of the Precambrian Penokian age. The landscape is a swampy terrain of till and outwash plains, the result of the advancement and readvancement of the Laurentide Ice Sheet. Three miles north of the town is the distinct ridge of the Winegar moraine.

"Millions of years ago," he explains to Eberhard, Frank, and Mika Two Knives, "there was something called the Penokian upheaval. A volcanic eruption."

They are taking a break from building the barn and his audience includes all the adults present. He points to the fieldstone foundation under the barn that they have made from rock unearthed in the field and a nearby ridge called a drumlin.

"Igneous rock is volcanic rock that gets heated, folded over like a piece of bread, pressed, heated, and folded again."

Eberhard, Frank, and Mika bring small rocks to him so that

he can identify them: quartzite, Archean gneiss, and black granite. He tells them that Fox Lake was formed when the Laurentide Ice Sheet retreated for the last time, pulling gigantic boulders from the ground and leaving a deep basin to be filled by underground springs.

After the picnic lunch, he walks around the nearly finished barn with Magdalena.

"How do you reconcile your scientific knowledge of this land with your belief in God?" she asks.

He pulls a flask of whiskey from his back trouser pocket and offers it to her. She shakes her head. He takes a pull, caps it, and puts it back in his pocket.

"I suppose much like you do," he responds, startling her. "It is a struggle I live with daily."

"You think I struggle with my faith?"

"How could you not? Your father is a well-known European scholar and a Darwinist. He educated you. Albert told me that he and his brother Raymond were his prize students. I understand that while Albert retains the faith, his brother did not," he says.

"I don't think that had anything to do with my father," she answers. "Raymond was always a very independent thinker. Yes, Albert retains the faith but he struggles with it. Your predecessor really tested it. Is that wrong?"

"Not at all. I think anyone with intelligence and an education would wrestle with the contradictions. I am suspicious of blind devotion, but then again there are people who are truly devout and I don't question it."

He takes out his flask again. She has seen the unease in him since his arrival and knows, in the coming years, alcohol will be the oil that eases the rift between his faith and his scientific knowledge. They reach the other side of the house and watch the others while they eat, laugh, and rest.

"You must miss your family. This," he comments, gesturing with a hand toward the field in front of them, "is a long way from Augsburg. Its civilization, its pleasures, and its educational pursuits."

"I miss it at times," she admits. "But we are not without some things. Raymond sends us books each month. My parents write letters, especially my father who keeps me aware of what is going on in Europe. And I'm learning new things. I travel with Marjaana when she delivers babies. She is getting old and most of the women don't want to go to the doctor in town." She catches a stray lock of hair and tucks it behind her ear.

"I could ask the same of you," she adds. "Why are you here? You are well educated and could have had a larger parish in a bigger town or city. Did they send you here or did you request it?"

"I requested it. Partly for selfish reasons. It is speculated that the land around Lake Superior contains some of the oldest rock in the world."

He closes his eyes, takes a deep breath.

"It is so beautiful here. I don't regret my decision. The Chippewa were described to me as being childlike and yet savage. I told the bishop that the English describe the Irish in somewhat the same way. He told me I was young, that I would learn once I got here."

"And what have you learned?" she asks.

"I am humbled by them. With all that they must do to survive. What they know about their history. With what they have lost. They are hardly childlike or savage although they do have a fear-some history of warring with the Dakota and the Iroquois."

She hears the sentiment in his voice and simultaneously remembers her father's warning.

"Be careful not to romanticize them," she cautions. "My father didn't spend much time in the United States but he did live for a while in South America and traveled to the Congo. He said that to romanticize a people and their culture was a form of conde-scension. That it creates illusions that eventually breed contempt. Because those romanticized cannot live up to the illusions they never asked for."

She stops, feeling uncomfortable with her pontification. It has been a long time since, other than Albert, she has had anyone with his intellectual stature to talk with.

"And what have you and Albert learned, living here?" he asks.

"They have their own way of doing things. They have their weaknesses and their virtues. Their ambiguities. Fox Lake is like any other community. They have bad people, good people, and those that fall somewhere in between. Just like us. They work hard but in a different way, in a different time frame. It vexes Albert," she notes ruefully, "but not enough to cause trouble."

She looks at the adults and children eating on blankets near the cabin. A mixture of Indian and white, French, German, Polish, men, women, and children. Even Jacob, Marie, and their infant daughter are here. She longs for Aino and Kyle, Raymond, her parents and sisters. She misses Alzbêta. She never thought she'd miss the Flats so much but she does.

"We wanted to raise our children among people from other cultures," she adds.

"You are exceptionally tolerant."

She glances at him, thinking he is provoking her. But he remains serious.

"I know what it is like to be perceived as different, to be judged, to be thought of as in need of conversion. I am not a full believer in the Catholic faith, Father. Or any faith."

She thinks back to her visit to Seven Corners, to the crust on the Mormon's eyes. She turns to face the priest. "I don't mean to lecture you. I want you to do well here. But I know you were sent here to convert them. I know the dictates of the Jesuit mission toward the Indians."

She holds up her hand when he opens his mouth to speak.

"Do not try to convert them. You will fail, and worse, you will lose their trust. I know you cannot speak ill of another priest but I can. Monsignor Fitzgerald was medieval in his beliefs. He was superstitious, ignorant, and a bully. A good many believed in his authority but Albert and I did not. They," she nodded in the direction of the reservation, "did not. It galled Monsignor Fitzgerald that they ignored him. I think you have good instincts. What you have been doing since you arrived is the best way. Not just with them but with the farmers and others in Chippewa Crossing as well. Ilmarinen and his father respect you. That is quite a compliment."

"Have you and Albert known Ilmarinen and his family long?"

"Since the first spring after we came here," she answers.

"He is very intelligent, almost sophisticated in his manner. I was surprised to learn that his mother educated him at home on the reservation. How is she treated in town as a white woman living at Fox Lake? Is she received?"

"She is not or at least not in the way you are thinking. She is respected as a midwife and healer. They call on her for that but the townswomen do not invite her to social functions. She does not go to any church although she was raised Lutheran, chiefly by her mother. Her father abided by an older belief—the Kalevala. Do you know about the Kalevala?" she asks.

"Some of it. I read that Finnish scholars accused Longfellow of stealing the rhyming sequence and meter of the Kalevala to write 'The Song of Hiawatha.'"

"I have a friend Aino who sings the runes of the Kalevala. It is beautiful to hear her sing. We met her and her husband when we lived in Minneapolis. They are now in northern Minnesota and we are here." She pauses, thinking of his original question. "As to being received socially, I don't think Marjaana cares about it."

He focuses his blue eyes on her. "Neither do you," he says.

THE BABY'S FACE does change but only to become more solidified in her resemblance to her dead grandfather. Magdalena told herself that the bond she did not feel with her daughter at birth would correct itself within a month or so. It is a natural consequence, she reasoned, resulting from experience and not one that she imposed.

But Magdalena weans her daughter at five months. She tells surprised and disapproving neighbors and friends including Marjaana that Hilda is maturing rapidly. She pries open the stubborn mouth and shows them the protruding tooth on the baby's upper gum. Albert does not believe it, knowing that Magdalena breastfed their two sons well past the age of fifteen months when both of them had teeth. He brings the subject up once and then leaves it alone, deciding that she knows best.

It is not the tooth. Magdalena cannot tell him what she feels when looking at the baby's blue eyes, so reminiscent of Albert's father in their cold, almost hostile stare or of the determined mouth that tugs painfully at her breast as if to get the chore of eating over with as soon as possible.

She writes to Aino who gave birth three weeks after Magdalena to twin girls.

I don't feel the same way as before. I don't understand why except that she looks like Albert's father and even has his will. The midwife here (who is Finnish!) saw it right away but was tactful. It is as though I gave birth to her but I am not her mother. Or rather, she doesn't want me as her mother. Is such a thing possible?

WHEN HILDA TURNS a year old, Magdalena sees that her initial distance was wrong and that its damage is irreversible. Hilda refuses Magdalena's hand when she begin walking, lurching toward Albert and the boys instead. Her husband notices it then.

"I don't understand why," he says one night in bed. She does not answer. He studies her faint profile and she knows what he is thinking, what he is remembering. How close Magdalena is to her mother and his mother, their letters going back and forth. How he wants the same closeness among his children and had hoped for a daughter who would resemble his wife or his mother.

He sighs. He is thinking of the baby born on the Flats. She had looked unmistakably like Magdalena. But Hilda resembles his father's side of the family: the blond curls that will turn more gold and not brown with age, the prim, disapproving lips so unlike the rosebud lips of the baby who died. Hilda has inherited her grandfather's eyes as well: a shade of blue like the north Atlantic on a sunny day, the color masking the duplicity of its depth. Hilda has also inherited Heinrich's unbendable will. The girl decides when and if she will allow her mother to hold and kiss her. And then there are times when Hilda gazes at Magdalena with nothing less than disdain. It troubles him. Hilda is the opposite with Albert and the boys; affectionate and adoring, easygoing and pliant in their arms. But Magdalena is rebuffed half of the time when she attempts to rock or hold Hilda. So she refrains from forcing her affection on the child, waiting instead for the child to come to her. He tells Magdalena that it is not natural for a girl to reject her mother, explaining that he is not blaming her. She tells herself that it is not natural for a mother to feel this way about her own child.

But then it occurs to her that her child may not be natural.

☩ ☩ ☩

THEY FINALLY BUILD A HOUSE, six years after their arrival. They order it in the winter of 1911 from the Sears, Roebuck catalogue. It has two and half stories, a diamond-shaped gable window just below the pitch of the roof, four bedrooms, a parlor, a large kitchen, and a large formal dining room. When it arrives in early June, they marvel at the modernity of having a house delivered and ready to be assembled. Jacob is working in Michigan but Ilmarinen brings additional men from Fox Lake, and Father Boland contributes when he is able as does Roman. But tensions arise over an old problem.

The different sense of time held by the Indians is something they had not understood when Roman Zelinski first mentioned "Injun" time. But now it is a source of vexation for Albert and at times Magdalena. Even after six years, it occasionally tests Albert's friendship with Ilmarinen and the other Fox Lake men who do not adhere to specific points on the clock—indeed they do not own a clock—but indicate vaguely that it will be morning, afternoon, or evening when they are able to fish, hunt, or work. Albert wants the house completed in the sequential order of days. But Ilmarinen and the Fox Lake men can come one day, and then not the next, so that the building of the house drags out over a month. Although it is mostly done and they are living in it, there are two rooms left that need to be floored with oak. Ilmarinen was supposed to come that morning and now it is two in the afternoon.

"How do they get anything done?" Albert asks, taking his hat off and sitting down at the table. He runs a hand through his hair, rubs his face in frustration.

"And yet they do," Magdalena answers. Her days have an order to them, one that she controls as she does the work chiefly alone. She puts a glass of cold water in front of him.

"He is not like Raymond—he is not a younger brother you can order about," she reminds him. "He offers his help and we accept it. Even though we pay him and the other men, it still doesn't give us the right to demand. They have lives, too. It is who they are and it is who we are."

She reminds him that Germans are famous for their obsession

with time, with their love of order. How Raymond and even he chaffed against the rigidity of their father's schedule.

"He may not have been as zealous as your father but my father insisted on order, on timeliness."

She thinks of Roman's complaint about hiring men from the reservation ("One day here, the next day gone"), about the references made by others, the stereotypes that get solidified over and over again in town at the lumber mill, the taverns, Fishbach's General Store. That the Indians waste land that should be farmed. That they are inherently lazy and stupid and drunkards. The latter is true only among a few, as it would be with any other people. Albert pointed out to Roman that there are just as many white men if not more who are drunkards. He tactfully does not include Roman's own weekend bouts at the tavern.

Magdalena is uneasy about making such opinions because in a different context it could be them. They read her father's and Raymond's letters about the growing anti-German sentiment in Great Britain and France. Her father sent them a clipping from the *London Times* with a cartoon depicting the kaiser righteously sitting on a giant clock with his sword held high. She remembers another British cartoon from her youth, one in which a rotund Bismarck was snacking on beer and pretzels at a beer garden, while Disraeli and other foreign leaders were peering at him from the tree branches above. As a girl, traveling with her mother to Paris and London, she learned of the negative connotations attributed to Germans. Ambitious, rude, pushy, loud, aggressive, and arrogant. She thinks of Ernst Hasse, the founder of the Alldeutsche Verband—the Pan-German League—and what he said, published in an Augsburg newspaper in 1891. *We want territory even if it belongs to foreigners, so that we may shape the future according to our needs.* Her mother was horrified, her father disgusted.

"How are we to travel in Europe with that hanging over our heads?" her mother asked, anguished. "Did you know the Alldeutsche Verband is distributing posters to the shops here? Ernst Geringer showed me one. It says, 'The world belongs to Germany.' Ernst refused to put that in the window. He burned it."

"Good for him!" her father said. "If an uneducated but intelligent man can understand the madness of it, hold his own against it, one should hope there are others."

But after Heinrich's death, Otto had joined the Alldeutsche Verband, much to Albert's disgust.

It didn't help that two days before, Eberhard and Frank cited their Fox Lake friends' disregard of set minutes and hours to reason a way of sleeping in, claiming it was unnatural to wake up in the dark. Albert was swift to correct them.

"You can have two different ways that coexist. That works for them. But we go by a time that is our own. So get out of bed and go up to the barn," he said, pulling them out of their beds.

Magdalena sits down at the new table, in what feels like an enormous kitchen, filled with southern light.

"Do you want to be like the Weirs?" she asks, reminding him of their nearest white neighbors, living on the acreage adjacent to their farm.

"God, no," he answers. "That man is so stubborn, so damn arrogant and ignorant. He doesn't get along with anyone. I thought he was going to shoot me that day, remember?"

THEY ALMOST NEVER SEE Joseph and Hannah Weir, and are only aware of their growing brood of undisciplined and sometimes unfed children because they wander through neighboring woods and across other homesteaded land. One cannot mistake a Weir child for they all look the same: white-blond hair, flat and wide cheekbones, and skin so fair it is ghostly when seen to be peering out from between bushes or trees. When they stop and ask for something to eat, they never say "please" or "thank you" but simply wait until given something to eat and drink before running off. Joseph Weir ambitiously purchased 160 acres and they assumed like many others from the area that he knew how to farm it and would hire help to clear so much land. A year earlier when it became apparent that he did not know farming and that he was getting deeper into debt, Albert rode over to offer his help. But he was turned away, with Weir yelling at him in German to mind his own business.

When Albert told the story at the dinner table that evening, five-year-old Hilda shocked them by saying, "They will die then."

"Don't ever say that!" Magdalena said with such vehemence that it scared the boys and Albert. In the silence that followed, she felt the horror of repeating her mother's words, of suddenly realizing her mother's fears. Since that time she cannot help herself. She watches her daughter for the same signs that her own mother dreaded.

BUT TODAY Magdalena is happy. She can walk up the stairs and look out from one of the front bedroom windows and see all the way down to the river. They are sitting in the kitchen with its large nickel-plated stove and two ovens, and the custom-made maple table large enough to seat twelve. Marjaana advised them to build an outdoor kitchen for canning, and it was Ilmarinen who designed it with Eberhard so that it blended in with the rest of the house.

"Maybe I should go over to the Weir place. They need help," she says, thinking of the times she has seen Hannah Weir in town. She is as pale, as undernourished as her children. She is always pregnant, her belly the only evidence of extra flesh, of life on her otherwise spectral frame. Magdalena would have approached her except that she had a sense of nothingness as though Hannah Weir was only an illusion.

"You will not go over there," Albert says. "I don't need to know the man well to know that he would see you as . . ."

The word he doesn't say hangs in air, almost as visible as the dust particles captured in the rays of the late afternoon sun.

HIS FATHER AND ILMARINEN sent him back for tools and the lunch they forgot, having gotten an early start to work in the far corner of the farm. Eberhard reaches the top of the slope near the Weir place when he sees a saddled horse grazing not far from the homestead's barn. He nudges his mare into the direction of the other horse, sidling up alongside the animal with a casualness that will not spook it. He reaches over and collects the reins, leading the horse behind him as he approaches the house. There are three children of indeterminate ages playing in the sunny but grassless yard. They stand up, dust-covered, and vacantly consider him with pale-blue eyes as he dismounts, tying the horses to the unfinished picket fence.

"Where are your mother and father?" he asks, uneasy at the near total silence of the place. He repeats, "*Wo sind deine Vater und deine Mutter?*"

They shrug and then squat to resume playing with pebbles and sticks. He decides to try the barn first, untying the horse and leading it toward the open flat tracked door.

"Mr. Weir!"

It is dark in the barn and he stops to adjust his vision before moving forward. He turns into what he thinks is an empty stall and is struck in the face by a boot. He stumbles backwards into the horse behind him, hears the clattering of its back hooves as the animal steadies itself. He stares up at the rafter above the stall, stares at the bulging eyes and the noose around Weir's neck. His stomach lurches and he leans over and vomits into the gutter. He stays bent over until the heaving is done. Then Eberhard stands up and tries to breathe evenly, concentrating on what to do next. He hears a brief childish laugh outside. He has to get the body down before Mrs. Weir and the children see it.

He leads the horse to the end of the barn and ties it up to the calf pen gate before walking back to the stall with a barn stool. He climbs up onto the right side of the stall and walks across to the middle, holding onto the rafter above with one hand. He reaches over to where the rope is tied and cuts it with the knife Kyle sent him for his fourteenth birthday. He hears the thud of the body hitting the stall floor, avoids looking at it as he climbs back down. He finds a horse blanket to cover Weir, feels the urge to vomit again at the rope-burned neck, the half-opened eyes. Then he walks out of the barn and toward the house, unable to think of what he will tell Mrs. Weir. The children glance at him with momentary interest as he enters the house. He is not there three minutes before running back out. He unties, mounts, and spurs his horse into an immediate gallop toward the direction of home.

MARJAANA ACCOMPANIED ILMARINEN that morning and stayed to help Magdalena with an abundance of cream that needed churning. Marjaana kneads the last of the butter between two pieces of cheesecloth. Magdalena is pouring the remaining buttermilk into a stoneware jug and then into three glasses when someone knocks at the back door. She gives a glass to Marjaana, one to Hilda who is playing with marbles under the table, and puts her own on the table before opening the door. A Weir boy in dirty overalls and no shirt stands there.

"Can I help you?" she asks, judging him to be about eight years old. When he does not respond, she asks in German, "*Kann ich dir helfen?*"

"Mama won't move," he says, wiping his nose with a dirty forearm. "*In der Küche.*"

Magdalena hears an approaching horse. She pauses, looks past the child to see her own son riding at a hard gallop toward the house.

"What do you mean she won't move in the kitchen? Is she sick?" The boy does not respond. He stares glassy-eyed past her at the buttermilk on the table and the half loaf of bread. She motions him in, gives him the glass of buttermilk, and cuts a thick slice of bread. He gulps down the milk, grabs the slice of bread, and runs out of the door like a feral dog.

"Just like a Weir," Hilda comments from underneath the table. "He didn't have any shoes on and his feet were dirty."

She opens her mouth to scold her daughter when she sees Eberhard dismount and motion her to step outside.

"Hilda, stay here," she says. "Marjaana and I are going outside for a few minutes."

IT IS SILENT when they reach the Weir place. The children outside appear to be mute and Magdalena tells Hilda to stay with them. Then the two women walk through the bare front room to the doorway of the kitchen in the back. Two children are huddled in the corner near the stove. A girl of about ten sits on the floor next to the table and holds her mother's hand, hanging limply over the table's edge. Hannah Weir is lying on the table, her eyes open and her legs bent as though she had attempted to sit up. The dirty brown skirt is pulled up over the knees and—Magdalena hears her daughter gasp.

She spins around, shielding Hilda from what she hopes her daughter has not seen and pushes her to the door.

"I told you to stay outside! Help the children make a fire and then boil some water in the washtub we saw lying out there. Keep away from the barn."

Back in the kitchen, Marjaana cannot get the children by the stove to leave.

"Go outside," Magdalena says, pulling the children to their feet. They stand but do not move. "*Geht raus*," she commands, and then louder, "*Geht raus!*"

They run out of the kitchen. She turns to the girl who appears to be the oldest at ten, maybe eleven.

"*Macht ein Feuer draußen*—make a fire outside," she instructs, prying the girl's hand from her mother's and pulling her up. "*Und füllt den Waschkübel mit Wasser*—and fill up the washtub with water.*"

Magdalena lifts the dead woman's arm and places it on the table. They hear the children's voices outside, listen as Hilda and the girl instruct the other children to build a fire, to draw water from the well, and pour it in a large wash kettle. Marjaana shuts the woman's eyes and sweeps a lank of hair from her face. They move to the end of the table where Hannah Weir is most exposed. The baby had been born but never took a breath, the umbilical cord wrapped around its neck. A girl. Her body is bluish yellow and covered with the milky vernix of birth. The arms are crossed and the hands fisted on the tiny chest.

"She died only a couple of hours ago," Marjaana says. She reaches forward to finger the hem on the skirt. "She was a pretty girl once. Got married at seventeen, pregnant of course. Had a baby every year for ten years. I came over here five years ago and then two years ago—when I knew her husband was not around. I offered to help her but she would have nothing to do with me. She didn't speak English well and I, of course, do not speak German."

"Was he an unkind man?"

"Not that I know of. I don't think he hit her. More like neglect out of ignorance. Joseph Weir only thought about farming. He probably assumed the labor would be like the others and left her to bear the child alone. Only it wasn't like the others and he found her too late and went mad." Marjaana pulls on one of Hannah's legs to straighten it. "She's getting stiffer. We better begin."

They work without speaking. Marjaana cuts the umbilical cord and ties it with waxed twine. The oldest girl brings in two basins of warm water. Magdalena tells her to keep bringing in more hot water. Marjaana rummages through the kitchen sideboard cabinet, finds a hard brown bar of lye soap and an old tablecloth. She rips the tablecloth into pieces. Magdalena walks into the adjoining bedroom, finds a trunk with clothes. A plum-colored dress and a cotton petticoat with hand-stitched lace on the hem had been carefully wrapped and put away. Magdalena spreads the dress on the bed and cuts the petticoat into large pieces.

They wash the baby first and wrap it in the largest piece of petticoat so that the ruffled hem frames the infant's face. Marjaana place the small body on the kitchen sideboard. They both push on Hannah's thighs and knees until her legs are flat on the table and cut away her clothing. They wash the bloody thighs, the swollen calves and ankles. They wash the milk-filled breasts, the stomach with its lattice of stretch marks, the hands as calloused and leather-tough as the feet. The girl comes and goes, emptying the washbasins of dirty water and replacing them with clean hot water. She stops a moment to watch them.

"*Mama ist gestorben?*" she asks.

"*Ja. Deine Mama ist gestorben,*" Magdalena answers, wondering where Hilda is but the girl leaves before she can ask her.

When the body is clean and wiped dry, Magdalena cuts open the back of the dress so that they can slip it on. They tilt the dead woman on her side and loosely sew up the back of the dress. Magdalena brushes and braids Hannah's hair.

Then they lift and carry Hannah Weir to the bedroom and lay her on the bed before retrieving the baby from the sideboard, placing the infant on Hannah's chest and folding her hands over the small body. The two women then walk back into the kitchen. One end of the table is soaked with blood and birth water.

"Ilmarinen and Albert will have to carry it out and burn it."

"What about Joseph? He is in the barn," Magdalena asks. It exhausts her to think of washing and preparing another body.

"We can't wash him in the barn and we can't carry him to the house. The undertaker in town will take care of him," Marjaana answers.

They hear someone enter the house.

"I found Mr. Weir," Hilda announces, swinging a knotted hoop of rope, "in the barn." Hilda puts the rope around her neck and briefly yanks it upward. Magdalena slaps her daughter, and lifts the rope from around her neck. Her daughter is momentarily stunned. Then she lifts a hand to her face and begins to wail.

"Don't you dare cry," Magdalena says. "Or I'll slap you again!" Hilda runs outside. Magdalena grips the edge of the soiled table. She fights the desire to follow Hilda and beat her.

"It is shock," Marjaana says behind her. "The girl doesn't know what she is saying."

"I wish," she chokes out, "I could believe that."

ALBERT, THE TWO BOYS, AND ILMARINEN arrive ten minutes later. They place Joseph Weir's body next to that of his wife and infant daughter in the back of the wagon that was in the barn, and cover them with blankets. Then the rest of the children climb in, sitting in a row on either side of their parents with two of them perched behind the buckboard's seat so that Hannah and Joseph Weir are surrounded by the white-haired, pale-faced waifs they created and left on this earth.

Marjaana pulls Albert and Eberhard aside. It is decided that Albert and Frank will drive the wagon to the funeral parlor in town, and Marjaana will take Hilda home with her to Fox Lake. Ilmarinen saddles the horse that Joseph Weir kicked out from under him so that his mother and Hilda can share his horse. Hilda's tear-stained face is stoic. She does not look at Magdalena or at Eberhard.

Mother and son watch them all depart before mounting the

two remaining horses, nudging them into a slow walk, silent and occupied by their own thoughts.

The first sight of Hannah Weir had almost knocked her down. Magdalena put aside her horror and other emotions and did what was necessary. The worst of it, however, had been her daughter's callous detachment in finding Joseph Weir. Her disobedience. Eberhard had told her to stay away from the barn. She hopes that Marjaana is right. That Hilda's response is a delayed reaction of feelings and that in a week or few weeks, the girl will show some emotion over this day. That such a tragedy might evoke some empathy into what she feels is an unnatural child. The only small comfort she can take away from the day is that she is now sure that Hilda cannot read people, that she cannot anticipate events or has a sense of the unknown. Her fault lies in her precociousness and tactlessness. She does not consider the effect of her words on others, or their feelings.

"I slapped your sister," she finally says.

"I know. I yelled at her. She deserved it."

It appalled Eberhard when his father told him what Hilda had done, how she had disobeyed his order to stay away from the barn. If he hadn't seen her cry over dying pets—chicks that didn't live in the first two days, a puppy with twisted intestines—he would fear her heartless. He has never understood his sister's coldness toward their mother while she idolizes him and their father, Frank less so. His father spanked him and Frank when they were younger but they could count the number of times on their fingers. Their mother has never had to raise a hand to them. She has a tone in her voice, a look that warns them as if she knows what they are considering.

"Don't feel bad, Mama," he says, seeing the distress on her face. "It's a good thing Hilda is going to school this fall. Wait until she acts up like that in front of the nuns. She is going to wish she was home all day again."

He pulls out a canteen of water and takes a long drink. It doesn't matter how much water he drinks, he can still taste the bile from vomiting. He has seen his mother's breasts but he has never seen a woman naked below the waist. He is not so much repulsed with what he's seen but afraid. It could have been his mother, dying like that in childbirth.

"Why didn't they ask for help?" he says. "Why did they fear other people so much? Why didn't they learn English?"

"I don't know. Joseph Weir was a proud man. Your Grandfather Kaufmann was the same way. He obviously believed that asking for help was a sign of weakness. And speaking English may have seemed like a betrayal to who they were."

Eberhard thought that a strange concept given that they were in an English-speaking country. He knew of the prejudice against the Fox Lake people and although he did not share it, could understand how people feared difference and therefore would not have asked them for help. His mother had explained it to him when they moved here. But they were the Weirs' nearest neighbors. They were German as well, spoke German. And they farmed.

"I would have helped him."

"I know."

His face still reflects the horror of finding them. Of an unassailable grief at not being more aware of how the Weirs' isolationist tendencies would bring them to this end. It bothers her that she did not ride over to the Weir place, did not attempt to make contact with Hannah Weir. Magdalena had not considered her sense of Hannah Weir as insubstantial and weightless as pertaining to death. She could not have predicted the tragedy either, although she always felt nervous when she spied a Weir child roaming their property like a pale spirit from Hades. Hilda had, though. Her young daughter had deducted through casual observation that those who isolated themselves risked an eternal exile. Magdalena remembered her mother's words about the Muellers. *Their deaths were sad. Like so many.* She cannot repeat that to her son, sharing his rage at the untimeliness of death. Of whom it chose.

Magdalena scans the sky, ascertains that there is about an hour of sunlight left. The sun looms huge on the horizon, its outer ring like the bloody red of the rope burn around Weir's neck. She shudders, knowing that under different circumstances, it could be them. They know now that the book that Raymond had sent to them—*Northern Wisconsin: A Hand-book for the Homeseeker*—was greatly exaggerated and full of outright lies in some parts. It was most likely the same book that lured Joseph Weir to this part of Wisconsin. They have since learned that the lumber companies, after decimating the land of its timber, colluded in the lie so that they could unload what they considered worthless land onto to unsuspecting immigrants. It upset them but did not deter them. Albert was like Joseph Weir in that he did not give up easily either. He did, however, ask for help. It was a necessity on the Flats and it is a necessity here to help neighbors and in turn be helped by them.

They had stayed when many others did not. She and Albert understood it, did not fault anyone who gave up and left. Joseph Weir would have been wise to do so before it had come to this. It was not like working an established farm or starting one on easy soil such as was to be had in southern Wisconsin or, they heard, in Iowa. They had created a farm in an area—and Albert said it, too—where a farm didn't really belong. It was too late for them. Not because of their financial and physical investment but because the land held them in such a way that they hardly knew how to talk about it.

One day, hoeing in the garden, Magdalena stopped and listened, thinking someone had spoken. During the spring thaw, all the way up at the house they can hear the river roar with the swell of water that nearly overcomes its banks. In the midsummer heat, the river murmurs and they feel drawn to the sound, stripping off their clothes to stand in the shallows of the Chippewa, entranced by the water moving past and occasionally splashing their legs. The boys are too young to remember swimming in the Lech River on the Kaufmann farm, and they had not gone swimming in the Mississippi because of its size and swift current. But their section of the Chippewa is mild during the summer and the children can splash in the shallows. One day Albert showed the boys and Hilda how to swim in a river, how to align their body with the surface and float, never fighting the current but using their arms as rudders so that they guided their bodies toward the shoreline where they might grasp an overhanging branch. When September arrives, the river speaks but not to them, its voice reaching into the sky to the passing geese and ducks who then settle on its surface.

They love the tamaracks whose needles turn mustard yellow in the autumn and then fall off, unlike other pines. The birches and aspens remind them of their five years on the Flats. The leaves flutter together like pennies made of crinoline so that when the wind blows through them they speak in a chorus of whispers. The birches' leaves turn a lemon yellow in the autumn, resisting release until the first violent storm of winter wrenches them from their branches. Each spring, Albert, Magdalena, and the children stand outside in reverential silence as large flocks of Canada geese pass over, and they do so again in the fall when the geese head south. Ducks fly over, too, the mallards like chattering busybodies in their flight. Magdalena is especially fascinated by the blue-winged teal, flying at a speed much faster than swallows and making a brief high whistle as they passed overhead.

She cannot evoke or feel the same poetic elegance about her birth home, even the countryside surrounding it. But how could she not? Bavaria had magnificent forests and breathtaking vistas. She mentioned this to Raymond during a visit from him the last summer, on break from his duties as a young history professor at the university.

"Because the land is still owned by the aristocracy there. The sense of possibility doesn't exist. You must gain permission for everything. Even if you want to just walk on a beautiful piece of land," he said, standing at the top of the slope that went down to the river. "Here," he joked, placing his foot on a small pile of rocks gleaned from the field, "it is not about permission because the only authority is this."

That is what killed the Weirs, she thinks, the horse picking up its gait as the house and barn came into view. *They obeyed the wrong authority.*

HANNAH WEIR'S PARENTS were dead and her siblings scattered— it was last known—in Minnesota, Wyoming, and Montana. Joseph

Weir appeared to have no next of kin. The children are to live at the convent dormitory until homes can be found for them or unless Hannah Weir's siblings respond to the ads placed in the major newspapers of the three states. Father Boland cannot break the religious law on suicides. Hannah and her child will be buried in the cemetery in town. Joseph will be buried in paupers' field just outside town a day later.

Oddly, Jacob Bleu attends the burial of Hannah Weir and her infant. Eberhard is the first to spot him waiting outside the wrought-iron gate of the cemetery, his eyes cast down as he listens to Father Boland deliver the Rite of Committal prayer in Latin. He lingers until the crowd has dispersed before approaching the priest and the undertaker. Eberhard wonders why Jacob is there but gives it no more thought than that, still stricken by their neighbors' tragedy.

A week later, his father purchases Weir's 160 acres and settles the debts. Ilmarinen rides over to help his father survey the acreage. He leaves his five-year-old son, Seppo, to play with Hilda before heading out with Eberhard and his father. They are a quarter of a mile from the Weir house when they find a fresh grave covered with rocks and cut cedar boughs in a young white pine grove.

"Good Lord!" his father exclaims. "That can't be who I think it is."

"It is," Ilmarinen answers. Having heard that Jacob was at the funeral, he rode over to the field where the whites bury their suicides, their poor, and their forsaken. He walked among the white unmarked posts that dotted the small field but found no fresh grave marked by a new post.

"Why?" his father asks, taking off his hat. "The man didn't like anyone, especially Indians. Did Jacob know him? Work for him?"

"Not that I know of. I don't know why Jacob did it. No one knows or understands what he does sometimes. But he must have had a good reason," Ilmarinen replies.

"I don't want him here. Jacob should have asked me."

"Jacob buried Mr. Weir here while it was still his land. He did not have to ask you," Eberhard says.

"Well, we own it now and I don't want him here."

"Why? Because he killed himself?" Eberhard asks.

There was a nun at the school who liked to frighten the younger students with a list of sins that would get them buried in paupers' field, until Father Boland forbid her to do so. Eberhard used to have nightmares from her stories and would avert his eyes when they passed that field on their way into and back from town. Now that he is old enough to travel alone into Chippewa Crossing, he stays off the road and takes his horse through the woods.

His father works the brim of his hat with his fingers. Eberhard wonders if his father is superstitious enough to think that Joseph Weir will haunt them, that his presence will bring further bad luck.

"Yes, but not because I think he should be buried in paupers' field," he answers, aware of Eberhard's fears. "I don't like the notion of your sister coming across this. Or any other children."

Eberhard looks up at the young pines swaying in the wind. They will be majestic and stunning when he is seventy years old.

"It isn't like you're going to cut down this grove and plow the ground up," he comments. "Look at the size of those rocks! Jacob must have had a terrible time digging the grave. This part is only fit for grazing, if that."

"So you think he should stay?"

"He's dead. Nothing worked out for him. Are you going to take this away from him, too?"

Ilmarinen steps out from the white pine grove, surveys the line of woods. "I'll cut down some of that hemlock there," he points "and stack the logs here."

"I'll help you," Eberhard says. "Only the three of us will know."

His father puts on his hat.

"And Jacob," he comments.

They mount their horses and ride farther on to look at the rest of the acreage. Eberhard lags behind thinking he's heard a child's voice, and turning the horse, scans the trees. It is quiet, the only noise being the swish of the boughs in the wind. Still he has a hunch.

"Hilda! If I catch you in there I'll slap you worse than Mama did!"

HILDA HAD PROMISED her mother that she and Seppo would play within calling distance, but the two children had followed the three men, listened to their conversation. In the ensuing days they shadow Ilmarinen and Eberhard as they cut the hemlock and stack the timber in a double-walled octagon shape, big logs on the bottom and smaller logs near the stop of the stack so that it looks like a beehive. The children wait on the last day until Ilmarinen and Eberhard gather their tools and head back to the Kaufmann place. Then they climb the stacked wood.

"There is a hole at the top," Hilda announces, reaching her arm down into it.

"Don't do that," Seppo says.

"Why not?"

"So Mr. Weir can breathe."

"He's dead, dummy," Hilda says, withdrawing her arm.

"Not breathe like that," Seppo explains. "It is for his spirit." He climbs down from the stack. He understands what his father has done. He has accommodated Hilda's father but has not gone against Jacob's reasoning, whatever it may be.

"Sister Theresa-Maria says that his spirit is in hell. That means his spirit is burned up. So he has no spirit."

"She's wrong," he answers. "Jacob got his spirit back."

THAT FALL, Hilda begins to attend school, and to their relief she forms close ties with four other children, two of whom are girls: Alice Charbonneau, and Jacob and Marie Bleu's daughter Ruby. The other children are Ilarminen's son Seppo, and the son of Alexandra and Ivan Fishbach, Peter. She blossoms overnight, becoming more responsive toward Magdalena and chatty about her daily activities at school. She does well in all of her subjects, although at the end of the first month Sister Mary-Agnes notes on her report card that while she shows remarkable self-assurance, she is willful and obstinate on occasion. "Still, she is surprisingly tolerant toward others," the nun had written.

But after the first month, Hilda begins to show a growing inclination toward religious zealotry that is not practiced at home. Her devotion to God increases considerably at school and tries even the most pious of nuns.

"It's a phase. She'll outgrow it," Father Boland says, thinking that girls in particular were prone to romantic notions about religion. They leave the rectory, hoping he is right and simultaneously knowing that he is not. Hilda assumes authority over mealtime prayers that get longer and longer until she embroiders them into missives that try all of their nerves. The last week of October, her long intonations of gratitude to the Lord finally crack Frank's patience.

"I think God gets it, Hilda," he says. "We are thankful for our food. Now can we eat?" She pushes out her lower lip, and glares at Frank.

"Hilda, we like it when you say the prayers but just make them a bit shorter," Eberhard cajoles. She stands up from her chair and stomps up the stairs to her bedroom.

"What is wrong with her?" Frank asks, rubbing his face in frustration.

"It's a phase," Magdalena answers, repeating Father Boland's observation. "She'll grow out of it soon."

A little while later, they hear her footsteps on the stairs while they are having coffee and dessert. They turn to see her standing in the kitchen doorway.

"I want to join the convent," she announces.

MAGDALENA AND ALBERT sit in the lamp-lit kitchen after the children have gone to bed.

"So dark," she murmurs, gazing at the window over the kitchen sink. They did not have streetlights on the Flats but there was always a neighbor who was up at some odd hour of the night and one could see a lighted oil lamp in a window. But here the only respite from complete darkness at night is a full moon. Then she can look out the window and see the fields and the line of trees by the river.

"Sometimes I think Monsignor Fitzgerald was right," she says. "She is a changeling. I have no idea what goes on in her head. She views things as if they are either right or wrong. No in-between. If this zealousness toward the faith gave her empathy, I would tolerate it gladly. But it does not."

Albert rubs his face. The boys had tested him as was natural, and when they were defiant it was almost always for a good reason. Two years ago, Frank was adamant that they buy a Henderson reversible sulky plow meant for rocky soil on hillsides. Albert said no but Frank kept after him, so sure that the plow would make things easier for them. The plow blades could be adjusted to cut a wide furrow or a narrow one. On hills it turned the land along the line of the slope rather than up and down, and because of the adjustable seat they could sit and drive the horses and not walk behind them. Albert eventually gave in, and was apologetic when Frank's reasoning proved to be correct.

Magdalena thinks of her own certitude at the age of five. But while her mother worried about Magdalena's precociousness in speaking, her fear was out of love and protection for Magdalena and the family. She can't quite name what it is about her daughter.

"Power," Albert says, startling Magdalena. "It's about power. Doing anything with Hilda always requires a negotiation of sorts. Spanking her doesn't seem to help. Sometimes it is as though my father is standing in front of me. She has his arrogance, his hardheadedness."

"I wish your mother was here," Magdalena says. "She would know how to handle Hilda." She recalls what Marjaana said when she returned Hilda the day after the Weir tragedy.

"I don't want to wish pain on any child," she said. "But Hilda needs to go through something significant in her life, something that will knock her down enough to make her think of other people and not just herself."

Albert reaches forward and encloses her hands.

"I think we should talk to Father Boland again."

"I guess it's not a phase," Father Boland admits. "I will rely upon Sister Augusta to handle this."

Two days after their visit to the rectory, Hilda is brought to the mother superior's office. She kneels in front of Sister Augusta's desk, her hands clasped in prayer. The nun tells Hilda that she is not required to genuflect, and to sit in the chair. Sister Augusta adjusts her wire-rim glasses, and then leans forward on her desk.

She sternly informs Hilda that humility, not righteousness and arrogance, is at the core of a religious life. Then softening her tone, the nun suggests that Hilda serve Christ by focusing on school so that she can attend college one day—a great achievement for women. She reminds Hilda that Christ supported the education of women and suggests that Hilda read the story of Christ's visit to the sisters Mary and Martha.

Sister Augusta's words lower the level of her righteousness to a tolerable level but do not stop it.

HENRY TWO KNIVES PREDICTED a harsh winter and no one could remember a time when Henry's predictions were wrong. The house is silent except for the occasional sound of Hilda, shifting under the covers of her bed as she sleeps off a cold. Albert and the boys are doing morning chores in the barn. Magdalena paces from window to window, touching the glass that not even frost has been able to lace over because of the snow packed against it. She opens the front door to the white tunnel that extends mainly to the barn. Last night she had read the first chapter of *Alice in Wonderland* to Hilda. Looking at the twelve-foot-high snow banks she wonders if they, like Alice, have been plunged into another world. She closes the door and rests against it, grateful that she is no longer in the cabin, that she can walk up the stairs and see out across the landscape, white as it is.

It began to snow in mid-November and did not stop. By January the lower part of the house was fully enclosed. Albert and the boys dug a network of trenches from the front door of the house to the barn, the chicken coop, the outhouse, and the smoke and ice-houses. Magdalena melted kettles of snow on the stove and sluiced the sides of the trenches with lukewarm water, creating ice walls that they hoped would not collapse with each snowfall. Albert attached a pulley system of ropes from the porch roof and then to each of the necessary buildings on the farm. No one is allowed to go out alone, and they have to grab the rope above them as an extra precaution should one of the trench walls collapse. The children cannot attend school, and rather than pay to have them board at the convent Magdalena tutors them at home. That fall they had purchased large quantities of flour, sugar, salt, and other store-bought necessities. A pig was killed after the first frost, and some of it was smoked while the rest was hung to freeze in the icehouse. They did the same with the three deer that Eberhard and Frank had shot, smoking strips of venison, freezing a few steaks, and canning the rest. They had tolerated the situation fairly well until the end of January. But then, tempers wearing thin, Frank and Eberhard got into a fight over a game of checkers. Eberhard had pinned Frank to the table when Albert pulled him off.

"Look at what you've done! Look at the broken dishes! Do you think money grows on trees!" he shouted. He grabbed them by their shirt collars and threw them out onto the six-by-six-foot cleared space on the front porch. "You want to fight? Stay out here and do it. Do a good job of it. I'll check in half an hour to see which one of you is alive."

Minutes later, the boys apologized from the other side of the door and Albert let them in. Frank had bloodied Eberhard's nose and Eberhard had split Frank's lip.

MAGDALENA PUSHES HERSELF AWAY from the door. Henry Two Knives also predicted that they would have an early spring. Normally she would look forward to it, especially this year given the harshness of the winter. But Eberhard will be leaving them in May to live with Raymond and attend the University of Minnesota. He turns fifteen in a week, already a grown man as he inherited the Kaufmann trait of maturing early. Facially he looks like Magdalena— the same dark eyes, thick black hair that curls, and sensuous lips. His skin is a lighter olive but in the summer he tans to such a deep brown that he was once mistaken for being related to Ilmarinen.

She knows it is time for a change. Eberhard has exhausted the school's resources. His grasp of Latin is excellent, thanks to Father Boland. He is proficient in the basic sciences except for chemistry, and his knowledge of world history is outstanding as well. The latter is a result of her father who sent Eberhard books with required readings.

"He's ready for further study," the priest said last fall. "He will grow dissatisfied if held back any longer."

She knows this to be true, knows that Eberhard is eager to return to the Flats, to see old friends, go to college, and spend time with Raymond. Although Raymond's career as a history professor was flourishing, he had returned home from a conference the previous autumn to find his wife, whom the Kaufmanns had never met, gone. His letter to them was brief, giving no explanation for the divorce.

"I doubt it was her fault," Albert said. "You know Raymond and women. It might do him good to have Eberhard there."

It isn't his departure to the Flats that makes her uneasy, it is his life after that. Unlike her mother, Magdalena does not see images of her children's futures. She only took Alzbêta's advice to a certain extent. She does not ignore that which is in her, which speaks to her, which causes her to see images. But neither does she hone it. She does not want to know her children's futures. Partly because she fears pain but mostly because it would be like stealing from them. Their futures are their possessions. She listens as they talk about their dreams and goals, often changing with age but as frequently too as the seasons. It is Eberhard's dreams that make her nervous.

"After college, I want to go to Germany. To visit Berlin, Augsburg, Munich. I want to see Grandma Kaufmann, Grandma and Grandpa Richter. And my aunts. I still remember them."

"Your grandparents are still trying to come here," she said, keeping her tone casual. "There will be no need to go to Germany after they emigrate."

"Mama, you've been saying that for ten years. Why is it taking them so long?"

"Your great Uncle Bernhardt doesn't want your grandfather to leave. And your grandfather is obligated to participate as a member of various boards of the factories. He is still trying to find a way to get out of it without breaking family ties."

"Eberhard is just eager," Albert said later, "to make his mark on the world. I wouldn't worry about it. It will take him years to save the money required to visit Germany. And I don't think your father and mother will encourage his visiting, as much as they want to see him and the other children. Raymond certainly isn't going to encourage him to visit Germany either."

✛ ✛ ✛

SHE WALKS INTO THE KITCHEN, checks the bowl of bread rising on the sideboard. Eberhard's fascination with Germany may
be their fault. Albert insisted that they not dredge up most of his
family history or speak of family members other than his mother.
He did not want to romanticize their past in any way. But they also
did not talk about the Kaufmann side of the family out of fear that
Otto was still looking for them. It is only natural, she realizes now,
to wonder from whence one has come. The lack of knowledge about
her mother's background still haunts her.

She remembers a question she once asked Alzbêta.

"Tell me something. What good is it to know or see something
ahead of time when you cannot change the outcome?"

"That is the sting of it," Alzbêta answered. "The toughest part
to bear."

RENASCENCE

Minneapolis, France, Germany
1914–1919

WINTER WAS BANISHED YESTERDAY.
Eberhard opens his eyes, looks to the window, and sees the dark receding and the light beginning. He gets up, dresses, and leaves the bedroom. His uncle's bedroom door is slightly ajar. Raymond was so drunk the evening before that he fell across the middle of the bed. Sometime in the night he must have righted himself and is now sleeping with his head against the headboard. His snoring is deep and Eberhard bets that he will sleep through most of the morning, waking up at noon with a terrible hangover. He indulged as much as his uncle yesterday during the Morena but he does not suffer the effects the same way.

"I could do that once. The gift of youth," Raymond commented yesterday with a mix of admiration, envy, and longing before tipping back another beer.

He butters two slices of rye bread, wraps them in wax paper, and tucks them inside his shirt. An empty beer bottle is on the table and he grabs it before leaving the house. He stops and sits on the steps to put on his shoes. Across the fence is the house he used to live in, which is now occupied by a young classics professor and his wife. They had moved in two months after Eberhard returned to the Flats. Raymond invited them that spring of 1912 to attend the Morena. They fell in love with the festival and the river community and bought his old house.

"Won't other faculty members think they're strange for living here?" Eberhard had asked Raymond. "Doesn't the History Department think you're nuts for living down here?"

"Oh, they've grown used to the fact that I live just across in the river rather than in faculty row," he answers, referring to the elegant townhouses ten blocks south of the university. "And given that

I study the history of immigration, the department chair thinks it only natural I'm down here."

He chuckled.

"As for them," he said, indicating the classics professor and his wife, "this is *la bohème*. This may not be Paris but this is a poor section of Minneapolis where life is dramatic, where art in all its forms is at the root level. It is a very befitting place for his wife. She is a painter and she plays the violin."

Eberhard looks at the clapboard siding, the full porch, and the enlarged windows. It is almost unrecognizable from the *bude* that Eberhard had first known, that his family had lived in for a year.

He stops first to fill the bottle at the community water pump in Carrie Finstrom's yard. It is quiet and only the most religious in the community will rouse themselves to attend church. Eberhard likes it this way, does not want anyone to know or see where he is going. He walks up to the top of the Flats and then beyond it to where the bluff is steeper, to where the deer path is. He bends down to look for human footprints other than his own and sees none, only the sharp hoof marks of the white-tailed deer that the Flats residents rarely see but know exist. One evening a month earlier Eberhard had surprised a group of does, at least three of which were heavily pregnant. For a brief moment, he and the does stared at each other. Then the does scattered upward, bounding into the nearly vertical slope underneath the shelf of the bluff. He puts a finger into a tiny hoof print. They have dropped their fawns. Only Honza has seen the sire of these fawns, a big buck that he says roams the river bluffs from St. Paul to Minneapolis and back. Eberhard starts walking again, follows the path beyond the western edge of the village. Then he enters the grove of birches and sits next to the large slab of limestone that has not been broken by weather or animals save for the grooves in its surface from where the deer lick it.

He came here the morning after his arrival three years ago. He kissed the limestone slab as though it was an altar, his gratitude at being back tearful. He cannot say what draws him to the grove, only that he feels an affinity for the place that is inexplicable. His uncle sometimes finds him here but does not linger to sit and talk. Instead Raymond tersely reminds him to come home. He used to think that it had something to do with Raymond's ex-wife. That the grove was a place of romantic encounter for them. She had left him in October 1911. It was only a few months earlier that Raymond had spoken of her, saying that she hated living on the Flats and he refused to move. Eberhard was secretly pleased that the grove had nothing to do with his uncle's marriage. But he still doesn't know what it is. He is perplexed at his uncle's attitude but not enough to pursue it.

He opens the wax paper and takes out a slice of buttered bread. The sunlight filtering through the birch leaves is warm, hinting of greater heat by noon. He puts out a hand and watches the leaf-shadowed light dance on it. His life, he thinks, reflects the light and the shadow at any given time. The light is his joy at being on the Flats. The shadow is homesickness, at being away from the farm. His mother had hugged him at the train station.

"I know this is the right thing for you to do and we want you to get an education," she said. "But I fear I will never see you again."

"You will always see me," he placated, but his arms trembled, giving him away.

Then he boarded the train, and as it got closer to Minneapolis his sorrow was replaced by a fear that no one would remember him on the Flats. Raymond picked him up at the train station in a motorized cab. Eberhard nervously chewed on a torn thumbnail as they crossed the bridge. They got out of the cab and walked to where the wooden steps were, shrouded by trees.

"You first," Raymond said, nudging Eberhard onto the first step. He heard movement as they got closer to the bottom, saw the dim outline of people.

"*Krátký fízl!*" a voice boomed. Honza lifted him off the last step, kissed him on both cheeks, and spun him around. Eberhard felt as light as a five year old in the Czech's bearish embrace, felt the tickle of Honza's soup strainer of a moustache, and smelled the beer and garlic sausage on his breath.

"Uncle Honza!" he exclaimed, kissing the older man back on each cheek. Then Honza put him down and an old woman stepped forward out of the thirty or so gathered at the base of the steps, wearing a familiar pendant.

"Oh my," Moira O'Flaherty said, reaching up to cup his face with her hands. "You look so much like your mother."

Then he was surrounded, the women kissing and hugging him, and the men pelting him with questions. His uncle reached in and grabbed Eberhard's arm.

"Follow me!"

The group moved down the street like a swarm of bees following a queen. They reached the house and Eberhard saw tables set up in the yard and out into the street, with dishes waiting to be filled with food. There was a barrel of beer, propped up on two wooden horses. Raymond moved ahead to usher people to the tables. Three women waved at Eberhard from the kitchen window, the glass fogging up from whatever was cooking on the stove. He waved back but did not want to go inside the house. He was not sure what stopped him. A hand rested on his arm.

"The dead are never far away," Moira O'Flaherty said. "Come, sit by me."

HE TAKES OUT the second slice of bread, folds it, and eats it in three bites. He tilts back the bottle of water and drains it. Then he lies back on the sparse grass and closes his eyes.

The Sunday after he arrived, his uncle surprised him by taking him to mass at St. Elizabeth's Church. Afterward they had a noonday meal, most of which was prepared by Honza's wife except for the dessert. Raymond had mastered the art of making Alzbêta's *Koláč*. They each ate a large prune-filled *Koláč*, dusted with powdered sugar. Then his uncle cleared the dishes from the table, put out two small glasses and a bottle of Slivovitz.

"I'm going to tell you what Alzbêta told me," he began. "Number one: don't bed any of the women from down here ..."

Although Raymond never pushed him, he did make Eberhard aware of his favorite brothel on Selby and Dale and gave him three French letters as a precaution. Eberhard went there out of curiosity. It was exciting and enjoyable but the condoms dulled the full sensations he experienced by the use of his own hand. There was something else missing in the experience as well.

"Jesus Christ! You're a monk like your father," Raymond said when Eberhard tried to explain his lack of enthusiasm.

"Papa is hardly a monk," he said, thinking of the passionate noises from his parents' bedroom that he'd heard all of his life. But it halted him for a moment, thinking of the similarities between him and his father. "I *am* like him. It has to be a special woman. I need it here, too." He tapped his head. A look of melancholy longing surfaced on his uncle's face.

"Not everyone is as fortunate as your father," he said.

He has not had sex since his last visit to the brothel and wonders if this is normal for someone his age. But he's been busy with school and jobs. One of the first odd jobs Eberhard did on the Flats was exercising Honza's horses. He has inherited his father's way with animals, horses in particular, and Honza saw it and trusted Eberhard from the beginning. Honza sends Eberhard and his son Marek out on delivery jobs alone. Eberhard also rigged a new fishing platform with Raymond's help, and he trolls the river in the fall for sturgeon and paddlefish, singing the song that Kyle taught him and Frank. Singing to ask Väinämöinen for assistance in landing the big fish. With the permission of the current inhabitants, he fixed up Kyle's old smokehouse. He now provides smoked fish for Christmas and for the Morena, selling the excess to the same butcher in the city that Kyle used to deal with, and adding to his savings.

He is also learning to play the *balalaika* from Sergei Demidov, a thirty-year-old Russian immigrant who fled Russia in February 1905 after the Bloody Sunday massacre killed his father, mother, and all three of his brothers. He had escaped to Finland, traveled through Sweden and Norway, and found passage on a cargo ship out of Oslo. Like Ian Brock, he made his way from New Brunswick through the rest of the Canada, entering by way of the Great Lakes and finally reaching Chicago where he worked in the stockyards for months. Another Russian told him to head north to Minneapolis where there was substantial factory and mill work. Throughout his entire journey, Sergei had kept his father's *balalaika* with him constantly. He made it known after he settled on the Flats that he would kill anyone who stole it. Honza declared him acceptable after he heard Sergei play, adding yet another instrument to the band that accompanied the Morena and other events.

Eberhard opens his eyes and sits up, wiping the crumbs from his pants. Squinting at the sky, he calculates the time to be about ten o'clock. Soon people will emerge for the day, and his uncle will wake up and wonder where he is. As he walks the deer path back, Eberhard considers if his uncle is lonely. He was still not himself when Eberhard arrived that spring, feeling the guilt of his divorce, but six months after that his concupiscence returned. Raymond keeps his liaisons above in the city, never bringing a woman back to the house. But lately, his uncle has been preoccupied with something else and has stayed home most nights. Eberhard does not know what it is, only that he catches Raymond staring off into the distance.

He stops by Honza's house to pick up Zena's famous cure for hangovers, which Honza refers to as "killing the pig." He promises to bring money over later to pay for it.

His uncle is sitting at the kitchen table, his head cupped between his hands. He looks up and sees the jar of viscous liquid in Eberhard's hand.

"No thanks. I think I'll suffer."

"Why?"

"Because I'm afraid that if I drink that stuff, the pig I kill will be me."

IT IS A MONDAY EVENING, the day after the Austrian archduke's assassination. They listen as Eberhard reads aloud the articles from the St. Paul *Pioneer Press* and both the Minneapolis papers. Raymond and Eberhard sit at a table by the river with Honza, Radim, Ian, and Sergei. Raymond listens and watches the river, its water moving as languidly as a couple out for a Sunday stroll across the bridge.

"They shot his wife, too," his nephew says, folding the paper and putting it on the table.

"A Serb," Honza comments. "If the archduke would have been traveling through Prague instead of Sarajevo, it might have been a Czech."

"Alzbêta would slap you if she were here," Raymond responds. "She would say the Czechs are not murderers."

"And the Serbs are?" he shoots back. "Every country has its boiling point."

"The Balkans have been boiling for a long time. What makes you so loyal to the Serbs?"

"It's not loyalty. It's because they have suffered under the Hapsburgs same as the Czechs. The Hapsburgs are finally coming to an end. Just like the czar." He drains his glass and Radim reaches over with a jug and refills it.

Raymond glances at Sergei fingering the strings of his *balalaika* and wonders what the brooding Russian thinks.

"You understand this could mean war?"

"Would that be new?" Honza says. "The Austrians and Hungarians have been trying to conquer the Balkans for a long time and they haven't succeeded yet."

Raymond motions for Radim to refill his glass too. He is relieved that Honza sees the conflict as contained to the Balkans. He doesn't want to explain the ramifications. A few months earlier, in January, he had received a letter from Richter.

War is imminent, he wrote. *It doesn't take a genius to realize the kaiser is waiting for the right opportunity to justify invading Belgium and, from there, France. We can't leave now. Rose's husband has been conscripted. Rose won't leave without him and Adelinde, Amalia, and Eva won't leave without me although I have begged them to. I am bound to my brother's business obligations. It is those same obligations that have, ironically, saved me from putting more scrutiny on the family. Right now every socialist is suspect. We can't even move to England because of the anti-German hysteria there. So we will endure what comes.*

Raymond immediately wrote to his mother, asking her to leave. He told her of a Franciscan order not far from Minneapolis—the Franciscan Sisters of Little Falls, Minnesota. Her response is also no, but for a different reason. She is the reverend mother now and her duty and loyalty is to her convent in Augsburg.

"So, professor," Ian says. "What do you think will happen?"

Raymond locks eyes with Eberhard. He wants to redirect that question to his nephew. Two days earlier, Eberhard told him he had joined the Minnesota National Guard and would be spending three weeks in July and three weeks in August training at Fort Snelling in St. Paul. A temper Raymond didn't know he possessed erupted. He shoved Eberhard against the kitchen door and slapped him.

"Are you crazy!"

"Uncle Raymond, it is the *National Guard*. Not the *army*. It means if we are attacked on this land, I will be a part of defending it. I'm not the only one. Marek joined," Eberhard said. "And four of my classmates."

"But you are only seventeen, not eighteen."

"Seventeen is the minimum age."

"With consent of a guardian or parent," Raymond said. "You forged my signature, didn't you?"

Eberhard shook loose of his uncle's grip.

"You left home at sixteen," he said.

"Jesus Christ! That was different. *Much* different," Raymond said, holding his forehead with one hand. "Why didn't you talk to me about it? Defending this country means defending *its interests* as well, not just the borders. Canada isn't a problem but Mexico is and the troubles down there are getting worse. And things are getting worse in Europe. The National Guard *is* an army."

"You would defend this country if you had to," his nephew countered. "If someone attacked the Flats, you would defend it."

"That's different," he bristled. "Have you written to your parents yet?" Raymond asked, thinking of his brother's reaction. Albert will hold him responsible.

"No."

"I'm not going to tell them. That is your responsibility. You'll have to tell your parents at some point. And *you better* tell them you forged my signature." He paused. "You might not be so enthusiastic about the National Guard after you complete basic training."

THEY ARE WAITING for his answer. Raymond feels an overwhelming sense of dread. His life is going to change—how he does not know. If it were not for his professorial and avuncular duties, he would obey the impulse of the moment. He would take off his clothes, walk into the river, and just float with the current, letting the river dictate his future.

"I don't know," he finally says and means it.

GERMANY INVADES BELGIUM on August 3, and France and Britain declare war. All mail from Germany stops, and Raymond, like Magdalena and Albert, finds it agonizing not to hear from his mother, from the Richters. Then the fall term begins and he is swamped with teaching, something he is grateful for as it keeps him from brooding.

He is reading and grading assignments from his second-hour class when the department secretary knocks on his door and delivers a letter postmarked with a London address but no name. He puts it into his briefcase, eager to finish the assignments. When he arrives home that evening, he finds a note on the table. Eberhard has finished studying and is at his part-time job as a cooper's assistant. He has left Raymond a warmed plate of *klobásy*, sauerkraut, and boiled potatoes with butter. Raymond sits down to eat when he remembers the letter. He gets up and retrieves it from his briefcase, using a table knife to slit it open. He reads the first line and is transported from the present to the near past. To what he thought was a memorable but benign meeting in October 1911.

RAYMOND HAD APPLIED FOR and was awarded a small grant to travel to Oxford for a conference and to deliver a paper on human migration in history. He wrote to Richter and told him that he would be in London and asked if he and Frau Richter could meet him there. They wrote back, affirming their travel to London but that they would miss his lecture by a day.

He was a junior professor, a minor speaker, and the auditorium was sparsely populated. One man, however, sat attentive in the middle row. He waited as Raymond finished speaking, then introduced himself as Captain Kell and they chatted for a bit.

"I would never have known you weren't born in America," he said upon learning Raymond's country of origin. "You have no accent."

"I do actually—American Midwestern—but I can't explain it.

I'm not as versed in the linguistics of language although I can pick up and acclimate to different accents."

"*Können Sie noch Deutsch sprechen?*" Kell asked.

"*Ja, fließendent.* I am also fluent in French, and passable in Czech and Slovak."

Kell invited him to tea at his home and then to the London Orchestra that evening. He learned that Kell was an army officer, that his father was a decorated veteran and officer of the Zulu wars, that his mother was the daughter of a Polish count, and that his parents were divorced. His education had been sophisticated: private school and then traveling through the whole of Europe and parts of Russia. After he married, he and his wife traveled to China to learn the language and to act as a British liaison in witnessing the Boxer Rebellion. He could speak five languages and had studied as a linguist. Raymond was about to ask him what his role was in the military when he happened to notice the book on the table next to the sofa. *The Invasion of 1910* by William Le Queux.

"You are a fan of spy novels?"

"Not really. That book was a gift," Kell responded. "I take it from the look on your face that you don't care for it."

"I rarely have time to read novels much less spy stories. But I have a colleague who loves them and so impressed upon me to read that book."

"What did you think of it?"

Raymond hesitated. He was aware of the growing anti-German sentiment in Britain. He did not feel that sentiment at the conference, but then again he was introduced as an American professor. And Kell was a British military officer.

"I think he exaggerates, to put it mildly. If Germany were a threat to Britain through espionage, then such muckraking and overblown prose would hamper if not really damage Britain's ability to detect such a grave threat. Historically, one of the greatest men in espionage was Sir Francis Walsingham who, I wager, would have considered Le Queux an idiot. Walsingham was a master of secrecy and discretion."

Raymond stopped, embarrassed by what he felt was a professorial lecture.

"I apologize. You obviously know your own history. I didn't mean to insult you."

"No apologies needed. I'm not the least insulted. My wife is currently reading the book. Le Queux is a popular author with the public though and a favorite of Queen Alexandra. Do you think there are no truths to his *faire des conjectures?*"

"I wouldn't say that. Just that his intention is to exploit prejudice and earn money doing it."

He picked up the book, looked at the cover.

"His writing reminds me of the Karl May novels I used to adore as a boy. Then one day Herr Professor Richter killed my adoration in one fell swoop. He said Karl May hadn't even been to the western United States and he was doubtful that May had even met an American Indian during his brief stay in New York City. He also said he was a terrible writer. And he was right."

"You were a student of Herr Docktor Richter?"

"Yes. My brother, Albert, too. His oldest daughter is married to my brother."

"I would like to have studied with him. A brilliant man. Unconventional as well. I admire that."

"He and Frau Richter will be here tomorrow. I'll be at the train station to pick them up."

"Might I meet them?" Kell asked.

"Certainly. Shall I bring them for tea?"

FRAU RICHTER KISSED HIM on each cheek at least twice and Richter himself could not stop shaking Raymond's hand when he met them at the train station. His former professor had lost more hair but otherwise seemed as vigorous as Raymond remembered him. Frau Richter—was it possible?—had become even more exquisite, her hair just as black as Magdalena's, her stature as elegant as always. And the sensuality of her person . . . he shivered when she kissed him, the effect making him feel like a young boy.

"Everything I hoped for you has come true," Richter said. "Look at you. A grown man, and an up-and-coming scholar!"

"We love your letters," Frau Richter said. "The Flats. What an extraordinary place you live in, what fascinating people. And now

Magdalena and Albert have a farm. How I would love to see them, see their farm. See Eberhard, Frank, and little Hilda. Meet the Indians Magdalena writes about."

Her voice caught. She stopped speaking, dabbed at her eyes with a delicate handkerchief.

"It is beautiful where they live, extraordinary really," Raymond said. "Everyone is healthy and happy. Except that they miss all of you very much. I have photographs to give you, sent to me from Albert and Magdalena."

"Yes, yes!" Frau Richter said. "We have a large package for you to take back. Full of good things for both you and for Albert, Magdalena, and the children. Unfortunately the rest of the family is not with us because we told no one of this trip except your mother."

"It was a precautionary measure," Richter said. "Your brother, Otto, is the head of the Alldeutsche Verband in Augsburg. They've taken it upon themselves to watch the train station. Who leaves and who arrives. Your mother arranged for a buggy from the Kloster to take us to Regensburg and we took the train from there. It is a disease, this pro-Germany movement so full of hate. A madness!"

"Your mother sends her love to all of you," Frau Richter said. "I visit with her once a week, and of course we work together in the Fuggerei. She is in good health and so happy, Raymond."

"Before I forget," Richter said, tapping his head. "Leo—remember little Leo? Peppermint Drop?"

"Yes. We've lost touch. What has happened?" Raymond asked, the image of his childhood friend suddenly at the forefront of his thoughts.

"He has tuberculosis. Their church gathered the funds so that the family could send him to a sanitarium in Switzerland. We gave generously of course, and I sent some books along for Leo to read. But it isn't looking good. He was never a strong boy and he was very weak the last time I saw him. I have the address," Richter said, pulling a piece of paper out of his vest pocket, "so that you can write to him. That would cheer him up immensely. He will of course keep your address confidential."

Raymond stared at the address for a few moments, thinking of

Leo as he last saw him, of their once-close friendship. And then he remembered his duty from the day before.

"You've been invited to tea by a Captain Kell. I don't know yet what his position is in the British military but he is very well educated and a great admirer of yours. I met him when I gave my lecture yesterday—"

"It was very successful, wasn't it?" Frau Richter interrupted.

"Well," Raymond blushed. "Not many attended but those who did seemed to like it. Kell did. You have a few hours to freshen up and then I'll take you to his home. He's a fascinating man, world educated. He's very eager to meet you. You should have much to talk about."

IN HIS HOUSE ON THE FLATS Raymond looks at the letter again. After Kell's brief introduction and summary of where they have met, he writes, "Would you be interested in aiding the British government in its war efforts? I have it upon good authority to ask you this."

Although the wording is ambiguous, Raymond knows that he is not being tapped for traditional military service. It is his language skills and his knowledge of Germany that are valuable. Kell, he thinks, must be in British intelligence. He wonders how Kell knows where his loyalties lie. Then it dawns on him that Richter told him. The two men had hit it off on their meeting, and the Richters remained in London for a week after Raymond had left. Although his former professor had never mentioned Kell in his letters since that trip, Raymond is now sure that the two men have stayed in contact.

He sees the paper is grease stained across the middle. The knife he used to open the envelope had a smidgeon of butter left on it. He thinks of the coffee stain on the letter Richter wrote back in January, the letter that, among other things, informed Raymond of Leo's death from tuberculosis. Of how he would have known Richter's mood before reading the letter. He could picture what happened. Richter was so preoccupied and upset while writing the letter that he misgauged the position of his coffee cup to his mouth. The coffee that spilled from his lips dripped onto his shirt, onto the letter, and smeared some of the ink. He had already written much of the letter and did not want to start over. So he carefully blotted the letter, waved it dry, and then rewrote over the smeared sections. It was the last line that stood out from the rest as it was on the un-stained bottom of the page.

Conrad said that all a man can betray is his conscience. I agree with that. I love Germany. But sometimes you have to betray the country you love in order to save it.

THEY ARE IN THE MIDDLE of what was once a white pine for-est. His father kicks the burned remains of the clear-cut trees and shouts curses that the light snow cannot muffle or cleanse. It is the cold that fogs his father's breath as it does his own, but Eber-hard thinks it could just as well be smoke, the rage like fire, the words—sinful, hellish, and damning—like burning nuggets of coal spit out.

It is Christmas Eve, and his first time home in three and a half years. Eberhard went to town that morning with his parents to pick up regular supplies and some special treats: six oranges, some candy canes, a bag of chestnuts, and some dried prunes. They stopped by the post office for mail before heading home. There were no let-ters or packages from Germany. He had not expected any but saw from his mother's face that she had hoped the German government would respect the holiday and temporarily lift a ban on mail leav-ing Germany. She turned to him.

"We aren't at war. I don't understand why mail to the United States is blocked."

"We are providing supplies to Britain and France," he answered, tactfully avoiding the other reason. His grandfather was being watched, having been a critic of the Kaiser and because his political beliefs leaned toward socialism. There was a letter from Raymond, which his father did not open until they got home. He helped his mother unpack the kitchen goods while his father read the letter.

"What does Raymond have to say?" his mother asked.

"I don't believe it," he said and left the house, the letter still in his hand.

"Something's wrong," Eberhard said. His father looked as though he'd been struck in the head.

"Go after him," his mother said.

"Goddammit!" his father shouts. He turns and looks at Eberhard as if seeing him for the first time.

"Did you know about this?" His father holds out the letter but he is standing beyond arm's length from Eberhard. Eberhard stays put, thinking it safer to do so.

"About what? Uncle Raymond left for the University of Toronto two weeks ago. I told you."

"Well he's not at the University of Toronto. He's not teaching. That stupid idiot has gone to Canada to enlist!"

He thought of the hug his uncle gave him at the train station. There was nothing in his embrace that spoke of something graver. If anything, Raymond seemed more worried about his house, and about leaving the Flats.

"That can't be. I saw the letter from the University of Toronto inviting him to teach for a year. He's gotten a leave of absence from the University of Minnesota."

His father leans over, breathing hard and bracing his hands against his thighs. He studies Eberhard.

"You really didn't know a thing about it?"

"Of course he didn't!"

Eberhard turns. His mother approaches, a shawl over her head. She walks past Eberhard and takes the letter from his father.

"That ass!" his father continues to seethe. "He left Germany to avoid becoming a priest or a soldier and look what he up and does! He's going right back into the muck of it. And he has the gall to say 'Please trust me on this.'"

His father walks to another stump and kicks it, sending pieces of rotting and burned wood in all directions. His mother folds the letter and tucks it inside her skirt pocket. They stand in a triangle, looking at each other, at the white clouds of their breathing. There is only two inches of snow on the ground, not enough to conceal the ugliness of the cutover, the big holes where the Krueger Lumber Company attempted to dynamite the biggest stumps out by blasting apart the long and gnarled roots that held each stump, and once tree, in place. Eberhard looks past his father to where the barbed-wire fence encloses this section of land. They haven't had time to work out the stumps, and instead allow the cows to graze on the grass that grows in between the tree remains.

"Albert," his mother says, breaking the silence. "This is upsetting but you aren't considering who Raymond is. He's done some stupid things in his life, but then again he came over here when he was sixteen. He is the reason that this," she waved her arm to indicate the farm, "all happened. Raymond is a survivor. This is obviously something he has thought about. He has a reason for this and for the confidentiality he is asking of us." She turns and looks at Eberhard.

"Only your father and I were to see this. You are to tell no one, not your brother and sister, your friends here and in Minneapolis. *No one.*"

He nods. His mother knows something that he and his father do not. But her face gives nothing away, and he is worried that she also knows what he has not told them.

"This is Christmas. Not the season to damn anyone. Raymond needs our love and understanding. Albert," she says, "you owe him that much. Come, let's walk back now."

But his father does not join them, heading in a roundabout direction that will lead him to the barn. His mother takes his arm.

"Your father's anger is not about hatred," she says. "It is fear."

"I know," he interrupts. "He just needs time to cool off."

He takes a deep breath, grateful that he has not yet told his parents about his enlistment with the National Guard. He thinks back to his uncle's reaction to his own enlistment, feels a sharp resentment over his uncle's now obvious hypocrisy.

"Are you not afraid for Uncle Raymond?"

"Of course I am. But while your uncle may be stupid in matters regarding love and women, he is razor sharp about politics. And he's like a cat except that he has more than nine lives. He has at least eighteen." She stops.

"In a strange sense, your uncle's letter has given me hope. He will find a way—I know he will—to contact your grandparents and aunts. And he will do all he can to make sure they are safe. Did he not tell you anything?"

He feels it then, the invisible hand of her scrutiny palming his head. He cannot look away because then she will know for sure.

"Not a thing."

EBERHARD WAITS UNTIL THE SUMMER of 1915 after receiving his engineering degree to tell them that he joined the Minnesota National Guard.

I am sorry, he wrote. *Please do not blame Uncle Raymond. He was and is as angry as I think you must be, Papa. He did not sign my papers. I forged his signature. It was cowardly not to tell you when I was last home but you were so angry with Uncle Raymond and I didn't want to add to that. Please understand that I feel proud of my decision. This will allow me to show that I am a good American, that we are good Americans.*

He informs them that they have nothing to worry about, that the National Guard protects the interior of the United States and is not a part of the regular army. Albert is mollified by Eberhard's reasoning.

But his letters that follow write of the subtle and then not so subtle taunts from the engineers he works with, and the growing anti-German prejudice in both Minneapolis and St. Paul. Only on the Flats does he feel free from innuendos. They begin to worry about his morale. His letters indicate a growing frustration and anger at the stupid comments of others.

Then, in the summer of 1916, he writes to tell them that he has transferred to the Wisconsin National Guard as they will be deployed to Texas to aid in the fight against Pancho Villa.

Albert leaves the house, red-faced with shame. It is his fault. Eberhard is afraid of him. Albert remembered the frozen expression on his son's face, his unwillingness to come closer as Albert swore at his absent brother and kicked the stumps. He thought he had understood the growing prejudice that Eberhard was facing but he does not. He has not heard any comments from the growing number of Finns and Norwegians homesteading in the area, and he assumes it is because they want no part of it, as the troubles of Europe are why they have left. There is some sniping from the small Irish and English population in town but the comments are always said under the breath, as Chippewa Crossing is at least three-quarters German and most of the businesses are owned by German immigrants. The conflict among the Germans is between those in support of the kaiser, those who are in favor of the U.S. entry into the war, and those like him and Magdalena who want to remain neutral. But now, of course, they cannot be neutral as Raymond is there working for the British. He circles the barn and heads back to the house.

"Did you read the rest of the letter?" Magdalena asks.

He saw two pages, not one, in her hand.

"Eberhard has been granted leave during May next spring. He won't have enough time to travel this far north but will be on the Flats for a week. He wants to see us."

He too wants to see his oldest son, needs to see him. But there is no way he can leave the farm at that time, nor can he spare Frank.

"You and Hilda will have to go," Albert replies. "Frank and I can't leave the farm. But we'll be fine without you for a week."

He questions his decision daily as they work through the fall and winter, tries to think of men he can afford to hire to take care of the place if he were to go. Ilmarinen is busy with his family. Jacob Bleu is logging in Michigan. Roman's drinking is of some concern as is Eddie Charbonneau's, as both men spend much time in the taverns. Father Boland would be ideal, but of course he cannot ask the priest. He looks at Frank from time to time, and thinks it is unfair to hold him back from seeing his brother. As if sensing his thoughts, Frank says to him one day, "Papa. It is okay. You can't work the place by yourself for a week. I'll be here too."

His agonizing comes to a halt as he and Frank wave at Magdalena and Hilda, watch the train pull out of the station. He is not on the train nor is Frank, and so the decision is made.

His humor is somewhat restored when Frank reads to him a list of the ships thus far destroyed in the war.

"Listen to this, Pa," Frank said suddenly. "'The SS *Wilhelm der Grosse*, a passenger ship converted to a merchant cruiser for the war, sank three ships before the British cruiser HMS *Highflyer* overtook her. Although the *der Grosse* did not sink, the crew abandoned her because they had run out of ammunition.'"

Albert laughs.

"Billy rolled over," he says.

THEY WILL CELEBRATE her eleventh birthday today in this place where her parents and brothers once lived, where her Uncle Raymond still lives, the place with the strange name. She is perched high up in the trestles underneath the bridge, having climbed it against her mother's orders. But her brothers climbed these trestles when they lived here and at a much younger age, and she will not do differently because she is a girl. From up here she can see all the features of the Flats and its residents. The wooden steps are barely visible because of the trees shrouding them, the steps she skipped down like Alice in Wonderland when they arrived two days ago, looking for the world of her parents' and brothers' stories, the world apart from what she has known. And it has been, although at first the crowded houses with their unpainted fenced-in yards, the dirt streets, the smell of fish, sauerkraut, and something called lutefisk invited her scorn. There was a mountain of coal, calling her as it did yesterday when she and Ilona and Erika—daughters of her mother's friend, Aino—climbed it. They returned to her uncle's house almost unrecognizable, their fair hair made black with coal dust, their faces and hands and even their eyelashes equally black. Their mothers were exasperated but Eberhard laughed and made them stand in the yard while he poured buckets of cold water on them, listening to them squeal.

She hears giggling below, hears her name being called and looks down to see Erika and Ilona sitting on a lower part of the trestle. She waves and then goes back to her consideration of the view in the mid-afternoon sunlight. That bear of a man who swung her mother around and kissed her on both cheeks and called her "Maggie" is lifting kegs of beer onto wooden sawhorses. The bear man's barrel-shaped wife, Zena, is dishing up food with her large and rough hands. Seated at the head of the longest table is old Mrs. O'Flaherty whose blue eyes glitter out of her soft, wrinkled face whenever they look upon Hilda, and who wears a pendant that she claims is more valuable than gold or diamonds. Dancing together is the Cornish man with a bad eye like Roman Zelinski, and his pretty Russian wife, Larissa, who brushed and braided Hilda's hair yesterday, telling her that she was lovely and that her hair was beautiful. Then there is Ilona and Erika's mother, Aino, bringing out loaves of fresh potato and rye bread from the limestone ovens. Aino was the surprise that Eberhard had for their mother. They hugged each other, wiped one another's tears, and hugged again for the longest time, keeping Eberhard and Hilda waiting on the steps.

"This is the first trip I've taken since we've moved to Pine City," Aino says. "I was so happy when I got Eberhard's letter. It is a good thing I put a little aside each year. Kyle had to stay home to watch over the farm with the neighbor's help. But he's happy we are here."

Hilda does not know what to think about Aino. When Aino looks at her, the green in her eyes changes and she feels as though Aino knows her, has seen her before, and can see into her soul.

Then there is her brother standing and drinking beer with other uniformed young men including the bear man's son. There were other soldiers at the train station but no one who was as handsome, wearing the olive-green tunic, breeches, and some things around the bottom half of his legs called puttees. He wears a hat just like those of the Canadian Mounties in her book on Canada. She was speechless with longing and with love when he swept her up in his arms at the train station, this older brother who means everything to her. Eberhard is taller than the rest of the men, and he has, as her mother put it, "filled out." He looks like their father in that his shoulders and chest are broad, and he has the same muscular leanness and easygoing way of standing. But his face, the face she adores and has missed, is a masculine version of her mother's. Unlike her mother, Eberhard does not scrutinize Hilda or watch her so closely. His brown eyes are warm and liquid, and his laugh or frown can change her mood and her sense of herself very quickly.

She hears footsteps above, the loud sound of heavy boots. She looks up but can only glimpse the presence of whoever they are by the sunlight they block out in the cracks between the bridge's flooring. She thinks nothing of it as people have been walking across the bridge all day. She looks back at the crowd below. Then a bottle is thrown from above her and she watches as it lands, hear the violent sound of glass breaking. Two or more beer bottles are thrown, just missing some of the people standing below. Then there are voices, chanting coming from above. The voices of men.

"We are going to hun-hun-hunt you down!"

The bear man runs toward the bridge, as does her brother, yelling at people to get out of range of the bottles. The chanting above continues, punctuated with "Come and get it, Fritz!" and "German pigs!"

More bottles are thrown, and to her horror one of them hits her brother in the chest. She screams, terrified that her brother has been hurt. It does not break upon impact but it knocks the breath out of Eberhard. He stares up at the bridge and then his eyes move down and he sees Hilda.

"Hilda! Stay there! Don't come down!"

She looks down at Erika and Ilona who have stood up and are holding onto the steel frames. They are shaking.

"Hang on!" she yells. Their faces turn upward, are wrenched with fear.

"You goddam sons of bitches!" the bear man yells. "You buy my beer and throw the bottles at me! Come down here and do that, you sons of bitches!"

Her mother is running toward Eberhard. But the bear man grabs her and pulls her away from the bridge, from the bottles. Hilda looks at the steps to see her brother disappear with a group of other men loping up the steps.

"Stay there!" her mother yells, looking at Hilda. "Ilona! Erika! Stay there!"

There is laughter above her. She feels warm water dripping on her head and looks up, only to have a stream of it hit her face. She smells the rank, salty smell of piss. Before she can react, thunder hits the bridge. The trestles vibrate as boots come from the other side. There is the sound of fighting: thuds of punches, swearing, bodies falling, bodies being kicked.

She hears their names being called. She looks down and sees her mother and Aino directly below.

"Mama!"

At first she thinks it is Erika and Ilona who have cried out. But it was her.

"Hilda, climb down now. Don't be afraid. I'm right here. I'll catch you."

And then she is moving downward, her shaking hands and feet working together. She drops to the ground and stands up, feels the stinking wetness of her hair and the front of her dress. Her fear, humiliation, and rage come forth in tears.

"They *peed* on me."

"Let's take them to the river," Aino says, grabbing each of her daughters' hands. They make their way against the crowd headed for the bridge. Mrs. O'Flaherty is already down by the shore, bent over her cane and livid.

"Holy Mary, Mother of God! They pissed on children!" she says as if it is a trespass as great as being hit. The girls are undressed until they are wearing only their chemises. Then Hilda's mother lifts her up, cradles her as if she were a baby, and wades into the river. Aino does the same with Erika, while Zena carries Ilona.

"Pinch your nose shut," her mother says. Then she lowers Hilda into the water until she is beneath its surface. She feels her mother move her back and forth and then she is pulled up, the piss and her tears washed away.

"All gone," says Aino. And her mother, Mrs. O'Flaherty, and Zena say the same. *All gone.*

THE FIGHT ON THE BRIDGE was quickly over as there were only five men who initiated it, against twenty young men from the Flats. The police broke it up.

"And for the first time, *the first time*, mind you," the bear man whose name is Honza said, "the police did not press charges against us. It was because of the uniforms. Are you going to arrest American soldiers having a celebration with their families? No!"

Her brother has a scrape on his cheek and his knuckles are raw and swollen. His lower lip trembles.

"Three of those men went to school with me. Graduated with me. They used to be my friends," he says.

"The Anglos have always been that way, for as long as I've lived here," Honza replies. "To them, people who come from countries east of Paris are Polacks, Huns, Bohunks, or Ruskies. Good enough to have work in the mills and the factories. But not good enough to sit at the table or be respected like any Anglo man or woman."

"Did you read the paper last Sunday?" Radim says. "A Lutheran minister was tarred and feathered for reciting a prayer for a dying woman in German. Three Germans at the mill have already changed their last names."

A man with a long red beard asks Eberhard and the other soldiers to take off their uniforms so that he can clean them. Hilda notices a groove in his right index finger.

"He's a tailor," Eberhard whispers to her, noticing her fascination. She watches her brother take off his uniform.

"Thank you, Zalman," her mother says, placing the folded stack of clothes in his arms. "Will you play your cello later?"

Zalman nods.

Hilda and Erika and Ilona have fresh dresses on, their hair still damp, braided into coronets. The sun is setting and people have returned to celebrating, but with an edge of sadness. She shifts from leaning against her mother to leaning against her brother now dressed in everyday clothes. There is a big cake with candles on the table for her birthday. Since Erika and Ilona's birthdays are in less than a week, the cake is also meant for them. The girls blow out the candles, and there is a rousing cheer for their health and happiness. Then Zalman plays a sonata and her mother sighs.

"Oh, Paganini."

The Russian man whose name is Sergei is asked to play his *balalaika*.

"Not for a few weeks," he says, holding up his hands. They are as swollen and bloodied as her brother's.

Eberhard turns to Aino.

"Auntie. Will you sing the rune of Aino?"

Aino blushes.

"Oh Aino, please," her mother says.

It is a story; a song that flows likes a wave, which sweeps Hilda into the water of it. She is hypnotized by Aino's voice, by Aino's eyes, which in the firelight are the green of new pine needles. The song is a warning to mothers to watch over their daughters. It settles in Hilda as if Aino has reached inside Hilda's chest and cupped her heart. She leans back into her mother, feels her mother's arm wrap around her. The world she thought she knew has shattered. She is no longer in control of what happens, is no longer so safe from harm. There is a bigger world, a world in which people hate other people based on where they are from. Hate her even though they do not know her. She remembers what Ruby Bleu said to her on the playground, after she complained about her mother.

"You are stupid, Hilda!" Ruby said. "You have *a nice* mother. And a nice father." She paused, narrowing her eyes and brushing a lank of black hair out of her face. "You think you're so good, so holy. But you're not."

On the walk back to Raymond's house, she pulls her mother aside, waits until the others are out of hearing.

"Would you force me to marry?" she asks.

"Never," her mother answers. "And if you still want to become a nun when you are sixteen, I won't stop you."

Hilda follows her mother into the house. She's not sure she wants to be a nun anymore. She wants to be a moon maiden, a woman who can stand on top of water and sing comforting songs to those on the shore.

"I HAD HOPED WILSON would keep us out of it," Albert says.

"I don't think he could have," Father Boland answers.

It is the customary Sunday dinner with the priest. Hilda and Frank have gone down to the river to fish, leaving the adults to talk over dessert. The priest is grateful for the beauty of the October day, for the good food and company. He rode out to the Kaufmann farm feeling his spirits lifted by the yellowing of the tamaracks, by the routine of the natural world, and not by what is occupying everyone's mind these days: the entry of the United States into the war. He prays that this will bring the now three-year-old war quickly to an end.

There are quarrels in the taverns, at the lumber mill, and at the general store. The State Board of Education demanded that schools remove from their libraries all books about Germany, written in German or by Germans. The priest argued that the Catholics of German and Eastern European descent in his parish want to stay neutral, not because they are patriotic to Germany but because they are patriotic to cultural traditions and to family members still living in Germany. He was not being entirely truthful. At least a quarter of his German constituents were in favor of Germany in this war. But news of German atrocities, especially in Belgium, has increased the anti-German hysteria.

And then there was the Zimmerman telegram, sent to Mexico's German ambassador, promising the support of Germany in getting back the land of Texas and California if Mexico declared war on the United States. It was intercepted by British cryptographers and presented to President Wilson as solid evidence that Germany was hostile to the United States. It does not help that in some parts of the state there is a strong membership in the Pan-Germany movement. Father Boland is affected by the disturbing news but refuses to have his German parishioners bear the guilt of actions they are not a part of. Rather than destroy the books, he has put them in the rectory's attic.

They do not talk much about Albert's brother. He briefly considers a tactful way of asking the question but relents, not wanting to cause discomfort. So he asks about their oldest son.

"Any news of Eberhard? What division is he with again?"

"The 32nd," Albert responds. "They are stationed at Camp McArthur, in Waco, Texas, but will be leaving for Camp Merritt in New Jersey before shipping out to France—he thinks, in February or March. He doesn't like Texas. The country down there is dry, apparently. Eberhard says he misses water and pines. We received a letter from his commanding officer just last week. Eberhard is outstanding in everything he does. He said that Eberhard 'has the gift of diplomacy' and that this aids greatly in maintaining the cohesion of his unit. That we should be proud of him."

"He's right," the priest answers. He cannot determine whether Albert's tone is one of resignation or acceptance.

"How is Frank?" he asks.

"Unhappy. He is bitter that he couldn't pass the military physical because of a heart murmur. He feels useless even though I couldn't do without him on the farm," Albert answers.

"He's gotten better. But he's still restless," Magdalena adds.

"Why don't you speak to him again of attending the university? Better yet," Father Boland says, "why not have Eberhard write to Frank and urge him to attend? That way, Frank can live in Raymond's house and go to school."

"Frank's never been keen on school. He's never been a scholar like Eberhard. He likes hunting and fishing more than reading," she says.

"But he likes farming?"

"Very much," Albert answers.

"The University of Minnesota has an excellent agricultural college. There are new methods to farming developing all the time. It would be more vocational, something Frank could relate to. Can you afford to let him go for four years? He could come back and be of even greater assistance."

They do not answer right away. Albert is pensive, Magdalena thoughtful.

"I don't want him to experience what Eberhard did. I don't know that it is safe," Albert says.

"What if he attended using Honza's last name," Magdalena says, turning to her husband.

"Or mine," Father Boland offers. "I could say he was my nephew."

"He would be expelled if it was ever found out," Albert replies. "And if he isn't expelled, he will graduate with a diploma that does not show his real name. I appreciate the offer, Father, but it's galling that we have to do that."

"It will not make him any less your son. There was a small paragraph in the *Milwaukee Tribune* last week—you may have missed it—about the University of Minnesota's dismissal of a political science professor who was German. If Frank were to go on for an advanced degree then changing his name would be problematic. But he wants to farm, not teach. When your brother comes back after the war, he may be able to petition to have Frank's name changed back to Kaufmann. Boland is a safe name to have at the moment."

"That would get you in trouble with the archdiocese if they ever found out," Magdalena says. "It is a lie. And a sin."

"It is a sin of commission. And I accept that. My duty as a priest, as I see it, is to protect innocent people."

"We can't let you do that," Albert says.

Albert gets up and walks to the dining room window.

"Frank Cervenka," he says as if to taste the name. "I still don't like it. That he would have to change his name to be safe!" He turns around. "But it would be more plausible, and if anything arose Honza could attend to it."

"Oh Lord," Magdalena says, covering her mouth, thinking of the possible outcome. She could see the big and coarse Czech sitting down with the president of the university, offering him a beer and plug of chewing tobacco, and filling his ear about what he thought education should be.

"Let's hope Frank doesn't do anything that would require Honza's presence," Albert quips with a sudden grin. The priest has never met the big Czech but the stories about him remind him of Roman Zelinski.

"We could write to Honza and ask him if there are two young men or even a couple who wants to move here and learn how to farm," Albert says, thinking aloud. "We could fix up the Weir house and put them in there. That way we'd be helping someone and getting help in return if Frank leaves. And I think having Eberhard pose the idea to Frank would work."

The priest is not fooled by Albert's sudden acceptance of the situation. He sees the sadness on Albert's face and can follow his train of thought. Albert knows his youngest son is restless. He does not want him to resent being on the farm. But he is losing the men he is closest to in life.

On his drive back to town, Father Boland wonders if he could have been such a devoted father, could have endured the leaving of children especially during wartime. It is a harder test than he has ever been asked to bear, and he feels some shame in being sheltered by a religious life.

FRANK RECEIVES A PACKAGE from his brother in mid-February. It is from Camp Merritt in New Jersey, and enclosed is a letter, a photograph of Eberhard in uniform, and two pictures of him with friends from the 32nd Division.

Uncle Honza will be thrilled to have you as his nephew in name! He's has been watching Uncle Ray's house but he needs someone to live in it. You would be doing Uncle Ray and me a big favor. And, he wrote, *college is fun. You'll see.*

As Father Boland predicted, Eberhard's letter persuades Frank to attend the university, and under the last name of Cervenka. Just after the letter for Frank arrives, they learn that Eberhard has shipped out with the 32nd Division to France.

Frank leaves in late April for Minneapolis. He has some remedial studying to do before he begins the fall semester, and the summer will also allow him to resettle on the Flats and get his bearings.

Albert had the tailor in town make Frank a new suit, one of blue serge. They are happy for their younger son. He has finally found some direction for his life, but their emotions are sober, anchored by the past year's events. They stand on the train platform and watch until they can no longer see the caboose. It is eerily reminiscent of the last time Eberhard was home that Christmas of 1914. In two weeks, they will be back at the train station to pick up the young Norwegian couple that Honza recommended to take Frank's place on the farm.

Albert hands the reins to Magdalena, telling her that he has some business to attend to in town and that he will catch a ride home with Roman. It is eleven o'clock in the morning. He walks into Schaeffer's Tavern and orders a beer. At four p.m., Father Boland answers the rectory door and finds Albert sitting on the steps, incoherent. He drives him home in the church's new Model T Ford. The priest hoists him out of the car, carries him into the house, and lays him on his bed. Magdalena asks him to stay to supper but Father Boland wants to drive back to town while it is still light. It is mud season and the roads are soft in some areas. She walks Father Boland out to the car.

"I wouldn't say anything to him," he says. "These are terrible times. Even the best of men fall down and I'd say Albert is more than deserving of some excess. And you as well."

He gets in, rolls down the driver's side window.

"I think you, Albert, and Hilda should make a trip to Ashland this summer, to see Lake Superior. I can find a couple of men to take care of the farm. I think you will find spiritual sustenance in the big lake."

She watches him turn around in the barnyard and then head down the driveway. *Sister Superior.* She has not thought of Tempy in a long time. Wonders if he is alive or dead.

TWO DAYS LATER in the spirit of hope and contrition, Albert takes some of their savings and buys a Model T, saying won't the boys be surprised when they come home. After that, whenever they buy something a little nicer, no matter how small, it is followed with the postscript of *won't the boys be surprised when they come home.*

Raymond had given them a post office box address in London to contact him in case there was an emergency. Magdalena did not feel it necessary to write to him when Eberhard was sent to Texas to fight against Pancho Villa. She knew that Eberhard would be all right. But she does not feel that now. She folds the letter and inserts it into an envelope. Her son being sent to fight in Europe is an emergency.

THEY SIT, listening to Schumann on the Victrola. It is early morning and Kell is home suffering from a bout of asthma, reclining on the sofa, his eyes shut. Raymond, who is no longer known by his real name for the duration of the war, picks up the phonograph's paper cover. *Kinderszenen op. 15, Scènes d'enfants.* Kell opens his eyes. He leans over to turn down the music.

"Do you like Schumann?" He cannot speak without the wheeze, the slight whistle.

"Very much."

"I do as well, especially this opus. My mother would play this when I was a child. Given the present circumstances, I suppose it is a bit unpatriotic. I miss other composers as well."

It is understood that the missed composers are Beethoven, Bach, Wagner, and Mozart. Three Germans and an Austrian.

Kell leans back and shuts his eyes again. His asthma is getting worse. When Raymond first met him it wasn't as apparent. But then it was October at Oxford and the season for blooming plants was over. Now it is May, six years later, and although Kell's family is now in a house in Camden Hill, having left their country home in Surrey, it seems the city also harbors allergens that test his lungs. It has been suggested at the Foreign Office that Kell's asthma makes him unfit to be the head of MI5, the Security Service. Raymond suspects the "suggestion" came from Friedrich Thomson of the Special Branch, a flamboyant braggart who loves publicity, covets Kell's position, and who takes credit for much of MI5's achievements. Thomson is close to the ministers who hold sway, who accept his flattery and find Kell's shunning of publicity and understated manner intimidating. Raymond is disgusted by the shallowness, the fickleness of the British ministers. After all it was Kell who broke an extensive network of German spies just before the war, crippling Germany's espionage within Britain. But the public didn't and couldn't know that. The arrests of the spies were attributed to Scotland Yard, thereby maintaining the cover of MI5's predecessor, MO5.

Kell's eyes roll underneath his lids, a sign of light dreaming.

Raymond leans back into his chair. It doesn't seem that long ago that he wrote back in the affirmative after receiving Kell's initial letter. Kell then responded with more details, including instructions to destroy the letter after Raymond had read it. Raymond sent the requested photograph of himself, and in early November 1914 he received the passport and other documents he would need to enter Canada and Great Britain.

"Alan Edward Davies," the custom official read aloud at the Detroit ferry crossing. "Enjoyed your time here, Alan?"

"Yes, very much," Raymond responded with the inflection of an educated south Londoner. He chose not to sit inside the ferry where it was warm so as to avoid engaging in lengthy conversation with strangers. He stood on the deck with his coat collar turned up and his hands in his pockets, marveling that the Detroit River hadn't frozen over yet. He boarded the train in Windsor for Toronto. In Toronto, he switched to a train that took him to Quebec, changing trains yet again for the training camp at Valcartier in the blue Laurentian hills. There Raymond presented his War Office pass, signed by Kell. After two months of basic training, he sailed out of the Gaspé Basin on an Atlantic liner carrying munitions, horses, wagons, and a small company of new Canadian infantry recruits for the port of Plymouth. No one guessed, during that entire time, that he was an American or German. He slid effortlessly into his new identity, even startling Kell who picked him up at the train station in London. After six more months of training within British Intelligence, he was then given a Certificate of Registration of an Alien Enemy for any travel he might make to Germany under the guise of a businessman, Fredrich Bergmann.

The maid opens the sitting room door bearing a tray of tea and toast with jam. She sees Kell, assumes he is sleeping, and hesitates. Raymond motions her in. He marvels at how the servants seem to glide unnoticed in rooms, bringing whatever is needed without pause. She silently puts the tray on the table and glides back out. Kell opens his eyes.

"Ah, tea."

He sits up, pours Raymond a cup and then one for himself. He puts two half slices of buttered toast with a dab of jam on a plate and hands it to Raymond. He himself does not eat. He takes a sip of his tea and then presses the cup against his lips and breathes in deeply.

"Bloody spring. I've been told for years to live in a desert climate. Maybe I will in retirement. Can't leave just now obviously." He drains his cup and refills it.

"You wanted to talk to me about something?"

Raymond takes Magdalena's letter from his inside coat pocket.

"I TOLD YOU I had a nephew, Eberhard, who was on the border of the United States and Mexico, fighting in the war against Pancho Villa. He is now in France. He came over with the American 32nd

Division in February. He's with the 128th Infantry Regiment. They are billeted in Petit Croix and Norvillard for training."

"And your brother—"

"Sister-in-law."

"Sister-in-law wants you to look out for him."

"Yes."

"That is only natural," Kell responds. "But you can't make contact with him. We can't afford to have you break cover."

"I know that. I don't want him to see me. But will you permit me to shadow him when I can? To stay informed as to the movements of the 128th? Do we have a reliable American military contact who would keep me informed?"

Kell reaches over with the teapot and fills Raymond's cup.

"Yes, we do. You'll have to maintain your British identity. You cannot slip, even once, into an American accent."

Raymond nods. He's not sure he has an American accent anymore.

"I realize it has been difficult for you, not having contact with your family," Kell says, putting on his spectacles. "I can open that avenue a little wider. You've been with us long enough for me to get a channel free of the censors. But my concern is an obvious one. Your family is of German descent, has a German last name. Since we are concerned about a spy network in the United States, such correspondence would be suspect. They live far north—Wisconsin—am I right?"

"Northern Wisconsin. Sixty miles south of Lake Superior. Where they live is still fairly remote. They live next to an Indian reservation."

As soon as he says it Raymond realizes the solution, and he could hit himself for not thinking of it sooner. He could send letters to Albert and Magdalena via someone on the reservation. He thinks of the storyteller Henry Two Knives. No, he wouldn't do. The name is exotic enough for censors in Britain and the United States to suspect it. But there is Ilmarinen Stone. He recalls that Ilmarinen, being half white and literate, does most of the outside business for the reservation. Mail going to his address and his name would not be so unusual. Raymond would write only every few months. Not enough to be considered steady correspondence. He will make it clear that they cannot write back.

"I think I have a solution," he says, and explains it to Kell.

"That's close to Canada," he comments. He pours himself another cup of tea. "You could send letters through Canada. I have a reliable contact in Quebec. The return address would be a Canadian one, not British. I think we can accomplish this."

Kell takes a sip of his tea.

"Thank you," Raymond says.

It is a miserly statement of gratitude but their relationship and Kell's demeanor has never contained hyperbole or expressed affection. They have a respectful, warm regard for each other but also a professional reserve.

"Our friend in Augsburg might want to hear news of his daughter and her family. We have an agent in Munich. I'll see what I can do," he adds.

MAGDALENA STANDS OUTSIDE Jacob and Marie Bleu's house, waiting for Marjaana who is still inside, and thinking how wet the spring has been. It has delayed Albert from getting in the fields, but here in this clearing by the bottomlands of the Chippewa spring is announced as if divinity reigns here. There is nowhere in the immediate twenty miles where the season is visually as apparent. There are the pines, of course, a darker shade of green, but in this clearing where the house sits there is an abundance of deciduous trees. She wonders if it is the silt from the bottomlands of the Chippewa that makes the leaves on the elms, sugar maples, silver birches, and box elders such an incandescent green. Yet it is that same abundance of water and the lowland dampness that is contributing to Marie Bleu's condition.

Marjaana comes out of the house.

"That woman is so stubborn. At least that ointment from Fishbach's store seems to help with her breathing. What's in it again?"

"Eucalyptus," Magdalena answers.

"I would have guessed it to be tuberculosis but Jacob says it is not, that the doctor at the sanitorium in Bayfield feels it is not. She's always been prone to colds but she's had this hacking for at least the past two years. Still I think we should take precautions."

As if on cue, Marie coughs so loud they can hear it outside. Magdalena ties a scarf around her lower face.

"I'm going in to talk to her. I'll send Ruby out, even if I have to push her," she says in reference to Jacob and Marie's eleven-year-old daughter. Ruby is as tough as Hilda and much wilder. She will risk being bitten by the girl if she uses physical force.

Ruby is still there, holding one of her mother's hands.

"Ruby, I need to talk to your mother alone. Can you just go outside for a little bit?"

Marie nods at her daughter. The girl is not happy about leaving but does so.

"Wash your face and hands," Magdalena calls after her. She sits on a chair next to the bed.

"*Marie, vous avez une infection grave des poumons. Vous devez aller à un hôpital. Nous allons trouver et obtenir parole à Jacob*—Marie, you have a bad infection of the lungs. You must go to a hospital. We will find and get word to Jacob."

"*Non, je sais qu'il va revenir. Ce sera la fin de cette semaine. Je dois attendre*—No. I know he is coming back. It will be by the end of this week. I must wait for him," she answers.

"*Comment savez-vous cela? At-il écrit pour vous?*—How do you know this? Did he write to you?"

"*Je sais juste*—I just know," she answers, adding, "*Prenez avec vous Ruby*—Take Ruby with you."

"*Je le ferais si je le pouvais. Mais elle devra être examiné par un médecin. Elle aurait besoin d'aller à l'hôpital avec vous*—I would if I could. But she will need to be examined by a doctor. She would need to go to the hospital with you," Magdalena answers.

Marie coughs, shakes her head.

"*Non. Puis elle reste ici avec moi*—No. Then she stays here with me."

There is no pushing Marie, and Magdalena leaves the house frustrated. Ruby runs back inside the house to be with her mother.

"Lord! She is stubborn."

"Of course. She is a Cadotte from La Pointe. She has always had the arrogance of the Métis, especially from up there. They think their French blood and history on Madeline Island makes them royalty. Until you came, none of us had much success conversing with her," Marjaana says.

"We can't leave them."

"What else can we do?" Marjaana replies. "We can't force her unless you want the sheriff to come out and physically remove her. I wouldn't advise that. That would be seen as more interference from the whites. We'll have to hope that she is right. That Jacob will be here by the end of the week."

JACOB DOES ARRIVE by the end of the week, to find his wife dead and his daughter catatonic with grief. He buries his wife and then takes his daughter into town where he has the local lawyer draw up guardianship papers. Then he rides up to the convent and leaves her with the nuns.

Magdalena had ridden over to the Bleu place in the early afternoon that Friday, to see how Marie was faring and to find out if she had left her missing bottle of laudanum there. She found no bottle and only the fresh grave. She rode home, finding upon arrival that Father Boland had driven out from town to tell them that Ruby was at the convent.

"WAS SHE THAT CLOSE TO DYING?" Father Boland asked.

"It is hard to say," Magdalena replied evasively, thinking of the missing laudanum.

"Why would he do such a thing?" Father Boland asked, as bewildered as the rest of them. They have congregated at the Kaufmann farm and are sitting around the kitchen table. "Bury Marie out there rather than in the cemetery. And leave Ruby at the convent."

"Ever since he came back from that school, his thoughts and why he does things are a mystery," Henry Two Knives commented.

"Like reburying Jacob Weir," Albert notes.

Henry Two Knives looks at Magdalena as if he knows something, as if he knows she suspects something as well. Then he shifts his focus to stare out of the window, speaks as though thinking aloud. "For Jacob to give his daughter away leaves us with no fight. It isn't our burden anymore. It is his, and I would not want to be him. It is a terrible thing he has done. To abandon his own child."

He turns away from the window and looks at Magdalena.

"You are all Ruby has now."

SHE DREAMS OF MARIE every night, can see her speaking but cannot hear what it is she is saying. Albert leaves to pick up supplies in town a few days later and Magdalena at first thinks of asking him to take Hilda with him but then decides that her daughter will go with her. Their relationship after their trip to the Flats had changed noticeably.

"It was terrible, of course, for all of you to go through that," Marjaana said when she heard about the fights during the Morena. "But it turned out to be the something that knocked Hilda down. That swept her off that righteous pedestal of hers. I'll bet being pissed on didn't feel good."

Magdalena rides over the Bleu place with Hilda sitting behind her in the saddle. The rock-covered grave is as close to the big oak as Jacob could get without cutting through the tree's huge roots. There is no headstone but carved into the oak's trunk is her name, Marie Cadotte Bleu, with the year of her birth and death. He carved a third line with the words, *Nous nous rencontrerons à nouveau*—*We will meet again*. Magdalena is sure he did not carve the marker on the day he buried his wife but came back to do so. The words are not so touching as the fact that he carved them in French. She listens, hears no human activity. Just the mating calls of Canada jays and chickadees. The incandescent green has grown darker but makes the clearing no less enchanting. There is now a road going past this place but it is far enough back that no one riding by would think someone had lived here. Still she has the feeling that someone is nearby, is watching them. She looks at Hilda, puts a finger to her lips.

"Jacob!" she calls. "I do not judge you."

It is a true statement. She woke up last night remembering her own reasons for burying her daughter, reasons that would be incomprehensible to everyone else except Aino and Raymond.

She takes out two hand shovels and a burlap bag full of iris bulbs from the saddlebag, tying the horse loosely so that it can graze on the lush grass that grows around the house. She gives Hilda half of the bulbs. They work across from one another, planting the bulbs along the sides of the grave and at the end where Magdalena guesses that Marie's head lies.

"If all goes well, they will naturalize and spread so that this becomes a blanket of irises," she tells Hilda. It was the flower Marie liked best, and that Magdalena's own mother cherishes. Magdalena planted purple irises during their first July on the farm, and often brought bouquets of them to Marie when they bloomed in the spring.

"*Presque comme des sabots de Vénus*—Almost like lady slippers," Marie said, explaining the wild flower that grew in the bogs of the Apostle Islands.

Hilda finds a bucket near the pump and fills it. She pours the water over the buried bulbs. Then she stands and contemplates their planting and the grave.

"Will you plant these on my grave if I die?" Hilda asks.

"You won't be dying for a long time, my girl. You will outlive me. But I would like it if you would plant irises on my grave when I die."

They stand for a few minutes longer. Magdalena did not explain to Marie the meaning of irises, what the Greeks believed about them, because she did not want to imply anything negative, given Marie's illness. Irises were placed on a woman's grave to summon the Goddess Iris who would then guide that woman in her journey after death.

She bends down, smooths the soil over a shallow spot. Since Marie borrowed traditions and beliefs from both sides of her ancestry, it couldn't hurt to have more spiritual help, even if it was from people as ancient as the Greeks.

FRANK STANDS IN THE DOORWAY of his uncle's house, a beer in hand. The city of Minneapolis has declared the Flats residents as unlawfully homesteading the river shore and bluffs. He cut classes early today and took the deed to the house and a copy of Alzbêta's will to the Minneapolis City Hall to prove his uncle's ownership of the house and lot. He insisted that they look in their records for a copy of the deed. They found it and he further insisted that they give him a document acknowledging that the house and lot, once owned by Alzbêta Dvorak, and then Magdalena and Albert Kaufmann, was now Raymond Kaufmann's.

"Are you a relative?" the city clerk asked.

"Yes, Raymond Kaufmann's nephew," he answered nervously. Fortunately, the clerk did not take it any further than that. He put the documents into the safe box under his uncle's bed when he got home.

It is almost October. He is homesick for the farm but he knows he has made the right choice in attending the agricultural campus of the university. He does have fun as Eberhard said he would, but not in the sense of social events and parties. Going to school at this level is different. He thrives at it, excelling in chemistry, biology, and agronomy. Next quarter it will be farm economics and animal husbandry. He has even gotten past being known as Frank Cervenka rather than Frank Kaufmann. It allows him to be someone he didn't think existed, has given him a sense of himself apart from his father and brother for the first time. He feels more like a man, and his growing confidence showed in his willingness to go alone to city hall.

He scans the houses below him. The appearance of city officials walking the streets, stopping and asking questions about who owns what house, how long they have been living there, and so on, has diminished any social resentments within the Flats, unifying them against the city. The city's timing is cruel. So far it has been a deadly September. The Pafko, Kovach, Novak, Karitesh, and Michenko families have each lost a son. Last week a telegram arrived for Honza and Zena. Marek was killed in the Argonne offensive. Honza's rage and then sobbing could be heard on both the upper and lower parts of the Flats.

They have also been suffering from the shortages because of the war, worse for them than for the city dwellers. Everyone plants a garden, but in a very short time Frank has become the intellectual of farming, bringing new seeds to them and showing them better ways to organize their raised beds, doubling their yield of vegetables. He has rebuilt chicken coops and showed them the risk of disease when mixing flocks of unknown birds.

He hears the approach of someone, looks down the street, and sees Honza. The older man is carrying a shotgun.

"Going duck hunting?" he asks when Honza gets closer.

"Rats," he answers. He sits down on the front steps, tired from walking. "Wood Street is having a problem with them. I said I'd shoot as many of them as I could. I just hope things don't get so bad that we have to eat 'em." He grimaces.

"I thought you might be out looking for city inspectors," Frank says.

"Those, too, the rat bastards."

Frank goes into the house and returns with another beer. They clink bottles, listen to the cicadas and crickets. Then a clarion call comes from above them and they watch a lone goose as it flies overhead. Honza wipes his face on his sleeve.

"I didn't want Marek to go over there," he says. "It isn't our fight, I told him. But it's hard to take insults when you are a young pup. Marek got tired of being called a dumb bohunk just like Eberhard hated being called a Hun. I don't know what it is with the Anglos of this city. *They came* from somewhere else, but if you ask them they just say they are Americans. Still we fight for America, same as they do. Pay the same price." He puts the shotgun on the steps next to him. "I wanted to stay out of it. But Ray told me that we couldn't bury our heads in the ground. That if the Hapsburg dynasty wins, it will try to rule the world. And I'll be dammed if I live under that yoke again."

He tilts back the bottle for a long drink.

"Have you heard from Eberhard? Or your Uncle Ray?"

Frank hesitates, thinking of the stories in the newspaper, the posting of the casualty list from the September 18 push forward in France. Eberhard survived it and Marek did not.

"C'mon. Tell me. I need some good news," Honza says, lightly punching his shoulder.

"I got a letter from Eberhard yesterday. I haven't heard from Uncle Ray since he left. Eberhard is okay. He's got a shrapnel wound in his left leg. His letters don't say much."

But in this last letter, Eberhard told Frank that he has kept a journal. And that if anything should happen to him, Frank should have it. Frank suspects the journal is filled with what Eberhard could not include in his letters.

"Neither did Marek's. His letters had some of the words cut out of them. The mail from the soldiers is censored."

"What do you think Uncle Ray's doing over there?"

"I don't know. But I can guarantee you that he isn't a foot soldier. With his brains and education, he's probably higher up in the chain of command."

Frank has the feeling that Honza knows more than he is telling. That he does have contact with Raymond. It is one of the paradoxes of Honza. He has a temper, is passionate about what he likes and equally vocal about what he doesn't like, can be crude but within seconds courtly and well mannered. It used to be said about Honza that what you see is what you get, but Frank knows that isn't true. Despite his lack of education, Honza is a thinker. And when he is told to stay quiet about something, he does, taking the secret into the depths of himself.

"You could beat Honza's brains out trying to get information but he won't give it. And besides, it will be your brains that get mashed if you get him riled," Eberhard had once said.

"What should we do about the city?" Frank asks, changing the subject.

"Well there are some here who will sell out and move on. But we got a lawyer and will fight it until your uncle comes back. Ray will know what to do."

He finishes his beer and gives the empty bottle to Frank.

"Remember that man who bought my big roan?"

Frank nods. He was mucking out the stalls in Honza's stable up in the Seven Corners neighborhood when Honza sold the horse. Honza grins.

"He asked who you were and I told him you were my nephew. And you know what he said?"

"What?"

"That you looked just like me!" Honza brays, slapping his knee.

That night Frank looks in the mirror, examines his face and ears for hair, slightly worried that his assumed last name could have a physical effect on his being. Then he looks again, realizing how ridiculous a notion that is. Honza pulled his leg, probably laughed all the way home. He sits at the kitchen table and begins to write a letter to Eberhard, to tell him what Honza told him, to make him laugh.

EBERHARD HAS HEAVED SO MUCH that it feels as though he's torn a muscle in his belly. He has dysentery as well and his ass is sore. A nurse and doctor have just finished changing the shit-soaked bedding under him.

"What's wrong with me?" he whispers.

"Influenza," the doctor says. "You and six other men. It's no wonder what with the rain and mud and cold."

"Where are we?" The doctor bends down.

"What did you say?"

"Where are we?" he repeats.

"We are still in the Argonne. You were too sick to be transported out. Do you know your name?"

"Kaufmann. Corporal." He stares deliriously at the doctor. Only the doctor's eyes are exposed, the lower half of his face is covered with a mask.

"Am I going to die?"

"I doubt it. You had a bad night but you have improved substantially. Here is the nurse. Drink as much water as you can and try to hold it down."

HE SLEEPS the rest of the morning and wakes at noon, feeling clearer in the head. The same nurse brings him a bowl of plain oatmeal and feeds it to him.

"You're a woman," he says. "An American."

"Yes. Both."

She suppresses a laugh. She has southern accent. Her eyes are as blue as Father Boland's, set off by strawberry-blonde hair, most of which is tucked under her white cap. Her skin and voice are like honey. At least that which he can see and hear in spite of her mask.

"You are so pretty."

Then she laughs. "Oh, when there are so few of us, the troops find us prettier by the day." She turns her head and he notices the bandage.

"What happened to your neck?"

"A tiny piece of shrapnel. I didn't realize I was hit until the doctor saw the blood running down my neck. It's nothing really."

He tries to sit up but she pushes him down.

"How long have I been here?"

"Four days."

"What is the date?"

"November 4."

SHE RETURNS TO ATTENDING the other men in the rows and rows of cots, most of which hold wounded soldiers. Despite many opportunities for injury, even death, he is unscathed after months of war except for a slight shrapnel wound in his left leg, and the war neuroses that all of them cope with: nightmares, tremors, fatigue. He heard one of the doctors call it *neurasthenia*.

Just three weeks before, the 32nd had broken through the Hindenburg line, known in the Argonne as the Kriemhilde Stellung. The 126th, 127th, and the 2nd Battalion of the 128th Infantry had worked their way forward into a wooded area between Bantheville and the Landres-et-St.-Georges. A patrol was sent out to determine the conditions for an advance. They reported back that despite the heavy shelling, the barbed-wire belt of the German front line was intact. The wire had to be cut before the 128th could go through. Eberhard was one of the chosen fifteen volunteers. They handed out wire cutters.

"I have my own," Eberhard said, lifting the long handled Kraeuter that he had found in a captured German trench at Romagne.

Eberhard went back out with the patrol and looked at the German front line through binoculars. It was a daunting task. The German belts consisted of six to eight rows of barbed wire interwoven to form a band approximately fifteen to sixteen feet wide. The wire used was hard and thick.

A smoke barrage was arranged to conceal them from the German gunners entrenched not more than thirty feet away. They had cut through the first five belts and were working on the sixth when a sudden wind came up and lifted their cover. A burst of fire cut down six men. Eberhard and the remaining men took cover and returned fire. The lieutenant signaled for them to crawl forward through the small opening in the sixth belt. They got close enough to the German trench so that the German machine guns could not be depressed into action. Two minutes later, the lieutenant looked at Eberhard and raised one finger.

"*Nicht schießen!*"

"*Wir sind es!*" Eberhard followed. There was a pause.

"*Wer ist wir?*"

They jumped up and into the German trench.

"*Hier!*" Eberhard yelled, shooting a startled gunner in the head and another one through the throat. It was over in minutes. The lieutenant was the only one who had been wounded, shot in the shoulder and left leg.

HE TURNS ON HIS SIDE, grateful to be on a cot facing the canvas of the tent and not another cot. The previous night Eberhard dreamt that he saw his uncle, there next to the cot. He was wearing a uniform and had grown a moustache. He spoke to Eberhard but Eberhard can't recall what it was he said. He has no idea where Raymond is, and on the few occasions that he has been tempted to ask his commanding officer he is reminded of his mother's words and keeps the temptation harnessed. He is sure now that his uncle is not a foot soldier but somewhere in the higher ranks of the British military, moving unseen.

He would like to have the delirium of the night before. Being clear-headed but weak brings on boredom, which in turn brings on rumination. Thinking was something he used to enjoy as it helped him make sense of the distant and immediate past of his experiences. At present he doesn't want to think about much of anything but he is helpless against the power of his memory.

THE FIRST MAN he had killed was during the surprise attack on German lines at Château Thierry. They went over the top, following a rolling barrage of artillery fire, and entered enemy lines. The man popped up in front of him, too close for him to fire. So Eberhard used his bayonet, stabbing the soldier in the gut and then the heart. The German soldier went down but took a while to die. After that Eberhard tried whenever possible to use his pistol or his rifle. He told himself that this was his job, shifting whatever he had previously believed into a hidden place in his head. But it was more than that. He *had* to survive this war and nothing would get in the way of that if he could help it. He had shot the two German gunners more easily than he would have a deer.

He has had many duties since May. He has manned artillery guns, has been on patrols with grenades in his pockets, and has served as a medic when the need arises. He's fixed harnesses and wagon wheels, and dug new trenches. He has miraculously escaped being gassed but has ministered to those who have been gassed. Witnessed their festering, blinded eyes and the choking as their throats swelled up. He has seen the human body decimated in every way possible: shot, burned, gassed, knifed, and blown up. He can walk through the stench of rotting corpses without covering his nose. He often worries that he is losing his sense of smell, that he won't recognize the perfume of a pine forest or the smell of fall leaves when he returns home. *The dead are never far away.* Here, he would tell Mrs. O'Flaherty, the dead are always present. There is no past for them or for the troops who are alive, who must see the dead every day. He has crouched in trenches where the walls are embedded with skulls from the previous three years. Limbs stick out of the mud and ground as though waiting to be assembled again, like dolls. The dead are with them always, reminders that holding a belief in the future is a luxury during war.

But it is the death of horses and mules that still gets to him. While the soldiers can dive for cover, the horses and mules cannot and take direct shell hits or are strafed with machine gun fire. The screams from those animals make him shake and tear up. When it is safe to do so, he walks through the carnage of animals and shoots those mules and horses mortally wounded but still alive. Their agony is burned into his memory. He will hear the screaming of horses for the rest of his life. The only thing worse is the sound of the wounded men in no man's land, men they can't get to who scream through the night in pain.

It is now evident even to the soldiers in the trenches that the German army is more demoralized than the Allies. The number of German deserters has skyrocketed; more have given themselves up as prisoners, desperate for food and sick of fighting. Some of them are thrilled when Americans capture them.

"I want to be a citizen of America," a young private announced to Eberhard, his hands still in the air.

HE GROPES THE SIDE OF HIS COT looking for his packsack. Inside is a letter from his mother that he has already read. So far he has received only one letter from his mother, but it is not because she hasn't written more, just that only one of her letters got through the tangle of communications. Her news was of the farm and how well Frank was doing although his father was still unhappy over Frank's assumed name of Cervenka. Mika Two Knives and two other men from Fox Lake had joined the army but that is all she knows. She does not know what division. Her letter was meant to be cheerful and newsy and on the surface it was. Yet he can read between the lines, knows the wound he has inflicted on both of them. He has written short letters, mostly to let them know he is alive. He writes funny vignettes of the vagaries of army life. He would like to write some of the truths of his experience, but those letters would not make it past the censors. He can still see the terror on his sister's face when the bottle hit him during the Morena.

But here he is among other American soldiers of German ancestry, with German names. He has fought with Italians and Jews from New York, men who speak Italian and Yiddish as well as English. He has fought with Poles, still so newly emigrated that their English is heavily accented with their native language. There are Czechs, Slovaks, Norwegians, Swedes, and countless others who are barely first-generation Americans. There are Mexicans from California, Texas, New Mexico, and Arizona. Like Mika Two Knives, there are other Indians. He fought with two Winnebagos from southern Wisconsin at Château Thierry, a father and son with the last name of Dobson. The father was in the 127th, and the son in the 128th. The son was killed first. The father, vowing revenge, went over the top and managed to kill four Germans before being riddled with machine gun bullets.

What he cannot write is whether or not his acceptance as a German American will hold true after he gets home, after the uniform comes off.

He feels sleepy and turns to lie on his back. Having the influenza will not get him sent home. After a few more days of rest, Eberhard will get sent back to the 128th, which is fine with him. He has something he wants to do.

But he needs the war to end first.

THE FIRST SNOWFALL has come earlier than it has in the previous five years, on the morning of November 12, and there are three inches of white everywhere. It is too early for them to portend it as an omen or a gift.

But that evening, Father Boland rides out from town bearing a telegram. For a few minutes they stand in the parlor and look at the telegram in his hand. Albert takes it from the priest and opens it.

"The war is over," he says in awe. "And Eberhard is alive and so is Raymond."

Magdalena and Hilda run outside and dance in the snow, kick it up like fairy dust while the men watch from the porch, overwhelmed by the good news. Magdalena swings Hilda around by her arms. All her fears were unfounded. Something in her ability to sense the unknown had taken the wrong road or else she sensed the fate of someone unknown to her.

Father Boland stays the night, leaving early the next morning to return to town and send a telegram to Frank.

Letters from Raymond and Eberhard arrive on the same day a week later. Eberhard will be staying for a few months longer as part of the Allied forces occupying the Rhine River, and Raymond is delayed as well although he does not explain why. They are disappointed that Eberhard and Raymond will not be home for Christmas but it does not dent Albert and Magdalena's joy at knowing their family has survived the war.

Eberhard has written, *I hope I won't be coming home alone.* They puzzle over the cryptic sentence until Albert says, "I'll bet he hopes that Raymond will be with him on the same ship when he comes home. That's what he means."

FOR THREE DAYS, Eberhard discreetly obtains what he needs, risking severe punishment for fraternizing with the local Germans if caught. Each day after drills and maneuvers and before he is scheduled to his assigned post, he slips away to meet a local black marketer exploiting the occupation of the American Expeditionary Forces. The first day he purchases a worn wool coat and winter cap. The second day, a pair of wool pants and gloves. The third day he exchanges some of his American money for German marks and pfennigs. He wraps the money inside the clothes and hides the bundle in the stone house where he is billeted on the outskirts of Coblenz. He shares a bedroom with four others, having chosen the bed in the right-hand corner because of an alcove a foot above the floorboards.

The evening of the third day, Eberhard visits the private guarding the new supply of horses in a stable just down the street, and he engages him in drinking and cards. He gets up at three a.m. and goes back to the stable where the private is passed out. He steals a horse, a saddle, and a set of saddlebags.

HE IS NOW TWENTY MILES from Coblenz. It is January and cold. He rides into a wooded area and changes his clothes. He leaves the breeches and puttees of his uniform under a pile of leaves but keeps his army jacket, stuffing it into a saddlebag. The other saddlebag is full of tinned rations, enough to last him the 250 miles to Augsburg. He watches as the horse drinks through the broken ice of a small stream. It is a big bay, muscled and in prime condition. An officer's horse.

He thinks again how long it will take him. They covered twenty miles a day on foot when they marched to the Rhine. On a good horse he can double that at an easy gallop, maybe even triple it if he stays off the roads and pushes the animal. He pulls out a map given to him by the old man who sold him the clothes. It's prewar and therefore dated, but the roads are the same. If all goes well, he will reach Augsburg in four days. He puts the map back in the saddlebag and mounts the horse, reining it away from the water. By now they know he is gone, but they don't know where. He has never spoken of having family in Germany to anyone, not even his commanding officer.

That evening he arrives near Bingen and risks going into the town. He does not dare speak English and is worried that he has acquired an American accent in speaking German. He needs to hear the dialect of German spoken. He is not prepared for what he sees, believing that the Germans who suffered the most were those in Alsace. But every person he passes on the street looks tired and gaunt. Even the children are pale and skinny. The small shop he enters has bare shelves.

"Do you have any pork?" he asks. The woman behind the counter shakes her head.

"No pork."

"Any beef?"

"No beef."

"Chicken?"

"No chicken. No meat," she answers as if he might ask about fish as well. She puts a small sack of potatoes on the counter. He purchases it, tries to engage her in small talk. She is not much older than he is and yet she looks far older. Her cheeks are hollow and her eyes are red-rimmed. He notices a wedding ring. A widow, he suspects, one of many from the war.

"Do you have any cheese? I'd like to take some home to my parents as a surprise," he asks.

"Take yourself home. That will be enough of a surprise," she answers.

He leaves, grateful for the short but confirming conversation. She sees him as another German soldier on his way home.

A DAY AND A HALF LATER, Raymond stops in Coblenz, having learned from his American connections that Eberhard's division is posted there. He is on his way back to England from Berlin, exhausted, his detachment nearly broken. He rode in a boxcar part of the way, and then on a bony horse for the rest of the journey. He is hoping to find someone with a car to take him into France.

Raymond sent a report back to Kell of what he's seen, what he knows. Berlin is in chaos. He dodged the left-wing demonstrators, the workers on strike, only to end up on a dead-end street in the industrial district of the western part of Berlin. He heard guns being fired and hid behind a pile of bricks. There he watched as the right-wing Freikorps rounded up supposed communists, socialists, and other suspect civilians, forced them against the wall of the building across the street, and shot them. He stayed behind the brick pile until the Freikorps left, shaking and with his ears still ringing from the machine gun fire. When he was sure it was safe, he ran past the dead lying next to the building without looking at them, desperate to get his things and find transportation out of the city.

I fear, he wrote to Kell, *that the communists are not the party to be worried about but rather the rise of a right wing, guarded by the Freikorps. There are bands of Freikorps roaming throughout the country and especially in Bavaria.*

He takes a room at a local inn not occupied by the American troops, bathes, shaves, and changes clothes to assume his identity as Alan Davies, British attaché. He locates the American Expeditionary Forces' temporary headquarters and meets with a Major Jensen. He explains that he is on his way to Cologne to meet with the British high command occupying that city. He expresses his admiration of the AEF and asks how the men are doing in their role as an occupying force.

"Overall they are doing well, considering the men want to go home now," Jensen says. "Morale isn't as high as we would like but it is understandable. They want to get on with their lives. Unfortunately, morale is at a low ebb just now with the 128th. One of their own deserted two days ago."

"Deserted? At this point in time?"

"I know. The only reason I can come up with is that he couldn't wait another three months to go back to the United States. We assume he is traveling through France to reach a ship heading west.

He stole a horse so he isn't on foot. We have alerts out at all the ports including England."

"Have you talked to the men in his unit?"

"Absolutely. None of them have any idea of why he deserted. His sergeant said he was every inch a professional soldier. Told them wonderful stories about his home in Minneapolis. That's where they think he is headed ultimately."

Raymond's heart begins to pound, sends up a roar in his head not unlike an artillery blast.

"What is his name?" he asks with forced casualness. "So I can pass it along in Cologne just in case he should go through there."

"Kaufmann. Corporal Eberhard Kaufmann."

RAYMOND MAKES IT OUT of the building and is running down the street toward the inn when he becomes violently ill. He ducks into a narrow alley between buildings and bends over against a pain in his chest and struggles to breathe. When it eases, he stands up and beats the brick wall with his fist. It never occurred to him that Eberhard might try to reach his grandparents. But of course he would. His nephew's blind and naive rationale is clear. There is an armistice and therefore it is safe to travel in Germany.

Raymond walks as fast as he is able out of the alley, the pain still in his chest, thinking of what he must do. First he must pen a letter to Kell to briefly explain his delay and to ask him to contact the Munich agent who will then contact Richter. Then he must purchase clothing and boots. The trains aren't running and he cannot risk driving a car through southern Germany when there are so few cars on the road because of the lack of petrol. So he must purchase a horse and saddle from the American Expeditionary Forces. If they won't sell him a horse, he'll steal one.

EBERHARD HAS RIDDEN FOR FOUR DAYS with very little sleep. He has no choice but to ride through the city of Ulm at midnight as the Danube is too big to cross on horseback. But the city is quiet and almost seems abandoned. He tells the guard at the bridge that he is heading home to family in Augsburg, intimating that he is returning from the war.

"*Gott segne Sie*," the old man says. *God bless you.*

His horse picks up a stone about ten miles out of Ulm. He pries it out with a pocketknife and is dismayed. It has cut the frog of the hoof and his horse is not only winded now but lame. He mixes snow with the dirt of the road and packs the hoof with mud. The horse bears the pain but moves no faster than a canter. They reach a small river that he assumes is the Lech. The horse balks and will not move any farther. Eberhard ties the animal to a thicket and then crawls under the branches to catch some sleep, wrapping himself against the snow-covered ground.

He does not have the usual fitful dreams of artillery and machine gun fire. For a few hours he sleeps deeply. He hears the pleasant syncopation of hooves, dreams that he is six years old and seated behind his father as they ride into town.

Then it becomes silent, and he is no longer asleep. He opens his eyes. Above him are four men in German uniform on horseback. One holds up his saddlebags, and the man next to him has his uniform jacket across his lap. It is the man with his jacket who speaks first.

"American soldier. You are a long way from home," the man with his jacket says, his breath clouding in the early morning cold. Eberhard guesses that he is the leader of the group. He is about forty, has graying black hair and a shrapnel scar on his left cheek. Eberhard stands up.

"I have family in Augsburg. I was born there."

The men look at each other.

"What is your name?"

"Eberhard Kaufmann."

"Oh Kaufmann! Kaufmann Gold?" the leader hoots.

"That was my grandfather."

"Then Die Pfeffernüsse is your uncle?"

Eberhard is confused. "I don't know. My uncle's name is Otto."

"Ja. Die Pfeffernüsse." The older man turns to the youngest in the group, tells him to dismount and tie Eberhard's hands. The youngest man looks at him hesitantly. He is about Eberhard's age and is wearing the top half of a German uniform over shabby trousers with holes in them.

"Why are you tying me up? There is an armistice."

"Not here. You are in Germany now," the older man responds.

Before he can tell them that he has other family in Augsburg, the older man nudges his horse forward and with the butt of his pistol, strikes Eberhard in the head.

EBERHARD REGAINS CONSCIOUSNESS lying across the saddle of his horse just as they reach the farm. His head is pulsing with pain but he recognizes the house, the courtyard, and the barns. They pull him from the horse, untie his legs so that he can stand. A tall, corpulent man comes out of the house, chewing on a cigar. He looks Eberhard over. Eberhard recognizes his Uncle Otto, even though he is much fatter than he remembers. He has huge jowls and his eyes are creased between layers of fat on his face. Otto removes the cigar from his fleshy lips and spits.

"He says he is your nephew," the leader says. He gives Otto the uniform jacket.

"Uncle Otto, it's me. Eberhard. Albert's son," he says, hearing his words slur.

"Albert's son," he repeats. "Come home, have we?"

His pig-eyed uncle stares at him for a long time. Finally he says, "Your father is a traitor. So is your Uncle Raimund, who is also a thief. It appears you are one as well."

His uncle turns to the leader. "He is a spy for the Americans. Take him out to the cottage by the river. I'll be there in a few hours."

"I am not a spy! I'm your nephew!"

The youngest soldier speaks up.

"Are you sure he's a spy? He wasn't carrying any weapons."

His uncle regards the young soldier with disgust. He turns to the older soldier.

"You teach him to question his elders? What kind of discipline is that for the German army?" he says.

The young soldier is told to retie Eberhard's feet and gag him. They hoist him over the saddle again but this time they cover him with a blanket.

HE IS TIED TO A CHAIR in what used to be the parlor, and he watches through the window as the sun moves westward. He was stunned when they arrived at the house where he was born on the Lech River. It is apparent that the four men have been living in the cottage. There are empty beer bottles and cigarettes butts on what he remembers as once being a polished wood floor. He does not know what the rest of the cottage looks like and doubts that he will get to see it. He is threatened with being pistol whipped again if he asks them questions. It would be a meaningless exercise anyway. Why would they believe him? He looks nothing like his uncle.

In turn, Otto bears no resemblance to his father or to Raymond. The man is huge, has the white eyelashes, eyebrows, and skin color of a Yorkshire pig. He shows no evidence of having served in the military and Eberhard wonders how that can be. Germany was even recruiting young boys at the end. He does not understand this strange band of men who captured him. Former soldiers, from what he can see. They wear their uniforms haphazardly. His uncle holds sway over them, as though he is their commander.

It did not occur to him to think of the Kaufmann farm. To visit there. The cottage and the river had never seemed part of the farm and hence he did not equate the larger ancestral house, barns, and surrounding land as home. Only the cottage and the Lech River. There had been no talk of Otto after they left Germany except once. Eberhard dimly recalls his Uncle Raymond talking to his father at the dinner table in their house on the Flats, alluding to "the Pfeffernüsse." His father told his uncle to shut up and his mother shot Raymond a warning glance. He vaguely remembers witnessing a fight between his father and his uncle. His only clear memory of his father's older brother was when they boarded the SS *Wilhelm der Grosse*. How he had ridden into the harbor. How he had shouted at his mother, called her names. How sick she had been afterward.

He relives his capture over and over, regretting giving his name as Kaufmann. He should have said *Richter*. But then again, who knows what that name might have done because of his grandfather's politics?

The young soldier appears in the doorway with a bottle of water. He removes the gag from Eberhard's mouth and puts the bottle to his lips. Eberhard drinks and then talks fast before being gagged again.

"I have grandparents in Augsburg. Immanuel and Adelinde Richter. They will pay you. My grandmother, Sister Hildegard, is mother superior at the convent. She will tell you I am not a spy," he says. The soldier's eyes widen and then just as quickly, narrow. He ties the gag back on and leaves.

He wonders how much longer they will interrogate him before they let him go. The most they can do to him is make him a prisoner of war, although that violates the conventions of war during a cease-fire. He hopes the young soldier contacts his grandparents.

RAYMOND ENTERS AUGSBURG four days later, just after the winter sun sets in the late afternoon. The horse the American Expeditionary Forces sold him on a memorandum of agreement was a better animal than he had hoped to get, but after four days of hard riding, the animal is lathered and exhausted. He walks the horse through side streets until he reaches the stables behind Geringer's smithery. The four other horses in the stable take little notice as they enter. He stalls the horse, gives it water and oats. He puts an ear to the door leading to the back of the shop and, hearing nothing, opens it and walks in. The shop is empty and quiet. Then he hears a murmur of voices coming from the storage room behind the counter. He stands next to it and listens. Even after twenty-three years, he recognizes Ernst's deep and resonant voice. The other man's voice is just as familiar. He knocks. The voices stop. He knocks again. Ernst opens it.

"I am closed. How did you get in here?"

"I came through the stable door. I need some postcards," Raymond says, "and my horse has a bad shoe."

"How bad?"

Raymond takes off his cap. *It is me*, he mouths. *Raimund Kaufmann*. Ernst looks him over. The big homely man has not changed much except that his hair and beard are white, his face redder and courser from years of working near a hot fire.

"Rai—"

"Friedrich Bergmann," Raymond says. Richter appears behind Ernst. He motions for Raymond to come in.

"My God! It is you," Ernst says. Raymond gives him a quick hug and turns to Richter. Unlike Ernst, Richter has changed dramatically. His glasses are thicker. His moustache and beard are silver, the only hair on his otherwise bald head. Raymond notices the stooped shoulders, the slight bobbing of his head, and the trembling of palsy.

"Herr Doktor Professor," he says, his voice breaking. Richter reaches forward and clasps Raymond's hand. Raymond can feel the cracker-like fragility of his bones.

"I wish we could have met again under different circumstances," Richter says. There is palsy in his voice as well. Raymond glances back at Ernst.

"Eberhard is here or is on his way—"

"Sit down," Richter says.

HE STARES AT THE SHELVES while they tell him. Two days earlier, a young soldier came into Ernst's shop, frantic and needing to be hidden. Ernst thought he was a deserter at first. He closed the shop and took the young man upstairs. He poured a glass half full of schnapps and gave it to the soldier, recognizing him in the light as his cousin's son.

"Do you know Herr Professor Richter and his wife?" he asked Ernst.

"I do."

"I've done a terrible thing," he said, before he broke down and cried. It took Ernst over an hour to get the full story.

"Are there many in the Freikorps here?" Raymond asks.

"Not really. Just this group. Your brother, Otto, and three of his cronies from the Alldeutsche Verband hired them to harass whomever they think harbors socialist ideas or was in favor of the armistice."

"Have they bothered you and Frau Richter?" he asks Richter.

"No. Because of Bernhardt and where we live, they couldn't dare."

"Where is this soldier now?"

"Still upstairs," Ernst says. "I have to find a way to get him out of Augsburg. The Freikorps are looking for him. His name is Louis. He is my second cousin. His parents and most of his family are dead."

Raymond turns to Richter. "Has he seen you?"

"No."

"Good. I want to talk to him."

ERNST BRINGS THE YOUNG SOLDIER into the kitchen.

"This is Friedrich Bergmann. He's not going to hurt you or turn you in," Ernst explains, pouring a glass of schnapps for each of them. "Tell him what you told me. Then we'll get you to safety."

The story comes out between bouts of intermittent weeping. Raymond almost goes mad with waiting.

"The Pfeffernüsse said he was a spy. But the American soldier denied it, said he was the Pfeffernüsse's nephew. Said he was the son of his brother, Albert."

"Did you believe him?"

"I didn't think he was a spy. He was unarmed. He didn't look like the Pfeffernüsse. He looked like Frau Richter who he said was his grandmother. Same eyes, same hair. Dark like she is. The Pfeffernüsse told him that even if he wasn't a spy, he was a deserter from the American army. And that we were doing the Americans a favor by executing him."

Louis then tells them that Eberhard was tied to a hitching post at the cottage near the river on the Kaufmann farm. That Otto ordered the four men to line up and raise their rifles.

"Do you know the rules of the armistice?" Raymond asks.

"Just that we were supposed to stop fighting. But the Pfeffernüsse said that didn't pertain to inside the borders of Germany." He pauses.

"I didn't shoot him. I couldn't. I shot over his head. After it was done, they told me to go inside the cottage and keep watch. I knew after they were done they were going to tie me to the hitching post and do the same thing."

"What did they do with Eberhard?"

"I don't know. I guess buried him but I don't know where. Away from the cottage. I waited until they left. Then I crawled out of a window and rode as fast I could into town."

Raymond stands up.

"Where are you from?"

"I was born in the Fuggerei. That's how I know Frau Richter. She would bring us food, clothes, and school books."

"Is there anything else I should know?" Raymond asks.

"The Pfeffernüsse told the American soldier that his father was a traitor to Germany. And that his uncle—Raimund I think his name was—was also a traitor and a thief. But it was more than that."

"How so?"

"The Pfeffernüsse told him he looked just like the gypsy whore who was his mother. But the American soldier didn't get angry. He *smiled*. He was so calm. He told the Pfeffernüsse that he was going to die."

"That the Pfeffernüsse was going to die?"

"Yes. And then the American soldier said, 'I am proud to look like her. I am proud of my mother and my father.'"

"How did the Pfeffernüsse respond?"

"He told us to fire."

THEY LEAVE THE WEEPING SOLDIER in Ernst's kitchen and walk downstairs to the storage room.

"What are you going to do?" Richter asks.

"I'm going out there to get Eberhard." He turns to Ernst. "I'll need a pistol, preferably a Luger with at least three magazines."

They watch as Ernst opens his safe. He produces two Lugers and five magazines.

"What about a knife?" He holds up a bolo knife.

"I've got one," Raymond says. He lifts his right pant leg so that they can see the hilt of the dagger protruding from his boot. He glances back at the bolo knife. "Where did you get that?"

"On the black market," Richter answers for Ernst. "I assume its Australian, from an Australian soldier. Obviously dead."

The blacksmith stands up, tucks the bolo knife into a sheath on his belt.

"I'm going with you," he says. "You can't do this alone."

"What are you going to do?" Richter asks again.

"It's best that you don't know," Raymond answers. "Where do I bring—"

"Behind the Kloster. Your mother is waiting for you."

ERNST SADDLES A FRESH HORSE for Raymond and then hitches up two other horses to a flatbed wagon. Raymond decides to go to the farm first. Ernst will follow with the wagon and wait for him a half mile from the cottage.

"You'll find Otto sitting outside the back door of the brewery. He likes to smoke out there after his wife goes to bed."

"It's January. Won't he be inside?" Raymond asks.

"Not Otto. Wait until you see him. He's so fat that he doesn't feel the cold. You know they tried to conscript him. But after a few weeks of training, they saw that it was useless. He was more of a target than a soldier. So they commissioned him to grow crops and make beer for the military," Ernst answers. "If he isn't outside then he'll be in the brewery."

RAYMOND RIDES UP behind the milk barn and ties his horse there, enters the barn through the hay door, and walks to the opposite door facing the courtyard. The gas lamp is lit. The lower part of the house is dark but there is a light in the bedroom where his parents once slept. He crosses the courtyard, the thin layer of snow just enough to muffle the sound of his boots. He moves down the right side of the house to the back of the brewery.

He smells and hears Otto before seeing him. The cigar smoke, the labored breathing. He peers around the corner. Ernst is right. His oldest brother is huge, sitting in a large chair that must have been custom made. The brewery is fully lit, casting just enough light for Raymond to see the details of his brother's profile. Otto turns to exhale the smoke in Raymond's direction. Raymond sees the heavy jowls, the folds of whitish pink flesh on his face, nearly eclipsing his eyes. The enormous belly, and the elephantine legs that dwarf the size of his feet. He is not wearing a coat of any kind. Just a shirt. His oldest brother sits and smokes as though he has had a full and satisfying day.

Raymond pulls out the Luger and in three steps is next to his brother, pressing the barrel into Otto's head.

"Where is Eberhard?"

"Who?" Otto asks, dropping his cigar.

"You know who he is. Eberhard is Albert's son. You met him two days ago. You had him killed two days ago."

"He was a spy," Otto sputters.

"He was not a spy. And he was unarmed. Where is he?"

Raymond moves enough so that Otto can see his face. Otto's face is wet with sweat. He smells sour and Raymond isn't sure whether it is from fear or from Otto's inability to bathe all of his body.

"Recognize me, Pfeffernüsse? I'm your brother. Raimund. *The thief. The traitor.* Isn't that what you told Eberhard?" He presses the Luger harder into the side of Otto's head. "Where is he?"

Then to his surprise, Otto gets cocky.

"Where he should be. Where he should never have been born."

Raymond transfers the Luger to his left hand, reaches down with his right to lift his pant leg, and pulls out the Cretan dagger that Kyle made for him.

"You always were a stupid pig," he says.

He sticks the dagger into the fat of Otto's throat. Otto's eyes bulge and he gasps. Raymond works the dagger down, and feels the tip scrape against Otto's sternum. Then his whole hand and part of his forearm disappear into the enormity of Otto's stomach as he works the dagger through layers of subcutaneous fat. Otto gurgles, choking on the blood filling his esophagus. It is like gutting a large and inert boar. Raymond feels something spill out and looks down. Intestines and the sudden gushing of blood. He stops just before the pelvis and pulls out the knife. His right hand and arm are bloodied up to the elbow. He steps back, puts the Luger back into his coat pocket.

"You had no cause to kill Albert's son. Magdalena's son," he says, watching the roll of Otto's eyes. "He was *innocent.*"

Then Raymond walks past the dying man slumped in the chair

to the left side of the house and into the courtyard. There is a pail of water next to the pump. He breaks the ice covering it and washes his hand and the knife. There is blood on the front of his coat, and covering the right sleeve. He will turn it inside out after he is done with what comes next. Raymond slides the knife back into his boot and heads back to the barn and to the horse.

ERNST BRINGS THE WAGON as close as possible to the cottage without being visible. The road leading to the small house by the river is overgrown, showing only recent signs of travel. It is a moonless night, so dark that the lit windows of the cottage appear to him like something from Grimm's Fairy Tales. The woodsman's house in *Hansel and Gretel*.

He met Raymond at the beginning of the road, smelled the blood on him but said nothing. They separated, agreeing that Raymond should come around the back of the cottage and meet Ernst near the front. Ernst gets down from the wagon. There is nothing to tie the horses to and so he hobbles their back legs. Then he trudges through the snow toward the small house, pushing a magazine into his own Luger.

Raymond's horse makes too much noise moving through the river thickets. He ties the animal to a bush and crawls underneath and in between the frozen branches until he reaches the twenty yards or so of open space behind the cottage. He sees the light from the windows, uses it to guide him. He trips when he is within thirty feet of the cottage and lands on his hands and knees. He remains still, listening for signs that the men inside have heard him, and notices the dark outline of horses tied to a fence behind the cottage. He lifts one muddy hand, becomes aware that he is on soft ground. That he has tripped on a large grassy clod of dirt. His hands clutch loose soil rather than snow. He crawls sideways and feels the loose dirt give, feels himself sink. He rolls until he is on hard ground, pushes himself up, and moves quickly until he is underneath the sill of the kitchen window. He peers through the window and sees a narrow view of the parlor. There are two men sitting in chairs, smoking and drinking beer. He recognizes the label on the empty beer bottles littering the floor. *Kaufmann Gold.*

The one soldier is talking to someone Raymond cannot see and he concludes that it is the third man. They are all in one room and armed, he is sure, with pistols.

He rounds the corner of the house and sees Ernst crouched beneath the parlor window. He signals for him to go ahead. Ernst walks up to the door and knocks. One of the soldiers opens it and Raymond listens while Ernst tells the soldier that Otto sent him, that he understands one of their horses is lame.

"Not one of our horses!" the soldier laughs. "But yes, we have a lame horse. Found him two days ago."

"I'd like to get back to town," Ernst says. "Can you show me where the horse is?"

It is the oldest soldier who appears, the one described by Ernst's cousin as being the captain. He watches as Ernst and the captain come his way. The captain is drunk, and weaves as he walks. Just as they come around the corner, Ernst shoves the captain to the ground and pushes his face into the snow. He holds his pistol to the soldier's head and says, "Shut up."

Raymond moves past them and into the house. He walks into the parlor. The two soldiers look up, astonished at his sudden presence. He lifts the Luger and shoots them. Then he walks back outside to find Ernst beating the captain against the side of the cottage.

"Ernst! Stop!" Ernst releases the soldier, who drops to the ground.

"Do you know him?" he asks. Ernst wipes his face.

"No. He's from Ulm. Says his name is Bauer."

Raymond looks at the captain moaning on the ground. His mouth is full of blood. Raymond nudges him with his boot, forces him to roll over. He spits out blood and several teeth.

"Where did you bury the American soldier?"

The captain coughs, points in the direction where Raymond fell.

"I think there is a kerosene lamp in the kitchen," he says to Ernst. He briefly watches the blacksmith walk back into the house. Raymond looks back at the soldier on the ground.

"You killed my nephew."

"The Pfeffernüsse said," he sputters, leaning over to spit out more blood, "that he was a spy."

"And you believed him? Why would a young American soldier travel through here unarmed?"

"I don't know. Maybe because *he was* a spy."

"Tell me, what did you do in the war?"

"I was a gunner," the captain whispers. Raymond can see the imprint of Ernst's fingers on the man's throat.

"You've come down in the world, shooting unarmed men. Did he threaten you?

"No."

"Did he show any hostility toward you?"

"No."

Ernst is back with the lit kerosene lamp.

"Get up," Raymond says. "Show us where you buried my nephew."

It is where Raymond suspects, where he fell just minutes before. He asks the captain to step back. Asks Ernst to lift the lamp so that he can look at the captain.

Then he shoots him in the head.

Ernst gets the wagon while Raymond finds a shovel inside the cottage. He is about three feet down when Ernst comes back and the big blacksmith takes over, digging out the last two feet. They lift Eberhard out, wipe the dirt off of him, and carry him to the wagon. They cover him with blankets and then a tarp. They return to the open grave, roll the dead captain in, and refill it. Then Raymond walks back into the thicket and retrieves his horse.

"What about the other two?" Ernst asks when he returns.

They go into the cottage.

"Give me your knife," Raymond says. He takes the bolo knife, wets it in the blood of one soldier and slides it into the belt of the other. He takes the pistols from their bodies, and fires into them before placing them back into their hands.

"What are you doing?"

"So it looks as though the captain killed Otto. Then they came back here and had a fight. One of them shot the captain and they buried him. Then they argued some more and managed to shoot each other." Raymond pauses.

"Do you think the authorities will see it the same way?" he asks.

"Probably. All we have is old men and they aren't going to waste the energy investigating."

"Even Otto?"

Ernst coughs, working the phlegm up out of his chest. He spits.

"Do you think anyone is going to cry over Otto except his wife and children? The war was hell but Otto was worse. That fat bastard. He pointed fingers at innocent people and accused them of being traitors," Ernst says. "He's the one who hired this lot, *the Freikorps*. There is nothing free about them. They are madmen for hire."

Raymond mounts his horse, rides up next to the wagon. Ernst places his hand on the tarp-covered body.

"I remember him as such a sweet little boy."

IT IS TWO THIRTY in the morning and the city is silent. Their hearing is heightened to a painful level, made so by nervous exhaustion. The hooves of the horses are especially loud on the cobblestone streets, their clopping is like drumbeats echoing off the stone buildings. Raymond follows as Ernst drives the wagon down Sternstraße, turns into an alley next to the Kloster of Maria Stern, and pulls up to the service door behind the Kloster. Raymond dismounts, remembers to take off his coat and turn it inside out before knocking on the door. A young nun opens it, silently gestures them in. He holds the door as Ernst uncovers Eberhard, pulls him to the edge of the wagon, and lifts him as though he were sleeping.

They are led into a kitchen with a large marble table. Richter and two nuns are there. Ernst lays Eberhard on the table and steps back. Under the light, Raymond can now see the mortal wounds of his nephew. He has been shot through the chest and belly numerous times. His face is untouched except for a bullet hole in the middle of his forehead. Despite the pallor of his skin, Eberhard looks as though he could have been alive just a few minutes ago. It is the cold, Raymond thinks, that has stalled decomposition. And for that he is absurdly grateful.

Richter walks to the table, reaches out a trembling hand, and lets it hover for a few seconds before he settles it on his grandson's chest. What could be held as disbelief, as unseen, is now seen and can be touched. Then a woman steps forward from the shadows and stands at the head of the table. Frau Richter is as lean as her husband, her cheeks sunken and her onyx eyes ringed with dark circles. Her black hair is threaded with silver strands and is loose, like a black and silver veil covering her shoulders and back. Her beauty is still there but has changed with time and with the stress and deprivations of the war. She is no longer earthy and sensual. She has become ethereal, her face mirroring that of Mary in the Pietà. He looks away, feels ashamed of his boyhood lust for her. She caresses Eberhard's face, lets the tears streak her cheeks.

"He looks so much like Magdalena," she says.

"And like you," Raymond says.

The interior door to the kitchen opens and shuts. A nun enters. A nun who has his mother's face.

"Raimund," she says, walking toward him. She clasps his face, kisses both his cheeks. Then she walks back to the table and gazes at her grandson. She places the tip of her index finger over the bullet hole on Eberhard's forehead and holds it there for a few moments. They watch as she raises the finger to her lips before making the sign of the cross.

"Sister Maria and Sister Barbara need to wash him. But first they will show you to another room where you will be given something to eat and drink. Raimund," she says, turning around. "I want you to come with me."

THEY SIT IN HER OFFICE, in chairs opposite each other. He does not know the protocol for touching her or addressing her now that she is a nun. He sees the face that he knew and loved as a child, the face that he has missed. Her hazel eyes are the same as is the oval of her face. But the skin on her face is intricately meshed with delicate lines like those of seine net.

"I know it startles you to see me like this," she says. "You left before I joined the convent. It has been twenty-three years since I've seen you. But at this moment, I am not the reverend mother or Sister Hildegard. I am *your* mother." She reaches forward and holds his hands.

He looks down at her hands and sees that his are covered with dirt and blood. He pulls his hands away, horrified that he has forgotten to wash them.

"I n-n-need soap and w-w-water," he says, his voice breaking. He shoves his hands between his legs to hide them, to control what feels like the breaking of his body.

"Raimund, look at me."

He does not want to look at her. She clasps the lower half of his face and forces him to look at her, just as she had done when he was a child.

"Mama. I have f-failed," he says. "I t-t-told Magd-d-dalena I would w-w-watch out for him."

Then he rolls forward, falls on his knees, and lays his head in her lap. There he turns to liquid.

SOMEONE COMES AND GOES from the room. He hears a bowl being placed on the desk. His mother strokes his head, sings under her breath. He does not know how long he has been crying, only that his head is heavy and that he is exhausted. Nothing more can come out of him at the moment. Her hand cups his face and lifts it. A cold cloth is pressed against his face, against his eyes.

"Can you sit up?"

He pushes himself back, gropes for the arms of his own chair and sits.

"Take your coat off," she instructs. He removes it and she walks to the door, opens it, and hands the coat to someone he cannot see—another nun, he assumes. She shuts the door, walks back to the table, and rewets the cloth in the bowl of ice water.

"Hold this against your eyes. In a little while, I will take you to another room to wash and change into clean clothes. We don't have much time. You must leave Augsburg soon."

"What will you do with Eberhard?" he asks.

"In a few hours, I will alert Monsignor. Frau Richter will tell him that Eberhard is her grandnephew, that he was released by the German army and was traveling to Augsburg to see her when the Freikorps killed him. That they left his body on their doorstep. He will be buried under her maiden name of Vargha. You understand why he cannot be buried under the name of Kaufmann or Richter?"

He nods. Eberhard was not from here, is clearly not a son of Otto's, and so it will be suspicious if a young Kaufmann is suddenly buried. He cannot be a Richter either because Bernhardt, like Immanuel, had only daughters and no sons. But Adelinde Richter's family is an unknown entity. It is much more plausible to have him buried under her maiden name.

He will have to consult with Ernst as their proposed story will conflict with what Frau Richter will say. They will have to get rid of the bodies in the cottage rather than leave them.

"And the monsignor will believe this?"

"Yes, especially given how much Eberhard looks like Magdalena and Frau Richter." She pauses. "How I would like to have seen him grow up."

He removes the cloth from his face, sees that his mother's calm demeanor is a mask. The black and white of her habit cannot change or make holy the terrible pain on her face.

"You know what I've done."

"Yes."

"I'm sorry it has caused you pain."

It is the only thing he can say. He is not sorry for killing Otto, knows that his feelings will never change about that. But Otto was also her son. He has to respect that.

"It could not be helped. None of you have given me as much pain as Otto. Even if there had not been a war, Otto would still be who he was. I have known since he was a child that your older brother had the seeds of evil in him. He's never had a conscience, no matter how hard I tried to instill one in him. He has harmed many people."

"You forget that Papa had much influence over him."

"Your father did bad things, did hurtful things, but even he had a basic level of conscience. He was callous at times to others, especially to his brother Gunter. Yet he still would have protected Gunter. He would not have killed him. I realized after your father's death that his attitude toward Gunter's suicide was really guilt. I think he felt he drove his brother to his death."

It becomes quiet then. In a few hours the dull state he is in now will change. He will cry again until he is exhausted. He has no idea how long the pattern will last. What he is sorry for is returning to her with blood, literally, on his hands. His mother breaks the silence and says, "I don't want you to go through life believing yourself evil for your actions. I have wrestled with my faith during this war. I have wondered where God is, why he allowed the killing to go on. I have asked Him to forgive Otto and at the same time asked Him to stop Otto from causing harm. He did stop Otto but not soon enough.

"I know you don't believe in God, Raimund. But there is no authority here that would have brought Otto to judgment. There are still people in Augsburg who believe in the righteousness of this war. Otto was one of them. He hired men to kill. Otto was an instrument of the Devil. I believe you were chosen to be an instrument of God."

Before he can answer, there is a knock at the door and his mother rises to answer it. She comes back with something in her hand.

"What is it?"

She holds up a broken silver rosary.

"Sister Barbara found this as they were undressing Eberhard. It was caught under his belt. He must have been wearing it."

He finds it odd that Eberhard would have been wearing a rosary.

"You don't recognize it, do you?" his mother asks. "This was my grandmother's. I gave it to Magdalena just before you all left the country. She must have given it to Eberhard."

She reaches for Raymond's hand, and puts the rosary into it.

"Take it back with you and give it to Magdalena."

"I'll have it fixed first."

"No," his mother says. "Leave it as is. Magdalena wouldn't want it fixed."

A HALF AN HOUR LATER, he gathers with the others in the kitchen. The nuns have dressed Eberhard in a suit provided by the Richters. His mother dismisses the two sisters, so that it is only Ernst, the Richters, his mother, and himself.

"I will tell Albert and Magdalena," Raymond says. "I ask that you not write to them of what you know, what you have seen. I know this is a terrible request. But the situation has larger ramifications.

Eberhard deserted. We know he did so with good intentions. I must rectify the situation enough so that he is remembered with honor, not dishonor."

"Raimund, I *have* to write to Magdalena," Frau Richter says.

"You will be able to," Richter says, stepping in to help Raymond. "But we must wait until Raimund tells us when."

Frau Richter comes from around the table and embraces him. He feels her frailty, her need to hold him. Then Richter surprises Raymond and encircles him with his arms so that both of them hold Raymond as if they will not let him go. Nothing can be said. Goodbye is too harsh and yet it is the truth. It is uncertain whether they will see each other again. Raymond feels a second round of uncontrolled sobbing threaten his cold stability. He untangles himself carefully, so as to not give offense.

"If you need anything . . . ," he says, wondering what it is he could possibly give them.

IT IS AN HOUR BEFORE DAWN. Raymond cannot risk staying for the mass and burial. He and Ernst stand in the alley behind the Kloster. The wagon and horses are gone as Ernst took them back to the stable while Raymond was with his mother. He came back to the Kloster on a single horse.

"We have a problem," Raymond says, and tells him the story that Frau Richter will present to the priest.

"We need to burn down the cottage then," Ernst replies. "Or better yet, blow it up. I can do that."

"No, you can't. It has to be me. I'm leaving. You still live here. Do you have explosives? And a detonator?"

"Yes. But do you know how to do it?"

"I learned it in basic training in Canada. I was good at it, surprisingly. What about Louis? I thought I would take him with me, get him out of Germany."

Ernst says nothing at first. His face is the color of rock under the dim lighting of the alley.

"Louis is dead," Ernst finally says. "When I took the wagon and horses back to the shop, I found him hanging in the stable."

We shouldn't have left him alone, Raymond thinks.

"Do you want to bring his body back here?" he asks.

"No. It is a suicide. That means I'd have to explain to the priest just what drove him to it, what he was doing for a living. They won't bury him in the cemetery anyway. That is why I have to blow up the cottage. I'm going to take Louis out there and put him inside with the others."

"Ernst—"

"Otto was buying a lot of dynamite on the black market, and storing it, I assume, somewhere on the farm. It will look as though he blew up the cottage and the men in it. And then someone, another Freikorps member, took revenge on him."

"That should work."

"Yes, but only if I get out there right away. I have your things packed, and a horse waiting. You must leave now."

A FEW WEEKS AFTER CHRISTMAS, Magdalena is walking from the barn to the house with a pail of milk when she feels light-headed. She puts the pail on the ground and bends over to get the blood flowing. Her heart pounds and she feels nauseous. She slowly rises and looks toward the house but does not see it. Instead she sees the bluff behind the Flats. She is inside the grove of birches, looking out toward the Mississippi. Her belly cramps and she shuts her eyes against the sudden pain. When she opens them the house is there again. She picks up the pail and continues on. Inside the kitchen she takes a pencil and makes a small check on the calendar hanging in the kitchen. It is January 12.

ON THE TWENTY-THIRD, someone pounds on the door at four A.M. A single rider from town whom they vaguely recognize gives them a telegram and a letter from Raymond. They open the telegram first.

EBERHARD WITH GRANDPARENTS RICHTER, AND
WITH GOD.

They stare at each other.

"With God?" Albert asks.

Magdalena opens the letter and reads it aloud. Raymond's

message is brief. Eberhard was killed by a Freikorps sniper while guarding his post in Coblenz. *This is not the Freikorps of the Napoleonic Wars*, he wrote. *These are bands of ex-German soldiers who are against the armistice. Who act as vigilantes for hire.* Raymond was granted release of Eberhard's body and took him to Augsburg to be buried in the Richter family plot. He ended the letter by saying he would be visiting the farm in late January on his way to Minneapolis.

Albert makes his way to the kitchen table, feeling the walls and the chairs as though he is suddenly blind. He sits down. They hold their positions in silence, as though they are the dead victims of an unforeseen Vesuvius. Albert sits at the table with his face in his hands and Magdalena stands near the door, holding the telegram and letter. She reads the letter over and over. They know Germany is in chaos, that there is rioting. Their worry after knowing Eberhard was alive was how to get food to her parents and sisters. They didn't think there were dangers to the Allied soldiers occupying Germany. It is incomprehensible that a son who survived the war should die during what they thought was a declared peace. Their silence is broken by the sound of bedsprings above their head.

"Albert," she says, walking to the table. "You need to tell Hilda. She'll take it better from you."

She watches him walk up the stairs. Moments later, she hears her daughter's wail and then Albert's sobbing.

The rest of the day is torturous, the news sinking in and becoming more painful as the day progresses. Albert works outside, obsessed with chopping wood. Hilda cries intermittently and refuses to eat. Playing upon her daughter's precocious taste for beer, Magdalena gives Hilda two glasses of heavy lager and some toast for supper. She falls asleep within an hour. Magdalena goes out to the icehouse, fetches five more bottles of beer, and puts them on the table in front of Albert, his face chapped from the cold. She opens a bottle and drinks from it.

"Go ahead," she says. "Drink as much as you want. I'm going to."

RAYMOND DOES NOT ARRIVE at the end of the month. They receive a letter from a Captain Kell, explaining that Raymond has been sick and is hospitalized. He assures them that Raymond is not in any danger, that he needs a month or two of convalescence, and will most likely arrive home with the rest of the American troops in April or May.

"Perhaps he doesn't want to come back," Albert says, folding the letter and giving it back to Magdalena. "I don't blame him. I'm sure he knows how angry I was over his enlistment."

"I don't believe that," she says. "We know so little of what Raymond's been through. He may have been wounded. He needs to hear from you, Albert. He needs to know you want him to come home. Especially given the letters we received from your mother and my parents."

Both letters expressed love, deep grief, and tried to provide as much solace as could be attempted in the written word. They also expressed gratitude for Raymond, for his intervention in preventing Eberhard from being dumped in a field like so many of the war dead. Both letters have an oddly defensive tone in regard to Raymond. *Raymond did the best he could in trying to watch over Eberhard. Please know that,* her mother had written. *He is in as much pain as you both are.*

ALBERT COULD NOT GET OUT OF BED for two weeks after the telegram and letter. The Norwegian couple who rented the Weir place did all the farm chores. Marjaana stayed with them and insisted that Magdalena rest as well. She cooked meals and cared for Hilda. At the end of those two weeks, Magdalena and Albert were forced to rise above the torpor of their pain because the farm demanded it and they had one child still at home and another struggling with the same pain, unable to be physically consoled by his parents. Others had suffered as well. They had known from Frank's letters that Honza's son Marek had been killed in the Meuse-Argonne Offensive. One of the Chosa boys from Fox Lake was killed in the Argonne as well. Mika Two Knives survived the war. They learn from Ilarminen that he is in the 32nd Division but his unit is occupying the Rhine River south of Coblenz. He will be coming home in May.

They endure the rest of the winter and find one day that it is spring. They discover that after the immediate grief comes rage, especially for Albert. If the duration of the Great War has made him a fool in his thinking, seeing significance in ordinary occurrences, its results return him to his educated perspective and realism but with a scarred sense of that history that Albert would later refer to as being logically irrational. Not only had Germany presented him and Raymond with no opportunity, no freedom of choice except to emigrate, it had now killed his oldest son.

For Magdalena the Great War represented one of Grimm's fairy tales. In exchange for the life she chose in America, her former homeland has claimed her first born. She reconsiders each of the words in Eberhard's letters, weighs them to divine what mood he was in, what he was withholding. The letter that seemed most like him was the one they received three months after he shipped out, after he arrived in France. She walks outside with the letter, rereads his description of the wine and bread he ate, the other soldiers he met. She lifts her face. It is a bitter irony that she must suffer his death while surrounded by the fertile, mineral smell of spring mud, and hear the call of robins, cardinals, and blackbirds.

After a month of discussion, she and Albert decide that they will become Americans in the fullest sense possible. There is much about their birth culture that they cannot let go of, so ingrained are some of its happier traditions. But they stop speaking the language of their birth in public and forbid their daughter to do so. Language, they reason, is the deepest part of identity, and they can control that identity by simply abandoning it.

Hilda has no particular loyalty for speaking German, especially since their visit to the Flats. She comprehends the language more than she speaks it, as her primary language since starting school has been English. The Germany of their selective stories is just that to her: stories. She has no knowledge or sense of politics. She cannot comprehend the vast scope of the war that has killed her brother. To her it is not the Great War but the Great Mystery. The adored brother whom she had not seen for three years walked into an abyss and never came back.

She has become withdrawn, eating very little and rarely speaking. She attends school but completes her homework with little enthusiasm. In their desperation to rouse her, they ask her, sometimes beg her, to say the mealtime prayer. She refuses. Magdalena gives Hilda the rosary that her mother had given her and asks her daughter if she would like to attend Saturday mass as well as Sunday, something she had nagged them about the previous fall. She fingers the rosary and then gives it back.

"No," Hilda says. "The rosary you gave Eberhard didn't protect him."

HILDA REVIVES A BIT in late April when it is her turn to bring in rocks for Father Boland's lesson on geology. They watch from the house as Hilda walks the river shore, filling her book satchel so full that she has to drag it. That evening she comes home from school with an empty satchel and a muddy dress with a torn sleeve. She silently walks past them on her way to the stairs, stopping only to hand them an envelope.

"SISTER AUGUSTA WOULD USUALLY BE TALKING to you about this but I happen to witness the incident firsthand," the priest begins. They are in the rectory's study. Ilmarinen is there, too, his wife home with their three-month-old daughter. Father Boland describes the rock pile on the edge of the playground where the students dump the rocks that they bring in for class. Hilda was dragging her satchel across the playground during the afternoon recess to add her rocks to the other mounds of specimens, when she saw Seppo Stone on the ground with his hands in front of his face, defending himself from a boy two years older.

"I had just walked out of the school to go back to the rectory when I saw the boys and then Hilda," he said. He watched in amazement as Hilda lifted the satchel and began to run with it. She picked up enough momentum to swing the bag, hitting the older boy across his upper shoulders and head. He fell a foot away from Seppo who scrambled up as his oppressor went down.

"Who is the boy?" Ilmarinen asks.

"Mason Krueger," Father Boland answers. Ilmarinen flinches, and Albert runs a hand across his face. The Kruegers are the leading family in Chippewa Crossing, having made their money in the lumber industry. The elder Krueger is a second cousin to the Pillsburys who own the flour mills in Minneapolis, and the very mill that Albert and Raymond had once worked in. Magdalena and Albert were surprised to learn they had a son in the school. They assumed the Kruegers were Protestant. But Mrs. Fishbach told Magdalena that Mrs. Mason Krueger Sr. was a Catholic and that her husband converted before they married.

"Mason is a bully," the priest says, "and he's done this several times before. He has a penchant for picking on the Indian children. That isn't all of it," he adds. He described how Hilda pushed the dazed boy onto his back, took out the largest rock from her satchel, and then stood on the boy's chest.

"If you ever touch him again," she said, "I'll bash your stupid head in."

She stared down at the older boy, her hands holding the rock above him, waiting until she was sure he comprehended her threat. Then she stepped off his chest, motioned for Seppo to follow her, and together they emptied her satchel of rocks onto the pile. The priest stood, mesmerized by her cool rage.

"I do not condone violence," Father Boland says, "and normally I would have intervened. But sometimes the Sisters and I cannot administer a fitting punishment or determine justice like children can among themselves in certain situations. And this was one of those situations."

"But the Kruegers!" Magdalena protests. "Have they said anything?"

The priest grins.

"They can't really say anything this time," he answers. "I warned them that if their son bullied another child, I would have him removed from the school. Oh, they've written to the bishop several times, saying that I am unfit to guide this parish. But a girl, and a younger one at that, has beaten their son. Do you think they will tell the bishop that?"

Magdalena leaves the men in the rectory, hears their laughter as she walks the short distance to the school to see the mother superior.

"I watched the whole thing from the window," Sister Augusta

says. "I wouldn't have thought Hilda had the strength to lift that bag. She has become so thin. We can't get her to eat much either."

She pours coffee into two china cups, giving Magdalena one.

"I know you've been worried about her. You have all suffered a devastating loss. So many in this town have, between the influenza and the war. But I think Hilda will be all right now."

"I hope so. She was very close to her oldest brother."

"And she is to you although it hasn't felt that way. Oh yes," the nun says, "I've been aware of your worries. I have had them myself and I am not her mother. I know you have worried over her disposition. But she does have a heart and a sense of morals. Hilda is such an intelligent girl but awkward in expressing feelings. She will always blow either hot or cold with emotions." The nun sighed.

"As you know, I've wrangled with your daughter's will on many occasions. She is a tough one. Yet she did us all a great favor and perhaps for Mason as well. It is not a charitable thing for me to say but it is the truth," the nun replies. "Unlike other girls, her sorrow did not come out in tears. It came out as anger. What better way to use that anger than to stop a young bully?"

RAYMOND BOARDED A STEAMER in Thunder Bay rather than ride a horse the remainder of the way into Minnesota and across to Wisconsin. He doesn't have the strength to travel that way. Even now, standing at the deck's railing, the cold wind off Lake Superior cuts right through him, through the layers of clothing he has on underneath an equally thick coat. He will go inside the main cabin in a bit, but for now welcomes the cold. It sharpens his mind. He needs to think some things through before he sees Albert and Magdalena.

He fingers the passport in his coat pocket. He left his wartime passport, his wartime identity, in Thunder Bay. He is no longer Alan Edward Davies or Friedrich Bergmann. He can be Raymond Kaufmann again. Professor Raymond Kaufmann, who lives on the Flats, who teaches history at the University of Minnesota. But the rest of the war cannot be left behind so easily.

He thinks of his conversation with Kell upon his return to London.

"I CAN'T HAVE HIS PARENTS be told that he deserted," Raymond said. "Not only because it would add enormously to their pain but because then they would have to be told more. And I can't do that—we can't do that. It is a huge security risk. Can we work with the American command to hush up his desertion? Or better yet change the story so that he can be granted an honorable discharge?"

"I think we can but I can't promise anything. I would have to go through Thomson and he would make it difficult," Kell replies.

"Can't you go directly to Lloyd George?"

"That would cause problems down the road. But I can speak to Hankey," he answers, in reference to the war secretary. "He will be able to make the Americans understand the delicacy of the problem. You are right. This could potentially damage the armistice." He pauses. "I say, are you all right?"

He saw the alarm on Kell's face just before he passed out. He woke up hours later, delirious with fever, in a London hospital.

HE HAD SENT A TELEGRAM to Ilmarinen Stone when he was in Thunder Bay. He can't face Albert and Magdalena at the train station. He needs the ride out to their farm to get back in their element, to feel a sense of place before seeing them. He also wants to thank Ilmarinen for agreeing to be the go-between, for accepting letters and telegrams.

He feels the inside pocket of his coat for the small book there. It is Eberhard's journal. He has written on the front page that it was to be given to Frank only. Raymond is not tempted to read it, cannot bear to hear his nephew's voice in words. He will give it to Frank when he returns to the Flats.

They will be docking in the port of Superior in two hours. From there he will find some kind of transportation to Ashland where he will board the train going south to Chippewa Crossing.

THEY ARE ASTONISHED when Ilmarinen shows up at the door with Raymond.

They invite Ilmarinen to stay for supper but he declines, wanting to get back to Fox Lake. Magdalena watches him ride away, knowing that he refused because he did not want to intrude on this homecoming.

Albert removes Raymond's coat and is shocked by his brother's skeletal frame. Raymond's skin is the color and texture of gray parchment, and the hair on his head has thinned. Magdalena's first thought is that he has had typhoid again or cholera.

They let Hilda ask questions, and they listen as Raymond consoles her. Hilda still won't eat much and Magdalena puts her to bed before supper. The three adults eat without questions concerning the war or Eberhard. They chat about easy things: Frank's education, the purchase of several more cows, the upcoming summer plans.

Raymond helps them clear the table. Magdalena picks up Raymond's plate and notices that he has not eaten much. She won't let him wash dishes and so he sits with Albert, drinking beer.

"This beer is as good as Papa's," Raymond comments. "Where did you buy it?"

"It is Papa's, in a way. I make it from memory. It isn't quite there yet but I'm still tinkering with it."

There isn't much else they can think to say that stays within the realm of small talk. The silence becomes unbearable.

"You should be getting Eberhard's discharge papers soon," Raymond finally says. "His commanding officer put Eberhard up for the Distinguished Service Medal. That should be arriving soon. He will also be receiving the Croix de Guerre. He was an excellent soldier."

They are hesitant to ask him the questions long on their mind because of his fragility. But Albert must know if Otto survived the war, if he is still obsessed about finding them.

"Do you know anything about Otto? About the farm?"

It is a dangerous question, as though speaking their oldest brother's name will bring hell down upon them.

"Otto is dead."

There is no mistaking the inflection of rage in Raymond's voice as well as the finality in which he responds.

"How?"

"He bilked the German military on a contract. He was shot."

"You are certain of this?"

"Yes."

His brother's face is stony. Albert is not fooled. Raymond knows more. But that is all right. To hear Raymond say it makes it a certainty. Otto cannot reach them anymore. He'll bide his time, ask his younger brother after he is more stable. He watches as Raymond studies the inch of beer left his glass. Then Raymond lifts his head and says, "Honza wrote and told me that there will be a memorial service during the Morena for Marek, Eberhard, and the other young men who were killed. I know you are loathe to leave the farm for even a day, but it would mean everything to me, to Frank, and to Honza if both of you and Hilda came. I will pay that couple you are renting to, to take care of the farm for a week. And I will pay the train fare for all of you."

"You won't need to do that. Of course we will go. It is what Eberhard would want us to do," Albert says, "and Frank needs us."

MAGDALENA LOOKS AT ALBERT. It is what they need. To go back to the Flats, to step out of their isolation and share their grief with old friends.

"I sent a telegram to Kyle and Aino. They will be there with their children," Raymond adds.

They talk awkwardly for a few minutes and then walk upstairs to bed. Albert, anticipating nightmares, instead falls into a deep sleep. Magdalena lies in bed awake, the questions she could not ask Raymond running through her head. Then she hears the front door open and gets up to look out the window. It is Raymond, walking away from the house in only socks, his coat over his pajamas. He is walking toward the river. Magdalena runs down the stairs, puts on her coat and boots, and leaves the house to follow him. There is a full moon, its lunar light reflecting from the frost-covered grass.

"Raymond!" she calls when he reaches the middle of the field. He turns and looks at her as if he doesn't know her. *Shell shock*, she thinks, remembering what Father Boland had said about the returning veterans, and describing its symptoms. She slows to a walk so as to not frighten him.

"Raymond. It's cold out here. You have no boots on. You'll get sick again."

She grabs one of his hands, rubs it.

"Raymond. It's me. Magdalena." She watches as his eyes direct their gaze from above her head to her face, the recognition coming slowly to his face.

"I have something for you," he says, and reaching into his coat pocket brings out a small box. She opens it and lifts out the broken rosary.

"I was going to get it fixed. But my mother said not to, that you wouldn't want it fixed."

He looks away and stares out at the field.

"He was wearing it when he got shot."

She examines the rosary in her hand, notices that it is broken between the first and second Our Father. She hears a strange sound and realizes it is coming from Raymond. At first she thinks he is choking and leans toward him.

"Breathe," she says. But he is not choking. He is sobbing so hard that he is hyperventilating. She pulls him toward her and holds him, waits for the worst of it to pass.

"Let's walk," she says, trying to turn him around to head back to the house. He resists and so they move ahead. At first his weight is on her as though he cannot feel or find his feet. His breathing evens out as they trudge through the rest of the field. They stop when they are close to the river. His crying has eased up.

She now knows what it is. He was not sick with typhoid or cholera. He was not shot or physically wounded. He is sick with what he cannot say, with what he's seen. Any questions she might ask of him would only be torture.

"Do you remember Verdun? Didn't you go there with your parents?" he asks.

"Yes."

"You wouldn't recognize it. The land around it. It has been bombed to hell like much of France. There are valleys now where there used to be hills. The trees or those that are still standing look like burned skeletons from Dante."

He wipes his face with his coat sleeve. The tears on his face are oddly solid in appearance, as though they are mercury.

"I never thought I'd see such beauty again," he says, sweeping his arm and then pointing up at the sky. "Here it feels like the war is just a bad dream."

"You can stay with us as long as you like. Albert has missed you so much and so have I."

"Has he? I would have thought he'd want to kill me."

"*Raymond, no.* Don't ever say that. It is just the opposite. He is ashamed that you are afraid of him. That he has instilled such a fear in you. He doesn't hold you responsible for Eberhard."

"And you? I said I'd watch over him."

"That was a terrible request for me to ask of you. There is no way you could have been by his side the entire time. Eberhard was a grown man. You did not fail him. You did not fail Albert or me. We were so grateful for your letters. It was an enormous comfort to know that my mother and father and sisters were all right. And your mother. Ilmarinen rode to town each week, regardless of the weather, to pick up the mail. He also picked up mail for the Chosa and the Two Knives families."

She holds him closer. "We want you to stay with us for the summer. Let us take care of you."

"I appreciate the offer. But I have to go back. It is the thing that keeps me alive. I have to go back to teaching and I miss the Flats. I miss my house. You know about the city? What they are trying to do?"

"Yes. Frank wrote to us about the city trying to reclaim the Flats. About forcing people out of their homes. Frank took the house deed to city hall to prove that you own the house and the land it sits on. We sent him some money—not much—to get legal help for some of the others."

He looks up at the full moon.

"How strange it is to be here. I feel like we are on a stage. Like we are in an opera. The light is just like being in a theater."

She smiles.

"That is what Eberhard used to say. He loved moonlit nights especially in winter. He and Frank would go over and skate on Fox

Lake in the middle of the night with Mika Two Knives and their other friends. He loved it here but not enough to come back here."

"Oh, he loved it here, Magdalena. He was torn between both places," Raymond responds. "Do you know the place he loved best on the Flats?"

She shakes her head. She can think of a number of places but not one that was best.

"The grove of birches up on the bluff. He went there when he wanted to be alone. I'd find him sitting on that limestone slab."

Now it is she who has trouble breathing. She can see the grove of birches as though they are in front of her, as though she has been pushed back to that January day. She marked the calendar on that day, the twelfth, because she thought she was pregnant. She thought seeing the grove meant that she had been forgiven. But her menses arrived two weeks later and she was left unable to understand what that day had meant. She steps back.

"Did he know about the baby?"

"No. I'm quite sure he did not. He just said he found it peaceful to be there. It was unnerving at first for me to find him there."

"On what day in January did he die?"

He hesitates.

"January 14."

He raises his hand, reaches out and touches her face with one finger, moves it lightly over her jaws, her nose, her eyebrows, and her cheeks. Then his finger stops in the middle of her forehead, and rests there.

"Eberhard was very proud of his resemblance to you," he says. She reaches up and removes his finger, troubled by his tracing of her face, of his marking of her forehead. She thinks it must be a benediction of sorts, one that only Raymond understands. She looks down at his feet.

"You will get frostbite," she says. She links her arm in his and turns him around in the direction of the house.

ALBERT LISTENS with the others amassed near the shore as Father Boland and the Lutheran minister from the Immanuel Evangelical Church lead the service. He watches the priest, thinks how natural he looks against the backdrop of the Mississippi. How the priest can evoke grace or a prayer anywhere and make it a church. It was his agreement with Raymond. Albert wanted Father Boland to attend and lead the prayer for the Catholics. He thought perhaps the priest from St. Elizabeth's would attend but learned upon arrival that the monsignor would not perform a memorial service if it were not held inside the church. Albert had guessed that would be the case, and wanted Father Boland who knew Eberhard, who knows their pain, and who is not so rigid in his belief of where God resides or where he can be called upon.

Then Father Boland concludes the makeshift Requiem Mass by leading them into reciting the Our Father and Hail Mary. Hilda and one of Honza's younger sons bring forth a large straw cross in which copper plates are embedded, each bearing the name of those men killed. They walk down the wooden pier, stand while the priest blesses it with holy water. Then swinging three times, they throw the cross on the fourth swing into the river. The crowd watches the cross drift south until it is no longer visible.

Aino comes forward and walks to the end of the pier. Facing the river, she begins to sing in Finnish, the soprano of her voice so pure that it rises, calls into the sky above their heads. There is a collective awe at Aino's voicing of their lament, penetrating even the most reserved among them. Father Boland's solemnity is betrayed by the tears that stream down his face and that he does not wipe away. Albert feels Frank sag against him on his left, and Raymond on his right. He wraps an arm around each of them, to shore up his son and his brother. He sees Magdalena, her face buried in her apron, the flour from her early morning baking dusting her arms. Hilda has her arms around her mother.

It is Honza who lifts the mood, who meets Aino as she steps off the pier and swings her up into a hug before he speaks. Then he stands stiffly in front of them.

"Today is the Morena. All the young men who are not with us today," he says, his voice trembling, "would want us to celebrate as if they were here. Eat and drink and dance, not in sadness but in remembrance and celebration of them. Let us begin!"

Albert is astonished by Honza's eloquence, although he heard the fugue of grief in his voice.

"Did you help him with that speech?" he whispers to Raymond.

"I did," Frank answers.

TOWARD EVENING, after much laughing, drinking, and dancing, Sergei Demidov brings out his *balalaika*. They sit at a table with Kyle, Aino, Honza, Zena, and Father Boland and listen. It is music unlike anything Albert has heard before. It is haunting and mournful, and yet rapturous. He looks across the table at Honza. The big Czech is weeping.

"That is proof," Honza says when Sergei finishes, "that the soul does not die."

THE LAST FIGHT

Minneapolis

1923–1950

H E WAKES UP, HIS MOUTH TASTING AS muddy and gritty as if he had been in the river. Unlike a new dream whose details do not linger into consciousness, Raymond has had this dream before, and it is more distressing because it persists, because he can remember every detail of it, and nothing about it has changed over the past eight months. He reminds himself to make a note in his journal of its occurrence. The last time had been two months earlier during the night after the funeral.

He gets up and shuffles to the kitchen. He stokes the burning embers in the stove with more wood, and fills the blue enameled coffeepot with water, throwing in a handful of coffee grounds before putting it on the stove. Then he sits at the table, the surface warm and yellow with sunlight from the window, and waits for it to boil.

He thought he could resume his life as it was before the war or at least a good measure of it. But he arrived home from one war only to face another. He is grateful to Frank for solidifying his claim to his house while he was in Europe, but the city is persistent. They claim that the majority of the Flats residents are squatters, that they haven't paid rent in years.

"I've been paying rent," Honza fumes, "but every year the landlord changes. I never see the landlord. One year it was a Mary Leland. Now it is this Smith fella."

"I thought 'twas taxes I was paying," Mrs. O'Flaherty says. "We came here and homesteaded because it was free. No one from the city wanted the land down here. Now they suddenly want it? For what?"

"Rent! I bought my house twenty-five years ago," Joseph Novak says. "From a man named Bolaug."

Unfortunately, he has no paperwork to show for it, like others who purchased their houses from the mysterious Bolaug. Raymond has legitimate paperwork so that they cannot evict him, but that does not stop the city from pressuring him to sell. He has retained an attorney for himself and for others on the Flats who want to stay. Just yesterday the city came forth with another offer.

"My answer is no," he said to his attorney. "Do they not understand? I don't care how much money they offer me. This is my home. This is where I will die."

He gets up and pours himself a cup of coffee. In his response to the city's latest offer, he reminds them that *those squatters* have had sons die in the war and are as American as anyone could be. He cannot fathom what business interests the Flats suddenly hold for the officials of Minneapolis unless they intend to build a road along the shoreline connecting the top of the bluff to the river shore.

"It would cost 'em," Ian Brock commented. "They'd have to bring in tons of landfill and rock to build up a solid bed to hold city traffic."

Raymond said nothing, knowing the city would spend such a sum of money.

He sits down again, notices that Zena is approaching from a distance with his breakfast. The Flats residents were shocked at his appearance when he came back. What they had imagined about the war was presented to them in the flesh. Not the bullet-riddled bodies covered in blood—as painful as such images were, they were too easy. It was his gaunt frame, his skeletal face. The sunken, vacuous eyes and the crepe that was his skin. The lack of an easy smile. He evoked pain from the top of his head to his bony feet. The men did not know what to say, standing around him in stunned silence at the bottom of the wooden stairs. But the women did.

"We'll start with an oatmeal gruel," Mrs. O'Flaherty said, placing a frail hand against his chest. "Then if that stays down, a boiled egg."

THE CITY FURTHERS ITS CLAIM in May 1923. Raymond is in his university office when the riot breaks out, when a landowner they have never heard of sends police down with a court order to evict fifteen families.

Katrina Brock, the daughter of Larissa and Ian, shows up at his office door, out of breath and terrified. He gives her a glass of water and after a few minutes she is able to tell him what is happening.

"The police tried to force their way into Zena and Honza's house. But Zena barred the door and began screaming. We heard her and ran over there. They are loading Honza and Zena's furniture into a wagon. After they are done there, they will come to our house."

"Run back and tell them I'm coming. Get as many of the women as you can and stand in front of Honza and Zena's house."

He calls his attorney, who will meet him down on the Flats with an order to stay the eviction. Then Raymond runs through the campus, across the bridge, and down the steps.

The women are beating back the police with fists, sticks, brooms, and even wet dishcloths twisted into small whips.

"Stop!" he yells, pushing his way through the women, praying that his attorney will show up soon. "You cannot do this. There has been a mistake."

He informs the officers that a stay of eviction will be arriving momentarily. Zena is so upset that she faints, falling across the steps of her house.

"It will be your fault if she dies," Raymond lies, grateful for Zena's timing. The police back off but do not leave. They sit near the wagon and wait. His attorney finally shows up an hour later with the stay of eviction.

"Goddamn! What I would have paid to see the look on those bastard's faces," Honza howls that evening, raising his beer in a toast. "What a mistake to come during the day! Thinking they would avoid *the men!*"

IN THE SPRING OF 1928, they are about to build new houses on the lower Flats, houses that will stand on stilt platforms much like the bayou houses in Louisiana so that the residents on Wood Street will not have to suffer the flooding of their lower floors, and

sometimes the whole house, every spring. Then the city of Minneapolis begins its condemnation proceedings. Raymond's neighbors
put their confidence in him, and Raymond himself is confident that
he can win the fight to save the Flats community.

"It is a living piece of history," he argued in court.

"It is a piece of living garbage," one of the prosecutors snickered.
The Flats was not sanitary, they went on to argue, not a fit place for
anyone to live. Raymond accused the city of false politics, playing
under the auspices of public health.

"I don't think that's it, Ray," his attorney says. "I'm guessing there
is a third party involved because they want the west bank pretty
bad. They say it is to expand the barge terminal down there and
turn the rest into a park."

"A barge terminal and a park? Doesn't that strike you as an odd
combination?" he asks.

He knows what it is, what the city is really accusing them of.
They have not assimilated into the blandness of American life, do
not support the melting pot theory as the nativism in Minneapolis
sees it. On the contrary, the Flats' residents prove assimilation. The
Flats is a living example of many ethnicities living literally side by
side. The only thing missing is other races. He is well aware that it
is their whiteness that has allowed them to hold out so long. The
Flats would have been wiped out ten years earlier had there been
Negroes, Chinese, Indians, or Mexicans living there.

IN 1935, he is still legally wrangling with the city when he is made a
Regents' Professor. At fifty-six he is the youngest professor to be so
designated, yet the city does not recognize the honor as giving any
heft to Raymond's claims that the Flats is a bona fide community.

He is so preoccupied with saving the Flats and with his work as
a professor that he pays just enough attention to what is going on
in Europe to be informed but not get wrapped up in it. It is Magdalena who is keeping watch, who updates him through letters.
She does not press him about his lack of interest out of sensitivity
for what he'd gone through during the war. But even the years after
the war remained difficult for all of them, gradually erasing what
positive ties they had to Europe, to Germany.

Richter had died in 1922 and his wife followed him a year later. It was devastating that the family could not go to the funerals because of the financial and political difficulties in traveling to Germany. Magdalena suffered severe depression after the death of her parents, so debilitating that she often could not leave her bed. Hilda's wedding to a local boy from Chippewa Crossing in 1925 finally made her come to the surface. Then, in 1931, just when Magdalena thought she would be able to get her sisters and their husbands out of Germany, they disappeared, and throughout the next years she continued to work with the Red Cross to discover what happened to them. Sister Hildegard died in 1934, surrounded by the nuns who loved her. They would have traveled to Germany for her funeral, but her final wishes were that they give the money they would have spent traveling to the Kloster to aid the sisters' work in teaching poor children.

Then one day a letter from Kell, out of the blue, wakes Raymond from his present concerns.

I'm still working but am put, as you Americans would say, on the back burner of the business. Not at the front of the action, I'm afraid. All of my worst fears about Germany are coming true. I feel so stupid not to have foreseen what the Treaty of Versailles would lead to, what damage it would cause. And yet it was there, plain as day. Our friend in Augsburg predicted this would happen. I feel his loss keenly. Hitler could only have come out of the Great War, was clearly formed by it. Despite all of the diplomacy being exerted upon that madman, there will be another war. As bad as the Great War, maybe even worse. But my influence is very little now. I am an old man from another time, another past, another war. Maybe even an old fool. I miss our conversations very much. Please let me know when you next visit London.

Raymond puts down the letter, feels the force of Kell's loneliness. It lances the barrier he has constructed against his own despair. He would gladly go to London to see Kell if his funds weren't so tied up in fighting the city. But even if he had the money, he fears what would happen in his absence if he left the front line of the battle. He also fears that a visit would ensnare him into becoming involved in the inevitable second war. And he won't do that. He's done his service. He won't abandon the Flats again.

Goddamn Hitler! he thinks. *Goddamn Minneapolis!*

There is a knock on his door. He puts the letter aside, gets up to see who it is.

"I can't do it any longer, Ray. I've got grandchildren now. I have to think ahead for them," Honza says.

He stands at the entrance to the house, twisting the cap in his hands. The lumber mill Honza had worked for went out of business in 1932. Fortunately, prohibition on beer had ended about the same time and jobs had suddenly opened up at the local breweries. Honza now worked at the Hamm Brewery in St. Paul.

"Where will you go?" Raymond asks.

"St. Paul. I found a house with stables on Phalen near the brewery."

Honza's big shoulders are hunched with misery and embarrassment. And exhaustion.

"There is no shame in leaving, Honza," Raymond says. "You did the best you could. You are right. You have to think about your family's future."

"Ray, why don't you move with us? You can't fight the city. When it wants something, it just takes it. There are czars and kings everywhere. They will get you sooner or later."

"Then let it be later," Raymond answers.

BY 1945 there is only a handful of them on the river flats. Raymond's persistent fight against the city makes news headlines.

REGENTS' PROFESSOR REFUSES TO LEAVE HOME ON RIVER FLATS

It gives him a few sympathizers but in response to the articles the majority of Minneapolis's inhabitants side with the city. In the fever of winning the Second World War, they do not want to see reminders of the past. Progress is the buzzword. The president of the university quietly implores him to take the city's settlement, as do Magdalena and Albert, but he will not give up even though he and old Mr. Novak are the only residents remaining, the rest having left earlier in the year. There are days when he can hear Alzbêta's voice. *You will represent us. Through you they will know that we are a good and intelligent people.* He regresses in his desperation, enough to temporarily believe in and pray for a miracle. He says the Hail Mary every night before he goes to bed.

BUT THE MIRACULOUS does not happen, and in 1950 he capitulates with sorrow. He has recently retired and can no longer deny the futility of his fight. Mr. Novak had died the year before and Raymond is the only one on the Flats. His house stands alone amid the rubble of bulldozed houses. He agrees to move, with the stipulation that it be the day after his birthday.

RAYMOND WAKES, feeling himself to find that he is dry, not wet. He sits up but the ache in his shoulder is so intense that for a few moments he feels faint. They celebrated his seventy-first birthday yesterday. He had reached up to get five wine glasses from the cupboard and lost his balance, falling down hard on his right shoulder. Magdalena made him stay on the floor while she cautiously palpated his shoulder. No bones were broken but she insisted that he go to a hospital. Raymond refused. He did take the aspirin she gave him and allowed her to ice his shoulder.

He hears footsteps in the hall and then a tap on the door.

"Albert?"

His brother opens the door. "Come in. Shut the door," Raymond says, unbuttoning the pajama top with his left hand. It slips off his right side. His brother grimaces.

"Jesus."

Raymond's shoulder and upper arm look as though there is an oil spill underneath the skin. He tries to raise his arm and discovers that he cannot move it above his chest without excruciating pain. Nor can he put any weight on his right hand.

"I think Magdalena should look at it again," Albert says.

"Not yet," he winces. "I need you to shave me and then help me get dressed. Where's Frank and the boys?"

"Outside arranging the furniture on the barge. It sure makes it easier to move your stuff. I wasn't looking forward to hauling all of it up the steps to the bridge. This way, we can just go downriver, cross to the other side, and have it loaded on a truck at that river landing just below your new apartment. It was good of the city to provide it for free."

Raymond refrains from making a sarcastic remark and gestures for his brother to help him. Albert wraps his arm around Raymond's left side and lifts him to his feet. They stop at the doorway to make sure Magdalena is still in the kitchen and then walk across the hall to the bathroom. Raymond sits on the toilet seat opposite the sink and mirror. Albert picks up the bowl of shaving soap, wets the brush, and works up a lather.

"Are you gonna make it today?" he asks.

"I have to," Raymond answers, his chin tilted up as his brother brushes the foam onto his face and neck. "They're bulldozing the house tomorrow."

His brother sighs.

"You're still a stubborn kid," Albert says, running the straight-edged blade up one cheek before wiping the foam on a towel. "It was time, Ray. It isn't as though you are moving to a junk heap. That apartment in Prospect Park is nice."

Raymond watches his brother in the mirror.

Yes, the new apartment is nice, but it will never be home. He feels his chest swell, his throat thicken with the congestion of grief. It didn't seem so long ago that they were both young men, working in the flour mills. Albert retains the leanness and muscle of a younger man from working hard all of his life as a farmer. His thick hair has turned white, contrasting with the intense blue of his eyes. He still has the strong and rugged German jaw from their father. The lines on his face, though deep, are smooth as though repeatedly washed over by water instead of years. Raymond, once considered more handsome, is now mistaken for being the older brother. He has gone bald, unlike Albert. The past ten years have not been easy on his body. His broad shoulders have slowly but noticeably eroded into slopes and his belly sits like a halved cantaloupe on the waistband of his pants. But he has inherited the same jaw and their mother's hazel eyes.

"You look good, Albert," he says. His brother straightens up and glances at him in the mirror, thinking Raymond is baiting him and sees that he is not.

"You too, Ray."

He bends over to work on the other side of Raymond's face.

"I wonder what Eberhard would have looked like now," he says, pausing to refold the towel around Raymond's neck. Raymond is startled.

"Eberhard would have looked like you and Maggie. Her eyes and hair. Your frame," Raymond answers. He gestures for Albert to keep shaving. He doesn't want to take the topic any further than that.

They have breakfast sitting on the boxes not yet carried to the barge. He drinks his coffee and watches as Magdalena deftly braids and then coils her hair into a chignon without a mirror, with hands that are seventy-three and not twenty-three. Her hair is pure silver now and she has never cut it. He thinks of those nights when Albert would brush it, how it aroused him and nearly drove him insane.

"Ready to go?" Frank says, poking his head in the door.

"I'm not going on the barge with the rest of you. I want to walk across the bridge," Raymond announces.

"But your shoulder—" Albert says.

"I'll walk across the bridge with Raymond," Magdalena interrupts. "We'll catch a taxi on the other side and meet you at the apartment."

They take their time walking down the remains of Cooper Street and slowly climb the wooden steps. They stop when they reach the middle of the bridge to watch the barge leave the west side of the river and pass below them.

"Do something for me," Magdalena says.

"Sure."

"Write about how it was. You are a famous historian. You can do that. Especially now that you have retired."

"For just the family or to publish?" he asks.

"Both."

"Does Albert know you want this?"

"No." She reaches back to secure a pin in her hair. "I've wanted to ask you this for some time. But I knew you wouldn't be able to consider it until you retired."

He feels her reading him.

"There are complications," he says. He refrains from telling her what she already knows. That publishing a personal history exposes the dead to questions and judgments that would force the living to answer and defend. Then there is that part of his history that he cannot legally admit to unless released by the British government. He has never told them about that part of his life.

"All the more reason to write the truth or at least what we know. What we went through in Germany. Why we left. I don't want you to just sit in that apartment and do nothing. You will not do this alone. I will help you write parts of it."

She is right. Yet while Raymond can write officially about other people and their hidden histories, the thought of writing an auto-biography brings into conflict another belief he adheres to: that every person has a right to his or her own secrets. He would be the first to admit that he has enough of his own. He knows what he is and would never deny it if confronted. He was born a sinner, then baptized with the holy water of Catholicism, and, when older, baptized again with the blood of his father's authority. He does not speak about his spiritual beliefs. He cannot deny there is a God or prove there is one. So he has remained quietly agnostic. No last rites for him when his time comes. He will die unrepentant over some things and repentant over others. But to broadcast such admissions in a published way is troubling. He looks at the sunlight on her hair, the expectation on her face. It is hard to refuse her. He considers the possibility of writing under a nom de plume, writing it as a memoir with all of their names intact until the final draft. Then he would change them as protection.

"Don't you think there are some things that should not be told?" he ventures. "You have secrets. I have secrets. Why not leave them that way?"

"I'm surprised at you, Raymond. What if those secrets unravel onto the future generations of our family without explanation?" she counters. "What if they are condemned by something they didn't know and should have?"

She rests her hand on his.

"I know that Eberhard was not killed at Coblenz. I know that he was killed on January twelfth, not the fourteenth. I talked to Mika Two Knives after he came home and he told me the rumors that went through the division. That Eberhard deserted. That's how he got so close to Augsburg. Not because you took him there after he died. And I know about Otto."

"Your mother told you?"

"Yes. She sent me a letter before she died. For exactly the same reason that I am asking you to write our history. I had a right to know what happened. We made a terrible mistake in not talking to the children about Otto, about the way it was on the farm. Eberhard might have lived if he had known. I think my grandchildren and the children after them should know how it was, *what it was.*"

He feels as though his chest is being ripped out.

"I didn't want to lie to you. I had to," he says.

"I know. I knew that whatever you had done was for the good. To protect us. And because you could not talk about what you did during the war."

"Did you tell Albert this?" he asks.

"Some. Not all."

"Are you asking me to write about Eberhard?"

"I'll leave that up to you to decide."

She turns away to wipe her eyes.

"This place," she says, "brings back so much."

"Do you want me to write about this, too?" He gestures toward the remains of the houses below, toward his house still standing until tomorrow. "And the baby?" he adds. He had found odd comfort in knowing that a child of his blood was buried on the bluff, and he often went up to the grove to sit just as Eberhard had done.

"Yes. Because we lived it," she answers. "But not the baby. I know that sounds hypocritical but I have my reasons."

Raymond looks at her hand resting on the railing. He has an urge to kiss it. He has spent years searching for a woman like her, would do almost anything for a woman like her. And yet, this is one request he is not sure he can grant her.

She reaches over, lifts up his chin so that he is forced to look at her. For a brief moment, he sees Frau Richter as she was the night he brought Eberhard to her.

"Raymond, I want you to consider this: if you write our history, it might get you back to the other side of the river."

He stares at her. He sees Eberhard as he is in his dream, remembers the miss of the hook, the terrible pain in his shoulder. Magdalena's prophetic words suddenly clarify an oddity. His dream has never changed, and yet it was only last night that he injured his shoulder.

EPILOGUE

Minneapolis
1968

THIS MORNING RAYMOND GETS UP AS usual, has a cup of coffee and a prune pastry that he has saved from the day before. He shaves, and then puts on his best suit. He waits until midafternoon, knowing that there will be few students on campus as the spring quarter has ended. Then he takes the bus on University Avenue, gets off in front of Folwell Hall, and walks with the aid of his cane to the river flats behind Coffman Union.

He sits on a bench close to the shore, watches the sun slide down in the sky. He is the last one alive of their generation. Albert had died in 1960, and just last week Magdalena died, rocking two of her great-grandchildren on the porch. Two days ago, he was diagnosed with liver cancer at the university's hospital. They want him to fill out admittance forms, then lie in a hospital bed where they have said they would make him comfortable during what time he has left.

He stares at the river in front of him.

If someone were to sit down next to him right then and ask him what he wanted, he would point across the river and tell them this:

I want the laughter of those years; that hysterical, gut-twisting howling that left us unable to speak and pissing in our pants. And the crying that often gave birth to such laughter. I want the poverty and difficulty of those years because it united us, because it forced us to see the humor in everything. It broke down the old ethnic disputes and hatreds that lingered from Europe. It was our fists swinging against poor housing and absent, parsimonious, and tyrannical landlords, patched clothes, long hours of manual labor in the mills and breweries, and sometimes living on a diet of nothing but sauerkraut and potatoes. Laughter was our only defense, the psychological serum that protected us. Sure, there was still some ethnic jabbing and teasing. But hatred was a luxury that none of us could afford because at some point, every neighbor was needed, every skill contributed. It made us a people.

And then there was the Mississippi, its bounties and its flooding gifting and cursing us like a God. But a God we understood, a God that was right there at our feet.

My God.

He gets off the bench and begins to work his way down the shoreline toward the Washington Avenue Bridge. His face and hands are scratched by branches and thorns by the time he reaches the other side of the structure. There isn't much of a shore but it is enough for him to stand on, to look across to the other side. He can see through the bright green foliage of the trees that the seventy-nine wooden steps are still there.

The Mississippi is high because of the spring rains. He looks down at his shoes, decides to keep them on. Decides to keep his clothes on as well.

He drops the cane, and walks into the river.

Acknowledgments

Although some characters in this book are based on historical figures, and many of the areas described exist (the Minneapolis river flats, Augsburg, London, northern Wisconsin), it is important to stress that this story is fiction and that the portraits of its characters are fictional, as are most of the events.

A significant component of this book is based on a historical river "village" on the banks of the Mississippi River in the heart of Minneapolis. That history would have been lost had the Works Progress Administration (WPA) writers of the 1930s not collected the narratives of the Flats and published them through the Minnesota Historical Society in a book, *The Bohemian Flats*. The value of their efforts cannot be emphasized enough. I also relied on the magnificent articles by journalist and historian David A. Wood; his account drawn from former residents of the Bohemian Flats was published in the *Minneapolis Star and Tribune* in 1984 and in the article "How Green Was Their Valley" for the Minnesota Historical Society.

Many other books, as well as my own immigrant history, were crucial to my research: *The Kalevala, an Epic Poem after Oral Tradition*, by Elias Lönnrot and translated by Keith Bosley (Oxford University Press); *Memories of Lac du Flambeau Elders*, edited by Elizabeth M. Tornes with a brief history by Leon Valliere Jr. (University of Wisconsin Press); *A Little History of My Forest Life: An Indian–White Autobiography*, by Eliza Morrison (Ladyslipper Press); *Defend the Realm: The Authorized History of MI5*, by Christopher Andrew (Knopf); *Strategy and Intelligence: British Policy during the First World War*, edited by Michael Dockrill and David French (Hambledon Press); *The Great War and Modern Memory*, by Paul Fussell (Oxford University Press); *The Guns of August*, by Barbara W. Tuchman (Ballantine); *Education for Extinction*, by David Wallace Adams (University Press of Kansas); *Boarding School Seasons*, by Brenda J. Child (University of Nebraska Press); *The German-American Experience*, by Don Heinrich Tolzmann (Humanity Books); and *Mill City: A Visual History of the Minneapolis Mill District*, by Shannon Pennefeather (Minnesota Historical Press).

The Fox Lake Reservation is fictional, as is the town of Chippewa Crossing. My birthplace's original name was Chippewa Crossing before it was renamed Glidden, presumably after some lumber baron. I used the former name fictitiously because it was, and still is, so descriptive of that region.

I am thankful to Claire Keegan, who granted me permission to quote a line from one of her short stories. I am also grateful to writer Elizabeth McCracken, who generously gave her time and advice, and to my advisor at Iowa, James McPherson, for his astute observations and wonderful stories. This book would not have come into final form without four excellent editors: Ali-Bothwell-Mancini, Elizabeth "Betty" Johnson, Laura Westlund, and Jean Brady. I received critical feedback and review from four generous and well-read readers: Amy Gillard, Lisa Blanchard, Barbara Stoltz, and my childhood friend Patti Galiger Schoenborn. I have long been supported by four literary mentors: professors Shirley Nelson Garner and Toni McNaron, Regents' Professor Madelon Sprengnether, and Elizabeth Johnson, Ph.D. This book would not have reached completion nor would my life have been sustained without Holly Sanger, who helped me survive the early years of the recession and graduate school.

The long arm of my former French publisher and now agent, Marc Parent, pulled me up to complete this book; his love, faith, honesty, and encouragement have been extraordinary. I think it was fate and good fortune that our paths crossed. My brother, Paul, is not only a supportive sibling but a tremendous source of information and shared memory, as is my cousin Barbara Stoltz, whose dark humor has kept me from the abyss. Their love and understanding have been a necessity.

ACKNOWLEDGMENTS

A huge thank you to all of the staff at the University of Minnesota Press. I thank Anna Jarota, Anne Lepage, Dawn York, Jeanine Ferguson, Todd Orjala, Erik Anderson, Doug Armato, Kristian Tvedten, Susan Doerr, and Anne Wrenn for their guidance, support, and kindness.

Finally, my gratitude to my readers.

MARY RELINDES ELLIS
was born and raised in northern
Wisconsin. She is the author of
The Turtle Warrior.